# CARSTEN STROUD

# CUBA STRAIT

POCKET BOOKS

New York London Toronto Sydney

This book is a work of fiction. Names, characters, places and incidents are products of the author's imagination or are used fictitiously. Any resemblance to actual events or locales or persons, living or dead, is entirely coincidental.

POCKET BOOKS, a division of Simon & Schuster, Inc.
1230 Avenue of the Americas, New York, NY 10020

Copyright © 2003 by Absaroke, Inc.

Originally published in hardcover in 2003 by
Simon & Schuster, Inc.

ISBN: 0-7434-6393-5

First Pocket Books printing June 2004

10  9  8  7  6  5  4  3  2  1

POCKET and colophon are registered trademarks of
Simon & Schuster, Inc.

Cover design by Jae Song

Printed in the U.S.A.

For information regarding special discounts for bulk
purchases, please contact Simon & Schuster Special Sales
at 1-800-456-6798 or business@simonandschuster.com.

## ALSO BY CARSTEN STROUD

*For Linda Mair*

## AUTHOR NOTE

I'm grateful to Phil Bennett of the Hinckley Company for helping me get my facts straight about the Talaria 44, and in particular for telling me how a real sailor would deal with a hurricane in the Straits of Florida.

They really worshipped him in Valencia, and he was killed before they ever had the time to turn on him.

—Ernest Hemingway, *Death in the Afternoon*

# CUBA STRAIT

# CUBA

For forty-five minutes the pilot waited in the cool darkness of the ancient wooden hangar, the picture of his daughters almost forgotten in his left hand. In the open doorway the sea wind off the Caribbean stirred up miniature tornadoes of ochre dust that floated across the dirt floor. The battered windward wall was pierced by nine thin blades of slanting yellow sunlight. Out in the arc of the bay, past the ragged line of dusty palms, a flight of gulls crossed the red disk of the sun, wheeling in unison over a sea filled with a churning golden light. It was the same clean light that he had seen as a child in the Platte River country, shining in the windblown yellow grasses that rolled away to the edge of his world. He hadn't been back to Nebraska since the Navy had sent him out to Hawaii in 1969. The picture of the two little girls in his hand had been taken on a beach in Oahu in 1973. The colors had faded; the bright ocean dulled, the sunset behind the girls a band of

1

pale orange light. Katie was three at the time, Eileen two. He had taken the picture, Ruth's hand on his shoulder. Forty-eight hours later, he went back to the Gulf of Tonkin, flying a Phantom off the USS *Coral Sea* on Yankee Station. It took the Navy three weeks to deliver the photographs to the carrier. They were on his bunk waiting for him when he got back from Pearl. He heard a sound that he took for a gull's cry, but it was one of the Cubans calling him. *"Oye! Señor Verde!"* It was time to go.

*Mister Green*—the words played in the silence of his mind. Green was his cover name for this . . . well, *mission* was not the right word. This *lunatic stunt* was closer to the mark. Mister Green sighed, got out of the old wicker chair, straightened his leather flight jacket, tightened the holster strapped to his right thigh, and stepped out into the light. The heat was strong on his cheek; the humid sea breeze smelled of salt and seaweed. A long ribbon of shadow rippled across the tarmac behind him as he covered the hundred feet from the hangar to the stone jetty, where the Kodiak Turbo Twin bobbed at the wharf. The wind plucked at the cuffs of his tan slacks and feathered his graying hair. At the far edges of the valley behind them, stunted scrub cypress fluttered and swayed under the unceasing winds off the Caribbean. Beyond the cypress, the distant cliffs of the Cuchillas del Pinal glowed with violet and deep rose light. Far away beyond the mainland, climbing up out of the southeast, he could see a high bank of thunderheads, vivid purple in the sunset, a storm front coming out of Haiti. Green tried to put the weather out of his mind. What mattered here was the plane itself.

He ran his hand over the fuselage, the Teflon-coated hide as warm and smooth as the barrel of a horse. She was rocking softly in the gentle swells, rising up under his hand. He ducked under the port wing, crouched down by the dockside and checked out the Number One engine cowling. Dry, clean, no streaks of oil or signs of hasty work badly done, no duct tape, no flimsy pop-rivet repairs, the usual trademark of feckless Third World mechanics.

He walked along the whole port side, touching it, stroking it, shaking the struts, leaning in close to rattle and tug at the float connections, the old famil-iar preflight routine running on automatic, the indelible residue of his twenty-odd years on a carri-er's deck. Under the floats, the water was as clear as a gin-and-tonic. Sequined fish darted away from his shadow on the lime coral heads. The Cubans watched him from the dock, both hard Indian faces tight with attention. He straightened, tugged at the port cabin door and pulled it open. He had to hold it against a sudden gust off the water. Sea spray scattered tiny glittering diamonds across the wind-shield. The cabin interior was spotless, the instru-ments in good order. There was a large emergency oxygen canister in a brace beside the instrument panel. The cabin smelled strongly of soap and disin-fectant. Someone had spent a lot of time and energy cleaning the interior. Green decided not to think about what may have happened to this plane's last pilot.

He stepped up on the ledge and studied the upper sections of the big wings. The paint job was perfect, a deep ocean blue on top, the undercarriage a light sky blue. Invisible against the ocean if she was spotted from above, invisible from the ground against a clear blue sky, painted with radar-suppressing latex: the Kodiak was a gem, as far as he could judge, in flawless condition, a very good plane. He hoped it wasn't going to kill him today.

Popping open the bulkhead hatch, Green looked over the cargo section, fifteen hot-pink bales, tightly bound in waterproof shrink-wrap, each bale averaging eighty pounds, for a total payload of twelve hundred pounds. Mounted on a solid metal skid, it seemed. Odd, because a wooden skid is lighter, and every bit as strong. Anyway, add the two saddle tanks, the auxiliary tank stowed aft and Green's own one hundred seventy-five pounds. One hundred and eighty-one, if he added in the loaded Glock strapped to his thigh and the fifty rounds of nine mill tucked in the breast pocket of his brown-leather bomber jacket. All in all, a heavy payload. Right at the plane's specified upper limit, a critical threat even without that big storm front he could see building over the mountains in the south. There was no margin for error. He tugged at the nylon straps holding the cargo. They thrummed with a deep bass note, piano-wire tight. The bolt-downs looked well set, the titanium racks solid. Good work, especially for

Indians. He stepped back onto the dock, walked over to the Cubans. Narcisse Suerta was waiting with his hands down at his sides, his face turned into the wind. The other man with him, from his look a relative, was much heavier. His thick black hair flew back off his temples. The hard light in his eyes was Neolithic.

"*Muy bueno*, Narcisse. Your people did well."

Narcisse had nothing to say to that. Green got nothing human off the man, only his close attention. The mark on his face, the carved tattoo of a palm tree and a thunderbolt, looked like a red smear. The second man, new to Green, bearing the same tribal scar, did not even look at Green; all his interest was focused on the plane. He was barefoot and wore white pajama pants, a Polo shirt, and a bright yellow inflatable life jacket.

"Who's this?" asked Green, nodding at the man.

"In a moment. Where are your papers?"

Green handed Narcisse the packet containing his passport, wallet, identification papers, his Rolex, his wedding ring. He put the snapshot of the girls into his jacket pocket, next to the box of 9 mm rounds. Narcisse looked as if he had something to say about the picture, then shut his mouth, took the sealed package without a word, handed Green a Timex Indiglo watch with a clear plastic band and a bundle of used American bills sealed in a plastic Ziploc bag. He glanced down at the Glock in the holster on Green's thigh.

"That's clean," said Green. "Nothing traceable.

Anyway, I'm keeping it. You'll want to stand off there. She'll kick up a big wash when I start the engines. I'll be doing a preflight check for about five minutes. How's the outside looking?"

Narcisse lifted up his shirt. Next to the Colt Python revolver shoved under his belt, there was a gray plastic Motorola radio.

"They are up there, on the ridge. If there had been anything, they would have told us. You should go as quickly as you can."

"Who'll be on the other end?"

Narcisse didn't like that question.

"I'm not told those things, Mister Green. I do the planes. You go now, okay? The American takes off very soon."

"You know the schedule?"

"There is no schedule. We have people in Caimanera, in the hills above Guantánamo. They know the plane. Everybody in Cuba knows the plane. When it takes off, our people phone. At this moment, the propellers are already turning. You need to go now."

"What about that storm front? I'm already too damn heavy. I get caught in that, I'll go down like a gutshot mallard. And the cargo with me."

Narcisse looked to the south, over the ridgeback of the mainland. A dark-gray squall line rode the mountain peaks and ribbons of lemon-yellow cirrus were spreading across the southern horizon. He shrugged it off, his plank-hard face tightening, his yellow-rimmed eyes narrowing.

"It comes. You will be in front of it. There is no danger."

*None for you, anyway,* he thought, but he kept it to himself. Doomed or not, he was going to have to fly this mission. He had no choice. With a dark heart he gave it one last try.

"We can do this another time. I take it this load cannot be lost."

"Yes. That is true. This one is the most important one of all. Castro's people are not stupid. It must go tonight."

"Who'll be on ground crew if I get back?"

"I will. I will show you lights once I hear from you."

Narcisse turned his upper body, gestured without looking up at the peak of El Caballete over his left shoulder.

"Up there, a red light blinks. If it does not, you land farther along the coast near Cayo Moa. We'll be waiting with a boat. If there was surveillance, or anything has happened, we will sink the plane."

*With me in it, if I give you half a chance.*

"I'll need some hot food. If I get back. And *cerveza.*"

Narcisse showed his upper teeth, one gold incisor glinting.

"If? You will come back, Mister Green. Many people would miss you very much, no? You have much responsibility. It is very important for you to come back safely. You understand me? Now forgive me. I must speak alone with my friend. Oh, yes. I forget. I have this gift for you."

Suerta pulled a small plastic packet out of the pocket of his slacks, handed it to Green with a reptilian smile, and backed away a few feet, watching Green's face with a fixed and avid expression that was an obscene parody of the gift-giver's expectant regard. Green held the package for a moment, looked hard into Suerta's eyes, and then opened it. Inside the package was a small brown hand, a human hand, purple with bruising and still crusted with dried brown blood, neatly severed close to the palm, the fingertips burned away, the fingers themselves broken and mangled.

Staring down at it, his breathing locked up tight, his face paling, he recognized the small silver ring he had given to Ottavio Colon fifteen days ago, a gift for the child, to amuse him while he and the boy's father, a local fisherman, talked quietly about Green's request—a private message for a girl living in Havana—and he had thought—he had hoped—after so much time without a word, that Ottavio and his father Fulgencio had made it all the way safely.

But they had not.

Suerta's people had caught them. After a time, in their Indian way, they had grown bored with the effort of hurting the child to punish the father and they had killed him; this gift was Suerta's way of telling Green not to try to send anyone to Havana again. Green composed his features and presented a stony blank mask to Suerta when he looked up again.

"Why was it necessary to do this?"

Narcisse lifted his hands, palms out, and shrugged theatrically.

"Consider it a lesson."

"For me?"

"For everyone here. The situation must be made plain to the local people as well. These fisherfolk, they run in and out of Havana with their catch, to sell in the marinas."

"Where is Fulgencio? Ottavio's father?"

A cynical shrug. Dismissive.

"*No sé. Desaparecido, quizas.*"

"Disappeared?"

"It is possible that his family killed him. It was he who cut off the boy's hands."

"His father did this?"

"We gave him a choice. He chose to live."

Green looked at Narcisse Suerta for a long while, and Narcisse held the look without a visible emotion. There being nothing more to say, their mutual hatred as clear as it could ever be, Green simply folded the package and put it into the breast pocket of his flight jacket. Still silent, his jawline tight and a muscle in his right cheek flexed with the effort of this silence, he climbed into the Kodiak.

Narcisse gave him an insolent bow and backed away twenty feet, turning to speak with the second man. Green got his breathing under a semblance of control, stilled his mind and settled into the pilot's chair, buckling his harness tight. Through the skin of the plane, he could hear Narcisse's voice raised, a harsh dialect that was probably mestizo, having some kind of bitter argument with the other man. The argument grew very heated. Then there was silence. Someone stepped onto the float and knocked on the door. It was Narcisse, his face very pale, his voice flat and hard, packed with resentment.

"It appears that you must take this man with you."

The big Indian was standing behind Narcisse, his face a stone mask, his body rigid. Green shook his head and frowned.

"No. Not in the plan. I'm heavy as it is. Not possible."

"It is felt . . . no. It is decided."

Green looked at Narcisse's face, could see there was no point in debating the issue with him. It had been Green's experience that the only way to win an argument with a man like Narcisse Suerta was to write your opinion down very clearly on a piece of paper and then nail the paper to the man's forehead with a nine-inch spike.

"Better get him on board, then."

Narcisse turned, spoke to the other man, a burst of rapid Spanish. Green felt the floats heaving as weight came on them; the Kodiak dipped. The passenger door popped opened and the man climbed inside, broad, powerful, heavy muscles sliding under his soft teal Polo shirt. A sterling-silver medal hung from a steel chain around his neck. His thick Indian face was blank, with a blood tint in his black eyes, the whites as yellow as old ivory. He smiled once, showing expensive bridgework and a single steel tooth. His smile was a thin one and did not warm his face. Green turned back to Narcisse, who was watching him intently.

"This guy's big enough to have his own climate."

Narcisse shrugged, said nothing. The man was leaning out of the cabin. The Kodiak rocked as he strained at something and now there was an assault rifle in his hands—an AK-47, old but well maintained, with a curved magazine. The muzzle was pointed more or less in the area of Green's right kidney, possibly without intent. Perhaps the man found it more comfortable that way. Green did not.

"Narcisse, this is bullshit. I don't need a keeper."

"This is not bullshit, this is Geronimo, my cousin. You can call him Jerome. He wants to see Miami again. He has not been there for many years. Many old friends. It is important to him. As you can see."

"He weighs a ton, for Christ's sake."

"Do not blaspheme, Mister Green. For myself, it does not matter. But Jerome is very devout. Our people are from Belize and Our Lord is respected there. Jerome is a true believer."

He watched Jerome, who was examining the control panel as if he had never seen one before. Green had a terrible insight.

"Has this man ever been in a plane before?"

Narcisse shook his head, flashed him a shark's grin.

"No. This will be his first. He is very happy."

As far as Green could tell, the man was as cheerful as a crypt.

"He's a believer? Then tell him to pray for us."

Green may have meant it as a joke, but Narcisse's face was solemn. He inclined his head and spoke with some gravity in his thick growling Spanish, a Catalanian proverb that Green had come to recognize. *"May no new thing arise."*

Six minutes later, the blue Turbo Twin hammered away across the water, her twin engines blared and roared, white spray showered the windscreen. She lumbered into the air with a staggering lurch that Green felt in his spine. She was dangerously overloaded. In the co-pilot's chair, Jerome's face was bone white, his body arched and rigid, one bare foot propped against the panel, the AK-47 clutched in his hands. A portrait of incipient panic. Green looked off to starboard, saw Narcisse Suerta at the jetty, a small white figure on the concrete wharf. Suerta's head was turning to track his bank to the northeast. Green recalled the night his Harrier had been targeted by an Iraqi SAM site during a Gulf War mission over Bubiyan Island. The pilots called it *"lit up and locked on."* That was it exactly.

# MAYBELLINE

MOTOR CRUISER *CAGANCHO*
CAY SAL BANK, STRAITS OF FLORIDA
9:00 P.M. EDT, FRIDAY, SEPTEMBER 20

When the emergency weather fax came in, Rick Broca missed it completely. He was out on the stern more than slightly distracted by a fourteen-foot tiger shark. Hours ago, he had anchored in a shallow bay a hundred yards east of the Double Shot Keys, in a lagoon so limpid and clear the forty-four-foot cruiser seemed to be hovering in the air above the coral. The sun was setting, a disk of orange fire gliding down into Mexico through an opalescent sky streaked with margarita green and flamingo pink. To the southeast, a storm front was rising up out of Cuba, an ominous gray-green stain spreading out along the horizon. Rick was on the swim platform, shirtless, in jeans and Top-Siders, the sunlight strong on his chest and shoulders, a camera in his right hand, Cisco beside him, the cat's eyes wide, his ears flat, a hard vibrating growl deep in his chest, both of them watching the yellow-and-black tiger shark circling a few feet off the fantail, its gills flaring, one slate eye tracking them as she made a turn through the coral, the sand stirring into eddies as she passed. A man could spend his whole life in the Keys and never see one of these. But she was here, a huge female, two thousand pounds at the least. Sunlight rippled along her broad scarred back, glinted off her ragged dorsal fin. Her jaws were half-open, showing razor-edged yellow teeth set into pulpy tissue as blood-red as an open wound. What was on her mind? She was . . . *interested*.

Back at Garrison Bight, around the Key West Marina, the charter boat captains had talked about this big female tiger they had named Maybelline—presumably after someone's ex-wife—rumored to cruise the fishing grounds off the Cay Sal Bank. She had been hunted by sportfishers all up and down the Santaren Channel, spotted by sailors as far south as Cuba; maybe fifty years old, never took a hook, supposed to have a series of prop scars on her big white belly, gotten when she came all the way up a swim ladder after a hooked swordfish, which she sliced off clean behind the gills and swallowed whole.

When she turned in the coral, Rick had seen enough of her pale white underbelly to make her out as female, but couldn't think of any way to get a closer look that didn't involve being eaten alive. Well, there might be one way. He had a loaded bolt-action .308 Remington in an oiled sheepskin case beside the bed in the forward stateroom. Three above the eye would probably kill her.

Killing something as rare and full of power as this

tiger shark for no good reason other than to be able
to tow her bloody carcass home for the amusement
of a gaggle of Key West grifters on the dock at
Garrison Bight struck Rick as unworthy, a kind of
crime. But she had to be the legendary Maybelline.
How many of these huge tiger sharks could live in
the same waters? And this one, blindly compelled by
her primeval code, would have eaten most of the
competition a long, long time ago. She was visibly
ancient, battle-scarred, hundreds of gouges and
badly healed wounds all along her flanks, small
chunks bitten out of her dorsal, an ugly puckered
furrow carved into her snout.

The shark showed no sign of emotion, no sign of
leaving. Her interest in them was strictly business.
She was trying to figure out how to reach them,
working out the odds. The mass of the boat's stern
behind Rick was confusing her. She knew they were
there. She could smell and hear them. She knew
they were meat. But the shape of the boat, the mass
of it, was making her uneasy. She was obviously processing the problem. When she made a decision,
Rick figured they'd be the first to know. Nineteen
more minutes passed in this suspended zone, Rick
almost hypnotized by the shark, his breathing shallow, his mind blank, before he finally registered the
faint chime coming from the helm station. The
weather-fax alarm.

He straightened, raised the Nikon and ran off sixteen frames. The shark, reacting to the sound of the
camera's motor drive, arched, lashed her tail, and

dove under the boat's stern, leaving a large whirlpool roiling on the still surface of the lagoon.

Rick stepped through the stern gate and stopped, looking down at the big tabby-striped cat. Cisco stayed right where he was, completely focused on the idea of this shark, sensing that it was still very close, his growl rising a few notes, his muscles tightening visibly. Rick reached over the stern board, scooped him up, held him high in the air. Cisco looked down at him, his tattered ears flat, eyes wide, body rigid, twenty-some pounds of muscle and bone, clearly not pleased.

"You thinking of going in there, you mook?"

Cisco's yellow eyes were crazy, battle bright. He twisted in Rick's grip, terribly strong, got his paws onto the thickly corded muscle along Rick's forearm, and flexed his claws, raking the skin. Rick, cursing with the pain, plucked him loose, dropped him onto a bench under the canopy at the pilot station, pulled the fax from the machine, spread it out on top of the control panel. The news was not good.

There was a major tropical storm coming in out of the south-southeast. The incoming front showed as a dense helix of isobars on a graphic overlay of the Florida Straits, a vortex of wind shear and atmospheric collisions. The density of the lines meant that it was a sizable storm, and moving fast. Rick had been in the Keys for three months, long enough to know what he was looking at, what it meant for a boat trapped on a bank of coral shoals ninety-eight miles out of Key West. He'd once made the mistake of thinking that a well-set anchor and room to swing a full 360 degrees in a shallow sand-bottom lagoon like this was a good way to ride out a storm. Although Rick had made a multitude of mistakes in his short but colorful career, mainly with women, he made very few of them twice.

He looked off to the southeast, over the white-water ridge where the Anguilla Cays and the change from pale green to dark blue marked the edge of the Santaren Channel. There it was, away in the southern sky over Cuba, a blue-black tower, pale gray wings, capped by a thunderhead, dark green and smoky gray, with flashes of lightning visible inside the belly of the storm. This one was a real contender, drawing energy from the cooling of the day, picking up speed and force over the warm ocean water, coming in fast.

He glanced at the radar screen. In the display the luminous sweep of the radar beam showed bright green against a black background that covered a circle thirty miles wide. The incoming front registered as a glowing green mass, solid as a wall. And there was something else. Inside the green mass, at its trailing edge, a small but very distinct red blip. An airplane. Something big, judging by the size of the radar return, and low. Just a couple of thousand feet off the water. Maybe a DC-9 storm-chaser from the weather watch or a patrolling Hercules from the Coast Guard.

A gust of wind swept across the lagoon, ruffling the surface, scattering the dying light across the bay like shattered amber glass. The cruiser stirred at her mooring, tugging at the Danforth buried in the sand. The anchor cable came up out of the water, pulling tight, droplets falling off the line. The stern came around slowly, the boat pointed her bow into the freshening breeze. Rick looked at the barometer. Dropping fast. *Cagancho* had a big monitor on the control panel, on the left of the radar display, called a Navigation Plotter, which was really a shipboard computer loaded with marine charts, running a navigation program that was linked to the boat's GPS—the Global Positioning System. If he wanted to know where he was anywhere on the screen, all he had to do was hit the LOCATOR tab and the monitor would show him his current position against a detailed background exactly like a full-color marine chart.

*Cagancho* was indicated by a green arrowhead, her position 84 degrees, 55 minutes west, 24 degrees, 5 minutes north, the northern range of the Cay Sal Bank. Due north of his position, the chart showed the westward arc of the Lower Keys, Big Pine, Ramrod, Sugar Loaf, an extended archipelago of limestone and coral that ended in the flat limestone slab of Key West. On the eastern range of the chart there was the big island of Andros and far to the south the saw-toothed northern coast of Cuba. Just to starboard there was a shoal of jagged coral called the Dog Rocks and the reef off his port bow was called Muertos Cay. Death Key? Take it as a hint, Rick. Now that he knew exactly where he was, it was time to be somewhere else.

He switched the twin Yanmar 420s on, listened to their deep burbling rumble through the decking, left the shift in neutral, went forward to bring in the anchor. Cisco followed him, padding across the long white sweep of the bow. The wind was rising sharply, ruffling Cisco's fur.

The Hinckley 44 slid forward as the anchor cable churned into the winch, a tiny bow wave foaming under the cutwater. As Rick crouched there, looking down into the lagoon, the tiger shark sliced across his bow, rocking the hull, flashing away in the direction of the Dog Rocks, her scarred dorsal leaving a spreading V of white water, two thousand pounds moving so frighteningly fast she was almost a blur. Rick made a mental note to stay out of the water for the rest of his life. Cisco watched it go from his place in the bow pulpit, gave Rick an over-the-shoulder look full of weary accusation, padded back to the cabin with his tail straight up, hooked at the tip.

The Danforth broke the surface, smelling of slime and saltwater. Rick clamped it home in its storage locker, closed the hatch cover, locked it, went back to the controls, shoved Cisco off the captain's chair. The boat drifted broadside to the wind. He let her bow come all the way around to the north, running his left hand through his short black hair, his right hand resting on the throttles, his sunburned face hardening up, thinking about tactics.

He was ninety-eight nautical miles southeast of Key West. The anchorage at Garrison Bight—*Cagancho's* home port—was on the northern shore of the key, the sheltered lee shore, like most of the marinas in the Lower Keys. It had a narrow harbor entrance that he'd have to negotiate under heavy seas and a bad head wind. There were easier reaches due north; some of the smaller Keys along the Florida coast were no more than forty nautical miles away. *Cagancho* would do thirty-two knots per in a dead calm, less in heavy weather, but he might have to outrun a following sea all the way in, or deal with ten-foot waves breaking over her stern boards and a cutting rain sheeting straight into the back of his head. And all the time he'd be closing in on a lee shore full of shoals and hidden rocks. No, Key West was out. And the nearer Keys as well. By the fax here, it wasn't a very deep front, more of a passing squall. A damn BIG passing squall, but not yet a major storm. Maybe it would be better to go right at the thing, take it three-quarters on the bow and let it pass over him.

This idea, only mildly insane, appealed strongly to his inner psychotic. But it did make a kind of lunatic sense. When you got off the Cay Sal Bank and into the channel, you had 350 fathoms—over 2,000 feet—of blue water under the keel and a straight run into the storm with no saw-toothed reefs to worry about and a world of sea room to maneuver. Both fuel tanks were topped. The boat was low and broad-beamed—no showy and irrelevant flying bridge to make her top-heavy and lunging—she was rock steady in big seas.

He'd have to mind the limestone shoals that made such a hazard of the Great Bahama Bank on his port side, but the Hinckley—driven by two high-pressure water jets—had no propellers and drew only twenty-seven inches at her deepest point; she could glide like a gull over shallows that would crack another boat's hull like a Christmas walnut. It was a wild thing to consider, but it could, with luck and close attention, be done.

Here, at the decision point, he found a quiet moment to punish himself, and being a good little dago mick from Queens, he didn't pass it up. Damn the shark and damn the cat and damn the God-damn weather fax. Damn himself most of all. If he'd been up at the controls like a grown-up, paying attention to business, he might have had time enough to make a flat-out run for the nearest key. There was an old oyster bar right on the docks at Matecumbe Key with a bartender named Caroline whose looks could melt a plastic Jesus—he could have been safe indoors and halfway through a frosted margarita and a bucket of chilled oysters by the time this storm hit the breakwater. He heard a low cry. Cisco was sitting on the deck a few feet away, staring up at him, looking, for Christ's sake, as if the cheeky little fur ball was fretting about his dinner.

"Hey, give me no grief, you psycho. Where the hell were you when the fax came in? What kind of a ship's cat are you, anyway?"

Cisco blinked at him, narrowed his eyes, blinked again, and chose the moment to lick his privates.

"Nice. Attractive. When you're through, you can do mine."

He cranked the wheel to starboard, heading for the passage between the Dog Rocks and Damas Cay. *Cagancho*'s bow surged, rose up, white water curving away from the slicing bow. She was doing fifteen knots in a few seconds. Rick adjusted the trim tabs, she came down onto plane with the storm a few points off her starboard quarter. On the radar, the red blip—well inside the storm itself—was closer, coming in at 1,500 feet off the water. He decided it was definitely a Coast Guard plane. They were all totally nuts in the Coast Guard, especially the pilots.

He engaged the auto-helm, chased Cisco down the stairs into the main cabin—ignoring the cat's scalded hiss—grabbed himself a yellow squall jacket, a Beck's beer, his blue ball cap with the New York State Police crest, shut and sealed the hatchway door. Then he got back into the captain's chair, popped the cap on the Beck's, shut off the auto-helm, took a long pull from the bottle, got a grip on the polished wooden wheel, and shoved the throttles forward.

*Cagancho* roared up, boomed out sharply, cutting a white-water arc over the lime-green seas. The boat was very fast, the seaway wide open. He looked at the front again, assessing it. The belly of the storm was filled with flickering white fire, the base deep gray and blurred with driving rain all along the squall line. The setting sun was shining on the face of it and broken light flickered along the line of jagged whitecaps being driven before it. It looked nasty, mean, and dangerous. *Cagancho* cleared the Dog Rocks in three minutes and shot out into the Santaren Channel, Rick cutting the wheel to starboard until his compass reading showed 135 degrees, a bearing that would take him southeast down the Santaren toward the Old Bahama Channel. Out of the chop and into much heavier seas, *Cagancho* wallowed and slowed—Rick throttled back, adjusted her trim and then accelerated again—the bow came back up, leveled out. *Cagancho* was cutting into nine-foot waves. Each time the keel smacked into the blue-glass wall of the wave, the boat would shudder, and two white wings of spray would burst out from under the bow.

In his three months cruising the Keys, Rick had learned to ride heavy seas standing up, hands on the wheel, taking each wave as it came, knees slightly flexed, belly muscles tight, working, his shoulders and arms braced. He could feel the true ocean under his keel, the mountainous groundswell that was always rolling far beneath the surface waves, the slower and deeper surge, the open sea coated with yellow foam, streaked with running lines of lighter green. It looked slick and slightly greasy and long ribbons of sea grass churned in his wake. The air got even colder.

Ten minutes of this, at twenty knots, the boat taking the seas at a slight angle, slicing into them and then riding up and over the waves, the front getting bigger and bigger, then the boat hit the leading edge of the squall line, the sunlight cut off like a thrown switch and he was inside the storm. Visibility dropped to a hundred feet, even less. The wind rose to a piercing howl all around him, drowning out the

engine noise. Black-and-green clouds raced overhead, shredded and flying. He could see the base of
the system above him, solid as a freeway overpass,
dense, gray-black with sun-bright flashes of lightning deep inside. The swells increased, their crests
white with foam, the gusting winds stripping off the
whitecaps. A sheeting rain came straight in at the
windscreen, drumming against the glass, bringing
the sharp scent of deep ocean, salty, rotten, carrying
with it an unwelcome intimation of his own mortal-
ity. Fighting a sudden wave of what felt uncomfort-
ably like fear, he turned up the volume on the
marine radio, checked that he was on channel
sixteen, braced himself against the pilot chair, his
eye on the compass. This was going to be rough,
rougher than he had anticipated. He could feel the
force of the wind slamming into the cabin ports and
the boat began to vibrate with the force of the storm.
He backed the throttles off to fifteen knots, put the
wheel more to port, trying to increase the angle and
take the rollers at three-quarters on. This made it
easier to ride the crests up and slip down the
troughs, but it was also narrowing the space
between his port side and the distant reefs of the
Great Bahama Bank. The world shrank to a small circle of ocean pelted with stinging rain, streaked with
flying cloud, the boat rising up one glassy green
wall, cresting the peak, sliding down into the trough
and rocking, the next green roller coming at her starboard bow, the sickening roller-coaster lift up that
one and at each crest, in that single fleeting instant

of balance, all he could see beyond this wave was the next one and the one after that, rank after rank, column on column, until they disappeared under a billowing curtain of cold rain and white water.

He found himself listening to the tone of the engines with a painful intensity, watching the seas as they came at him out of the sheeting rain, glancing briefly at the compass bearing and the sonar screen—the three-dimensional display showed him the ocean floor three hundred fathoms forward and down in a holographic display of thin green lines that twisted and reformed as he passed over the valleys and peaks of the seabed—then a quick look at the radar screen beside it—*Cagancho* was at the dead center of this storm, around it a whirling green mass—and that red blip. God, it was damn close.

Rick squinted out through the rain-streaked windshield. If he was reading the radar correctly—he couldn't be—this plane was dangerously—at that moment something massive burst through the bottom of the cloud base—less than nine hundred feet off the waves—it seemed to be coming right at Rick's head—four shimmering silver prop circles as big as the boat—wings out a hundred feet—he could even see the windscreen on the plane—the wipers flicking—in the small part of his brain that wasn't involved with regretting his imminent death, Rick heard his own voice—*Hercules—it's a C-130 Hercules*—he got a fleeting glimpse of white letters painted on the army-green fuselage—USMC—then the transport plane went over his head no more than seven hundred feet off the radio mast—four engines roaring like volcanoes—the sound deafening—the force of the prop wave flattened the sea underneath it, stopped the boat in her tracks, shoved her sideways—the deck tilted as Rick lost control—and then the Hercules was gone—swallowed up by the squalls, leaving a swirling whirlpool of shredded cloud and the reek of burning kerosene. Rick, cursing, fought the wheel—she had canted wildly to starboard as the Hercules had gone over and the seas were pounding hard on the port side—he throttled up and cranked the wheel to port—was reaching for the marine radio to report a Hercules in distress—it was the only explanation— when a second plane—this time much smaller— a twin-engine floatplane—came hurtling out of the cloud base and flashed in at him no more than 150 feet off the water—so close Rick could see the white blur of the pilot's face—black holes for eyes— another face beside him—it went over him with a snarling yowl as the twin props feathered—he heard the plane's engines sputtering—they were so close to the ocean that wind spray was choking the intakes— he saw the plane yaw and tilt—recover—the wings flexing—then it was gone too—almost into the same hole in the storm that the Hercules had cut out of the cloud bank.

Rick looked at the radar screen. There were two red blips, almost merging into one as he watched, one very large, the Hercules—it was gaining altitude—and another, very faint—both blips bearing 315, moving away fast—the seas were still pounding the boat and Rick had to contend with the wheel, which was fighting him as the ocean tried to turn the craft sideways and roll it over—she was answering, though, he could feel her coming back into the wind—the next time he had a moment to check the radar—two full and memorable minutes later—there was only one blip on the screen. The larger one. The Hercules.

The military transport was still gaining altitude, almost at the northwestern edge of the storm—as he watched the red blip break out of the green mass—her bearing was 310—a course that led right to Key West—it had to be the Gitmo shuttle—the regular supply flight that he had seen every Tuesday and Friday—the Marine Corps Hercules that flew from Guantánamo base on the southeast coast of Cuba to the Key West Naval Air Station. No other blip. Nothing else in the entire sweep of the radar. He watched the green line as it circled the screen; there was no doubt at all. One huge red blip; the Hercules, heading away. The other plane, the twin-engine floatplane, was nowhere on the radar screen. Was it so close to the other blip that the return was lost in the backscatter? Or was it gone? Was it down in the water? Rick plucked the handset off the VHF, thumbed the call tab.

"*Securité! Securité! Securité!* This is the motor cruiser *Cagancho.*"

He throttled back, let the boat come around to port a couple of degrees. The force of the storm seemed to be lessening, but it was still very strong and the wave height was rising, as they usually did in the trailing edge of a big squall. He listened to the radio. Nothing.

"*Securité! Securité! Securité!* This is the motor cruiser *Cagancho*."

"*Cagancho, this is Royal Navy vessel Blackjack. Switch to channel twenty-two.*"

A British accent, male, young, calm, very naval.

Rick hit the selector, clicked over to channel 22.

"*Blackjack,* this is *Cagancho*. Do you have a light plane down, vicinity eastern edge of the Cay Sal Bank?"

"*What's your position,* Cagancho?"

Rick looked at his GPS.

"Eighty degrees, thirty minutes west. Twenty-three degrees, forty-two minutes north. Nine miles northeast of the light at Anguilla Cay. I was buzzed by a C-130 at nine hundred feet. Right behind it, underneath it, there was a float plane, a twin-engine Kodiak, I think. Engines failing. Two people aboard, at least. It's off my radar now."

"*Cagancho, our base has the American Hercules on radar. They reported catastrophic command and control malfunctions in their onboard computer system. U.S. Coast Guard has scrambled a C-130. They advise us there is no other flight plan filed for this sector. Repeat, they advise no other flight plan filed by any aircraft. They have observed no second radar return. We observe no second return. Repeat. There is no other return. Are you sure of the second plane?*"

Rick took a full fifteen seconds to think about his answer.

"*Blackjack,* I am positive. I had two blips on my radar as they went over. I lost the small one. And I had a visual confirmation. Small twin-engine float. Dark blue fuselage, light-blue undercarriage. No markings. Possibly a Kodiak. Couldn't have gone more than a few miles northwest bearing three-one-zero."

"Cagancho, *what are you?*"

"I'm a Hinckley, a Talaria forty-four footer, jet boat, twin diesels. American flag. I'm in heavy seas here. I'm singlehanded. I am not in distress. My name is Broca. Rick Broca. I'm a civilian."

Oddly, he found that very hard to say. But it was true. He was a civilian, nothing more. Those days were gone. With the dead.

"Cagancho, *do you wish to respond?*"

"*Blackjack,* I don't own this boat. Besides, I'm miles out."

"Cagancho, *we are currently deployed on a rescue mission. We have a sailboat in shoals on the Andros bank, under a lee shore. Rudder gone. You are the nearest vessel. We will advise the U.S. Coast Guard base at Key West and follow up as soon as we have this craft secured. Will you respond? There's no one else. Cagancho? Will you respond?*"

Rick looked out across the bow. The green waves were marching in, the tops shredded by gale, the clouds streaming over his head. But at the edge of his southern horizon line, he could see clear sky and a twilight glow. He was almost out from under it. And what had he seen? And how did he know the plane was down? Maybe it was still out there, but flying so low it was under his radar horizon. And why was it any business of his? He'd informed the Royal Navy. That was all he had to do. It was up to them, and the U.S. authorities.

The problem? This wasn't his boat. It belonged to Jake Seigel, his million-dollar boat and particular pride. If anything fatal happened to *Cagancho*, he'd gouge the replacement cost out of Rick's heart with an ice-cream scoop. Rick had been in business with Jake Seigel for eight months, long enough for him to see the lizard beneath the Santa Barbara tan and the Armani wardrobe. He throttled up and *Cagancho* butted through a rogue roller that had to be fifteen feet at the crest, slipped down the broad green back of the wave in a dizzying rush. The light in the southeast was changing into a deep purple. He looked back over the stern boards. The storm was bigger and blacker than ever, gaining power every second. It was on its way to being a tropical storm; perhaps, with a little persuasion, even a hurricane. And night was coming on. Damn. God damn.

"*Blackjack,* this is *Cagancho*. I'll respond."

"*Very good,* Cagancho. *Look for a debris field. We can detect no EPIRB or ELT signals from that vicinity. Can you monitor one-two-one point five megahertz?*"

They were talking about the safety devices known as Emergency Position Indicating Radio Beacon— EPIRBs—water-activated radio transmitters that were mandatory gear for planes and larger water-craft in the Caribbean. *Cagancho* had one on board, in a red metal case right next to the pilot wheel. In these waters, EPIRBs broadcast their distress signal at 121.5 megahertz.

"*Blackjack,* I can monitor one-two-one point five, but I'll come back to your channel twenty-two every fifteen minutes. Time check?"

"*Cagancho, the time is twenty-one hundred hours, fifty-eight minutes. We acknowledge your intention to come back to channel twenty-two every fifteen minutes. Good luck to you, Captain Broca.*"

Captain Broca. Rick caught the meaning. The man was saying, you might be a civilian in a borrowed boat, but, in this storm, you're a sailor, and this is the sea, and you have your duty right in front of you. Rick bristled. He didn't need stiffening, especially from some pencil-neck Limey gearbox with a tea-and-crumpets accent. He kept his temper, managed a civil good-bye.

"Thank you, *Blackjack.* Switching."

He punched 121.5 into his radio, let out a long breath and brought the wheel around quickly, throttling up hard as he did so, the stern swinging around quickly, carving a foaming white swath into the face of the following wave. He felt the boat's forward rushing rise as the big roller came up under her from the stern boards. The bow was pointing down, right into the glassy green wall of the wave in front of them. He pushed the throttles to the bar; a huge explosion of white spray from the twin water jets that propelled the boat—the long navy-blue hull came up slowly—blue-green water foamed across the pulpit and sprayed across the bow almost to the windscreen—*Cagancho* rode up the wave, the force of the following sea weakening as she gained speed. He pointed her northwest on compass bearing 310—right back into the storm.

Rick never did manage to put together a coherent memory of the next hour, only a few vivid images; a terrible wave that broke over the stern boards leaving a lake of dark water that bubbled and boiled back down the scuppers at the stern, the weight of the water pushing the stern down, lifting the bow, the sickening feeling as he waited for the boat to power out from under it, a sizzling crack of lightning that arced from one side of the sky to the other—lit up the seas like the midnight sun—Rick saw his shadow in flickering violet on the side curtain—a reverberating peal of thunder so loud it hit the front of his chest like a flat-handed blow—much later, a freak moment of silence during which he could hear Cisco complaining through the sealed cabin hatch, switching back to 22 to report nothing at all to *Blackjack*—*very good* Cagancho *carry on*—you pompous dork; I'm not in the Royal Navy yet—not a peep on 121.5—then the growing awareness that the intensity of the wind was dropping to a bearable howl—the waves less punishing—the sea rolling but no longer like a bucking horse—the light changing—Andromeda was overhead and low in the north he could see the Great Bear and part of Draco over the shoulder of a cloud bank, a pale half-moon riding the edge of the cloud inside a halo of mist—he was almost out from under, with the Dog Rocks a couple of miles south-west of his position.

In a few more minutes, it was over. He was in a gently rolling current with streamers of thin cloud overhead. In the north-northeast, he could make out the receding bulk of the storm, sheet lightning like pale-blue fire inside it, around it the stainless-steel stars piercing the mist, the veil-like sweep of the Milky Way running sidelong up the night sky, a broad river of luminous pink dust. A cool wind, the sea rolling gently, his own breathing, Cisco bitching with real conviction.

He throttled down to a slow cruise and the quiet rushed in from everywhere, the roar of the diesels settling to a dull throbbing beat. He put on the auto-helm, walked back to the stern and stepped out onto the port catwalk, then went forward to the broad white bow, feeling a cool salty wind on his face, the boat rising and falling on a gentle rocking swell. He drew in a long breath, let it hiss out between dry lips, stretching his arms and flexing away the stiffness in his back.

Although a man could rot faster in the Keys than anywhere else in the world, Rick was still hard, well muscled: he had managed to stay in shape by spending a few hours every week fighting pickup matches at a boxing gym in Key West. At this point, he felt like a man who'd gone fifteen rounds with a bark chipper. He badly needed a shower. And some hot coffee. He walked back to the controls, cut the engines, listened very hard.

He was alone out here. He could feel it.

Aside from the soft hissing of the wind and the lapping of water along the keel, there was silence. In all of the wide rolling sea around him, from the faint white curl off his port beam, where the Gulf Stream was racing northeast around the Dog Rocks, all the way into the northeastern horizon, where a soft yellow glow against the night sky marked the lights of the Florida coastline, there was nothing to be seen. No flashing emergency strobe light. No debris. No distant air horn sounding a distress call. No signal from any EPIRB. No radar return. All the way up the channel, he'd kept an eye on the sonar and he had seen nothing unusual on the ocean floor. Certainly no debris from a light plane, although there was plenty of litter and junk down there and a few ancient wrecks. Even some unexploded bombs in two hundred feet of water, about two miles northeast of his position, according to the chart, dumped there in 1967. But nothing new.

No wreckage. No flotsam. Nothing at all. He stood there for a while longer, listening carefully, but all he could hear was Cisco working himself up to a stroke down in the main cabin. He picked up the handset.

"*Blackjack,* this is *Cagancho.*"

"Cagancho, *this is* Blackjack. *What's your position?*"

"*Blackjack,* I have the Dog Rocks two miles off my port side. I'm in even seas, under a clear sky. I've run off thirty-two miles on a general bearing of three-one-zero. I've had my sonar on, and the radar, and

I've monitored one-two-one-point-five for any locator signal. I have detected zero. Nor have I received any distress calls on sixteen or twenty-two."

"*Roger,* Cagancho. *Any debris in the channel?*"

"Nothing, *Blackjack.* Have you received any distress calls?"

"*Negative, Captain Broca. You're still certain of your sighting? The floatplane following the transport?*"

"I stand by it, *Blackjack.*"

"*Right, then. We'll log this at twenty-two hundred hours, fifty-five minutes this date and send in a formal report. My name is Bonden. I'm the captain. You're a brave man, sir, and our whole crew would be honored to buy you a drink anytime and anyplace you choose. Are you all right? Any damage?*"

"No damage, *Blackjack.* I need fuel."

"*Do you have enough to make port?*"

"Affirmative. By the way, did that Hercules get home?"

"*Yes, it did. Arrived safely Fleming Key. Apparently they managed to bypass the damaged computers and fly by brute force. Took both the pilot and the copilot to hold her on course. Very near thing. We'll break off, then. We have a ship under tow and are making for Port Simon. We'll file a commendation.*"

"Roger, *Blackjack.* Thank you. *Cagancho* out."

# GREEN

Was Cisco going to get tired anytime soon? Apparently not. Rick went down the ladder, popped the hatch and stood aside as Cisco ran up the steps from the big main cabin, backlit by the warm yellow glow from the cabin lights. The cat made his extreme disapproval of Rick Broca and all his works very clear as he sauntered up to the control deck and jumped up onto the captain's chair. Rick rubbed the cat's badly chewed up ears—Cisco liked to start unprovoked fights whenever he was on shore leave and his choices were seldom wise—and looked out across the water.

According to the radar, the storm was heading west by northwest. The night promised to be a calm one. He could run back toward the Dog Rocks, cruise around them to that big shallow lagoon by Muertos Cay, drop the anchor, lay up for the night, take *Cagancho* back to Key West in the morning. Seigel and his current pull toy were flying in on

Monday. Seigel was planning a fishing run up the Keys and across to Nassau. *Cagancho* was a floating tribute to every electronic device known to modern high-tech sportfishers. Seigel wanted to bag a record black marlin and take it back to L.A. to astound the yokels. He wanted this thing very badly, and yet for years had bagged nothing but snappers and wahoos. Maybe this trip, Seigel would get his trophy fish. Rick hoped so. It might make the man easier to work for.

If he got into the marina by Saturday, he'd have time to clean up the boat, restock her, hand her over to Seigel in perfect condition, then maybe get the hell out of the Keys and go back to L.A. He had technical reads to do on another batch of shooting scripts, and a possible consultation on a new police pilot Seigel's television subsidiary was trying to pitch to HBO. Golly. What fun.

Whoring for dollars, sucking up to stainless-steel MBAs like Jake Seigel, peddling his law enforcement skills in bits and pieces from a rented fake-Spanish bungalow out in the valley complete with an above-ground pool full of mud-brown water, a concrete front yard spray-painted puke green and a navy-blue Jimmy stuffed under a rickety carport made of rippled orange fiberglass. Just like every other busted-out or broken-down ex-cop working the movie hustle out in Hollywood. How the hell he had gotten here, he couldn't remember. Well, actually, yes, he could, but he didn't want to.

Whatever had led him to this place in his life, it

was time to go back. He switched on the engines, slipped into drive, let the boat glide in to clear the northern part of the shoals, planning to pass them to port with a clearance of fifty yards. He was at the southern edge of the Gulf Stream, the great Mississippi of current that ran through the Straits of Florida, halfway up the Eastern seaboard and, eventually, all the way to the coast of North Africa. It called for some judgment, especially when you were in tight around jagged shoals and flint-edged reefs.

The sound of the Gulf Stream streaming around the Dog Rocks was a gentle soothing hiss; a soft blue light from the half-moon off his bow bathed the inner banks. He was bringing her around to starboard to run west of the shoals and into the anchorage when something solid struck the boat up near the cutwater, thumped along the port side. Rick's heart blipped, he put the boat in neutral, picked up a four-cell Maglite and leaned over the side.

Something was bobbing in the stream, just under the surface, passing toward the stern a yard off the hull. There was a gaff hook in a rack by the stern boards. Rick used it to snag a piece of webbing, tugged it up to the surface. It took him less than a second to realize what he was looking at. Bracing himself against the rail, he set the gaff in tight, held his breath, dragged the obscenity on board and let it flop onto the deck. When it hit the boards, Cisco flattened, hissed at it and backed away into a corner, spitting like a frying pan full of bacon. He put the Maglite onto the mess.

Well, he'd seen worse when he was a state trooper, including a young hitchhiker in Lake Placid who'd been beaten to death with a shovel, set on fire, and, much later on, half-eaten by a black bear. However, this was still pretty impressive.

It was recognizably human, in that a head with much of its facial features remaining was still connected by a webwork of sinew and gristle to a shiny pink spinal column and a few bitten-off stumps of bone—all that was left of his rib cage—the whole grisly assemblage miraculously held up by a partially deflated yellow life jacket. There were some stringy remnants of the upper torso, part of the right shoulder, some sections of his right arm. The chewy bits, was Rick's guess. After all, nobody really likes gristle.

The man had been very strong, with a powerful upper body densely packed with muscle and sinew, but below the sixth vertebra there was little to speak of. The expression on what was left of his flat Indian face was at best disapproving. Being eaten alive often has that effect, even on a normally cheerful person.

Looking at his face, Rick concluded that, had they met in life, they would not have liked each other very much. Around the neck, wrapped into a few shreds of teal material that might once have been a Polo shirt, there was a shiny necklace of steel beads. Rick reached down delicately, fingertips only, his pinky finger held out to the side as if he were at tea with the vicar, managed to lift it over the skull, held it up in the light. At the end of the necklace there was a large sterling-silver scapular medal with an image of Saint Christopher, the patron saint of travelers, and on the obverse face, an inscription:

> *Por Geronimo*
> *Y la regla de ocha*
> *—Narcisse—*

Rick figured this guy's immediate travel plans were limited to a free cruise down some carnivore's alimentary canal, so he set the necklace aside. There was a box of green garbage bags down in the galley. He brought three of them up, stuffed each into the next to make a triple-strength package, somehow managed to get . . . what's-his-name . . . into the bag. He didn't go in easily, had a tendency to flop around a bit, not all of him was reliably attached to the rest of him, and those particular parts had to be rounded up and gotten back into the garbage bag.

He noted with queasy semiprofessional interest that some of Geronimo's meatier bits were still pretty warm, much warmer than the ocean he'd been floating in. In gastronomic terms, you could describe Geronimo as *market fresh*. Which seemed to suggest that whatever had been dining alfresco on this hapless mook had pushed itself away from the picnic table only a few minutes—or seconds—before Rick arrived. He had found several very large triangular shark's teeth scattered through the wreckage, yellow, oddly familiar. Looking at the bloody devices in the palm of his hand, a line from

Chuck Berry came to mind: *Maybelline, honey is that you?*

During the cleaning-up process, Rick developed a renewed respect for all the Crime Scene Unit guys he'd been happy to abuse during his ten years as a New York State Trooper. In a few ugly minutes, he had the majority of Geronimo stowed away fairly well. He used the twist ties to seal the bag, lifted the package up, dropped it into one of the fish freezers in the stern, stood over the cooler, feeling that there was something he should say. Finally, he got it out.

"Geronimo, I see you've already met Maybelline. Maybelline, the chunky Latin entrée you just scarfed down was a hapless mook named Geronimo. I hope you two crazy kids can be happy together."

Cisco listened to this speech quite gravely and then went back down the stairs to the main cabin without further comment. Rick felt that he may have offended the cat, but decided that he was being too sensitive. He used the ship's pump to hose down the deck boards, pulled in a shaky breath, laughed once, slightly manic, went back to the port rail. Where there was this he figured there'd be more. He was right. He played the Maglite over the water, saw something shiny bobbing in the running seas about twenty feet off the bow. Rick turned on the engines again, moved her forward very slowly, keeping the flashlight on the object, which was drifting eastward with the current at almost ten knots.

It was a section of sheet metal, curved, maybe a yard long and a foot wide, riveted, twisted, and bent from a major impact, kept afloat by a lining of flotation cells. Navy blue above, light blue underneath. Part of an airplane float? Rick snagged it with the boat hook, managed to get it on board, almost certain that it was debris from the missing plane. He set it down on the floor of the stern and went back up to the con, intending to call the Coast Guard and report the wreck, but instead got quite distracted by the sonar screen.

It was showing metal on the seafloor, sixty feet down, a section of wing about fifteen feet long, some scattered smaller parts, a shattered float with a large section of strut and cable still connected. The path of the debris led away south, right toward the Dog Rocks.

Steering by the sonar screen, he brought the boat closer in toward the shoal . . . more debris on the sloping wall of the shoal . . . a section of fuselage . . . an engine, with the props bent at crazy angles, dug into the gravel bottom . . . more parts that could have been bits of the fuselage . . . a huge section came into view, right at the base of the Dog Rocks, in fifty-six feet of water, vaguely conical, maybe fifteen feet long, part of its starboard wing still attached.

*Christ.*

It was the entire nose section, the pilot cabin itself, snapped off cleanly in back of the exit doors, right where the wing section began. In the sonar image, it seemed to be relatively intact, sheered off as if it had been cut with a blowtorch. In the holographic image on the sonar screen, he could make out the surfaces of the windscreen, the curve of the forward cowling, lying in a debris field about twenty by fifty feet, right at the edge of a drop-off that bottomed out at three hundred feet.

As he studied the screen, it struck him that there was something wrong with the images. Exposed interior pieces of the wreckage showed up clear and strong in the sonar return. But the returns from the exterior surfaces, the painted surfaces, came back much weaker, and scattered. He adjusted the gain, but the effect did not go away. He'd spent weeks playing with all the electronic toys that Seigel had indulged himself in; he knew their capabilities by now. The plane had been coated in some sort of radar-suppressing paint. It was the only explanation. Rick flicked on the infrared fish-finder mounted in the hull below the forward trim-tabs.

On the television screen, the pieces of debris showed up as reddish glows against a soft green background. Which meant they were still cooling. He saw a thin line of smaller red pinpoints rising up out of the wreck, rising in a slanted line, moving with the current but coming up toward the surface, expanding as they rose. Hydraulic fluid leaking from a severed control line? Gasoline? Oil from a ruptured tank?

He brought the boat in another few feet, until the wreck was right underneath him, turned her bow southwest to put her nose into the current roiling around the rocks, set the water jets to stabilize her, so close to the reef he could hear the surf breaking on the rocks. He went to the side, looked down into the black water. Something was foaming on the surface, inside a lake of greasy water reeking of kerosene. As he watched, another thin stream of beadlike objects rose up and were taken immediately by the current.

This wasn't oil, or hydraulic fluid. They were bubbles. Air bubbles. Regular as breathing. Coming up from the cabin section. He went back to the infrared screen. There was a very faint but evident reddish glow around the cabin windscreen. Rick was pretty certain that he had seen two faces in the windscreen of the floatplane. If someone was still alive inside that cabin—not damned likely unless he had some sort of air supply—he wasn't going to last very long. On the other hand, there was the Maybelline factor. He hesitated for a while, watching the faint glow inside the cabin section.

*Why was this his problem? Besides, he'd already done ten years as a cop, most of that time spent helping out assorted numb-nut civilians who had usually done something heroically stupid to get themselves into trouble in the first place and who frequently turned out to be as grateful for his assistance as a bucket of rabid badgers. If he simply called the Coast Guard and let them deal with it, well, who would ever know? He didn't even have to tell them that there might be someone alive in the wreck. There sure as hell wouldn't be, by the time they got here with a dive crew and a derrick. Well, so what? The planet was too damned crowded anyway.*

Swearing softly to himself, Rick went forward,

took out the Danforth, let it run out through the port cleat, the cable slipping away into the water, fifty-four feet of it running off by the red marker bands before it went slack as the anchor struck the bottom. He went back to the controls, let the current take the boat northeast, running the cable out to over a hundred and thirty feet—nearly to the bitter end—until he could feel the tug of the anchor. It felt like it had a good bite. It had better. If the Danforth slipped and the boat drifted away into the deep water channel only a few hundred yards away, the Gulf Stream could take this boat all the way to Africa. Cisco was sitting on the deck, watching with detached feline interest as he pulled off his squall jacket and his jeans.

"Look, cat. I'm going down there. If I'm not back in an hour, you take the boat to Key West, tell them that Timmy's in really really bad trouble."

Cisco gave him a meaningful look that might have meant, *Damn straight, oh my Captain. Key West it is, and bring back the cavalry.*

Or not. Seigel, an avid sportsman, had two complete Scuba rigs stored in the equipment locker, fins, wet suits—one big enough for Rick—twin Dacor tanks that Rick had filled two days before at Garrison Bight. The broken cabin was lying on a ledge of rocky shoal fifty-odd feet down, an easy dive, except for the current that was running northeast at almost ten knots, the southern edge of the Gulf Stream. Rick was suited up in two minutes, but he wasn't very happy about this whole rescue idea.

If Maybelline was still around—and still a tad peckish—there was an excellent chance that the final seconds of his life would be quite spectacular and involve more than a bit of hysterical shrieking. He offered up a brief but devout prayer that Geronimo had been a very substantial guy, a stick-to-your-ribs kind of guy with lots of fiber and that Maybelline was off in a quiet cove somewhere far away, humming a Broadway tune and picking her teeth with one of Geronimo's pinkies.

He paused on the swim platform as another stream of bubbles surfaced through the oily seas. The kerosene scent of aviation fuel was thick, almost overwhelming. He heard a grating sound, looked back to see Cisco behind him, playing with Geronimo's silver necklace, tossing it around the deck, obviously using denial to cope with his desperate anxiety for his beloved shipmate in this perilous hour.

"Hey, Cisco—are you playing around like that because you're using denial to cope with your desperate anxiety for your beloved shipmate in this perilous hour?"

Cisco stopped toying with the necklace long enough to give Rick one of those upside-down cross-eyed cat stares and yawn hugely, showing Rick his fangs and the pink ridges of his upper jaw. Then he blinked twice and went back to the necklace.

Rick figured he had his answer. His hands shook only slightly as he slipped the Maglite onto his wrist strap, put the regulator in his mouth, inhaled deeply: he waited briefly for some timely access of courage to still the tremble in his right knee, gave it up as hopeless, and stepped off into the black water. Inside a rush of foaming bubbles, he arced, kicked out for the anchor line, fighting the current, got a firm grip, went down it hand over hand, his skin crawling with barely suppressed panic, the heavy Maglite bouncing on his wrist strap. The rope angled down into a complete blackness, Rick was swimming blind, but he wasn't about to stop anywhere on the way down to turn on the Maglite. Until he was safe on the bottom, he had no way of covering his back. If there was anything out there in the black water—naturally he was thinking mainly of Maybelline—well, she could come at him from any direction—below—above—behind—until he could get himself down to the seabed. But nothing did.

He was moving so fast, kicking so hard, that when he finally reached the anchor, well set into the rocky slope of the shoal, he damned near broke the lens of his diving mask on its ringbolt. He used the anchor as leverage, spinning around to get his tanks on the ground, breathing much too fast, his chest pounding, the pressure of all that water making his ears throb. He squeezed his nose shut, equalized, felt a hissing pop inside his skull, and the pain stopped. He had made it down.

He turned on the Maglite, moved the spotlight around him. It penetrated into the blackness, a thin tunnel of gray-white light, the beam filled with drifting motes. As the light hit it, a school of colored fish flashed like sparks from a fire, then disappeared into the black water. Beyond the school, Rick could see a curve of blue metal. The cabin section. He took a second to calm himself, let go of the anchor, fought the vicious current, kicked out toward the cabin, holding the light on it and staying as close to the seabed as he could.

It lay on its right side, a bit flattened by its own weight, but it looked fairly intact. Rick braced himself against a rocky outcrop, put a hand on the side, slapped it twice. At once two loud booms sounded from inside the cabin. Rick flinched with the shock, although the extremely slim chance of a survivor was why he was down here on this suicide mission in the first place. He came around to the windscreen, put his light on the glass. A man's white palm, pressed up against the glass, moving across it, flat as a snail's pod. Rick shifted the light. A man's face, gray hair waving in the water, his eyes underwater huge, blurred, and unfocused, with something in his right hand—a large red cylinder. Compressed air? As he watched him, the man inside the cabin put the tank's nozzle to his mouth, pulled in a lungful, shouted something to Rick, the air exploding out of his round blue mouth in a muffled cry, meaningless, thick with panic. The bubbles spread out along the inside of the windscreen, found a crack in the frame, and flew up in front of Rick's face like fireflies, swallowed up in the dark. Rick turned the light on to his own body, held up his hand, palm out.

*Wait. Be still.*

He put the light back on the man. His face was bleached of any color, his pale-brown eyes filled with horror. He managed a nod, then put the cylinder nozzle back to his mouth. Rick tapped the glass three times and let go. Kicking away toward the upper side of the cabin, Rick found the door, lifted the handle, put his fins on the wall, jerked it hard. The door shifted an inch. He heard a metallic shriek. Stuck. The frame was twisted from the impact. The other door was buried in the shoal.

He'd have to come at him from the sheared-off section of the plane, a risky thing to do. He could easily get snagged himself, or rip his air hose on a piece of metal. He had no choice. Pushing off hard, he glided down the length of the cabin until he reached the place where it had cracked open. In the glow of the Maglite, it looked like a steel cave, a tangle of broken metal and struts, the interior a maze of bent spars and popped bulkheads. At the far end of the cave, he could see the man strapped into the pilot's chair. Why was he still in the chair? Because he couldn't get out? Or wouldn't get out. Had he seen what happened to Geronimo?

Rick went in, feeling the sharp-edged sheet metal tear at his wet suit, stuck for a moment on a spur, strained against it—a *pop*—he was inside the cabin section. Sheltered from the current, it was calmer inside. Bits of gear drifted into the beam of his flashlight. There was something tubular caught on a broken spar—a rifle. An AK-47. What the hell was this guy doing with an AK-47?

He floated over it and came up to the man. He was big, looked to be in his fifties, wearing a leather jacket, tan slacks. He was twisting in his chair, watching Rick come up, one arm outstretched. When Rick reached him, the man's grip on his upper arm was massive, crushing. Rick took the regulator mouthpiece out and handed it to the man, who popped it in, took a breath that must have lasted fifteen seconds, exhaled explosively, and immediately took another. Rick held his breath, waited patiently. The man was close to panic, with every reason to be there. If he was going to calm down at all, air would be the only thing to help him.

While the man was pulling in more air, Rick put the light on the man's legs and saw the problem. The man's left knee was pinned under a section of the control panel. He was trapped.

He was also wearing a pistol in a holster strapped onto his right thigh. From the grip, Rick made it out as a Glock. He felt a tapping on his shoulder, shifted the light to the man again. He was holding the regulator mouthpiece out to Rick. His expression was a bit wild, but he looked like he was under more control. Rick took the regulator, inhaled twice deeply, offered it to the pilot again. The man shook his head, lifted the red cylinder, took a pull from the nozzle.

It occurred to Rick that breathing right off the nozzle of a compressed air cylinder was very tricky, took some training to get it right. With no regulator attached, you had to control the feed very carefully, or you'd drive so much air into your body that you'd literally pop a lung. Or force an embolism. This man had survival training. Although he was clearly in the final stages of nervous collapse, he hadn't let the situation kill him. He had himself under tight control, sliding along the razor's edge of panic but not yet lost.

The man lifted his frame off the chair, smacked a hand on the control panel twice. Rick nodded, indicating that he understood, that the man's leg was pinned. He shone the light around the interior, looking for a tool of some kind, but there was nothing in the wreckage other than litter, scrap, and broken struts that had snapped off some sort of storage racks.

He pushed off, drifted over to the tangle of broken metal, got a grip on a protruding shaft and tugged it hard. It slid free, a two-foot length of what looked like titanium. He swam back to the pilot with it, who was watching him with ferocious attention. He nodded rapidly as Rick reached him, then he grabbed the long bar out of Rick's hands, rammed it into the panel, driving it into a slot between the altimeter and the radio, smacking it home with three blows of his fist. The sound, although muffled in the water, was solid and the frame of the cabin shook from the force.

This man was extremely strong, but there was too much sharp metal around his leg. If he slipped or jerked the wrong way and opened a femoral artery down here, he'd bleed out in a minute. Rick stopped him with a touch on his left shoulder, handed him his regulator again, watched him calm down a couple of degrees. Rick had plenty of air left in his double tanks. At fifty feet, it would last them both perhaps another half-hour. He held up his hands, palms out.

*Slowly. There is time.*

He handed it back to Rick, even managed a distorted smile, put both hands on the bar, braced himself in the chair, heaved upward. Nothing. The console creaked, but did not shift. He banged the end of the bar again, resetting it. Rick tried to move in to help, but there wasn't enough room. Because the man was strapped in and had the leverage, he was able to bring much more force to the effort. All Rick could usefully do was to stay by him and watch.

The big man wrapped his hands around the grip again, set himself, heaved it upward again. There was a loud grinding sound . . . the man kept pulling . . . a muted screech of metal giving away . . . more pressure—a sharp cracking sound as the console gave away, the bar flew up, and he was free. The fabric over his left knee was ripped and a thin cloud of black blood drifted up from a green-looking gash above the kneecap. Rick watched the shapeless black cloud dissipate into the cabin and felt his throat tightening.

*Blood in the water. Blood in the water.*

Ignoring his wound, the man scrabbled at the harness release, his panic resurfacing. Rick could see that his chilled fingers were too numb to open the buckles. Rick came in over the man's left shoulder, pulled the release; the belt slipped away. He had to hold the man down in his chair, the man's eyes widening in anger, to force him to take the regulator again. He waited while the man took three long breaths, the bubbles making a rushing sound and collecting on the upturned windscreen, a silvery oblong like liquid mercury. Under his hand Rick felt the man's shoulder vibrating with cold and fear.

He pushed away from the cockpit, shone the light back along the cabin toward the sheared-off end, put it back on the man, who nodded twice, pulled on the regulator again, handed it back to Rick. The pilot stopped to pick up the red cylinder, then pushed himself off the chair, drifted over to Rick, getting a grip on Rick's dive belt. They eased their way carefully through the hanging clutter until they got to the opening, where Rick put his light on the anchor cable, a gray line rising in an arc off the seafloor about fifteen feet away. Pausing to give the man some air, then taking the mouthpiece back, Rick shoved off toward the anchor cable, feeling the weight of the other man tugging on his belt. Back in the current, they had to fight all the way across the seabed to reach the cable. When they reached it, the man tapped Rick on the shoulder. When Rick put the light on him, the man pointed up the cable and shook his head.

Rick looked at him, raised both hands, palms up. *What?*

The pilot tapped his own chest, then held both

hands out, put his palms together and drew them apart, then held up the red cylinder. Rick understood. The man had been breathing compressed air for . . . Rick had no idea how long. Judging by the size of the cylinder, as long as an hour, possibly. If they went up the anchor line too fast, he could have an embolism, as the nitrogen inside his saturated bloodstream expanded into microscopic bubbles. It was called decompression sickness. The bends. If he ascended too fast, it could cause a strokelike blockage in a major artery, paralyzing him. Or killing him outright. He gave the man the mouthpiece again and while he was inhaling, checked his air pressure gauge. They had used up more than he had estimated, probably from a combination of fear and the effort involved in prying the console off his legs. They had perhaps fifteen minutes of air left at this depth, not enough for both men to come up slowly, not enough to give both of them a critical five-minute decompression stop at ten feet below the surface. He shone the light on the cylinder, reached for it. The man let him take it. Rick turned the nozzle slightly. A thin stream of bubbles ran from it, flying upward into the blackness. Then only a few. Then nothing. It was empty. The man watched this, then held the mouthpiece out to Rick, shrugged his heavy shoulders. Rick let the tank fall away.

It was fifty-four feet to the surface in a straight line, through black water, a blind ascent, and they'd surface into a current that could easily drag them so far away from the boat they'd never be able to reach it. And Rick wasn't very keen on the idea of thrashing around on the surface with God knows what coming up from the deep water below. The only semi-safe method was to follow the anchor cable up, a run of a hundred and thirty feet before they reached the boat. Rick had been down no longer than twenty, maybe thirty minutes, too short a time to require a decompression stop.

If Rick let the man have the tanks, Rick could surface without them, blowing out air as fast as he could. With luck, he'd have some minor pain in his inner ears from the ascent, but nothing serious. It would leave the other man enough air to decompress at twenty feet, then again at ten.

Rick slipped off his depth indicator, gave it to the man. It showed a depth of fifty-two feet. Rick held up his hand, five fingers spread, made a fist, spread out five fingers, did this four times—*twenty feet*—did it again twice—*ten feet*—the pilot nodded vigorously.

Rick undid the straps holding the twin Dacor tanks, lifted it over his head, held it out to the man, who at first shook his head, then seemed to understand what Rick was doing. He reached for it—and stopped, his eyes widening. Rick felt a pressure wave ripple across his back—the man reached for him, jerked him into the seafloor—Rick turned, put the Maglite out in front of them. Both men watched as a huge striped shape glided through the beam less than twenty feet above them. It was Maybelline. As they watched, she moved slowly, ponderously, through the thin gray beam, her terrible mouth open slightly, her gills pumping, her tail sweeping back and forth. Rick kept it on her and tracked her until she slipped into the complete darkness beyond the reach of the flashlight. The pilot gave Rick's back a forceful shove. Rick took his point.

*Fuck the decompression. Let's go.*

Rick flicked the beam around, trying to find Maybelline. Nothing but blackness and the wall of greenish rock at their backs. He picked the scuba tanks off the rocks, slipped them back on, gave the mouthpiece to the pilot, watched as he pulled in two breaths, took it back, inhaled deeply, pointed his thumb to the surface. The man nodded vigorously, his face blank and stiff.

Rick gave him the Maglite, then he crouched, looked up along the sloping line of the cable. It seemed to stretch away for miles into a black infinity. He wrapped his hands around the anchor cable, fought his screaming nerves for a second, kicked off hard, the man right with him, his left hand locked around Rick's dive belt, the Maglite circling around them, Rick going hand over hand up the cable, both of them blowing out air as hard as they could—black water all around—forty feet—their own air bubbles cascading up in the bobbing light of the flash—Rick felt his inner ears pulsing—a terrific pressure building inside his skull—the anchor line slick against his palms—the drag of the pilot's weight—twenty feet—the big hull looming over their heads—ten feet and silvery bubbles fluttering around the hull—then thumping into the cutwater—letting go of the cable

and striking out for the swim platform at the stern—
forty-four God-damned feet away—but with the current now—Rick looking down into the deep and
seeing nothing—his hands on the swim platform—
the pilot in the water beside him—heads breaking
into the air—Rick gasping from the dizzying pain in
his ears—a wild scramble up onto the platform—the
man tried to sit there but Rick kept him moving—
Maybelline had come up onto the stern boards
before—he followed the man's stumbling form as he
pushed through the gate and fell onto the stern deck.
Rick slammed the gate. They had actually made it. As
Rick pressed his nostrils shut and blew hard, trying
to clear the terrible pressing pain in his ears, the
phrase *in one piece* came into his mind.

The pilot lay on his belly, breathing hard. Rick
watched him as Cisco came up from the cabin and
padded across to him, giving the soaking-wet
stranger a wide berth. Rick shrugged off the gear, his
lungs heaving, and half-crawled across the deck to
the man, who rolled over onto his back as Rick
reached him. His eyes were on the night sky filled
with brilliant stars, the pink band of the Milky Way.

"Christ, I thought I'd never see those things
again."

His voice was hoarse, resonant, definitely
American, something Mid-western. Rick kneeled
over him.

"You okay? Any bends?"

The man put both hands on his upper chest.

"Feels crinkly under the skin. Nothing else. I

guess we'll have to wait and see. Unless you've got a chamber on board."

"Damn. Forgot to pack one. How long were you down there?"

"Man. Who knows? An hour, I think. Maybe less."

"Can you sit up?"

The man grunted, put out a hand. Rick pulled him to a sitting position, stood him up, stumble-walked him to one of the stern settees, got a couple of big beach towels from one of the lockers. He handed one to the man, who buried his face in it, rubbed his hair vigorously, coughed a couple of times, and watched as Rick wrapped the other towel tightly around his bleeding knee. When Rick had finished, the man turned to look out at the water.

"What was that thing?"

"Maybelline," said Rick.

The man looked at him with a bleary hazel eye, red-rimmed.

"It had a name?"

"She's known around here."

He grinned, his seamed face creasing even more.

"Too fucking right she is. What was she, a tiger?"

"I think so. I've only seen the one."

"That was the biggest damn shark I've ever seen. Why didn't she go for us?"

Rick hesitated.

"I think she'd already eaten. Can you walk?"

The man leaned back against the stern rail, vibrating slightly, his gray hair wild, his face drawn and old-looking, his hands crossed over his lap. He closed his eyes and pulled in a long weary breath. Rick stood over him, considering the man's state of mind. He'd been through something that would have driven most people insane. If he needed a moment, Rick was happy to wait.

"I owe you," the man said, after a while.

"Damn straight," said Rick. "And I owe you too. I totally locked up when I saw Maybelline. If you hadn't given me a hard shove at the right time, I'd still be down there."

The man grinned once more, a fierce look, his teeth very white against the tan, his color rapidly returning.

"I hope to sweet Jesus I never go through anything like that again. I cannot believe I'm standing here. I could tell I wasn't too far down. The pressure wasn't strong, you know? But when I tried to get up and I couldn't . . . I had some bad . . . if I'd had a knife, I was going to try to cut my way out . . . but I didn't have a knife . . . the stuff that runs through your mind . . . people you're leaving behind . . . things undone . . . I was going to use the pistol when the oxygen ran out."

The man looked to be fighting a breakdown. Rick could hardly blame him. When Maybelline had passed through the flashlight's beam, the shock, the fear had been unlike anything he'd ever felt in his entire life. It was time to change the subject or they'd be having an Oprah moment.

"Oxygen? Was it pure oxygen? In the red tank?"

"Yeah. In case the cabin pressure dropped."

"Then I don't think you're going to have the bends. Not enough nitrogen in the mix. I hope so. I'm Rick Broca, by the way."

The man looked up, weaving slightly, put out a hand.

"I'm Green. Charles Green."

Rick took the hand, shook it. It was cold and hard.

"You did well down there. You military?"

Green looked surprised by the question, then shook his head.

"Not at all. Are you?"

"No," said Rick. "You a drinking man?"

"Only on days with a 'd' in them."

"How about three fingers of single malt? Over ice."

The man smiled then, his tired face creasing up into deltas and furrows of deeply ingrained humor.

"Skip the ice. I've taken on all the water I can hold."

# LA LUNA NEGRA

Forty-five minutes later they were sitting in the main cabin below, Rick in jeans and a towel, Green in one of Rick's sweat suits, his knee bandaged, leaning back on the padded benches that ran around the polished teak dining table, a CD of Harry James playing softly. The interior of the boat was lined in teak, with tulip-wood trim, shining brass highlights, marine lamps glowing warmly on the bulkheads, a stainless-steel sink and fridge, a stand-up shower and head, storage lockers and closets with teak doors, a forward stateroom under the bow with a large double bed. Rick had a big pot of chicken soup brewing on the propane stove. They were each nursing short, squat crystal glasses filled with ice and Glenfiddich and a splash of bottled water. Cisco was out on the stern, up on the fish locker, picking at the latch. Trying to get at Geronimo, Rick guessed. Rick didn't want to think about Cisco's motivations.

He was watching Green and listening to his breathing, but so far there was no sign of anything

61

that might be the bends. Maybe it really was the pure oxygen he'd been breathing, or an amazing constitution, or was it simply a side effect of fear? If Green got through the night without any symptoms, Rick was going to write it up for those science geeks in that ocean institute up at Marathon Key.

"Why the Glock?" asked Rick.

It was lying on the galley countertop across the cabin, next to a plastic Ziploc bag full of money and what looked like an old photograph of two tiny blond-haired girls standing beside a sand castle on a tropical beach somewhere, a long gray warship in the distant background, palm trees framing the shot. Green had set it out on a piece of paper toweling, carefully flattened it out. While Rick had been in the shower Green had field-stripped the pistol, a Glock 17, and dried the parts off with more paper towels, sprayed the pieces with some WD-40 that Rick had under the kitchen counter, then put it all back together. Rick had been in the shower no longer than three minutes. If the guy wasn't military then he was a cop.

The magazine was on the counter beside it, empty, also sprayed with oil. The bright brass rounds with the black tips were lined up neatly, sixteen nine-millimeter soldiers in a tight rank beside the box magazine. His clothes, the bomber jacket and the slacks and the rest, were hanging on hooks in the stand-up shower, dripping water. A cheap Timex watch on his left wrist, too small to cover the ring of pale skin underneath it where, quite recently, there had once been a much bigger and more substantial watch. No passport, Rick had noticed, and no wallet. No ID of any kind. Maybe it was still in the wreck. Maybe not. The cop in Rick was wide awake.

Green glanced at the pistol, shrugged it off.

"Hijackers. Thieves. Bums. I fly all over the islands. Not every passenger is a good guy."

"You're a charter pilot, I take it?"

"Yeah. Tourists. Sometimes freight. Odd jobs."

Thinking about the radar-suppressing paint and the AK-47, Rick was quiet for a few seconds and Green took the time to look around the interior.

"This is one hell of a boat. Whatever you do for a living, you must be damn good at it."

"Not mine. It belongs to a guy in L.A. He's in the business."

"The business?"

"Sorry . . . the film business. I've been there less than a year. Already I'm calling it the business. Like there's only one."

Green smiled, and then jumped a bit as Cisco leaped up onto the tabletop, padded over to him, ears forward, tail up. Rick swatted the cat off the table, gave Green an apologetic look. Cisco hissed at Rick, jumped back up onto the bench, standing beside Green and glaring indignantly at Rick over the guy's chest. Green rubbed the cat behind the ears. Cisco immediately settled down beside him, purring like a piston engine.

"Damn," said Rick. "He won't let me near him."

"I get along with cats," said Green. "We used to—"

He stopped and a spasm of something like pain passed over his face. He recovered, reached for the scotch. Rick watched his hand as he lifted the glass. It was shaking very slightly. Was it the bends? They could take up to thirty-six hours to develop. You knew it when they hit you.

"You need to get to shore," he said.

"Do I? I guess so."

"You won't be guessing if the bends set in and you're nowhere near a hyperbaric chamber. They have one at Trumbo."

"Trumbo?"

"The naval base in Key West."

Green was quiet for a while, his thoughts invisible to Rick. He decided to shake the guy a bit, see what came loose.

"So what's the story?"

Green gave Rick a hard look, then realized the meaning.

"The crash?" He leaned forward, rubbed his hands over his face, ran them back through his hair, staring at the tabletop. In that moment, Rick thought he looked eighty. Something was weighing on this guy. Something unpleasant. Green sat back, sipped his scotch.

"What happened? That God-damned squall happened. It topped out at ten thousand feet, too high for me. I was way overloaded. So I was coming in low, trying to get under it, and I caught a wave right in the props. Water up the intake cowling. The engines started to pop. Started to miss. I tried revving her, but it only seemed to foul the plugs up. I feathered the props, hoping for a glide and some clean air to dry out the intakes, but she dove like a fish hawk and I barely got her off the water. It was too rough to put her down anywhere. She kept missing and I kept fighting her and I covered . . . hard to say. . . . Seems like I fought her for a week. I got out of the worst of the squall. I could see the shoreline lights due north so I figured if I could get her on the northern side of one of the Keys, I could put her down in flat water. All the way, it was ten feet, twenty feet off the water, trying to get some altitude, the thing is pitching and rocking—then, when I think I'm going to be okay—*bang*—I run smack into the tip of a huge swell—the port float hooks in—she dips—the port wing catches too—the props shear off and the port engine start to shake apart—I kill that one but now I'm way too low and the next wave is right there in the windscreen. I'm going around in a spin cycle—the plane is breaking up all around me—the water comes up at me. I go straight into it like into a brick wall. When I come to, I'm in a very wet, very black place. I can't get out. I'm going to die. I didn't. That's pretty much it. I'm going to do my best to forget all of it. And, Rick, again, I thank you. From the heart. How did you find me? What made you look in the first place?"

Rick decided to give him a piece of the truth.

"You damn near took my radio mast off, down by Anguilla Cays. I saw you go over. I heard the engines. I knew you were in trouble. I put her about and came back, looking."

Green looked right at him, very awake.

"You saw me go over?"

"Close enough to throw you a beer."

"You said you 'put about.' You mean you were going south, into the squall?"

"I was doing southward what you were doing northward. Trying to get out from under the storm. My way worked."

"Then you turned around? You came back? Why?"

"Excellent question. Remind me to ask my shrink as soon as I can afford one. Did your troubles have anything to do with the Gitmo shuttle? And why you were tailgating it like that?"

Green looked at Rick for a long moment and Rick held the look, waiting for the man to decide which way he was going from where they were. A hissing sound from the galley distracted them both. The soup was boiling over on the stove. Rick made a move but Green stopped him. Rick let him.

"I'll get it."

Green slid around the table, crossed to the galley, and lifted the pot off the element, setting it down on a tile next to his Glock. He had his back turned to Rick. He picked up the Glock in one easy motion, turning as he did so, the muzzle now pointed in Rick's direction. Not at him, but close enough to make Rick's belly muscles jump. He leaned back in the banquette, put both hands on the table. Green kept the Glock on Rick through these motions. The look on his face was complicated and Rick found it hard to read. Both men said nothing for a minute. Then Rick smiled, laughed softly.

"Goodness. Was it something I said?"

The expression in the man's face changed, solidified into something closer to sorrow. Rick couldn't help but smile at him.

"Damn, my friend," he said, "a Hercules is a very big plane. I'd have to be doing something really interesting with underage twins to overlook it when one of them comes flying out of a squall line about eight hundred feet off the deck, not to mention a few seconds later, when a second plane fires out of the same hole in the clouds, only this time much closer to the deck, barrels off into the clouds again right on the Herc's tail rudder, engines sputtering, clearly knee-deep in shit."

The muzzle of the Glock was aimed right at Rick's head. He could look right down the black hole. Light from one of the overheads was shining into the muzzle and he could see a section of the rifling, the soft sheen of milled steel inside the barrel. He picked up his scotch, took a sip, held the heavy glass in his right hand, feeling the smooth chill of the crystal, the solid and satisfying weight of it, the way the clear white light from the ceiling shone down on the ice and the scotch, the taste of it in his mouth, as sharp and biting as the smoke from burning leaves. Cisco was lying on the bench a few feet away, snoring audibly. He figured cats were required by the union to be of no practical use whatsoever. If this were true, Cisco was the

Jimmy Hoffa of the cat union. Rick was finding it difficult to fake this jaunty devil-may-care-I-laugh-in-the-face-of-death facade while his genitalia seemed to be undergoing a total and possibly irreversible retraction. Green's bitter laugh cut the silence.

"Are you really as calm as you look?"

Rick shook his head slowly.

"No. And if you keep pointing that thing at me, I'm going to embarrass both of us. Listen carefully. I'm not a cop. I'm in the movie business. That ought to make you feel better. We do nine things before breakfast that would gag a wolverine. Whatever you're into, I have no intention to get in your way. Maybe I can help you make a decision. Here. Catch."

Rick tossed something toward Green. It tumbled in the light, golden and black. The Glock never moved. Green caught it with his left hand, held it in his palm, glanced at it, came right back to Rick. Lying in his palm was a nine-millimeter round, steel-jacket with a nasty black tip. Rick was smiling back at him.

"You lined up sixteen rounds next to your magazine there."

Green couldn't help but look down at the magazine and the file of brass soldiers. Then he looked back at Rick, pulled the slide on the Glock, saw the empty chamber.

"And you knew this Glock has seventeen rounds. Very nice. You're no more Hollywood than I am. You're either a cop, or federal, or military. Which is it?"

"None of the above. I'm a technical advisor for

the guy who owns this boat. His name is Jake Seigel. Paradigm Pictures? Cop films, action movies. I'm supposed to know all this stuff."

The man's face was getting rockier.

"What about the ball cap over there?"

Rick glanced at the hook by the forward stateroom. His navy-blue New York State Police cap was hanging there, drying off.

"I have about twenty of those. Feds. Fugitive Squads. Cops give them away like business cards. I am not a cop. Or anything like it."

Green looked uncertain. Rick tried for an open sunny expression. Since his lean Sicilian face was a tad battered from several years of club fighting—he wasn't as good at it as his mother would have liked—and he had a number of abrasion scars in the skin around his deep-set pale blue eyes, and his nose took a detour on its way down his face, innocence didn't shine from him as brightly as it used to, say, when he was six. But the muzzle dropped a few inches.

Rick stood up, came across to the counter, stepping around Green to get the pot of chicken soup. The aroma was magnificent. He couldn't recall when a simple bowl of chicken soup had ever smelled quite so fine. And it was very nice to be alive as well. Green stepped out of the way and, after a moment, set the Glock down by the magazine, dropped the seventeenth round onto the teak. He walked away to the table, sitting down with a heavy sigh, his face lined and haggard under the lights. Rick turned the stove off, poured out two mugs of soup, carried them over, put one down in front of Green, sat across from him with his own. Steam curled up from the mug. The boat rocked softly in the current streaming around her bow. They both drank some in silence. Green leaned back, sighed.

"How'd you know I wasn't going to shoot you?"

"You could have shot me when I was in the shower."

"How'd you get the round out of the Glock?"

"While I was working on the chicken soup."

"What if I had reloaded it? I'm quick enough."

"I was going to throw the glass of scotch at your head. It's a heavy glass, and I'm a sneaky rat-bastard. I freely admit it."

"I'm beginning to see that."

"Did your flight have anything to do with the Gitmo shuttle?"

Green paused, shook his head.

"I took a lightning strike when I got close to the trailing edge of the storm. I was having compass problems. Everybody knows the Gitmo shuttle runs all the way to Key West. That's where I was going. I tried following it and when it came down so fast, I went into the squall right behind it. Then everything went to shit."

The lie about "compass problems" was so handless Rick didn't have the heart to call it on him. His doomed flight was all about the Gitmo shuttle and Rick had a pretty good idea why. The Caribbean Basin was one of the world's most heavily watched sectors. The U.S. had multiple geosynchronous surveillance satellites stationed above it and routine AWACS flights to back them up. Anything that moved on, under, or over the Caribbean Basin was bagged and tagged by every agency from the DEA to the NSA.

Now a deeply lunatic pilot might try flying under a larger plane, hoping that the big return from something like a Hercules would create so much backscatter that he could fly in—or out—of the U.S. undetected. He'd have to be tucked right up under the thing, a suicidal stunt given the prop wash and the turbulence around the Hercules. Also, the crew would have to be a parcel of bonehead lifers, a not impossible requirement in the Marine Corps. Radar-suppressing paint would certainly help. His compass trouble was complete bullshit. Maybe when the guy was in better shape he'd come up with better lies. So now was a good time to keep asking questions. Rick wasn't a cop anymore but he still had all the instincts in full working order.

"What was so important in Key West that you had to fly through a tropical storm to get there?"

Green didn't answer, his face closing up. Rick sighed.

"What's this? Client confidentiality? Modesty?"

"I was carrying a passenger."

"Oh yeah? Where is he?"

"I wish I cared. Out there . . . somewhere. Why?"

Rick reached into his pocket, rooted around, brought his hand out, dropped the steel necklace onto the table. It lay there on the teak surface, a coil of bright metal under the light. There was dried blood around the engraved portrait of Saint Christopher. Green looked down at the medallion, turned it over, read the inscription.

"Where is he?"

"You're going to have to be more specific. Which part?"

Green stared at him.

"Well, some of him is in the fish locker. The chewy bits."

"You think—what's her name? Maybelline?"

"I'm learning to recognize her work."

"Is that why she let us go?"

"Isn't it pretty to think so? Thing is, bumping into what was left of Geronimo here was what led me to your location in the first place."

"So . . . so you weren't actually tracking me?"

"Tracking you? Hell, no. I was being a Goddamned Boy Scout, if you want to know. And look where it gets me."

"I couldn't figure out . . . how you managed to find me. All I could think of was that you . . . knew something about the flight."

"Nope. I'm totally innocent. It's a first for me."

This came as a shock to Green, that was clear.

"So, you weren't looking for me. Finding me—down there—that was . . . luck? Simply my dumb luck?"

"I'm afraid so. Life's a thin line. I'm glad I did, if that helps?"

"How did you find me anyway?"

Rick told him about the electronics on board, about Seigel's fascination with swordfish and marlin, the sonar and infrared fish-finder gear. Green listened with quiet but increasing attention. When Rick got to the part about the debris on the seabed below them Green interrupted him with a question.

"How much of the plane is down there?"

"What I could see? The pilot cabin, sheared off at the wings. One of the floats, bits and pieces."

"How about the cargo section? Anything like that?"

"I saw a debris trail that led in toward the Dog Rocks, and found you stuck there on a ledge about fifty feet down. I stopped looking after that. It drops off fast when you get by the Cay Sal Bank. If you had crashed a few hundred yards east of here, you'd have found yourself in almost two thousand feet of water."

"Two thousand feet?"

"Damn close."

"Can your gear—can the sonar read at that depth?"

"Sure it can. But whatever's down there is going to stay there unless you have some serious deep-sea gear. A minisub, at least."

"So you saw nothing that looked like a cargo section?"

"Not a thing. But like I said, I stopped looking when I saw the cabin. If you ask me, I think your plane pretty much disintegrated on impact. I'd ask for a refund on the purchase price, if I were you. If you like, we can do a cruise back along the debris path, see what we find. You after anything in particular?"

At that point, Cisco snapped fully awake and began to do that cat-mojo thing Rick had seen him do many times before, popping upright, bristling, staring wide-eyed at absolutely nothing, fully alert, his ears forward, body tensed, humming with brilliant attention. Rick watched him do it, thinking *the brain of a newt*.

"No . . . I mean, there was nothing I can't replace."

Rick didn't believe a word of it. The guy was a lousy liar, which made Rick think more kindly of him. His entire professional career had been one long and wearying verbal sparring match with a succession of depressingly gifted liars. This guy was refreshing.

"No payload, Charlie? Nothing on board other than what's left of Mister Sharky-Treats over there in the fish locker?"

"Payload? No. There was no payload."

Green stopped asking questions then and considered the medallion in silence for a few seconds. Rick watched Cisco bristle up like an electrocuted hedgehog at totally zip. Man. Now the psychotic little nitwit was actually growling. Cisco the method cat. Green skipped the medallion across the tabletop, sat back again.

"Well, at least that fat prick was good for something. If he hadn't jumped out of the plane at exactly the wrong fucking time, we might have made it to Key West. The man had never been in a plane before. The Herc came down almost on top of us, forced me onto the deck. This chicken-shit clown lost it a while after we crossed over you—I remember seeing your boat—long white upper deck over a blue hull—he popped the God-damned cabin door and stepped out onto the port float just as that fucking wave came along. She dipped, the float caught the wave. That was the end of it. We—"

Both men jumped as a huge blast of noise hammered through the hull. A horn. A ship's horn. It sounded again, a bull's brassy bellow echoing across the water. Rick looked at Green, held up his hand, and went up the steps to the pilot deck. A floating island of lights was idling out in the channel, less than seventy feet off their port rail. It looked to Rick like some kind of big sportfisher, a Bertram or a Hatteras, maybe sixty feet long, with a two-level flying bridge. Her engines were muttering and burbling in the current. He could make out several men on the bow and two more on the upper bridge. She was flying an American flag at her stern. As he watched, a searchlight flicked on at one side of the tower, blinding him, and a man's voice, American with a touch of Cuban or Mexican, came from the ship's loudspeaker, friendly, relaxed. Jovial.

"Are you in trouble, *Cagancho?* Can we assist you?"

Rick stepped out of the cabin and onto the stern.

The light followed him out and he stood there, inside the beam, one hand up to shade his eyes.

"Yes. You can get that damned light off me."

It didn't move.

"Turn the God-damned light off," Rick shouted, angry, shielding his eyes from the brutal glare. The man on the bullhorn ignored the request to turn off the light.

"You are okay, then? You are *simpatico*? You need anything?"

"Who are you?"

"We are *La Luna Negra*, out of Miami. Who are you?"

There was motion around the stern of the sportfisher. From the stairwell, he heard Green's voice, a hoarse whisper—"Don't let them come aboard"— and the sound of metal sliding on metal. He was loading the Glock. Rick didn't answer him. Something about the sportfisher was wrong. The davits. The rack above the stern, where the tender would usually be—it was empty. These big cruisers always had a Zodiac or a couple of Jet Skis on a davit. Where was the—

A gentle thump. The boat dipped. Rick sensed the weight shifting, spun around and grabbed the gaff hook as a man with a pistol came up over the starboard side rail, Indian or mestizo, blunt-faced, his skin almost black—the man's brown eyes widened as Rick stepped into him, struck him across the side of the neck with the gaff, feeling the shock of the blow all the way to his shoulders. The gaff hook punched into the man's throat, ripping deep into the flesh. The man screamed and reeled, blood sheeting over his chest.

*Man. What if he's a cop?*

On the deck of *La Luna Negra*, the man with the bullhorn was yelling at them—something threatening, in gutter Spanish—but nothing about being cops. Rick let go of the handle and shoved the man off the rail. He fell back into the Zodiac in the water below him—his scream choked off by the blood filling his throat—sprawling—knocking another man down into the boards—Green stepped up beside him as the other man, trying to get his balance in the rocking Zodiac, lifted a machine pistol. Green shot him three times with the Glock, the smack of the rounds punching into the man's body lost inside the earsplitting crack of the weapon. The man fell back into the waves.

The other man was still thrashing around on the wooden floor of the Zodiac, squealing faintly, trying to pull the gaff hook out of his throat. Green put a round into his forehead and then two more rounds into the nose of the Zodiac. Air began to rush out of its punctured hull. Somebody with a heavy weapon was firing at them from the cruiser, firing wild, the rounds spattering into the waves very close to the waterline, blue-white fire flickering out from somewhere to the left of that huge searchlight. Green turned directly into the glare of the light—aimed the Glock—steadied his right hip on the portside rail—fired another four quick rounds—the searchlight snapped off and they heard glass shattering across the water. There was a flicker of blue fire from the group of men on the bow and a pattering sound like hard rain on the hull, then the rhythmic thumping percussion of full-auto fire.

Rick ran forward, killed all the lights on the boat and started the engines. He backed the boat against the pull of the anchor cable. White water roared up around the hull. The cable pulled tight, the bow dipped, held fast by the Danforth. More full-auto fire from across the water; Rick heard the rounds skipping off the deck, and one shattered the port window a foot from his head.

Green was firing back at them with the Glock—seven rounds in a rapid staccato—each shot a sharp cracking boom—a cry of pain came across the water—*cingada!*—the full-auto fire stopped abruptly and then Green was up beside him, crouching below the shattered window, fumbling with his leather jacket, pulling out a box of rounds, dropping them onto the deck, the rounds rolling across the floor.

"The anchor," said Rick. "Cut the rope."

"With what?" said Green, jamming rounds into the magazine, his face lurid in the green glow of the instrument panel. They both heard the sound of engines accelerating from over the water. Rick looked out the broken window. The big boat was closing in and someone in the bow was firing at them with a pistol, somebody good. Two solid booms echoed across the water and two heavy rounds smacked into the superstructure by the pilot chair.

"In the galley."

Green finished loading the Glock, tossed it to Rick, went down the stairs. Rick heard him crashing around below. Then he was back on deck and running along the catwalk on the starboard side, away from the incoming fire, something glittering in his left hand. Rick put the Glock out through the broken window, fired several rounds into the bow of the big white boat, hoping to hit one of the dark shapes silhouetted against its cabin lights.

A white bow wave was curling around the cutwater of the cruiser. He could see a man at the wheel in the upper bridge. He put a wild round out in the general direction of the figure and saw the radar dome behind him shatter. A fluke, but he'd take it. Green was crouched at the bow, his shoulders working, sawing at the line. The shooters in the bow must have seen his figure against the white deck, because rounds were snapping by his head. That had to stop.

Rick aimed the Glock into the press of men on the bow, emptied the magazine into it. Why those mooks didn't kill their own cabin lights he couldn't guess. He saw a dark figure tumble off the bow, the shooting faltered and then Green was shouting at him. He could feel the boat slipping backward. He spun the wheel to port and hit the throttles.

Green stumbled across the heaving deck, ran back along the catwalk and fell into the stern as Rick brought the boat up to plane, the engines maxed out, the jets blowing a fountain of white foam behind them. He looked back to see the sportfisher, still closing, a very fast boat, maybe even faster than the Hinckley.

He took the boat around the western side of the Dog Rocks, putting them between him and the other boat and ran flat out across the moonlit sea on a course that took them deep into the shoals and reefs of the Cay Sal Bank, *La Luna Negra* following in their wake, a huge white prow gaining fast, men with weapons on the bow.

Green stepped up beside him, lifted the Glock out of his left hand, went back to the stern in a low crouch, took a position behind the fish locker and began to reload the magazine.

"Forget that," Rick shouted. "I've got a rifle in the forward stateroom. Rounds in the nightstand."

Green was past him before he got all the words out, laying the loaded pistol on the panel in front of Rick and disappearing down the stairs into the main cabin. Rick twisted around, saw the cruiser coming in at full speed. How could such a big damn boat move so fast? He cut the wheel to starboard and headed out across the shallow waters of the banks, into total darkness, nothing but moonlight and his sonar to steer by, all of his lights out except for the glow from the control panel, running flat out at thirty-two knots with both engines howling, the jets streaming white water. The Hinckley was light and fast, but not as fast as this damned sportfisher. And someone was standing in the bow of the pursuing boat, with a large weapon, a black shape against the running lights on the cruiser. He saw the man steady himself on the pulpit frame, lift the weapon, aim it—short, tubular—oh please.

"Green. What the fuck are you doing down there? Buggering the cat? There's an asshole back here with a LAWS."

Green's head popped up at the cabin door, the .308 in his hands.

"How the fuck am I supposed to find a fucking rifle down there without a fucking light? What LAWS?"

Rick jerked his head over his shoulder. Green stared back at the boat, took in the figure struggling to center the antitank weapon, shook his head sadly.

"Man. I'd zig if I were you."

"Thanks for your input," said Rick, who began to saw the wheel back and forth. The deck heaved as the Hinckley dug in to port, sending a huge starboard bow wave off into the dark water sparkling with moonlight, then another wave on the port side as he cut back. Their wake ran out behind them in a weaving white V, the cruiser a pale gray mass dotted with running lights slicing after them across the phosphorescent sea. There was a long table in the upper cabin, behind the navigator's chair. Green sat down at it, took an elbow brace on the table and steadied the Remington. Rick kept sawing the wheel back and forth, cutting the boat right and then left. After a minute, Green took his eye away from the iron sights and snarled at him.

"I can't hit a damned thing unless you go straight."

"Neither can he. And you told me to zig. Do what you can."

"On your head, then," said Green. He bent over the rifle again, while Rick's back muscles tensed up waiting for the LAWS to put a rocket right up his— Green fired—the flat crack of the rifle stunning inside the cabin—Rick heard the slide working—the brassy *ping!* of the spent casing hitting the deck—the bolt sliding home again—another shot—the bolt working again—a third deafening crack.

"Shit. Give me two seconds of straight," said Green.

Rick cursed softly, stopped working the wheel, took a straight run. Two seconds only and then—the rifle boomed out. Rick turned to see the man with the LAWS pitch over the side and disappear into the huge white waves curling out from under the bow of the cruiser. Christ, he thought: the man shoots like Gunny Hatchcock. Who the hell *is* this guy? Immediately, a row of blue sparks flickered on the flying bridge and a string of rounds stitched their way across the stern boards, sending wood and fiberglass chips flying into the air.

*Jesus Christ. Seigel will pop a carotid.*

He had the throttles pushed forward right to the bar, cutting the boat right and left in broad irregular arcs, trying not to get predictable. Green kept up a steady focused fire with the .308, shot after careful shot, working the bolt like a machine. Rick was watching his sonar and the GPS chart. In the screen, the bottom was an undulating three-dimensional wire-frame picture of the shoaling bottom.

Green had emptied the Remington and was reloading the magazine. He looked at the sonar screen, saw the bottom rising up sharply, saw the depth readings.

"What are you doing?"

"You want to drive?"

"No."

"Then—with respect—please fuck off."

He turned again to look behind him. The cruiser was less than a hundred feet back, so close he could hear the deeper rumble of its engines over the howl of the Hinckley's jets. Green watched it coming for a moment, shook his head again, shoved the magazine home and slapped the base, went back to the table, settled in, braced. The first deafening crack of the weapon came a second later. Rick heard the bolt working. Calm, deliberate, no hurry at all.

*If this mutt's a charter pilot, I'm Agnes of God.*

The sounding numbers were flicking across the top of his sonar screen. Thirty-six feet. Thirty-four. Twenty-eight. In the screen, a long narrow shelf was undulating, reforming as the radar return came in and the machine made its calculations and laid out the 3-D wire graph. Ahead of him, over the white bow and the spray flying wide, he saw nothing but a flat field of shining water pale white under the half-moon, not even a ripple where the reef was lying. Twenty feet. Nineteen. Ten. The bottom was shoaling out fast. There was no fire coming from the cruiser. Green fired one last time, worked the bolt, looked into the chamber.

"I'm out," he shouted. "All you had?"

"Yeah. What are they doing?"

"They've stopped shooting. I think they intend to ram us. If you're interested. I'm getting seasick, by the way."

Rick could hear the cruiser's bow wave, the hiss of her cutwater slicing through the water. He looked back. They were less than eighty feet off his stern. He stopped zigzagging, held the wheel steady, saw the speed climbing again. In the sonar screen the bottom was coming up very fast, a wall of reef less than a hundred feet away. The cruiser's bow was much closer, figures on it, holding weapons. Green could make out individuals, separate Cuban faces. He came over to the navigator's chair, picked up the Glock, looked at the sonar screen, then at Rick.

"Mind if I point this out? That's a shoal."

"And you're a Zen master of the stunningly fucking obvious."

Green looked at him, nodded, shut his mouth, took the Glock, walked back to the stern. Rick heard him firing, then a faint crackle as the fire was returned from the cruiser's bow.

"Stop shooting."

"Why?" Green shouted. "Afraid I'll piss them off?"

"Just stop."

Green stopped. Rick watched the sonar screen, the bottom rushing up like a virtual-reality graph of an explosion. Eight feet. Three feet. The boat raced in toward the shoals, the cruiser hard on her stern, forty feet back. Closing fast. Rick braced himself against the chair. As if that was going to help. Held the throttles hard down. Held his breath, too, watching the numbers flickering on the screen.

*Three feet six inches.*

*Three feet two inches.*

*Two feet ten inches.*

*Three feet nine.*

*Six feet seven.*

*Nine feet nine.*

They were through. Rick turned to shout at Green. "Get down."

Rick saw Green turning to say something. Beyond his black figure the huge gray-white cruiser was flying across the water right in their wake, no more than twenty feet off the stern, cutting a glittering white spray out of the shining water—a second more—Rick watched her come on—*please—please—* and then *La Luna Negra* struck.

Struck hard.

The big white bow flew up out of the water—men were tumbling off her decks—the fishing towers flexed, and then snapped off—over the howl of their jets and the deeper snarl of the diesels they heard the impact—a sound like a big tree falling—a terrible rending crack—the cruiser tilted crazily to port—her black under-keel visible in the moonlight—white water foamed up all around her port rail—her engines roared—her props spinning in the air at her stern—her momentum carried her forward—they could hear her keel grinding over the rocks—then a rushing bow wave as she hit the deep water beyond the reef, and the sudden silence as her engines choked out.

She slipped free of the shoal and settled onto her port side, rocking in the white water, big waves cresting away from her, and men jumping into the water all around her, tiny black dots thrashing in the moonlit sea. Rick looked away, cut the wheel to starboard, and checked the compass.

He came back around to bearing two-seven-one—a line that would take him west right across the banks toward Double Shot Keys—and dropped the rpms by twenty percent. The note of the twin Yanmars softened to a deep vibrato. Then he set the auto-helm and walked back to the stern, where Green was leaning on the fish locker, watching the wreck of *La Luna Negra* rocking in the swells.

"Well," he said. "That was a moment."

"Yes. It was," said Rick, sitting down heavily on the settee by the stern gate. Green was staring out at the wrecked cruiser falling far astern, at the white wake streaming out behind them. Neither man said anything for quite a while.

Finally Green spoke.

"What was the name of that boat again?"

"I think it was *La Luna Negra*."

"*The Black Moon*?"

"Yes."

"Tell me, Rick, back when you first saw me, when you figured I was going down, did you put it out on the VHF?"

"Yeah. I got a callback from a Royal Navy ship."

"They ask you your position?"

"They did."

"When you got to . . . where was it?"

"The Dog Rocks."

"The Dog Rocks. Did you give them your position then?"

"Oh yeah. So I guess they were your business associates, hah?"

Green was quiet for a long time.

"What does this boat draw, anyway?" asked Green, still looking back to the wreck, a distant white blur almost invisible against the broad flat plain of the ocean. Rick rubbed his hands across his face, feeling a wave of exhaustion pulling him down.

"Twenty-seven inches. Slightly less at speed."

"You took a hell of a risk."

"This is a forty-four-foot boat. Most people expect it to draw a lot of water. They obviously didn't think I could go anywhere they couldn't. But *Cagancho* is very light, has no props, only the jets. That Hatteras draws three times the water. But she was fast. Too fast."

"Damn straight. She was a rocket."

"So I took a chance."

Green nodded.

"I guess you figured for the tide, right?"

"No. I guess I figured, what the hell?"

"What the hell?"

"Yes. What the hell."

Green was quiet for a while longer. They both stared out at the long white wake spooling out behind them, the moonlight on the ocean, the night sky filled with stars. Finally, Green said:

"Cubans. I think they were Cubans."

"Cubans?"

"Yeah. You know. From Cuba. Cubans from Cuba."

"I'm very glad to hear that."

"You are? Why?"

"I thought they were cops."

# KEY WEST

MOTOR CRUISER *CAGANCHO*
TEN MILES SOUTHEAST OF KEY WEST
7:20 A.M. EDT, SATURDAY, SEPTEMBER 21

A mango-orange sun had cleared the eastern horizon, flooding the seas around them with a soft pink light. The breeze that always freshened at dawn was ruffling the peaks of the churning surf, and the U.S. flag on the stern mast was snapping and flowing. In the northwest a low bank of white cloud marked the island of Key West, still below the curve of the ocean. They were breasting a rising swell on the port quarter, taking the rollers slowly, at the end of an eighty-mile northeasterly run bearing two-nine-nine that had brought them all the way from Double Shot Keys. They were alone on the ocean, except for a tiny white sail that was cutting a notch out of the western horizon. Cisco was out on the foredeck, sprawled on the boards, sleeping soundly, his fur stirred by the wind. Green and Rick were on the pilot deck, Rick at the wheel, Green in the navigator chair, both men watching the light that was filling up the world.

Green had fallen asleep in the chair around the time they cleared the Double Shot Keys, four hours ago. He was awake now, and back into his own clothes, the rumpled tan slacks and the leather jacket, stiff and salt-stained. There was a constraint, an imposed silence, on them both, each man waiting for the other man to speak, neither man quite ready. The adrenaline had slowly ebbed away, leaving them slack and empty. Rick was keeping an eye on the fuel tanks. Both gauges were close to zero. Miles back, he had cut the engine rpms down to a slow cruise, the boat gliding in near-silence across the water.

Eight miles out, Rick shifted, looked at the ship's clock, picked up the VHF radio. Green sat up and watched him, a wary look surfacing in his lined face. Rick ignored him, keyed the radio.

"Key West Marina, this is *Cagancho*."

There was a period of silence, then an answer, a female voice, young, very worried. A French accent, Parisian, perhaps, or Geneva.

"*Key West. Rick, is that really you?*"

"Hey, Zeffi. Good morning."

"*Good morning, Rick. Where are you? Are you okay?*"

Rick looked at the chart monitor.

"I'm eight miles southeast of Whitehead Spit."

"*Oh Rick . . . we were all very worried about you!*"

Rick glanced at Green, held up a hand.

"You heard me on the radio?"

"*Of course we did. We monitor the emergency radio twenty-four hours a day. Our Coast Guard relayed your transmissions all the way back to the Keys. We all heard*

*you talking to the British ship, and then you went right
back into that storm after that missing plane. So brave.
Everyone was cheering for you here. Are you coming in?"*

"Yeah. Zeffi, can you do me a favor?"

*"For a hero, I will do anything."*

"Can you call Enzo Vumbacca over at Land's End
Marina? See if he has a berth available? Tell him I'm
coming in. I have some damage and I need it handled this morning. Early."

*"It was very bad?"*

"Bad enough. Paintwork, some fiberglass on the
stern is marked up. Port-hole glass gone."

*"We saw it on the news. You're lucky you got through it."*

"Zeffi, I'll see you later, okay?"

*"I'll call Enzo. He's always there. See you later, then?"*

"Count on it. *Cagancho* out."

*"Bye, Rick. Be safe. Key West out."*

Rick put the handset back in the cradle, leaned
back into the pilot chair, stretched hugely. Green
was watching him carefully.

"Who's Zeffi?"

"She's the dockmaster at the marina."

"A friend, I take it?"

Rick sent Green a hard look. He smiled back.

"Yes. She is. Coffee?" asked Rick.

"Sure," said Green. "I'd like that."

"Take the wheel. She's still on auto-helm. Just
keep an eye out for deadheads, anything drifting. If
you see any boats, let me know."

Green took the helm, and Rick went below to
brew some coffee. The Glock was lying on the

dinette table. He did a press check and saw a round in the chamber. From the weight of the piece, he figured it was fully loaded. The .308, empty, was lying on the double bed in the forward stateroom. He stuffed the pistol into his belt, pulled a white T on to cover it, put the coffee on to brew, and, to ease his conscience and to avoid reality for another sixty seconds, gave the Remington a quick wipe-down with a cloth soaked in lanolin and sprayed a burst of WD-40 down the barrel. Then he sat down behind the dinette, thinking, *Okay, now what?*

In a few minutes, too few, the coffee was ready.

He poured two cups, black, and carried them up to the main deck. He sat down in the navigator chair and handed one of the cups to Green, who took it with a nod and sipped it. Key West was visible in the north, a flat island under a cloud bank. A silvery sparkle was rising into the air at the eastern edge of the island, a jet taking off from Key West International. Rick knew there was a Florida Highway Patrol station right near the terminal. They ran regular patrols out of the Salt Ponds near the terminal, high-speed pursuit boats mainly, forty-footers, each one with a 50-caliber forward and a pair of light 7.62s on each rail. He could see one of them, a low gray gunboat shaped like a barracuda, running parallel to them, a mile off their starboard bow.

"Okay," he finally said to Green. "Please explain this."

Green finished his coffee, set the cup down.

"Rick, I can't get off the boat at any marina."

"How about you tell me your real name? For a start."

"I don't want to get you involved."

Rick had to laugh at that one. Even Green smiled.

"It's true, anyway. I can't get you any further into this."

"What is this, anyway? In the Keys, it's always one of three things. Guns. Drugs. Or cash. Usually all three."

"Not this time."

Rick considered the man in the pure morning light. His face was seamed and weathered, a man who had spent a long time in the sun in a dry climate, gray hair wavy and long, a big muscular frame.

"As a liar, my friend, you're a disaster. I admire you for that. The world is crammed to the rafters with highly gifted liars. I'm already involved, so let me give you my reading on this. Okay?"

"Yeah. Fine," he said, with a shrug. "Knock yourself out."

"You're using a Glock with the serial numbers erased and flying a Turbo Twin with no markings, radar-suppressing paint, dark blue on light blue to make you hard to spot from above or below, a float plane so you can land in any lagoon or shoal in the Keys. You came in underneath the Gitmo shuttle to avoid the satellites and the AWACS all over the Caribbean Basin. Only a seasoned pro could even attempt that. In my opinion, someone who had been a military pilot, a combat pilot. The Gitmo shuttle runs from Guantánamo in Cuba to the Key West

Naval Air Station at Trumbo every Tuesday and Friday. You were under the inbound flight, which means you picked it up somewhere near the coast of Cuba, because you needed to get under it before it got too far from Cuban airspace and before your own plane could get picked up by the surveillance satellites. To do that, you had to have the help—or at least the permission—of the Cuban authorities, because ever since we moved those Al Qaeda mutts to Gitmo they've been getting real scratchy about aircraft in their zone and shoot them down whenever they can. You've had survival training, and you handle yourself in a firefight like you've been there before. Often. You have no identifying papers, no possessions at all other than a snapshot of a couple of kids on a beach somewhere, a bundle of U.S. bills, and a cheap watch that doesn't quite cover the space on your wrist where your real watch used to be. You're what they call 'covert.' Before we got into the running fight with *La Luna Negra,* you told me you were overloaded and that was why you were running low under the storm. Then you tell me you were only carrying one passenger and you had no cargo. So why were you overloaded? And finally there's this little curiosity."

Rick tossed a small plastic bag across to Green, who caught it in his left hand. He didn't open it. He knew what it was.

"Maybe you can explain that for me. Looks like a human hand to me. A child's hand. Your thoughts? Views? Comments?"

"Where'd you find it?"

"In your jacket pocket."

"Searching my things, are we?"

"Damn right. So what's with the hand?"

"It belonged to a little boy. His name was Ottavio Colon. He was eight. I hired his father to run an errand for me. They were taken by a man named Narcisse Suerta, an Indian."

"Who then tortured and killed the kid? Why did he do that?"

"To teach me a lesson. Actually, he didn't do it himself. He told me he had the boy's father do it."

"His father?"

"I guess it was that or take a bullet."

"He should have taken the bullet."

"I couldn't agree more."

"This Narcisse sounds like a man in urgent need of a couple of rounds in the back of his head. What was the lesson?"

"I'm not going down that line. I can't."

"Charlie, what the screaming hell are you into? Whatever it is, I can help. And you're going to have to tell me because I think you were running something in on that aircraft, and whatever it was, you're probably running it for the Cubans, and that makes it very difficult for me to let you do it."

During Rick's dissertation, Green had tried to put on a series of innocent expressions, each of them slightly varied. The first two didn't fit at all and the third, though initially promising, ended in parody. He gave it up and, when Rick finished, tried for a diversion.

"Why? Presuming you have any of that right. Which you don't. You're in the film business, you said. What do you care?"

"I'm an American citizen. We're not as trusting as we used to be before September eleventh. And I don't like Castro."

"Neither do I. Look, Rick . . . there's more to this."

"You're what, then? CIA? ONI? DEA? Any one of those three-letter outfits will do. How about you level with me, for a change?"

"If I really were CIA or DEA or anything like it, would I admit it? While we're having our heart-to-heart, how about you level with me. For a change."

"About what?"

"Use your own argument. We both fought our way out of that hijack on the Cay Sal Bank. You held up your end pretty well. So the same rules apply. Maybe you're not a cop, but you were."

Rick was quiet for a while. A flight of pelicans swept by off the starboard bow, floating on outspread wings. They weren't alone on the ocean now. Aside from the Highway Patrol gunboat still running along a mile off their starboard rails, there was a chain of fishing boats heading south, and a cruise ship was hull-up in the far west near the Marquesas Keys, dragging a white snowstorm of gulls off her stern. They could make out individual buildings on Key West, low rambling wood and stucco blocks painted in carnival hues, and the Navy yards off Whitehead Spit were coming up on their port side. They'd be into the shoreline approaches very soon.

Rick was trying to figure out what to say. And why. He decided to try the truth.

"Yes. I was a cop."

"New York City?"

"New York State Police. I'm retired."

"How old are you?"

"Thirty-four."

"Young to be retired. Especially in the middle of a war. Most guys your age are signing up, not bailing out."

"I guess."

"I'm picking up an undertone here that says you didn't leave in a good mood. What happened?"

"That's none of your fucking business. With respect."

Green smiled, raised his hands.

"See? We've all got secrets."

"Mine don't involve smuggling drugs."

"Neither do mine. So why aren't you a cop anymore?"

"What does that have to do with anything?"

"I'm trying to figure out how to handle this whole situation. I have to trust you, I can see that. But I'd like some help."

"Christ . . ."

Green waited, in silence, looking at Rick's face.

"Charlie, you're a nervy prick, I'll give you that . . . okay. What the hell. You ever hear about a shooting at a high school in upstate New York? In a town called Carthage? Two seventeen-year-old geeks brought some semi-auto weapons into the school, killed nineteen other kids, and two teachers?"

"Yeah. Who hasn't? Last year, in the fall. I remember seeing it on CNN. The killers had been playing some video game called Mega-Death. CNN called them 'The Mega-Death Killers'? I saw the video—"

"I was there. I had just come off a task force thing in New York City—I was ejected after a witness I was escorting got hit by a truck while we were crossing Centre Street—a couple of other problems too, some Fourth Amendment stuff. I screwed up on a case. Badly. Then along came September eleventh. Like everybody in the city, I went down to do whatever I could. There's no need to go into the details. Everybody knows them all by heart. We were there for six weeks, day and night. Somewhere in that time, I lost my sense of humor, I got hard to live with. So I transferred out of the task force and went back to Albany. Then I tried out for ESU."

"Emergency Services Unit? Like the SWAT team?"

Rick made a low growling noise that came in well short of a laugh, shook his head slowly, smiling at the unintended irony.

"Oh yeah. The death-and-glory boys. Mixed bag of troopers from all over the state, all of us in our early thirties. No kids, no hotheads allowed. No siree Bob. We were 'serious men.' Trained day and night, practiced at Fort Drum. Hostage scenarios, bank-robbery scenarios. Takedowns. You know the drill. Black gear, HKs, military precision, MOUT training, the whole urban combat rat-fuck."

"Rat-fuck?"

"Oh, we did a few good things. Stopped a couple of armed robberies, and we backed up the Fugitive teams, even nailed some people connected to Hussein. Mostly we supported the uniforms whenever they had a high-risk arrest to make. We were good PR for the State Police and, of course, the cameras loved us."

Green waited for it. The Mega-Death Killers had been a national news story. The latest in a long series of high school shootings, but things had gone badly. Very badly. If Rick had been there, he felt sorry for the guy. Rick was quiet for a while, pulling the memory out of the ground, prying the lid open.

"Anyway, early November, a Thursday morning, beautiful late fall day—remember that November? How it was like late summer—went on forever? Well, that day, we get a call from the harness bulls in Carthage; two kids in a high school have started shooting. People are down. The security guard has bugged out at a dead run, the useless shit. So we roll on it, in our very own Blackhawk, God help us, twelve of us in the duty watch, under a new top kick named Harry Wilson Cargill . . ."

Rick's voice trailed off. Cargill. His round face white, wet with sweat . . . shouting at Rick as he went down that flagstone walkway . . . the pile of bloody clothes in the school library that turned out to be a dead girl . . . Donny throwing his police radio against a breeze-block wall . . . Harry Wilson Cargill . . . the gutless son of a bitch.

"Okay . . . so this Cargill, he's in charge. I'm on

one of the Contact teams, me and a guy named
Thornborough. Donny. Cowboy kind of guy, lots of
nerve, a very good cop . . . Delta sets up the perimeter and we're ready to go in—I mean the contact
units—and this . . . person . . . this Cargill . . . he
won't let us go. Get this, hah? We can hear gunfire.
Inside the school. Kids are dying right *now*, you see.
And this . . . thing . . . won't let us go in after them.
I mean, what the fuck is all this combat gear for, all
the guns, the MOUT training at Fort Drum, the CQB
drills, if it doesn't mean that we're the guys who go
in and stop the bastards? I mean, what the hell else
does it mean? If it's not for real, then it's God-
damned theater. Right? But Harry Wilson Cargill
says no."

"Why?"

"Why? Well, golly, Charlie, we had to assess the
threat, didn't we? We had to secure the perimeter.
We didn't know how many shooters there were. We
had to go slow. We had to study the floor plan. We
had to gather 'intel' . . . we had to do sweet dick.
Which we did. For twenty minutes we all sat there
on our useless chicken-shit butts while those two
fucks inside went from room to room, firing, reloading, firing. Listening to music on their headphones.
That rapper numb-nuts. Eminem. I ever meet that
kid, he's a dead man. One of the students had a cell
phone and she's in a bathroom, in a stall, I think,
anyway that's where we found her later . . . and
she's calling her mother, who puts her on to nine-
one-one and we can hear her screaming on the radio

and then the door gets kicked open and we hear gunfire. An entire fucking magazine. The Crime Scene guys had to use a scraper to get her into the bag. Cargill is in the command vehicle. So I leave my post. I . . . appeal to him, right? To his better angels. I know he's a gutless fuck . . . but I'm asking as nice as I can . . . all this time, the children are getting lit up inside that school, the parents are crying, and the only people our guys are roughing up are those poor kids who managed to stumble out of the place alive. Oh yeah, those victims, we had them run a half-mile with their hands up, cord-cuffed them, patted down every one—they might be armed, hah? And the network choppers are up there getting it all on the evening God-damned news, you follow? Do you, Charlie?"

Green followed very well, and said so, quietly.

"So . . . I go back to Donny and we look at each other and he says, 'Well?' and I say, 'Right' . . . and in we go."

This had been the main feature of the news that same evening. Green recalled sitting in his house in Denver and watching the footage, some Live Eye chopper, as two men in black combat fatigues ran into the main entrance of the school. Nobody followed them inside. They went in alone.

"So we do . . . in we go. And nobody came in with us."

"What happened?"

"We looked. We walked through the halls, stepped over dead kids. Blood pools. Followed the bloody footprints. And we found them. They were in the cafeteria. Listening to that Eminem fuck. One of them—what's-his-name—had a cue ball cut and pierced eyebrows, those stupid baggy jeans—he's sitting on the floor with a Big Gulp and a Beretta next to a dead girl. He has her shirt pushed up and he's playing with her breasts and talking gang-banger shit to the other mook. He was calling her his 'skanky bitch-ho.' They didn't see us coming."

This part Green did not know.

"I thought they committed suicide."

"Yeah. . . . Well, I guess they did."

Green looked at Rick's face, and let it pass.

"Of course, we're immediately suspended. They took our badges, our pieces. Stopped our pay. Officially disavowed by the Chief himself. Maverick cops, you follow? Unstable. Two weeks later, Donny Thornborough kissed his wife and kids, went down to his rec room, racked up a Tom Waits CD, had himself a nice cold beer, put on a motor-cycle helmet, and stuck the muzzle of a Colt Python into his mouth. The helmet was to keep his brains off the wood paneling. It worked too. Mostly. Three days later, after his funeral—no honors, no police guard, only the rest of our stick, and his family—I cut a quiet deal with the New York State Police force. I resign voluntarily. I forfeit my 401(k). They in turn drop the pending charges, and I'm officially history. After that, even the Army wouldn't take me. I know because I tried. Answer your question?"

Green had nothing to say to that. That was fine with Rick. What was there to say? They were a hundred yards off the Whitehead Spit. They could hear music coming from the beach, and kids were playing in the surf. It was a beautiful day in the Lower Keys. Really. A lovely day.

"Rick, I've got two thousand dollars in that plastic baggie. Take a thousand for the repairs, please. And put me ashore somewhere on this side of that beach. Can you do that?"

"One thousand bucks isn't going to fix this boat."

"I'll send you the rest. Whatever it is."

"Yeah? To where?"

"Wherever you say?"

"Charlie, what was on that plane? What were you carrying?"

Green's face changed. Rick saw the man pulling back, and was filled with a kind of pity for him. Whatever his troubles were, they were killing him. It wasn't fair to keep poking at him. He'd already decided to put him ashore wherever he wanted to go.

"Okay . . . you don't want to tell me about the cargo. How about you at least let me know what's forcing you to help the Cubans?"

That rocked Green; the way he shut down and the changes that passed across his face made that plain.

"Nobody's . . ."

"That's bullshit. You were in the military—my best guess is the ONI because that's the one agency you didn't repeat a couple of minutes ago—Charlie, don't even bother—and here you are, flying some sort of covert mission out of Cuba. There's no way the Cuban government could make you do that unless they had something to use against you. And if they do—whatever it is—then you need help, Charlie. Help. Ask for it, my friend—it's right here. Just ask."

Green's face was tight and closed; his silence hummed with the effort of not speaking what he clearly wanted to say.

Finally . . .

"Rick . . . there's no help for it. If I go to . . . our side . . . then it's all too late. There is no help anywhere, Rick. No help at all."

His struggle ended there. Rick saw him brace himself again, but the conflict still on his face was as visible as a burn. Rick felt a deep sadness coming off him, and found he had no heart to push him any further. One thing was clear: the Cubans had some kind of leverage on him, and whatever it was, it was deeply vicious.

"Okay, Charlie. Just tell me this. Was there anything on that plane that could be used to hurt American citizens?"

Green, brightened, shook his head.

"No. Absolutely not. It was nothing like that."

"Do you actually know what you were carrying?"

That stopped him. Green's face settled into a look of simple misery and Rick felt another surge of pity for him.

"No . . . they never told me what the cargo was."

"So it could have been anything? Drugs? Cash? Anthrax?"

"The pallet was loaded before I ever saw it. Every item on the pallet was shrink-wrapped in heavy plastic. All I did was fly the load out. But I checked it over as much as I could and it seemed to be paper bundles of some sort. Nothing like ordnance or chemicals."

"Okay. Never mind about the payload. There's bugger all we can do about it anyway. What about our friends? Will they show up in a cranky mood?"

"The Cubans? They're not looking for you."

"They know the boat. I put a gaff hook through a guy's neck. That's a picture going to stay with me for a long time. He had to be somebody's relative. Latinos are a vengeful crowd."

"They're not going to be looking for you. The only reason they'd look for you is to find me. And they won't have to."

"Why not?"

"Because I'm going back. Look, Rick . . . we're right off the beach here. There's the town a hundred yards away. You put me on shore right here in the shallows, I'm calling them as soon as I find a phone."

"Calling who? The guys who just tried to kill us? What's your major malfunction, for Christ's sake? I just saved your life. Are you totally whacked?"

"Possibly. It's been said by other men."

"And why the hell are you going to do it?"

The line of Green's mouth made it clear he was

through talking. He put the helm around and headed for the beach. There was a long sandbar running parallel to the shoreline, about fifty feet out. It was as far as they could go. Green killed the engines and let *Cagancho* glide over the pale green water toward the bar. White surf was curling gently over it. The bow slid up onto the bar and she came to a stop, rocking gently in the waves. Rick lifted his T, pulled out the Glock, handed it butt first to Green, who tucked it in under his leather jacket. The shore breeze was ruffling his hair, and the sun on his lined and unshaven face made him look old and tired. Rick had the uneasy feeling that he was looking at a dead man. Cisco came back from the bow and settled down on the deck between them. Green bent, rubbed the cat's ears. Cisco rolled over on his back, stretched out, yawned mightily, baring fangs.

"Stress is going to kill this animal," Green said.

"Oh yeah. He's a trembling wreck."

"You'll clean up the boat? I'll send the money."

"I will. And I don't need the damned money."

"I don't care. Tell me where to send it."

Rick sighed, looked out at the beach, back to Green.

"Key West Marina. Get it to Zeffi Calderas."

"Zeffi Calderas. Your friend. Okay."

"You better go."

"Rick, I can't say . . ."

"Then don't. Go. Try to take care of yourself."

Green went through the stern gate and onto the

swim platform, stepped off into the water. It reached his knees. He gave Rick a twisted grin and a crisp salute, turned, and walked away through the surf without a backward glance, reached the shore, threaded his way through the people on the sand and disappeared into the town.

# AKA CISCO

Jake Seigel took an hour to go over *Cagancho*'s damage repairs in her berth at the marina, Rick standing on the dock watching him. Seigel's date, a kid named Cory Bryant—maybe twenty-five, hair as shining black as a crow's wing flowing down over his shoulders, a deep honey-golden tan, pale green eyes, a carved, perfect body, and a well-cut face marred by a surly expression of chronic self-satisfaction—was stretched out on the bow, in what looked like the bottoms of a pair of gauze pajamas. Pretty obviously naked under this. Wearing Rick's blue police cap. Oiled up and catching the rays, with Cisco, the faithless mook, curled up beside him, sound asleep. Rick had marked him down early for a self-absorbed and totally useless parasite. He didn't think too much of Cory Bryant either.

Jake Seigel stepped off the side rail and onto the dock, walked around to the stern, and stood there, his sunglasses pulled down on his nose, looking at it. Frowning, which wasn't like him. Frowns created wrinkles and Jake Seigel had no lines on his face at all; he always looked as if he had been freshly misted with an aerosol spray of Botox and then lightly dusted with fresh cinnamon.

Eighty or eight, the man was hard as salted pork. Corded, deeply tanned, a short man, his round skull covered with a thinning coat of silvery hair, cheekbones like a Cherokee, a thin-lipped slash of a mouth; he spoke with a Boston accent and dressed like a Princeton undergrad, circa 1953. Today, it was white linen pants held up with a striped silk tie, slim leather sandals, a white dress shirt open at the neck, far enough to show you his chiseled pectorals, the perfection of his collarbones, the unlined skin of his neck, sleeves furled like white linen napkins on his sinewy forearms. A very tasteful glimmer of gold here, some rubies there, and a heavy gold ring with a Choate crest, where, Rick was reasonably certain, Seigel had never been. Rick was still wearing the yellow squall jacket, his faded jeans, a white T, and his battered Top-Siders; Seigel made him feel like a dockside rounder pleading for a day job.

Like most very wealthy men, he was drumheadtight with his cash and miserly with his possessions. Cleaning up *Cagancho* before Seigel arrived had been a matter of professional survival for Rick. The bodywork alone had cost him close to eleven thousand dollars; sanding her down, reworking the Kevlar hull, painting, sanding again, lacquering. Buying and rigging a new Danforth anchor. Digging a few bullets out of her keel—some hard cash there, to keep that quiet—and Enzo Vumbacca's stony look of silent disapproval to see him out of the marina afterward. Most of the money came out of what was left in his bank account, the rest went on his Amex card, and all of that was due in full in about two weeks. Although paying for the damage was the right thing to do anyway—it wasn't Seigel's fault that Rick had stumbled into a running firefight out of sheer dimwit fecklessness—it was also a political necessity. It hadn't taken Rick very long to realize that the reason the rich stayed rich was that they had the essential chill required to say no to a thousand legitimate claims on their time and money. Jake Seigel had that quality. You didn't screw around with his stuff. Not ever.

Rick's three-month stay on *Cagancho* had been one of Seigel's few spontaneous gestures, an offer made during an evening cigar walk along the Santa Monica Pier after a long dinner celebrating the signing of a deal to make a film based—barely—on Rick's time in the ESU. Seigel's offer wasn't obviously conditional on Rick's personal availability for the rest of that warm November night but when he realized that Rick really wasn't staying over, his warmth and his charm—he had an amazing capacity to make strangers feel as if this meeting was the start of a deep and lifelong friendship—had visibly but tactfully receded. It had been the first—but far from the last—time that Rick had thought of him as reptilian. It was a lizardlike withdrawal—slow, delicate, inexorable. *Sadly, I find our time together is draw-*

*ing to a close. Ciao, bella.* Like most of the L.A. people Rick had met, the hard-core professionals who really ran the town, Seigel had no rearview mirror. You were either in his immediate future, part of a production package, necessary to a deal, holding the rights to something he needed, or you were a human speed bump, dimly registered and totally forgotten a hundred yards down the two-lane blacktop that ran all the way to his own personal, fully guaranteed, and richly deserved California sunset.

Seigel looked up at Rick over his gold-rimmed Ray-Ban Aviators, lifted a hand, index finger curved slightly. Rick walked over, stood at the stern. Seigel made a sweeping gesture, taking in the entire curve of the stern board where the name *CAGANCHO* had been painstakingly reproduced in gold leaf across the sapphire hull.

"You know why I named this boat *Cagancho?*"

"Yes. He was a gypsy bullfighter. Hemingway wrote about him in *Death in the Afternoon.*"

Seigel had only told him about six times. Seigel grinned. He had a severe Hemingway addiction.

"This lettering is brand new, Rick."

His voice was flat, nonjudgmental. Cold.

"Yes, it is."

"Well, it looks quite fine. Who did the work?"

"Enzo Vumbacca's people. Over at Land's End."

"How much?"

"Not much."

"You didn't have to pay for it, Rick. I have insurance."

"They'd raise your rates. I know how much you love this boat. I wanted to return it the way I received it."

Hearing that it wasn't going to cost him anything brightened his mood considerably. He smiled at Rick, warming up.

"How bad was it?"

"Messy."

"All this from a storm?"

"I got driven onto a reef on the Cay Sal Bank. The stern took most of the punishment. But the hull's Kevlar, very tough. Enzo's tech guy X-rayed her ribs and did a full-keel sonogram too. Hull's perfect. Not a strut out of line. She's a very well-built boat."

"How did the port window get broken?"

Rick had been praying that Seigel wouldn't notice that, a prayer that had obviously gone unanswered by God.

"A pelican."

"A pelican?"

"Yeah. In the storm. Disoriented. Dazed. He flew right into it."

"That must have been a real bitch of a storm."

"It was. Caught me flat-footed."

"What about the storm faxes? Didn't they put one out?"

"They did. I missed it. I fucked up."

"Is that a new anchor forward? Looks like it."

"Yes. I had to slip the cable by the Dog Rocks."

"Now why did you have to slip the cable?"

*Because I was getting lit up by some lunatic Cubans, if*

*you really want to know, and a guy I pulled out of fifty feet*
*of water had to cut the cable so we all wouldn't die. Does*
*that work for you?*

"The Danforth got fouled when the squall hit and
the tide was at full rip, so I couldn't go down to free
it without someone at the con to keep the boat
steady. Cats can't steer all that well. No opposable
thumbs, you see? Their paws keep slipping off the
wheel."

*Steady, Rick. Steady.*

"Man you had a hell of a time. Lucky you got
through."

"Yes. I am."

"Okay . . . well she looks wonderful. I'm sorry
you had to shell out for the repairs. You *are* okay for
cash, Rick?"

There was only one right answer to that. Seigel
disliked poverty and treated those people he even so
much as suspected of it as if they had a contagious
skin disease. Rick had learned to present well in L.A.
It was a survival skill. In this business the only way
to get work was never to look as if you needed it,
that you only worked to beguile the tedious hours
between polo matches and trips to Tuscany.

"I'm fine, Jake. Totally."

*Totally? Rick, listen to yourself.*

"How's the read coming?"

This in reference to the shooting script that Rick
had been working on, the one that was loosely—very
loosely—based on Rick's short-lived career with the
ESU, centering around the Carthage shootings. The

working title was *Rough Justice,* although that hadn't been focus-grouped yet. It was into preproduction and there was a rumor that Vin Diesel was on board, playing Rick.

In the script, he and Donny were written up as a pair of psychocops whose idea of a professional fire-fight was to do slow-motion somersaults through the lobbies of famous hotels with their HKs on full-auto, then chill out with a couple of quarts of Cuervo Gold and a midnight race through the Mojave Desert on matched black Harleys. Rick couldn't recall doing anything remotely like that, although he had once fallen off a Vespa scooter on Astoria Avenue, and when he was sixteen he and a cousin had gotten reeling drunk on tequila, after which they celebrated by getting their stomachs pumped at a local ER. The scriptwriter was a nineteen-year-old hotshot from UCLA whose name sounded like Lance Zowie. Rick had met the kid during the first weeks of the project. He'd pronounced him-self "totally stoked" to be writing it, that Rick was "an awesome dude," that he wanted to "talk Rick's talk" and "walk Rick's walk" and "get down with death."

Jesus wept.

In the initial draft of the treatment Rick talked like a brain-damaged dyslexic surfer on Thorazine. Get-ting the worst day of his entire life interpreted by a semiliterate screenwriter with a moth-eaten goatee and then fed back to him as a slow-motion *cirque de soleil* for violence-addicted mall rats not a whole lot different from the two Eminem-clones that he and Donny had materially assisted in their bid for immortality was a truly life-altering experience, transcendent. But he had taken the money. And spent it. The last of it, as it happens, on fixing Seigel's boat.

"I FedExed it last week. It should have been on your desk Wednesday. Didn't you get it?"

"Cory and I were in Maui. It's his birthday month. He's a Virgo. I'm a Leo, but we've worked that out. He's on the cusp."

"Is he? Thank goodness for that."

Rick had spent an entire month going over it, doing the fact-checking, verifying even the smallest technical questions, finally running it past a legal adviser, the last pages of it finished in a dazed rush during an all-nighter to catch the ten o'clock FedEx pickup and meet Seigel's deadline. His apparently entirely unreal deadline, since Seigel and Cisco's newest best buddy had buggered off to some private resort in Maui to compare star signs by moonlight.

"By the way, Rick . . . about the cat?"

"What about him?"

"Well, I think Cory likes him. Can we keep him for a while?"

"Keep him? I thought he was yours?"

"Mine? No. What made you think that?"

"He was living on the boat when I got here. Zeffi Calderas, at the marina office, she said he's always lived on *Cagancho*. She's been feeding him ever since *Cagancho* docked here."

"I've never seen him before."

"She told me his name was Cisco. He's not yours?"

"No. His name is Cisco?"

"Yes. I guess it is. I mean, it is now, anyway."

*Is there anybody in the Keys without an alias?*

"So he stays then. I found this, by the way. Is it yours?"

He pulled a piece of paper out of his pocket, held it out to Rick, who took it. It was Green's picture, the two little girls on the beach, the palm trees, the gray warship in the distance.

"Yeah. Thanks. Where was it?"

"In between the cushions on the dinette sofa. Who are they?"

"Family."

"It's an old shot. It got wet, I see."

"Yeah. In the storm."

Rick was deeply rattled by this reminder of the past few days, a visible relic of an episode of brutal violence that even now was receding into a dream-like unreality. There'd been no sign of any Cuban interest in him, or in *Cagancho*, in the forty-eight hours since he'd put Green ashore at Whitehead Spit on Friday morning. For the first few hours afterward, Rick had lived in a condition of painful hyper-vigilance, a state that had gradually moderated as the time had passed. If the Cubans wanted him, they'd have come for him already. Green had obviously been right. Rick wasn't the target. The snapshot brought the images flooding back. He took a breath, smiled at Jake.

"Thanks, Jake. For finding it, I mean."

"You're welcome. I never think of you with family, Rick."

"No?"

"You never talk about anyone. Are your parents still alive?"

This was Seigel's *taking an interest* routine. His whole body was centered on you, his forceful attention beamed right at you, his voice low and caring. Rick could tell him his parents were working as transvestite hookers in a Chiang Mai brothel and he'd forget it an hour later, ask you the same question, with as much intensity.

"They're fine. Still working in that brothel."

"What?"

"Sorry, Jake. What was the question?"

"You look like shit, Rick. Is everything all right?"

"Fine. Couldn't be better. Look, you're all geared up and loaded, the tanks are full, the galley's stocked. The tide's running. If you're going to make Nassau by nightfall, you better get going."

Jake and Rick looked around at the sprawling marina filled with sailboats, charter boats, tramp fishers. The closing days of a warm and perfect September and Key West was still packed with every kind of human animal you could hope to see; assorted New Age dimwits, second sons and remittance men, thieves, pimps, hookers, hustlers, all the chronically pointless people who floated through the Keys like the chaff from a junkyard fire, and boats to match each type—a sleek Sea Ray Sundancer moored next to a rusted junk-rigged hulk, stainless-steel deep-sea trawlers with huge prows and nets drying on the stern, offshore boomers fifty feet long and two feet high, blue-water sailors and weekenders and tourists in their cuddy cabin Bayliners crawling up and down the Intra-Coastal. Entire swarms of those pesky Jet Ski things that Rick had always wanted to use as target practice. In a way, Key West was like America's appendix; whatever was of no use whatsoever to the rest of the country ended up down here. And now he was beginning to feel he belonged here too. It was time to go. Jake breathed in deeply, grinned fiercely at Rick.

"I love this place, Rick. It's so . . . valid."

"Valid?"

"Yes. Authentic. So different from L.A. L.A is so unreal."

"This place can be unreal too, Jake."

"Not this place. I can feel his spirit even now, after all those years. The truth of the place, its fundamental integrity, that will always survive. It lives in the blue shadows under the palms. In the hard true light on the beaches. In the deepest reaches of this all-surrounding sea. That will endure. He will always be alive here."

"That would be Hemingway."

"Yes. The Old Man. And somewhere out there, Rick, somewhere out there, she's waiting for me. We have an appointment, she and I. Our destinies are linked. I feel this, Rick. I feel it here."

He struck his chest with a clenched fist, his voice

thickening with real emotion. He was talking about his black marlin.

"I wish you the very best out there. And thanks, Jake. I really needed the downtime."

"Know you did, man. I've been there too. We carry the mark."

Rick was reasonably certain that the only incoming fire Jake Seigel had ever faced was a wicked forehand at the Bel Air Country Club. Maybe "the mark" was a tennis ball welt. Rick helped him cast off and watched as he worked *Cagancho* out of the berth and threaded her through the moorings toward the narrow gap that led to the open sea. Out beyond the breakwater, the brilliant ocean was seething with motion and light. Ragged shreds of high cloud raced across a perfect blue sky. *Cagancho* glided across the harbor and made the slow turn into the open sea, her white bow gleaming, her curved blue hull slicing the swells. He could see Jake under the roof, standing at the helm, Cory Bryant in the stern, still wearing Rick's navy-blue New York State Police ball cap—he had it on backward, naturally—relaxing on the settee, and Cisco walking along the port rail, his tail up, his steps light and carefree.

*Sadly, I find our time together is drawing to a close.*

Rick waved them off, feeling strangely alone, and strolled along the pier toward the cab ranks, carrying his leather kit bag. Zeffi Calderas was waiting for him at the office door, holding a brightly wrapped package in her hands, smiling at him, her long red hair shining in the light, wearing a pale green cotton sundress that covered but did not entirely conceal her sweetly rounded body. She stepped up and kissed him on the cheek as he reached her—she smelled of lemon and soap and her lips were very soft—and handed him the small package.

"What's this?" asked Rick.

"Don't open it yet. Wait until you get home."

Rick felt a sharp twinge in the lower belly that developed rapidly into a guilty and perfectly justified regret. Zeffi and he had been friends and lovers for weeks. She adored him and he knew it damn well. Being a guy, he took that for granted. Being a rat, he was still hoping to make a clean getaway.

"Zeffi. I didn't get you anything."

"I know. You're a man. Are you leaving?"

"I have to. I'm out of money, and L.A. is where they keep it."

"I'll miss you, Rick."

"I'll miss you too. I'll give you a—"

She reached up and put a finger on his lips, shook her head.

"Don't promise to call. Then, if you call, I can be surprised."

"Zeffi . . . if somebody asks for me at the office, say I'm gone. You don't know where."

She gave him a long considering look.

"Are you in very much trouble?"

"I don't think so."

"I think perhaps you are."

Rick smiled, kissed her, and went down the jetty to the cab ranks, where he caught an old Checker cab that smelled of ganja, with a driver who smelled of curry, out to the Key West International Airport. The air-conditioned chill of the big terminal was a shock, the concourse echoing with voices and the rustle and stamp of tourists and the squealing of their children. In a cold, dark bar decorated with neon palms he drank several very large margaritas served in oversized frosted martini glasses and read a day-old copy of *The Miami Herald*.

He had been out of touch for months, but it looked like business as usual on the deadly-earnest-and-supremely-dimwitted international front. In the editorials section the headline was more than mildly irritating for a man whose political views were slightly to the right of Vlad the Impaler:

UNITED NATIONS AND EUROPEAN UNION JOIN WITH
AMNESTY INTERNATIONAL, DOCTORS WITHOUT BORDERS
AND OTHER HUMAN RIGHTS GROUPS TO DEMAND
UNITED STATES LIFT ALL TRADE AND TRAVEL
SANCTIONS AGAINST CUBA

Apparently Callista Fry, the United Nations Human Rights Commissioner, judging by her photo a cranky-looking dweebette with a face like a Chippewa hatchet and a bad case of helmet hair, was in a terrible tizzy about "starving Cuban children" and "economic terrorism disguised as globalization," and was threatening to send a team of UN inspectors composed of people from Amnesty International and Doctors Without Borders to Cuba to "expose the tragic consequences of the United States' cruel and heartless persecution of the Cuban people." Robinson also hinted darkly that "intense international pressure" would be brought to bear to free Cuba from the "oppressive military intrusion that is Guantánamo Bay Naval Air Station."

Man, thought Rick, it would almost be worth the bus fare just to watch the MPs at Gitmo manhandle a posse of Tilley hat–wearing mooks in cargo pants and granny glasses who showed up at the front gates in a hissy fit backed up by nothing beefier than a snippy letter from Sister Callista Fry back at UN headquarters.

Rick read a few more lines until his blood pressure was back up to the near-critical level normally required for survival in Los Angeles; then he pitched the rag into a circular file and watched the light change out over the water until they called his flight. Number 9497, United Airlines, nonstop to LAX.

In the window seat, jammed up next to a very large, very damp woman in a baggy acid-green T-shirt that read *"My Parents Went Into Therapy And All I Got Was This Lousy Abandonment Issue,"* over purple Spandex bicycle shorts, he watched the ocean curving away toward Cuba, shining with silvery light, and then the pilot came on the PA to tell them they were at 33,000 feet, in a voice that reminded him of Charles Green, that deep Midwestern drawl, which made him think of the wrecked floatplane lying in deep water somewhere off the Cay Sal Bank, and her mysterious payload, whatever it was, and why it was so important to so many people, and pulling Green out of the water off the Dog Rocks, which reminded him of Maybelline. And thinking of Maybelline brought him all the way around, finally, and much too late, to Geronimo Suerta, to what there was left of him anyway.

Rick's face went tight and his breathing changed so abruptly that even the large damp lady in the Spandex shorts beside him looked up from her airline MRE and stared sideways at him over her heaping spoonful of chicken paws. Rick looked the way he did at that moment because Rick had finally remembered that what was left of Geronimo Suerta was still in the very same place he had put him at the beginning of that long and difficult night, tagged and bagged and stuffed inside that fish locker on the *Cagancho*.

# LOS ANGELES

Rick spent the last two hours of the flight to LAX staring at the overheated grip of the Airfone in front of him and trying to come up with a comforting interpretation of the fact that, in spite of his increasingly desperate attempts to reach him, Jake Seigel had never answered. By the time the jet began its third slow bank over Dockweiler Beach and the window next to his left shoulder showed him a limitless stretch of Pacific under a blue velvet sky with a trace of a pale green corona in the far west, he gave up on phony optimism and faced his real fear: the *Cagancho* was missing.

He had burned $89 in phone charges trying to raise Seigel's cell number in the first half hour after he had realized that Geronimo's carcass was still on the boat, and another $136 waiting on line while Zeffi at the Key West Marina tried to raise the boat on her VHF radio. Results: one hundred percent negative.

The silence from the *Cagancho* was deafening. By

the end of her fifth attempt Zeffi had picked up his sense of urgency and Rick listened while she called the Coast Guard and told the bored female dispatcher that the boat was out of radio or cell-phone contact. They both knew that the Coast Guard wouldn't organize a serious search until the boat was missing for twenty-four hours unless they picked up a signal from her EPIRB.

Well there *was* no emergency signal. Zeffi had checked that frequency as soon as her fifth attempt to establish radio contact had failed. The Coast Guard would—and promptly did—assume that the boat's skipper was ignoring the VHF and had his cell phone shut off. The Florida Keys were filled with party-boat cruisers carrying married men with no strong desire to hear from wives and sweethearts back on shore. As far as the Coast Guard was concerned, the silence from the *Cagancho* didn't mean a thing, since no distress call had been made from the boat and there was no EPIRB signal.

Rick had heard the dispatcher telling Zeffi precisely that over his cell phone as he was cruising high over the Rockies with the Colorado River a shining silver thread on the burned-brown wrinkled hide of the southwestern desert. Now they were coming in for a final approach to LAX and the city was wheeling into full view, a bowl of glittering lights from the low dark mass of the San Gabriel Mountains in the north all the way south to the saw-toothed Santa Ana range beyond Anaheim.

The flight attendant, a middle-aged woman with

fine lines around deep-set brown eyes and a trace of Savannah in her soft voice, put a pale hand on Rick's shoulder and asked him to put his seat belt on, giving him a sympathetic look as she spoke, aware that this passenger had spent most of the flight making increasingly tense calls on the Airfone to a party that never answered. Rick tried for a smile, managed a furtive cheek twitch and some bared teeth that must have made him look like a rabid ferret, but she patted his shoulder anyway and made a soothing sound and then walked away down the aisle, moving gracefully across the deck of the aircraft like a sailor.

They came in fast and hit hard and then the jets spooled up, braking; Rick felt his seat belt tightening across his belly and his breath coming in short shallow waves. Okay. Get a grip here.

Maybe the Coast Guard dispatcher was right. It was quite possible, perhaps even likely, that Seigel had simply turned his cell phone off. And the ship's radio as well. He and Cory Bryant were a new couple. Why not try for some romantic isolation? There was always way too much pointless cross talk on the marine radio, even on channel sixteen, which was supposed to be reserved for emergency calls. And everybody on vacation hated their cell phones. Especially anyone in the film industry, where you were always being pestered by writers with a stunning new concept or actors with a petty complaint. In the same situation, it was what Rick might have done himself. Why assume the worst-case scenario?

Rick's police experience provided the immediate

answer: because if you do, you'll never be disappointed. He also knew that if Seigel's cell phone was turned off, he'd get a system message telling him the client was unavailable. No. Seigel's phone was on. No one was answering it. Rick plucked his gear off the luggage conveyor and worked his way through the crowds of tourists and the tight-packed scrums of Asian businessmen, walked out into the steam-heated smoky reek of an L.A. evening. He eyed the conga line at the cab stands and flagged a white limo instead, told the compact young Filipina at the wheel to take him to 16 Beachwood Drive in Burbank and could they possibly maybe make the trip without the rap music set on "stun"? She grunted, turned it down to a muted torment and rolled up the glass divider without a backward look, flooring the huge stretch Lincoln hard enough to knock a crystal decanter of cheap brandy off the shelf beside him. Rick took this as a rebuke, which it was, and realized that he was back in Los Angeles and this time he was knee-deep in self-inflicted shit. As usual.

He decided he'd pissed the driver off by bitching about her taste in music. Or maybe he was too damn white. It took them an hour and a half to get anywhere near Burbank—a constellation of red-and-blue flashing lights by the exit for Santa Monica Boulevard turned out to be a six-car pileup that delayed them for thirty minutes while the troopers sorted out the living from the dead and finally waved them through—which gave Rick lots of time to fight the urge to make yet another useless attempt to reach Seigel's cell phone. Fight it and fail.

He reached into his yellow squall jacket, pulled out his cell and tried to resist it for less than a second, then punched in Seigel's number, something he had done so often in the last few hours that his fingertips were a tad tender. He watched the back of the driver's head and felt the thudding percussion of the rap through the floor of the limo. The line began to ring, as it had every other time. They were making a snaking run along the western edge of Beverly Hills. The canyons and cliffsides were packed with homes lit up like landing strips for an alien invasion. The line rang. A red Porsche passed them on the inside lane, doing at least 150 miles an hour, followed a half-second later by an ice-blue Shelby Cobra, its engine snarling and popping. The line continued to ring. The driver banked hard onto the Ventura Highway, blaring an outraged horn at a hat-jammer in a brown Taurus diddy-bopping through the on-ramp. The ringing stopped—Rick sat upright, listening to the silence, every nerve awake—a burst of static—more silence.

"Jake? Are you there? Jake?"

No response. Rick had a strong sensation of something—someone—some kind of presence at the other end of the line. There was another burst of static, a crackle of sun-flare radiation breaking up the beam a thousand miles over his head.

"Jake . . . Cory? It's Rick. Are you there?"

A click. And the line was dead. Rick stared at the

cell phone in his hand as if it could explain itself. Had someone answered the phone? Or was it one of the normal connection anomalies you got every day when you used a cell phone? Rick felt his temper beginning to rise, and tried to fight it back. Where the hell was Jake Seigel? What the hell was going on? Was all of this the overheated imagination of a crisis-conditioned ex-cop? He sat back into the leather seating, put the cell phone into his jacket pocket, and felt a piece of paper inside.

Taking it out, he flicked on the tiny reading lamp above the seat and studied the picture in his hand. Green's two girls. A sand castle. Somewhere tropical. And not a recent shot, faded, the colors pale. The girls were obviously sisters, both blondes, both with delicate fine-boned faces, slender, wearing matching two-piece bathing suits, navy blue with white trim. Judging by their open delighted smiles, the person taking the picture was someone they liked. In the background, maybe a half-mile, framed by distant palms and a low jetty with spidery cranes silhouetted against the setting sun, and out in the bay a sleek naval warship with either a gun turret or a missile launcher visible on the foredeck, a small forest of radar and radio antennae and a high conning tower amidships, under a vague scrap of a pennant, and a small indistinct shape on the rear deck that might have been a helicopter.

He'd need a good scanner and some image-intensifiers to get a better look at that ship. If he could identify the craft—it was certainly naval, although not necessarily American—maybe he could ID the kids as well. Maybe. And then what?

The driver's bonehead death race along the Ventura Highway seemed to put her in a more mellow frame of mind. She threaded her way through the tree-lined suburbs of Burbank until she found Rick's rented fake-mission bungalow on Beachwood, dark and deserted under a low stand of listless palms, rolled to a stop, and pressed a button that released the trunk lid. She stared straight ahead, wrapped up tight in a stony silence, and left Rick to get the hell out of her vehicle anytime soon, thank you very much, you ugly albino peckerwood.

He tipped her enough to prompt a display of her sharp teeth and in reward for his generosity she allowed him to get his own damn bags out of the trunk as well, pulling away sharply as soon as she felt the weight come off the tail, the trunk lid snapping shut like a leghold trap three inches from Rick's left hand. Watching the limo rumble away under the palm trees, radiating gangster rap at a level powerful enough to knock starlings off the power lines, Rick recalled the old line about the difference between New York and L.A.: in New York, when they say "Fuck you," they really mean "Have a nice day," and in L.A. it's the other way around.

The flagstone walkway up to his door was littered with rolled-up copies of the *L.A. Times* and when he shoved open the heavy wooden door with the iron-grated window, he had to push back a mound of junk mail. The house smelled of stale cigarette smoke, mold, and something brutally fetid that might have been a dead walrus under the front porch if Burbank had a problem with roaming herds of free-range inland walruses.

He walked through the front room, across the creaking wooden floors, taking in the antique wicker lawn set and the artificial palmetto plants that passed for his living room furniture, bowed low under the archway that led into the Thirties-era kitchenette, where he flicked on the stained-glass ceiling light, held his breath, opened the ancient pale green GE fridge, and found out what was making the house smell like a Mexican morgue after a three-day brownout.

Several cardboard boxes of what had originally been takeout Thai had, in Rick's prolonged absence, made an executive decision to transform themselves into an alien life-form that had already managed to gain a foothold in the salad drawer and was fully committed to an aggressive advance along several interior fronts.

Rick lifted a bottle of Beck's beer out of what might have been a flying column cut off from the main army and slammed the door shut. He opened up the tiny stained-glass window over the sink, turned the ceiling fan on full, put a Winton Marsalis CD into the Bose on the kitchen counter, and leaned against the black-and-white tiles, staring into the darkness beyond the hallway, thinking hard about the *Cagancho* and Jake Seigel and Charles Green.

After a few minutes, no wiser but slightly revived

by the chilled beer, he pushed himself off the counter and went down the low hall into his bedroom. He dropped his bags onto his huge mahogany four-poster bed; the landlord had generously included it as part of the deal and it had been several weeks before Rick heard from a neighbor precisely why he had been moved to do so, after which Rick had torn the bed apart, cleaned it with Lysol and bleach, and bought a new mattress-and-spring set and brand-new sheets in a pattern of pale fern leaves against a sunset gold.

Rick turned on one of the bedside lamps, bronze jaguars with amber shades, and sat down in front of the old bamboo desk he had placed against the outside wall, inside the curve of a leaded-glass bay window that overlooked the backyard pool. The desk held his Dell laptop, a Palm Pilot with all of his L.A. connections and a few police contacts, and his phone. It had a flashing red bar over a big LCD screen that listed the number of new callers he had. Thirty-six. He didn't feel much like listening to a packet of aimless chatter right now, but it might take his mind off the Seigel thing. Hell, there might even be some good news. He lit up a dried-out Davidoff cigarillo, put the photo of Green's girls on the desk beside the phone, picked up the handset, punched in his access code, and listened for a while.

There was a series of calls from Mike Mendel, Rick's agent at Constellation, a twenty-four-year-old hustler out of Rutgers with a voice like a cello who weighed about a hundred pounds including his earrings, his pierced eyebrow and his goatee. Rick had told Mike Mendel where he was going and for how long, but apparently it had slipped off Mike's desktop along with the probable whereabouts of Rick's last check from Paradigm.

"—*Rick, it's Mike. I got a call from somebody at Brad Grey's company. He wants you to send him a bio. I need a new one. The one I have is out of date. That's the Brad Grey, Rick. Call me.*"

"*Rick, it's Mike again. Where the hell are you?*"

"*Rick, it's Mike. I lost your cell number. Call me?*"

"*Rick, get back to me. This could be big.*"

"*Rick, forget it. It wasn't that Brad Grey. Sorry.*"

Okay. Which Brad Grey was it?

"*Rick, this is Mike. I heard from some people at Rangoon. They need a guy to do a technical read on a script. You're it. I'm sending it over by FedEx. By the way, now I remember. You're on vacation. Do it when you get back, okay. Usual rates. Also, Paramount wants to know, will you do scripts on spec? They have a treatment but they think the script should be written by a cop. I told them you'd think about it. Call me when you get back, okay?*"

Scripts on spec? Since when was Rick a writer?

And "on spec" meant "for free." Working "on spec" in Los Angeles was the last refuge of the totally doomed. Once you got that tag, you might as well go on up to Yreka, rent a double-wide with a view of Mount Shasta, crack that first jug of Ripple and start drinking your way through your renal system. Now the creditors checked in.

"*Mister Broca*"—she mangled the name quite wonderfully—"*this is Govinda Suni at Pacific Gas and Electric. Please call us about your account as soon as you get this message. Thank you.*"

"*Mister Broca, please call Justin Ventura at American Express about your Gold Card account as soon as you can. That's Justin Ventura. Have a nice day, Mister Broca.*"

At least Justin Ventura at American Express knew how to pronounce "Broca." Rick listened to a few more calls, deleting as he went, ignoring the calls from creditors. He'd get around to them when they ripened. Most of the calls were from business associates and casual friends he'd met while working for Jake Seigel. There were a couple of surprises, but the biggest one was the last one, tagged less than an hour ago:

"*Mister Broca, this is Adriana Colon at ATT. Can you give me a call when you get this message? The number here is: Two one three. Three five one. Four one four five. I'm here until four in the morning. It's important. Please call me back. Thank you.*"

ATT was Rick's cell phone service. He'd paid that bill in full a few days ago, on his Amex card, as it happened. And it wasn't his experience that the collections people at ATT left their names or worked until four in the morning. He checked his watch. It was almost two A.M. He picked up the handset and punched in 213-351-4145.

"*Security. How may I direct your call?*"

Security?

"I'm looking for Adriana Colon. This is Rick Broca. I'm returning her call."

*"One moment."*

Rick listened to a cut from *The Buena Vista Social Club* for about thirty seconds, then a young woman with a Latino accent came on, very brisk and guarded.

*"Hello, is this Mister Broca?"*

"Yes. You were trying to reach me?"

*"Yes. Can you hold on while I call up your account?"*

"Sure. But I'm fully paid up. What's the problem?"

*"I am speaking to Mister Rick Broca?"*

"Yes. I told you who I was. You called me."

*"And what number are you calling from?"*

"My home number."

*"What number is that?"*

"Don't you have Call Display?"

*"Yes, we do. What number are you calling from?"*

"Can you confirm for me that you're really with ATT?"

*"Yes. You can hang up and call Directory Assistance. Ask for North Central District security office. They'll give you this number. Do you want to do that?"*

Rick thought about the last few days.

"Yes, I do."

*"Fine. I'll wait for your call."*

Rick dialed 213-555-1212, asked for and got the number for ATT North Central District security office, dialed that number.

*"Adriana Colon, Mister Broca. Are you satisfied?"*

Rick was.

*"Now may I have your home phone number. The number you are calling from?"*

"Two one three. Seven two seven. Three nine three two."

*"And can you tell me your date of birth?"*

"July twenty-first. Nineteen sixty-eight."

*"And, for confirmation, what was the exact amount of your last bill payment? And the date you paid it? And the method?"*

"The exact amount?"

*"Yes, please."*

"Man . . . it was . . . three hundred and seventy-seven. And change. I paid it on . . . Tuesday, September seventeenth. I used my American Express card. What the hell is this all about?"

*"Mister Broca, we're following up on what might have been an attempt to breach our client security. Have you used your phone within the last twenty-four hours?"*

"Yes. I used it about . . . an hour and a half ago."

*"Did you call a number outside the continental United States?"*

"No. I mean, I called a cell number. It's a local number, but the subscriber was traveling."

*"So it was on ROAM?"*

"Yes."

*"The number you called . . . was it registered to a company called Paradigm Pictures?"*

"I don't know. The man I was calling works for them."

*"Have you called our Accounts office in the last few hours?"*

"Accounts? No. I've been out of town."

*"Well, our computers . . . we have a system that allows*

*us to monitor calls made from . . . people who make suspect calls. About an hour and a half ago, one of our people in Accounts got a call from someone who said he was you. They used your cell phone number to support that claim. They said that our bills were not reaching them, and they wanted to confirm your home address."*

"My address?"

*"Yes."*

"And they used my name?"

*"Ahh . . . yes. The caller identified himself as 'Rick Broca.' If this caller intercepted a direct call from your cell, then his digital display would have given him your full name, since our records suggest that you programmed your phone with your name."*

"Did your account person give out my address?"

*"No, sir. They called me. That's why I'm calling you."*

"Did your account person have Call Display?"

*"Yes. She did. The number was not your own cell number. Nor was it your home phone. The caller, he was not . . . convincing."*

"What was the number he called from?"

*"Area code three oh five. Five three two, two three one one. It's a Miami number. The National Hotel, on Collins Avenue, in South Beach. It's the general number for that hotel. Do you know anyone who might be staying at that hotel? Or working there?"*

"No. I don't."

*"Well, we wanted to let you know. About this attempt to get your home address. Your home number is not listed, is it?"*

"No. It isn't. Neither is my cell number."

"*Have you given out any business cards that might have your number on it, Mister Broca?*"

"Not in the last few weeks. Over the year, of course."

"*May we suggest changing your cell phone number, then? Just to prevent any . . . inconvenience.*"

"Yes. I will."

"*Just call Customer Service during business hours.*"

"I will . . . what was that Miami number?"

She read it out again, slowly. Rick wrote it down, thanked her a couple of times, pushed the disconnect tab, and held it there. Someone at the National Hotel in Miami either had possession of Jake Seigel's cell phone, or had been called by someone who did. And it was clear they were looking for Rick as well. Jake Seigel. Cory Bryant. The *Cagancho*. It was all right there. And what the hell was he going to do about it?

A dark wave of fatigue washed over him, and a sudden depression that went bone-deep overwhelmed him, bore him down. He pushed himself up from the desk, stripped off his clothes, and walked halfway down the hall to the bathroom—stopped—and came back into the bedroom.

He knelt down, reached under the four-poster, pulled out a heavy stainless-steel lockbox connected by a titanium chain to a ringbolt set into the floor joist. He pressed the code sequence on the touch pad on top of the lockbox, popped the lid, and took out a blue-steel Colt 45 semi-auto, still wearing a soft sheen from the polishing rag, slipped a loaded seven-round magazine into the grip, and tapped it home. He stood up, worked the slide, chambered a round, lowered the hammer down carefully, and flipped up the thumb safety. He went back down the hallway to the bathroom, where he set it down on the back of the toilet seat and had a shower. A very long cold shower. Then he shaved, toweled himself dry until his skin felt raw, wrapped the towel around his waist, picked up the Colt, and walked back into the kitchen, where he spent an hour cleaning out the fridge and the rest of the kitchen and another ten minutes cooking himself a bowl of macaroni and cheese.

He salted it lightly, put some HP sauce on it, and ate it sitting at the round pale-pink Formica table by the kitchen window, a light summer wind flowing in through the open window, carrying the scent of cut grass and palmetto. He cleaned the dishes, put them away, wiped the counter off, and went to bed, falling onto the fern-patterned top sheet like a man falling backward into a field of new snow. The brightly wrapped gift that Zeffi had given him when they said good-bye at the Key West Marina was sitting on the night table. He picked it up and took the paper off gently. Inside a box covered in midnight-blue satin he found a solid gold puzzle ring. He tried it on several fingers, and found that it would only fit the third finger of his left hand, where it glimmered in the light. Third finger of his left hand. The place where a wedding ring would go. A puzzle ring. The implication was clear even to him. How had she worked out his ring finger size? And when? It came to him that Zeffi Calderas was a more complicated woman than he had realized.

He laid the Colt across his belly and watched the ceiling fan turning slowly, listened to a skylark regretting its youth, wished for things to be all right with Jake Seigel and Cory Bryant, and knew damn well they weren't.

After a time, he slipped into a dreamless sleep with his right hand resting on the Colt, his chest rising and falling slowly. He had slept for one hour and fifteen minutes when, at one minute after 6:00 A.M., the phone rang. He caught it on the third ring, dazed and stupid. When the call ended two minutes later, he was wide awake.

# INDIGO NINE

Rick put on a good suit for this one—a very good suit, a lightweight navy-blue pinstriped single-button by Zegna, along with his best white dress shirt and a pale blue silk tie with a gold collar bar, black loafers buffed and shining. He left the Colt in the Jimmy, along with the New York State Police badge the men on his ESU stick had presented him with when he resigned. As he went up the steps and crossed the huge plaza, the building looming over him, a white stone temple thirty floors high, he could feel his heart rate rising and he worked at calming himself down. By the time he pushed his way through the massive glass doors and entered the main concourse—chilled to the dew point and the atmosphere humming with federal power—he had himself pretty much in hand. He walked by the bunker where the security guards were dug in behind a granite emplacement so high you could

141

hardly see their shaved heads and joined the lineup by the metal detectors. There were two separate lineups, one for law enforcement people, prosecutors, people who were part of the big machine, and another line—much longer—for the civilians, who were definitely not part of the big machine. The female security guard, short, steroidal, with small pink eyes and bad skin and her yellow hair in a mullet cut, shaved on top and long around the neck, looked him up and down, resented his height, and made a production out of running him through a secondary scan, then let him pass with a scowl.

The information board listed the main FBI reception on the fifteenth floor. Rick rode up with a crowd of well-dressed, highly scented, and extremely fit young men and women dressed in varying tones of gray or dark blue, white long-sleeved shirts and ties for the men, starched blouses and tight skirts for the women, heavy black shoes for everyone. They all wore plastic-laminated ID cards on silver chains around their necks, the FBI crest a shining hologram to prevent forgery. Sensing an outsider, they all stared straight ahead, unsmiling, silent, a trance of zombies, watching the numbers change on the panel. Rick found it hard not to grin. He used to think that being a part of the big machine was a sacred duty, that to live your life in the service of it was the greatest possible good. Well, they looked like bright young kids. They'd figure it out eventually.

A bell bonged, the doors glided apart, and Rick stepped out into a reception area that should have belonged to an investment bank: a broad charcoal granite floor with the FBI crest inlaid with what looked like lapis lazuli and solid-gold wire, and beyond this gleaming expanse—well beyond it— under another FBI crest, this one carved out of wood and painted in gold leaf and satin blue, there was a low rosewood desk the size of a four-door sedan, at which sat a very large, very bald young black man in a light brown suit who appeared to have been born without a neck. He looked up from something hidden behind his large folded hands—Rick hoped it was a Game Boy but doubted it. The black man's face was as impassive as a stone god and he spoke from way down deep in his belly. Maybe he practiced.

"How may I help you, sir?"

"I'm here to see Special Agent in Charge Diane Le Tourneau."

The man inclined his head, checked a clipboard to his left.

"Your name?"

"Broca. Rick Broca."

He extended his left hand, pink palm up, fingers splayed out.

"ID."

Not a question.

A blunt command to a meaningless civilian.

This is what is commonly known as "the insolence of office." There was a great deal of it going around these days and most of it in law enforcement. Rick suppressed a hard word, handed him his California driver's license. The man took it, held it under some sort of black-light machine, checked the photo, gave it back, jerked his head in the direction of a couple of Eames chairs in a corner of the reception area and snapped out a curt "Wait over there."

Rick stood in front of the desk for a while, staring at the bumps and veins on top of the man's skull as he pretended to read whatever it was he was hiding behind those huge hands. After a while, the tension became too much for him. He lifted his head—Rick thought of a bad-tempered buffalo with a migraine—and asked Rick if there was a problem.

"I think the word you were searching for there was 'please.'"

The man blinked at him.

"Please?"

"Yeah. Please. As in 'please wait over there.' You can say 'please,' can't you? It's easy. I can sound it out for you, if that'll help? PUH-leeze. Please."

No reaction other than a brief contraction of his pupils. A long silence thick with the man's internal struggle, Rick watching him with the first genuine sense of real enjoyment he had felt since his flight in from Key West. *Please*, he was thinking, *please get up and come around the desk*. Finally, the man spoke.

"*Please* wait the fuck over there."

"Good. Was that so hard?"

Walking away, Rick regretted that. It was pointless, childish, and they'd make damn sure he waited a whole lot longer. He was wrong. He had barely made it to the waiting area when a section of wood paneling behind the rosewood desk opened silently and a tall broad-shouldered blond woman some-where in her mid-forties walked out into the lobby, looked around, saw Rick standing there, and came across the floor, smiling.

She was wearing a two-piece emerald-green suit in raw silk. It caught the downlight from the ceiling pots and shimmered as she crossed over the FBI crest, hitting hard on her high heels, her hips full, working smoothly under the silk. Watching her move, Rick felt an artery in his neck pulsing under the shirt collar.

She was perhaps six feet tall, deep-set blue eyes spaced wide in a strong tanned face, her skin lined and creased around the eyes and tight over her cheekbones, as if she had lived in the desert for a while, her hair a golden bell that flowed around her shoulders. She had well-turned legs and the kind of body that was created by God as a scourge for the lewd and lustful. Her grip was exactly strong enough, her lips quite full, with a scarlet gloss, her voice deep, a trace of the south in the way she drew out the vowels in "a pleasure" and "thank you for coming in so early." By the time she let go of his hand, he had forgotten his last name. Could not bring it to mind. Totally gone.

"Broca, is it? I knew a Broca at Quantico. He was an instructor. Close-quarter combat. Lou Broca?"

*Broca. That's your name! You're Rick Broca.*

"No relation? Mister Broca?"

"I don't think so, Miss Le Tourneau. My family's mostly still back in Sicily. In Giarre."

"You came alone?"

Rick resisted the urge to look behind him.

"Yes. Why not?"

She shrugged, smiled again.

"Well, why don't you come back to the board-room? We're sorry about having to call you at such an unholy hour. Did Tyler fill you in on why we needed to see you?"

Rick had a pretty good idea what was going on but he gave her what was intended to be a blank look, a puzzled air.

"Not much. He said you were dealing with a matter that involved the film industry and that you would appreciate it if I came down to talk to you personally. He was very persuasive."

She nodded, led him through the panel and down a long silent corridor into a large office area filled with desks and agents, people working at computer screens, groups of men and women talking, all of them young, good-looking, and conservatively dressed, the smell of coffee and the sound of a printer whirring in a corner, low murmuring chatter, and the staccato clicking of keyboards. A wall of windows looked out across a swaying green sea of palms and sycamores toward Westwood and the sprawling grounds of UCLA. They reached a set of double doors in brass and rich mottled oak.

Rick followed her through them and into a large corporate boardroom, featureless and bland in taupe and beige, windowless, and a long oval table with a brushed steel finish, at which sat three men.

One was a hard-looking older man with very short, very white hair, a blunt, eroded face, deeply lined, wearing a uniform that Rick realized was Coast Guard summer whites. This did not come as a surprise. The second man looked like a pile of dirty laundry with a bloated corpse inside it, rumpled, seedy, with the bright, veined face of a heavy drinker. And the third, lightly muscled, very trim, tanned a deep bronze, aggressively handsome, leaning back in the chair with his feet up on the table, sockless in thin brown Italian loafers, wearing tan linen slacks and an olive-green golf shirt, smiling broadly at Rick, his long golden-blond hair brushed back off a rough-cut and slightly avid face. He looked like the golf pro at a Bel Air club; very Ivy League and apparently having a wonderful time. Rick made him right away for a Beltway barracuda, and was not disappointed. Le Tourneau made the introductions.

"Gentlemen, this is Rick Broca. Mister Broca, I'd like you to meet Commander Harrison Lee of the United States Coast Guard. Next to him is Dunford Buell. Mister Buell runs the Cuba Desk at the Defense Intelligence Agency in Washington."

This was the pile of dirty laundry, who nodded once, without expression, grunted, and folded his soft pink hands over a spinnaker belly incompletely covered by the highly stressed material of a shirt that may once have been white and a very fat orange-and-green plaid tie, badly knotted and much too short.

The third man, the smiling Beltway barracuda in

the green golf shirt and the tan slacks, stood up and came around the table with his hand out, shook Rick's hand in a hard bony grip and spoke much too cheerfully for Rick's taste, in a strong clipped accent with the flattened tones and the hard vowels of Back Bay or the Chesapeake. His cologne was light and smelled of lime and sandalwood. Rick could see him playing touch football on Martha's Vineyard, or sailing a wooden ketch off Nantucket, looking tanned and splendid in a force-five gale. The guy probably woke up looking splendid and stayed splendid all the damn day. Rick hated people who looked splendid. He wanted to punch them. He didn't, usually. But he wanted to. If the man was picking this up, it didn't faze him in the slightest. His voice actually had a chuckle in it, right at the back there. Maybe he *should* punch him. Just this once.

"Mister Broca, I'm Cameron Chennault. I'm with State. Thanks so much for coming down. Diane, can one of your people run up some coffee? Rick—may I call you Rick? They call me Cam. Will you have some coffee? Wonderful. Please, have a seat. Well, Rick . . . here we are. You came alone? He came alone, Diane? Really? Well, that's fine. That shows a cooperative spirit. Diane, perhaps you'd like to fill Rick in on the situation?"

Rick took a chair on the far side of the table, his back to the door, and tried not to look the way he felt. Le Tourneau let a moment of silence draw out noticeably while she reestablished the principle that this was in fact her boardroom and not Cameron

Chennault's playpen. Chennault, apparently in no way a fool, took the point and composed his face into an attitude of quiet attentiveness, resting his long-fingered brown hands on top of a file folder in front of him.

"Well . . . Rick," she began, and then waited as one of the solemn young men Rick had seen in the elevator came silently into the room carrying a large wooden tray with a sterling-silver coffee service and porcelain cups with the FBI crest. After he had gone, she sipped at her cup, set it down, and looked at Rick, something in that not-unfriendly appraisal carrying a subtle warning.

"Early this morning—at around oh four hundred Eastern Daylight Time, Mister Chennault's associates in the D.C. office got a communication—through what the State Department calls a 'back channel.' This source is in a position to know some of the operations of the government of Cuba as it pertains to foreign relations. As you are aware, we—our government—does not maintain diplomatic relations with Cuba and what limited contact there is has historically been handled by the Swedish consulate in Havana. Apparently, at some point during the night, a source inside the Cuban armed forces contacted the duty officer at the consulate and told him that elements of their coastal command had intercepted a vessel that was attempting a covert penetration—those were the terms employed—a covert penetration of Cuban sea defenses. This vessel was U.S.-flagged, and was detected by shore

radar defenses well within the twelve-mile limit that
Cuba has declared as its territorial waters."

*There it is,* thought Rick. *Always expect the worst.
You'll never be disappointed.* Just to take the mickey out
of Dunford Buell, for whom he had already con-
ceived an active dislike, Rick asked Le Tourneau who
this unknowable "source" actually was. The question created a stir of unease around the table. Rick
watched it the way a man watches a coin spinning,
wondering who would slap it flat on the table with a
snarl. Not surprisingly, it was Dunford Buell.

"What the hell kind of a cop were you?" he rumbled in a strangled eruption that reminded Rick of a
dyspeptic goat. "She said 'a source'—we're not here
to educate a small-town street cop in the operations
of the nation's intelligence systems."

"No?" said Rick, his dislike of Buell escalating
into open hostility. "How do I know any of this is
true, Mister Buell? I'm small-town cop enough to
figure out that I'm being interrogated here, and that
basis for that interrogation is some unnamed
'source' in some unnamed official sector of . . .
what? Cuba? Stockholm? Pluto?"

Le Tourneau stepped in to head off what promised to be a stream of vituperation from Dunford
Buell.

"The channels are of course classified, Mister
Broca. But I think we can say that the . . . communication . . . arrived in Mister Buell's office from a
covert source inside Cuba who is well-placed to provide midlevel intelligence on the operations of the

Cuban intelligence service, a source who has consistently provided reliable information that we have always been able to confirm from independent sources. We have every reason to believe this recent information concerning your friends is accurate. Does that satisfy your concerns, Mister Broca?"

Rick had kept his eyes locked on Buell during Le Tourneau's soothing interjection. The only time his expression varied from open and unalloyed contempt was when Le Tourneau mentioned that the information arrived "in Mister Buell's office." At that point, Buell's pupils had narrowed to pinpoints and his face had taken on a waxy tint like warm suet. It came to Rick then that perhaps Buell was defending something here, something that had to do with his own office. Why? What was he concealing? Rick was painfully aware that his position was a hard one to defend—he'd engaged in a running firefight in which an untold number of men had died and said nothing about it to any U.S. authority—but there was something else going on here and Buell's animosity was the key.

Le Tourneau watched Rick for a time with her unblinking and intelligent regard, and Rick got the definite impression that she understood exactly what he was doing with Buell. After a time, when the tension in the room had dissipated slightly, she went on in a tone that suggested a happy collegiality in which they all shared.

"Well . . . to go on. Two American citizens were found on the vessel. They were taken into custody by the authorities, and the vessel was put under tow by a Cuban gunboat. That vessel is moored at the government docks at Marina Hemingway in Havana and is being subjected to a forensic examination. The civilians are being held in an undisclosed location and are currently being interrogated by members of the Cuban intelligence service, the DGI, or Dirección General d'Informacion. This organization is the Cuban equivalent of our CIA, at least in terms of its function within the Cuban power structure. The Cuban government, according to our sources, is preparing an indictment of these American citizens on several charges, including—as usual—espionage, among other subsidiary charges. And, as well, they will be charged with murder. A capital offense in Cuba."

"Murder?" said Rick.

"Yes. Apparently the Cuban authorities found the corpse of a Cuban civilian on the boat."

Dunford Buell had been following this with close attention, and now he leaned forward and spoke directly to Rick, his voice low, surly, and packed with accusation.

"The phrase used was 'the partial remains' of a Cuban civilian."

"Yes, thank you, Dunford," said Le Tourneau. "The 'partial remains.' The charges being prepared also include allegations that this same vessel had previously fired upon and caused the sinking of a large Cuban fishing boat in the Straits of Florida. With considerable loss of life, we are told, and these deaths will also form part of the indictment. Would you like to know the names of these two American citizens now being held by the Cubans?"

Rick had no response to this, but then none was expected.

"Their names are Jacob Ezra Seigel and Cory William Bryant. We believe these people may be familiar to you?"

"Yes. I work for Jake Seigel. He's the head of Paradigm Pictures."

"And this Bryant person?"

"He's an associate producer. He works for Paradigm as well."

"And you know them quite well?"

"I've been in business with Jake for almost a year. Mister Bryant I had just met."

"Tell us, Rick, what it is you do for Mister Seigel. Your general responsibilities."

"I'm a technical adviser on police details. And an armorer."

"A weapons handler. You're a retired police officer, I see."

"Yes."

"But you're so young," she said, smiling. "Why have you retired?"

There was no way she did not know why Rick was no longer with the New York State Police. The FBI had been a big part of the after-incident inquiry. He and Donny Thornborough had both been interrogated by a couple of supercilious pricks from Albany.

"I suspect it's all in your files, ma'am."

"Yes. It is."

"So, with respect, can we get to the point here?"

"Certainly. I was only curious. I'm not without some sympathy in that regard, Rick. I saw the television coverage too. They've tried to incorporate some of the lessons learned from that incident in the HRT training at Quantico. The cost of that indecision was tragic."

"Yes. It was. More than you know."

She looked at him for a moment longer, while Rick, noticing that none of the other people in the room had asked Le Tourneau to explain the reference to his retirement, not even Commander Lee, the taciturn old Coast Guard salt, sitting ramrod straight in his chair, his face expressionless and cold. It was obvious that they had all been completely briefed on the Short Life and Hard Times of Rick Broca. Le Tourneau looked oddly troubled for a moment, and then went on.

"Well . . . the Swedes tell us the vessel we're talking about is a Hinckley Forty-four named *Cagancho*. Are you at all familiar with this boat?"

"Very. I came back from three months in the Keys. I spent most of that on the *Cagancho*. I know the boat very well. I handed it over to Jake and Mister Bryant yesterday morning and took the next flight out for Los Angeles. I got in last night around eleven."

"So you were on board the *Cagancho* as recently as last week?"

"Yes. I was on her until I reached Garrison Bight in Key West around nine on Saturday morning."

"And Mister Seigel and Mister Bryant had flown in from Los Angeles yesterday, I understand."

"Yes. You can check the passenger manifest."

"We did. So, you were in the Keys for three months?"

"Yes."

"Doing what, Rick?"

"Reading screenplays. Fishing."

"Alone?"

"No."

"Who was with you?"

"Cisco."

"Cisco?"

"Yes. He's a cat."

"Anything unusual happen in that time?"

"Yes."

"Anything involving other vessels?"

"Can you be more specific?"

"Certainly."

She turned to the Coast Guard officer.

"Commander Lee, you had some information?"

"Yes," he said, in a kind of rasping whisper. He leaned down and extracted something from a case by his feet, placed it on the table. It was a stainless-steel Nagra recorder. He pressed PLAY. Rick heard his own voice, faint, sounding extremely tired, and broken up by static, but clearly his voice.

"Blackjack, *this is* Cagancho."

"Cagancho, *this is* Blackjack. *What's your position?*"

"Blackjack, *I have the Dog Rocks two miles off my port side. I'm in even seas, under a clear sky. I've run off thirty-*

*two miles on a general bearing of three-one-zero. I've had my sonar on, and the radar, and I've monitored one-two-one-point-five for any locator signal. I have detected zero. Nor have I received any distress calls on sixteen or twenty-two."*

"Roger, *Cagancho. Any debris in the channel?"*

"Nothing, Blackjack. *Have you received any distress calls?"*

"Negative, *Captain Broca. You're still certain of your sighting? The floatplane following the transport?"*

"I stand by it, Blackjack."

"Right, then. We'll log this at twenty-two hundred hours, fifty-five minutes this date and send in a formal report. My name is Bonden. I'm the captain. You're a brave man, sir, and our whole crew would be honored to buy you a drink anytime and anyplace you choose. Are you all right? Any damage?"

"No damage, Blackjack. I need fuel."

"Do you have enough to make port?"

"Affirmative. By the way, did that Hercules get home?"

"Yes, it did. Arrived safely Fleming Key. Apparently they managed to bypass the damaged computers and fly by cables. Took both the pilot and the copilot to hold her on course. Very near thing. We'll break off, then. We have a ship under tow and are making for Port Simon. We'll file a commendation."

"Roger, Blackjack. Thank you. Cagancho out."

Lee hit the STOP button.

"This recording was made by our technicians at NAS Trumbo on Key West. It's a conversation between a British naval vessel—HMS *Blackjack*—

and, as you heard, an American vessel named *Cagancho*."

"Is it usual for Coast Guard technicians to record radio transmissions, Commander Lee?" asked Le Tourneau.

"No, ma'am. This happened to be recorded during an emergency incident involving a United States Marine Corps Hercules en route in this sector of the Florida Straits. A radio operator assisting with the emergency mission heard a channel twenty-two reference to a floatplane in the same sector as the Hercules. He monitored and recorded the exchange. There were several radio transmissions between *Cagancho* and HMS *Blackjack*. This was the final exchange. The recordings seem to reflect Mister Broca's belief that a small floatplane was in close proximity to the Hercules, and may have been damaged by a collision. He was asked by the captain of the British ship to assist in a search of the sector, and he complied."

"Very admirable, was it not, Commander?"

"Yes, ma'am. It was a brave thing to do. There was severe weather in the sector and Mister Broca ran a serious risk in rendering assistance. The British authorities subsequently did file a Commendation with our HQ in Newport, Virginia. I have a copy of that report with me, and it verifies the substance of this tape."

"I see. Rick, does this recording sound at all familiar to you?"

"Yes. Of course it does. I was risking my life at the time. That tends to leave a strong impression."

"Would you care to tell us what was going on?"

"It seems pretty self-explanatory."

"We'd like you to fill us in. On the entire incident. That's why we're interviewing you this morning."

"This is an interrogation. Not an interview."

"Do you wish to leave?"

"No. Not yet."

"Why not?"

"Let's say you've got my attention."

"We do? I'm so pleased. Well, Mister Chennault, would it be appropriate if we ran your video?"

Chennault lit up in a dazzling smile.

"Oh, Rick, you're going to love this."

He said this in a jolly chuckling tone that grated on Rick's already abraded nerves, and then grinned at him, his pale blue eyes wide, his wind-burned reddish skin creasing around the eyes. Rick braced himself for whatever was coming and kept his mouth shut.

Le Tourneau pressed a button on the side of the boardroom table, the room lights dimmed, and a flat-screen monitor about four feet across descended silently from a slot in the ceiling. The screen brightened, and they were looking at a high-resolution film of the Straits of Florida, obviously taken from a satellite.

Rick could make out the northwest coast of Cuba, all of Andros, and a great slice of the southern tip of Florida and the Keys. It was a moonlit night, but the far western reaches of the image still showed the faintest tint of pale purple light. In the upper part of the image, Rick saw the last traces of the squall he had fought his way through, breaking up over the south Florida mainland. The running time marker on the edge of the screen showed 0103 hours.

"Okay," said Chennault, his voice resonant in the pressing darkness, clearly enjoying the technology, "this feed was from our Indigo Nine bird. It covers a section of the Straits of Florida that includes the northern coastline of Cuba and the lower Florida Keys. This is the big picture, but in a second we're gonna zoom in on a reef called the Cay Sal Bank."

The image enlarged, changed, the islands and channels of the Straits zoomed crazily closer—the visual effect was like free-falling out of an aircraft at thirty thousand feet—and they were looking at an overhead image of two tiny boats, both with white decks. Even at this height, the equivalent of a hovering camera a thousand feet up Rick easily recognized the *Cagancho,* and the big Cuban Hatteras sportfisher, *La Luna Negra,* both of them lying off the Dog Rocks less than a hundred feet apart.

"Incredible," said Harrison Lee. "How the hell do you get that kind of detail at night? Is this from the NIMA system?"

Chennault laughed.

"National Image and Mapping? No sir. This is classified, Commander. Some of it's thermal, the rest is image enhancement, digital analysis . . . there was a half-moon, which helped when you can use light-intensifiers. We ran a recognition program on the boats. The smaller one is a Hinckley Forty-four.

Built in Maine. A Talaria model. The other one is
a Hatteras, a big sixty-eight footer. Couldn't get
a name off either image. That Hatteras is a three-
million-dollar boat. Watch this, everyone."

In the image, tiny puffs of blue-white flowered
and died.

"That's gunfire," said Chennault. "Semi-auto
from the Hinckley, full-auto from the cruiser. Now
the Hinckley runs for it."

The satellite image showed it clearly, as if the
camera were only a thousand feet above the deck, a
tiny red dot running forward to the bow, pausing a
moment—Rick knew it was Green, cutting the
anchor cable—the smaller white arrowhead backing
away from the mooring and then powering up, cutting a silvery trace across the dimly shining surface
of the ocean.

"Now the big Hatteras goes after it. And there's
more gunfire. Lots of gunfire. A running fight. Quite
impressive."

The firefight played in total silence, except for the
hum of the air-conditioning in the room, and Dunford Buell's congested breathing. Rick watched the
images running, remembering what it was like, feeling oddly distant from it, as if it had happened to
another man in another life. Maybe it was an effect of
the God's-eye view. They could clearly see tiny flow-
erings of blue-white light on the bow of the pursuing
boat, and smaller answering shots coming from
somewhere around the stern of the smaller boat.

"You can see the pilot of the Hinckley cutting the

wheel. He appears to be taking evasive action. Those small red images on the bow of the Hatteras are men. They appear to be firing on the Hinckley, and if you look close—there—you see some return fire coming back at them from the Hinckley."

In the video image, the small white arrowhead suddenly straightened its course and accelerated. The distance between the boats increased slightly, but then the pursuing boat began to gain.

"He's running for it. But that Hatteras is too fast for him."

"Christ," said the Commander, a whisper in the silence.

"Okay, this is it," said Chennault. "Watch what happens."

The small craft was moving very fast, but the larger boat was closing. Still closing. Almost on top of the smaller boat. Then the Hatteras rocked, jerked wildly to the left, rose up, and rolled over onto its port side, settling fast. In the image they could see eleven small red dots falling off the hull, the warm red color cooling through purple to pale green, and then, one by one, each dot winking out. Eleven men drowning.

"What happened?" said Lee.

"Hit a shoal," said Chennault. "Foundered right there."

"Why didn't the lead boat strike?"

"Hinckley only draws two feet. The Hatteras draws six."

"Damn, that's fine!" said Lee. "A very fine tactical move."

"Okay," said Le Tourneau. "We've seen enough."

She tapped the button. The screen went black and the room lights came slowly back to full. Everyone in the room was looking at Rick. There was a silence as the flat screen glided upward and disappeared with a hydraulic click.

"If you got that," said Rick, after a pause, "then you must have been able to see what happened to *Cagancho* last night."

Chennault looked at Le Tourneau, then back to Rick.

"We tried. It was . . . inconclusive. There was heavy traffic in that sea lane. Thousands of boats. We're still analyzing the images."

"You managed to find that sequence."

"We knew where to look. And when. You reported your exact position to HMS *Blackjack*. Our source in Havana had already told us that the seized boat was named *Cagancho*, and the Coast Guard had reported this previous radio contact with a boat with the same name to their superiors in Newport. When we asked the Coast Guard what they knew about the missing boat—a routine check in any matter involving a marine incident—the audiotape was already in their system, and they shared the information with State as a matter of course. Naturally, we started our scan at that first point of contact, timed it to begin at twenty-two fifty hours and searched that position. We got that footage. Searching through all the data stream looking for a random hit would be brutally expensive, in money and man-hours. We asked head office for more lens time but Homeland Security gets priority and they had another operation in the area. So the data stream got switched. This is all we could extract before they redirected the satellite."

Rick thought Chennault was lying, keeping something back. Once they'd tagged a boat with the geosynchronous satellite, why couldn't they stay on it for as long as they wanted to? He was thinking very fast, because in a moment they'd be asking him some very hard questions and he hadn't yet decided how much to tell them about Charles Green. But Chennault was definitely lying. Rick could sense it, see it in his easy smile and slightly hooded eyes.

"Okay, did you pull out the feed on the sector where the Hercules got into trouble?" Rick asked.

"Yeah, of course. It was part of the Navy's after-incident investigation. The video stream shows the Hercules taking off from Guantánamo. We tracked it all the way up to the southern edge of that storm, where we lost it until it came out the other side. There was no sign of anything—of any other aircraft—anywhere near enough to have been affected by its rapid descent. No floatplane, Rick."

Dunford Buell grunted, leaned forward, pulled a flattened pack of Kools out of his shirt pocket, extracted one, put it in his mouth, and left it there, making no effort to light it. He coughed a couple of times, looked at Le Tourneau for a nod, and turned back to Rick.

"So, kid . . . it's your turn. What the bloody hell are you up to? What the fuck happened down there?"

Rick looked at him, considering. Had they really started scanning the satellite feed at twenty-two fifty hours? If so, had they seen him go into the water after Green? Unlikely, even with that frightening technology. Some instinct was telling him to keep it simple. The instinct had no helpful suggestions on how to do this.

"I'm not sure myself. I was moored at the Dog Rocks because I was dead tired. I had run right into a major squall, I had fought it all the way down the Santaren Channel before I got out from under it, and then I turned around and went right back into it."

"Why?" asked Lee, in a flat but interested tone.

"You heard the tape. I got buzzed by that Hercules, and right after the Herc went over, I saw a floatplane—no markers—it looked like it was in trouble—props feathered, weaving—and then it was gone into the squall center. I had both blips on my radar, and then one disappeared, the smaller one. I put a call out on sixteen, got the *Blackjack*, and they asked me to go back along the flight path and see if I could find wreckage anywhere along that bearing."

"Yeah, I know. But why agree? You say on the tape it's not even your boat. You're a civilian. You had no obligation at all."

"I don't know. It seemed like something I had to do."

"Laws and customs of the sea?" said Lee, without irony.

"I guess. Yes, sir. You want help at sea, you should be prepared to give it as well. Right now, I wish I hadn't."

Buell cut in.

"Did you find anything? Any wreckage?"

*There it was.*

"No. Nothing at all."

There was a long silence, which Rick recognized as a calculated attempt to force him to fill it with nervous chatter. He kept his mouth shut. Why he had decided to keep Green out of this was a mystery he'd have to sort out later. He hoped it wouldn't be in a jail cell. Buell coughed, reddened even more, swallowed something unpleasant, probably an insult. If they had started the data scan earlier, now was when they'd spring it on him. Some saner portion of Rick's mind was asking very pointed questions down in his limbic system. Such as, why are you covering for Charles Green, you complete moron?

"So you're at the Dog Rocks. You're moored there. You're tired. What happened next?"

"I was at the edge of the Gulf Stream. Something hit the side of the hull. I fished it out. It was a body. Part of a body. In a life jacket."

"Part of a body?" said Buell. "Describe it."

Rick did, in some detail, including the ID tag around the neck, and his conclusion that the man had been attacked by a big tiger shark he had seen on the banks earlier in the day. Buell was writing while Rick talked, looked at his notes when Rick finished.

"And this . . . these partial remains belonged to someone named Geronimo? Is that your contention?"

Rick ignored the implication.

"I know that the name tag read *Por Geronimo* and seemed to have been given to him by someone named *Narcisse*. It was a religious medal, Saint Christopher."

"Do you still have that ID tag?"

"Yes. It's in my kit bag at home."

"What did you do with the body?"

"I triple-bagged it and put it in the fish locker."

"We may want to see that ID bracelet."

"Whenever you want. Send a car."

Le Tourneau had a question.

"Would a forensic examination support your . . . contention . . . that this Geronimo person was the victim of a shark attack?"

"Yes. No doubt at all. I found several large triangular teeth in the remains. Shark's teeth. Big ones. And the body had been ripped up, shredded. That's what sharks do."

Buell again.

"Why did you put the remains in the fish locker?"

"He was . . . a person. I figured maybe someone somewhere would want to bury him. A relative. This Narcisse guy, maybe."

Chennault stepped in.

"What kind of a life jacket?"

Rick understood his meaning.

"It was the kind you'd find on an aircraft."

"You think this Geronimo was on that aircraft?"

"I never found it. I have no idea whether it crashed or disappeared off my radar. I don't know where he came from. I know the life jacket was not the kind you see on boats. That's all."

"What did you do with the body when you got to Key West?"

Rick looked down, sighed, looked back at Chennault.

"I left the damn thing on board. In the fish locker."

Chennault's reaction was echoed around the table.

"You *what?*"

"I know. It's unbelievable. I totally forgot about it."

"How the hell does a man *forget* about the half-eaten human carcass in the fish locker? He'd have to be a complete idiot."

"Yeah. I couldn't agree more. What happened after, I guess it drove it out of my mind. I have nothing to say in my defense. It was flat-out criminally stupid. I take it that's the body the Cubans are saying was a murder victim?"

Buell leaned in with as much menace as he could manage, which was more than enough for Rick to decide he really hated that man. Buell seemed to derive some grim inner satisfaction from his own corrosive bitterness, as if he were feeding on it. Or it was feeding on him.

"Oh yes. And since it's their forensic team doing the autopsy, they'll come to whatever conclusion Castro tells them to. This is Cuba, kid. They'll claim you cut the guy up with tweezers and a salad spinner if they feel like it, and there's not a damn thing we can do. Thanks to you. You put your friends right into it."

"I can testify that—"

"Testify in what trial?" said Chennault, laughing softly. "You're going to go to Havana and demand . . . what? As Dunford has so delicately observed, this is Cuba, not America. Cuban trials make pro wrestling look like a sacrament."

Buell had his head down, scribbling madly in a rumpled notepad, while Chennault made another precise notation in the file folder in front of him. Rick knew he was being recorded and could have objected to that under the Fourth. He didn't.

"Okay, Rick," said Chennault, putting his pen down, folding his hands and grinning at Rick again. "Tell us about the Hatteras."

"I was moored. Having some chicken soup. I hear a ship's horn, I go up on deck, and there's this big white sportfisher out in the channel, maybe a hundred feet. They've got a huge spotlight on me, and some guy with a bullhorn is asking me if I'm okay, do I require assistance? I ask them who they are, they say they're *La Luna Negra* out of Miami, but they don't take that spot off me even when I ask them to. It's right in my face, blinding me."

"So of course you got your gun and shot at them," said Buell.

"Look at your satellite feed again. Maybe you'll see a small Zodiac right off my starboard rail. I'm standing at the port side, and they tried to put two men over the rail behind me on the starboard side. The hail was only a diversion."

"So you maintain. We'll see. What did you do then?"

"There was a gaff hook on the stern board. I picked it up and I used it. I stopped them from coming on board."

"With the gaff hook?" said Chennault.

"Yeah."

There was a general silence as the image developed.

"Yow," said Chennault. "I'll bet that left a mark."

"It did."

"Were they in any kind of uniform? Did they show any kind of badge or identify themselves in any way?"

"No. They just started shooting."

"And you shot back?"

"Yes."

"With what?"

"A bolt-action Remington. We keep it for the sharks."

"Really. A bolt-action? Then how do you explain the semi-auto fire we saw coming from your boat?"

"I don't. That was your call. Not mine. I was there."

"Okay . . . they're shooting at you," said Buell. "Did you ever wonder why? Give the matter some more thought?"

"I was a tad busy, Mister Buell. I figured they were pirates."

Chennault loved that.

"Pirates! How jolly . . . was there a parrot? Anybody with a hook? Was there rum? Did they say 'avast' and 'belay'?"

"Knock that off, Mister Chennault," said Lee, in a hard tone. "You know damn well that drug traffickers are always trying to hijack mule boats in the Caribbean. A lot of pleasure boaters convoy up if they're going to make a long crossing anywhere in that sector."

Buell stepped in again, his tone even more openly vicious, his puzzling but unmistakable vendetta for Rick becoming painfully obvious to everyone in the room. Buell pushed on, apparently unaware of how the others were reacting to him.

"So you're being attacked by these 'pirates.' And you return fire. And you run. Tell me something. How is it you can steer a forty-four-foot ship through dangerous shoals and, at the same time, put out a pretty good rate of return fire using a bolt-action rifle? I mean, that sounds amazingly . . . dexterous. Nimble. Incredibly fucking *nimble*. You must be quite the multitasker, kid. Wouldn't you agree?"

"I did what I did."

"And you did it alone? Explain me something, Mister Broca—at the beginning of this confrontation, the infrared shows us a figure running forward to the bow of your boat. You remember this?"

"I do."

"The figure is doing what there, Mister Broca?"

"I was cutting the anchor cable."

"You were cutting the anchor cable. I see. And

who was driving the boat while you were doing this?"

"No one. I had the engines reversed to keep the boat steady."

Buell closed his eyes, and then opened them. Rick had an image of a toad swallowing a bug. Buell's mouth was wide and wet-looking and Rick was finding it very hard not to put a fist into it.

"I see. All alone. As I said. Very fucking nimble."

Chennault again.

"Too right, Dunford. Okay, Rick . . . you fight off these pirates single-handed while steering a forty-four-foot boat through dangerous shoals, you lure the Hatteras onto a submerged reef, killing all aboard—only you come back to tell the tale—and then you . . . what? Crack a frosty Miller? Have a ship's biscuit? You go home, Rick. Back to Key West. Where you say what? About this entire amazing adventure?"

"I said nothing."

"Yes. We know. Nothing at all. Why not at least mention it? Why not say to the guys around the bar that night, hey, people, you'll never guess what happened to me today. I fought some pirates. I killed a guy with a gaff hook and I sank their ship. Plus I found a dead body and stuffed it into the fish locker. Somebody pass the pretzels. No, instead, you paid several thousand dollars to have the boat repaired, you handed it over to your boss with a corpse in the fish locker—I presume you forgot to mention that to him—and then you flew home to your cutesy neo-Art-Deco Burbank bungalow on Beachwood. And here we are with an international incident brewing, your boss in a Cuban hellhole, and you right dead bang in the middle of it. Care to venture an explanation of this, Rick?"

"What I did was self-defense—as you can clearly see from that video—and it was done in international waters. I know the law, Mister Chennault. I know it too damn well. A lot of good men in similar situations—in self-defense situations—are spending this afternoon eating chipped beef and lima beans off tin trays in a prison commissary somewhere. I don't find the justice machine all that reliable. I try to stay clear of it, especially when it's starting to redline. Of course I feel responsible for all of this. I *am* responsible. I regret it deeply, and I'd undo it if I could. But I can't. But I do intend to fix it. You want my advice, if you really want to help sort this out? Go to the Cay Sal Bank, take a good look at the wreck of *La Luna Negra*, see if there's anything on it you can use. That boat is connected. Find out who was on it."

"The boat's gone, son," said Lee. "Someone with a salvage barge raised the hulk Saturday night, heaved it aboard with a crane, and took it to Cuba."

"To Cuba. Not Miami?"

"To Cuba."

"How do you know?"

"One of our patrol planes saw the barge working. By the time we got a cruiser there, they were under way in open waters. They raised a Cuban flag and refused to heave to for boarding. There was nothing we could do. At the time, we had no legal reason to force the issue. If you'd reported the confrontation, we could have been more effective."

"Did you run the name of the boat? *La Luna Negra?*"

"They had the hulk covered with a tarp. We couldn't board to check it. As I said, Mister Broca, if you'd reported the incident . . ."

"Yes. That's true, sir. And I apologize for that. Now, with your permission, Miss Le Tourneau, I think I'll go. If you need me for anything else, I'll be at home or on my cell. You have my numbers."

This galvanized Buell—as much as you can galvanize a hogshead of salt pork—he got to his feet with a grunt and pointed a meaty finger at Rick, his mouth ugly with suspicion and what? Fear?

"You don't go anywhere, kid. I haven't heard anything from you that makes me believe you were some innocent tourist in all of this. You have the Cubans stirred up like a nest of wasps. I mean hornets. Bees. Fucking bees. My operations chief—I mean our intelligence operation—I have people in trouble all over the Caribbean Basin at this moment. Good people at risk, some of them dedicated and courageous Americans, and they're at risk because you decided to engage in some sort of vigilante combat for reasons which I suspect have more to do with your balls than your brain, and now you have the God-damned nerve to stand around in a room full of people who have spent their lives in service of their country while you fucked around in the Keys smoking dope and getting your blah-blah'd by skanky underage hookers—No! Fuck this, Diane. There is no fucking way. This son of a bitch is not walking away. I want him taken into custody. I want him . . . debriefed. And by my own people. You hear me?"

Rick waited in silence, his face impassive, but inwardly surprised at the feral intensity of Buell's hatred. Since Buell had thrown the last part of his tirade directly in Diane Le Tourneau's face, Rick was curious to see how she'd react. She sat there expressionless for a few seconds, wrapped in a quiet aura of power and control that contrasted vividly with Dunford Buell's choleric but somehow impotent rage. Finally she spoke, in a velvet voice that contained an undertone of regretful but firm reproach.

"Dunford, the . . . operational difficulties . . . you have been experiencing in your own department are unfortunate. Some of that can be attributed to your policy of recruiting civilian advisors from the exile community. This has not had the results you were looking for. May I remind you that I warned you against recruiting civilians, no matter how well-placed they may be with the exile community. There's a reason why we stick to professionals in this trade. But you ignored that advice. Now we— Cam, Harrison, and I—share your grief and your concern. But it has to be said that these . . . anomalies . . . began to develop long before Mister Broca here became entangled in what has always been a volatile part of the world. I have read—we have all read—Mister Broca's file. I have personally spoken with two of our people who have had professional dealings with Mister Broca when he was employed by the New York State Police. His record of public service—and by that I mean *operational* service, Dunford, not merely analytical service, but service in the field, during which he put himself in harm's way in the most literal sense of the phrase—his record is impeccable. So, as the agent in *charge* here, as the person directly responsible for the investigation here, I do not intend to see one of our own citizens subjected to an inquisition by representatives of your agency who are, understandably but perhaps rather too vigorously, trying to deal with issues that, however distressing to us all, are in the final analysis not only internal but—forgive me—in a sense self-inflicted."

This . . . disquisition . . . was given in tones of compassionate serenity tinged with sympathy and regret, which forced Buell to silently endure what was in actual fact a public disemboweling. Rick, watching her face as she talked, found it necessary to restrain himself from inappropriate speculation about Diane Le Tourneau's private life, particularly as it pertained to lingerie and champagne.

Buell's face, when she reached the end of her speech and sank the slender blade of her last observation with a matador's grace, was indescribable and still remains to this day one of Rick Broca's most cherished images. He was also alive to the critical fact that Diane Le Tourneau had made an enemy for Rick who would last him all his life. He became aware that there was a long silence and that all three people were staring at him expectantly. Time to split. He stood up, still half-expecting a phalanx of Buell's DIA enforcers to burst into the room and cord-cuff him. Diane Le Tourneau gave him a long considering look, and then rose and offered her hand.

"Thanks for coming in, Rick. You will stay in town, won't you?"

"Are you going to file charges against me?"

Dunford Buell wheezed, started to say something, but Le Tourneau lifted her hand, silenced him without looking.

"Not at this time."

"Can you do anything for Jake and Cory?"

"I assume you'll notify the senior executives at Paradigm right away. Have whoever is in charge there call my office and we'll send our people out. There'll be an FBI investigation, of course. There's a chance that this abduction is not related to your confrontation with the Hatteras. I doubt it. You take care of yourself, Rick. If these people are looking for payback, you are in a very dangerous position. I was going to offer you protective custody."

"Please don't. Lean on these sons of bitches. Get Jake back."

"We will."

# REAL LIFE

The Paradigm Pictures lot took up several acres along the Los Angeles River in Burbank, in between the Lakeside Golf Club and the Warner Brothers' lot. Rick drove the Jimmy up to the gates, which Jake Seigel himself had designed to look like the entrance to the old city of Babylon, complete with the huge stone images of Nebuchadnezzar on either side of the carved bronze gates, set into a wall made entirely of yellow limestone blocks quarried in Billings, Montana. The walls were twenty-five feet high, and stretched for a quarter mile in both directions along Riverside Drive. The security guard was not, however, dressed in the costume of a Babylonian guard. Jake took his security too seriously for that. The ex-Trojan defensive end in the dark-brown Wackenhut uniform watched Rick's truck rolling up the field-stone drive, already checking the license against the computer. He stepped out of his bunker, squinting in the hard light of a brutal sun, tugged at his belt, leaned down into Rick's driver's side window with one hand on the butt of his Smith.

"Good morning, Mister Broca. Can I get you to roll down your back windows there?"

They were heavily tinted, like the kid's bug-eyed alien sunglasses. Rick rolled them down. The guard—whom Rick did not recognize—gave the interior of the truck a long, careful look, and then checked Rick's ID card.

Waiting, Rick wondered how long it would take the press to find out about Jake's abduction and what kind of effect the news would have on the general staff at Paradigm.

The guard nodded, went back inside the bunker, and the bronze gates slid back in complete silence, revealing a large compound filled with hundreds of what seemed to Rick in his current state of mind as depressingly cheerful people, all dressed in sloppy beachwear, weaving around a maze of sound stages, equipment parks, trailers, and, on the far left, down an avenue shaded with cypress trees, the sandstone-colored fake-Navajo adobe blockhouse that housed the top brass of Paradigm Pictures. He had an eleven o'clock appointment in that building with Sheila Leventhal, Jake Seigel's wife, and the senior VP and Operations Chief of Paradigm Pictures. He hadn't told her why he needed to see her but his insistence that she have one of the corporation's legal advisors attend had caught her attention nicely.

Rick did not work out of the HQ, and he had no

intention of going in there to see her until he had a chance to spend a few minutes taking care of something vital back in his own office. Once Sheila Leventhal heard Rick's story, she'd probably have him thrown off the lot by eight guys like the bug-eyed alien at the gates.

He had been assigned a neat little pen in a cubicle farm on the second floor of a hangar-sized steel barn far out in the backlot, with a scenic view, through a gun-slit window above the coffee machine, of the employee parking lot and the construction equipment yard. The big air-conditioned space was packed with young people fresh out of college, many of whom were still semi-thrilled to actually be in the film industry and were therefore prepared to work in a large windowless hamster cage for the cash equivalent of food pellets.

Rick had no idea what most of these young kids did for Paradigm, but they all did it with exactly the same kind of bright chirpy energy that you found in the better breeds of parakeet. He parked the Jimmy in his space in front of a cardboard sign with the name BROCA spray-painted on it. No sense wasting real money on a parking sign. They changed far too often for that. In Hollywood, the only thing that was truly "forever" was how long it took for Accounts to cut you a check.

He took the back stairs and went straight down the aisle to his cubicle, where he cleared his desk—three months of dust had settled on the silver-framed photo of the Aegean taken from the courtyard of his parent's crumbling stone villa in Giarre—selected whatever personal papers he figured he'd need, including an old Day-Timer full of police contacts right across the country, stuffed all of this into his battered steel briefcase. Then he took a final and deeply regretful look around the cubicle. Regular employment that didn't require being shot at or thrown up on—frequently at the same time—had been very nice. He went back down the aisle, avoiding contact with other inmates of the cubicle farm. This was not difficult, since the entire cast of gerbils had changed almost completely in the three months Rick had been gone. He stopped at a large open section with a card taped by the entrance that read GRAPHICS.

This central section contained several huge digital copiers and one very expensive scanner the size of a hospital bed, along with other peripherals and a Macintosh computer equipped with a high-resolution laser printer. There was a young black woman at the computer, staring into the screen, frowning, her hair in a Dred cut, delicately boned, with a silver ring in the dead center of her lower lip. She didn't look up as Rick came over, but spoke over her shoulder.

"You're Rick Broca."

Rick had no idea who she was.

"Yes. I'm sorry, I don't—"

"Nobody does. I'm Talia-who-works-the-copier. You're the guy we're doing the movie about. I'm supposed to be a time-marker thingy on the preproduction crew soon. That's how I know you. Is there something you need?"

"The movie's not really about me."

"I know. Reality never works for film people. What's that?"

She was looking at the photograph in Rick's hand. He showed it to her, catching a light scent of patchouli and fresh shampoo from her hair as she leaned over to look at it.

"It's old. Really old. Who are the girls?"

"Daughters of a friend."

"They'd be all grown-up. They're cute little things."

"Yeah. Is there any way we could scan it into this computer?"

"Sure. There's a drum-scanner over there. What do you need?"

"I need to get a good look at that boat in the background. The gray one. It looks like a naval vessel."

She studied the shot, holding it up close. Rick realized she was a bit near-sighted. And she was beautiful. And beautifully black.

"Is this Hawaii? This looks like Hawaii to me," said Talia, standing up and walking over to the console of the drum-scanner.

Rick followed her across.

"I don't know where the shot was taken. Why Hawaii?"

"These palms here? There's something different about palms in Hawaii. Low, like this, and the way the trunks lean. These flowers here, I think they're called hibiscus. And these are mandevilla. You see them all over Hawaii. And the land itself, all jagged, volcanic."

"How do you know?"

"I was born there. On Molokai. And no, I'm not a leper. Plus, that probably is a Navy ship in the background there, and Hawaii is a big naval center."

"So's Guam. And the Philippines. And Okinawa."

"Guam doesn't have palm trees like that. And it's flat. And Manila looks like a bomb went off in a junkyard. I've been there. We went on a school trip, part of my history major. It totally, like *totally*, sucks. I don't know about Okinawa, but I'll bet it totally sucks too. Let's see what we can do with the scanner."

She loaded the photo, closed the plate, hit SCAN. After a few seconds, she touched the keypad and inserted a floppy disk. She hit SAVE and extracted the disk, gave Rick back his picture, walked across to her station, loaded the disk, and clicked on a Photoshop icon. The screen flickered, and there was Rick's photo, enlarged to the size of the monitor. The image was crystalline, but washed out.

"I can adjust the color to get rid of that fade. Here."

She clicked on a color bar at the bottom of the screen. The photo shimmered and then seemed to catch fire, the pale orange of the setting sun shifted to a deep amber, the robin's egg sky darkened to indigo, the washed-out green of the palms deepened into a rich emerald, the girls became a warm golden brown. Rick saw they both had sea-green eyes. Talia selected a grid and placed it over the steel-gray ship in the background, double-clicked. The screen blinked off, came on again, and the picture of the boat took up the whole screen. Enlarged like this, Rick realized she was a very big craft. If the cranes on the wharf were any indicator of scale, the vessel had to be almost four hundred feet long. She carried a radar dome on top of her superstructure, above a small forest of antennae. There were two boxlike gun emplacements on her forward deck, and a rack of antiaircraft missiles in a multiple-tube launcher. More guns aft, and a chopper on the rear deck that looked like a Bell Jet Ranger, an early model. Right forward, under her port rail, there were white letters painted aft of her cutwater. Rick tapped the screen over the letters, which were too broken up to read.

"Can you get those numbers up?"

"Maybe. This is very high magnification. But once we get the outlines, we can trim the pixels one by one and see what we get."

Rick had no idea what the hell she was talking about. Talia placed a grid over the forward bow, double-clicked. The image jumped again, but it was still a confused maze of white and gray rectangles. Rick started to say something, but Talia held up her hand and said, "Patience." Some sort of image-refinement program must have been running, because the maze of white and gray squares resolved itself, sector by sector, into clear numbers:

"There you go," said Talia, radiating quiet satisfaction. "Do these numbers mean anything to you?"

"Not really. How about you?"

"Well, there's lots of Navy all over Hawaii. Every country shows up at Pearl sooner or later. Most of the naval ships I've seen have these big white numbers or letters on the bow. I think they're called hull numbers. Like a license plate."

"Can you print this out?"

"Just the letters, or the enlargement of the whole boat?"

"The boat. As clear as you can make it."

"We have a color laser here that makes prints you can't tell from film proofs. Wait a second. There."

A large printer across the room bleeped, began to run off a glossy eight-by-eleven-inch copy of the image on the screen.

"Damn, you're good."

"Thanks. Is this going to be part of a movie?"

Rick looked at her, smiled, retrieved the picture. It was slightly fuzzy, but considering the original size, a damn good likeness of the ship. He realized that Talia was waiting for an answer.

"Part of a movie? No, Talia. This is real life."

"Good," she said. "I miss real life."

# SYMPATHY

There were three of them waiting for Rick in Sheila Leventhal's large and light-filled office. Apparently it was his day for threes. There was Sheila Leventhal herself, very short, angular, with a helmet of coal-black hair and a hawklike face, ageless, leathery skin pulled much too tight across her cheekbones, her frame as gaunt and skeletal as a starving cat, wearing a pale peach blouse and a beige skirt, standing in front of the thirty-foot-wide window wall, holding a small bottle of Appolinaris, and, over by the armoire, leaning on the ledge, sinewy arms folded, Vincent Dyle—known as Vin—Paradigm's head legal advisor, twenty-nine, Phi Beta Kappa and Law Review, out of Yale, in white riding pants and dusty black leather boots, a Polo shirt, sweat-stained as if he'd just gotten off his horse. Which he had. Dyle was holding a heavy glass full of something green and bubbly, and looking damn sulky. And Jack Cole, head of security for Paradigm, ex-LAPD, shaped like a blunt instrument, with a DI's haircut and an expression of chronic suspicion, still very much the Ramparts Division pit bull in spite of his well-cut tan suit and his heavy brown wingtips.

The atmosphere in the room was charged and tense. Neither Dyle nor Jack Cole reacted in any way to Rick's arrival, other than to send him a matched pair of fixed and hostile stares, but Sheila lightly set the Appolinaris down, bared her teeth in a sardonic smile as she floated over the football-field-sized Navajo-patterned carpet in a soundless glide and offered Rick a hand that looked like it had been freeze-dried and felt like a bundle of dry sticks. Her head was slightly too large for her anorexic frame and her pale hazel eyes had a tendency to glitter that Rick had often found unsettling. She was a formidable woman, extremely intelligent, profoundly rich, with the ethics of a feral stoat.

"Rick, so nice to see you again. But you don't look rested."

"I wish I were, Sheila."

"I'm sure you do. Now, Rick, I've had an interesting call."

Rick's belly contracted slightly.

"Yes? From whom?"

"Barry Cohen, at the *Times*. You know him?"

"I know *of* him. He owns the paper."

"He's the chief shareholder. He's also a big stakeholder in our firm. He's quite concerned, Rick, and so are we. Does your request for an urgent meeting have anything to do with his call?"

"Probably. What did he want?"

"One of his senior people in the D.C. bureau is picking up a buzz over at State. He says it's all unconfirmed, but apparently there's some flap with the Cubans and the rumor is that this involves my darling husband. Jack here has had a long but inconclusive conversation with a very charming person from the FBI office on Wilshire. Special Agent Diane Le Tourneau. I believe you have recently come from there? She speaks very well of you, by the way. Some of her people are on their way over, to explain what she called 'the incident.' She wouldn't give the details over the phone, but she confirmed that the situation involves Jake and some young person named Cory Bryant. So, Rick, is this why you're here today?"

"Yes. It is."

"Should we sit?"

"Perhaps you should."

She nodded, walked back to her desk, sat behind it.

"Go on, Rick. We're absolutely riveted."

Rick took a breath, and laid it all out for them. The tropical storm last Friday evening, the Marine Corps Hercules, the floatplane behind it, the search, Geronimo's body, and the attempted hijacking of the *Cagancho* by a party of unknowns on a big Hatteras named *La Luna Negra*, unknowns who might have been Cuban. They listened in silence, in a perfect unreactive silence, perfectly still, and let him tell the whole story. He only left out two details—Charles Green and the wrecked aircraft. When he reached the point about the corpse in the fish locker, Vin Dyle shook his head and sighed, but other than that they all waited him out in an increasingly hostile silence. He laid out the sequence of events involving his flight from Key West and his failure to reach Jake's cell phone or the ship's radio. He ended with his meeting down at the federal building this morning and the news that *Cagancho* had been taken by the Cubans, that Jake and Cory Bryant were being held by the DGI in Havana. Rick felt he'd said all he could reasonably say without beginning to babble or beg. When they realized he was through, Sheila looked at him for a long time and Rick held her look. She turned to Vin Dyle, shrugged her shoulders.

"Well, Vin?"

"First thing is the shareholders," he said. "If there's a panic about Jake, we'll get pounded on the NYSE. We also need to get point men onto every project Jake was running, talk to the core group, the directors, the talent, say we're acting on Jake's orders, that he's taking a little downtime to go fishing—they know his Hemingway fetish so it won't surprise them—and reassure them all that it's business as usual until he gets back. We'll have maybe forty-eight hours before State and the FBI get so deep into this story that someone will leak it to the press, that is, to press we can't control. When it does, we then respond that we'd love to talk but our hands are tied because of the FBI investigation and a request from the State Department, and at the same time we put it out to our media contacts—on deep background—Barry Cohen can spearhead the push—that Jake has been detained in a minor matter—something about fishing in Cuba's territorial waters—that the State Department assures us of his release within a few days and that the more PR the Cubans can get out of this the worse it will be for Jake."

Sheila listened to this with no expression at all, no outward sign of concern for Jake himself. Dyle took a moment, then went on.

"We can hold that position for several days, two weeks at the most. It's very likely that Jake will be home by then. He's an important executive at a major entertainment corporation. Cuba may be communist but they love the U.S. dollar. Two thirds of their GNP lies in the black-market trade with Cuban exiles and American citizens who go to Cuba through Canada or England. So I doubt they'll fuck with him. They'll make some noise, denounce the capitalist swine, and quietly send him back home on his own boat the next day. We gave them Elian Gonzalez. They'll give us Jake Seigel. Hell, maybe we can turn it into a movie."

"What about this Cory Bryant person?" she asked. "What's our exposure there?"

"I had my girl pull the contracts from HR. Apparently Jake had negotiated a contract for this kid as an associate producer."

"I haven't seen it."

"No. It was coming to you next week, according to Shelly."

"Am I to understand that this Cory person is a young male?"

"Yes," said Dyle, without inflection. "Twenty-four."

"And his contract hasn't been signed by anyone at Paradigm?"

"No. He signed, but we haven't yet. And we have all the copies, including his. Our position will be that there simply is no contract."

"Was he represented by counsel? Or worse, an agent?"

"No. It was a simple offer, without complications. He was handling the deal by himself. He may have—he certainly talked about it with his friends, I would have to assume. They all do. But, absent documentation of any kind, we can safely dismiss it as the normal kind of industry backchatter. I think we're in the clear."

"What if he made copies to impress his friends?"

"Forgeries. Fakes. Maybe Jack can pull his record—if he had any kind of police contact, drugs, mischief, petty theft, we can make him look like another cheap hustler. West Hollywood is top-heavy with thousands of low-end losers exactly like this kid."

Listening to this chilly dismissal of the human reality of a living being was making Rick slightly sick. It was also becoming pretty clear that Sheila Leventhal was just as happy to see Jake taken out of the picture. As second-in-command, and one of the largest shareholders, she was now running

Paradigm, which made her one of the most powerful women in Los Angeles.

"So he—or his family—Jack, find out if this Cory person had family—can't come after us for whatever happens to him, since there was no—there *is* no—official connection with our firm. Legally, Cory Bryant was a private guest on Jake's boat. Am I right, Vin?"

"If nothing surfaces to the contrary, and we keep it that way, then his presence on the boat was purely . . . social. That makes him Jake's problem. Not ours."

"Good. So, Vin, understand me here, and make sure everyone else does. If Jack finds out that this young man has any family, any connections of any kind, there will be no courtesy calls or expressions of sympathy, certainly no suggestion of support, from *anyone* in the company, under a penalty of immediate dismissal. No communication of any kind. We do not know the boy."

"I'll see to it, Sheila," said Dyle.

"Jack, do you hear this? I'll hold you equally responsible if anyone of our people compromises this order. It may be that this person had friends or contacts in the company, probably someone very junior, out in the gerbil bin—that was Jake's usual cruising ground—or the commissary. It's up to you to enforce this throughout the company."

"I hear you."

"Good. Now, do you agree with Vin about the Cubans releasing him after a ritual sideshow of some kind?"

"Maybe. This body is a problem. Broca, are you dead certain the guy was killed by this tiger shark?"

"I'm sure he was killed by a shark. They don't leave cards."

"Yeah? How? I mean, sharks eat the dead, don't they? How do you know he wasn't killed by something—or someone—else, and that fact will show up in a forensic exam?"

"I know."

"How?"

"I put him in the bag. He was still warm when I did that. He was *fresh*, if you follow me? Warmer than the sea around him. He had been killed minutes, maybe seconds, before I found him."

Jack Cole looked at Rick for a time, not kindly, then turned back to Sheila.

"Okay, if it's the body of a Cuban national, then they may not be able to let Jake go without a trial. A show trial, but even at one of those, things don't always turn out the way the people running it intended it to. But, short answer, yes. I think they'll let him go."

"And if they don't?" Sheila asked.

Rick knew that Jack Cole was ferociously loyal to Jake, who had hired him after a beating scandal at Ramparts had turned into a general race riot all around South Central and the chief had hung him out to twist for the amusement of the media. Rick looked at his face, waiting for his reply. There was the real possibility that Jake might never make it back, Jack had to know this, and Jack Cole was Jake

Seigel's man, not Sheila's. Jack Cole's answer had to bridge two possibly conflicting loyalties, and was necessarily a careful one.

"If they don't, if something goes really sour, and if you agree that it's in the best interests of the company, I think we should put together a private mission to deal with the situation unilaterally."

Vin Dyle reacted to this.

"Don't be infantile, Jack. Paradigm can't launch a commando mission to rescue one of its executives from a foreign power. The legal, the financial liabilities would be unthinkable. And it would anger State, the FBI. If it failed, which it undoubtedly would, and if the Cubans took it out on Jake, he could sue us later. If he survived."

"I'm not talking about a commando mission, you dumb fuck," said Jack, rounding on him, the cop inside boiling up. "I'm talking about using Wackenhut to help us negotiate a private release. Wackenhut does that kind of thing all the time. They maintain a team that does nothing but manage hostage negotiations for executive personnel. They contact the Cubans privately and work out a back-channel compromise. That way, State never gets involved."

"How expensive would that be, Jack?" asked Leventhal.

"I don't know, Sheila. Not cheap."

"Vin, do we have insurance on Jake?"

"Do you mean kidnap or hostage insurance?"

"Any kind of insurance?"

"Life only. No kidnap. It never came up."

"So Jake's worth more to us dead than alive, is he?"

A long strained silence. Then she smiled.

"It was a joke, people. A joke."

"What can I do?" asked Rick. All three heads turned to look at him, as if they had forgotten he was there.

"Do?" said Sheila Leventhal. "How charming, Rick. How touching. Jake would be quite moved. What can you do? I'm sure Vin here will agree that your reckless actions approach gross criminal negligence. Certainly breach of trust. You've put the firm in a terrible position and perhaps—God forbid—cost us the life of one of our most important executives, and my own, my sweet, my dearly beloved husband. So of course we'll happily sue you into penury, Rick. Penury. Poverty. Deep blue ruin. Until then, what you can *do* for us, dear darling Rick, is to go. Depart. Leave. Fuck off."

Rick held his temper with real difficulty. He was getting tired of abuse. Especially abuse he'd earned. A lot of this showed in his face and the rest was in his voice, which was thick with anger.

"I've already cleared out my office. But hear me, Sheila. And these two can witness it. I've heard nothing from you, or from anyone down at the federal building, that makes me feel that Jake and Cory Bryant are going to get out of Cuba anytime soon. The FBI has at least one CIA freak out of Langley cruising around at the shallow end of this thing looking for some way to fuck with the Cubans. Just so you know, if these people show up today, most of the growling and the snapping will be done by a mutt named Dunford Buell, but the one to watch is Cameron Chennault. He makes noises like a connected fixer out of D.C., but I think he's CIA. If he is, he won't give a rat's kidney about Jake unless there's something in it for him. So . . . I've asked you what I can do. You've told me. Get this straight. Jake Seigel is not my friend. He's actually a self-centered prick. None of that's important. What matters here is that I went to work for him. I took his money. That means I back him up when he needs it. I started this thing. I'll finish it."

Vin Dyle jumped on that.

"You've already been told to—"

Rick didn't bother to look at him. This was between Sheila and him. But he shut the kid up anyway.

"Nothing more from you, Dyle. Not one more word."

Dyle flushed, started to speak, then shut his mouth.

"Good decision. You're a bright boy. Now, what I will do, Sheila, I'll keep Jack Cole here informed. If I find there's anything you can do to help Jake, I mean really help him, I'll get word to him. Jack. Is that okay with you?"

Cole looked surprised. "What are you going to do?"

"I was a cop. I'll figure something out. Yes or no?"

"Yes," said Cole. "If you get anything, let me know."

Cole put a meaty paw the size of a baked ham into a side pocket of his suit and drew out a thin sterling-silver card case with the crest of the LAPD Ramparts Division engraved in gold and blue enamel, extracted a card and handed it to Rick with a stony look on his blunt instrument of a face that did not quite reach his eyes, in which Rick detected the unmistakable glitter of sympathetic amusement.

"Here," he said gruffly, "these are all my numbers. You get anything that will help Jake, you call me."

Rick looked down at the card and slipped it into his pocket.

"Thanks, Jack. I'll be in touch."

Cole nodded once and his lips twisted into a grimace that might have been interpreted as a wry smile if it had lasted longer than a nanosecond.

"You do that, Rick. Good hunting. Stay safe."

# KELLEHER

Although he scanned his perimeters and watched his mirrors all the way from Riverside Drive and across Burbank to his house, Rick caught no sign of surveillance. He fully expected watchers from the FBI, perhaps even some Wackenhut people put on his case by Sheila Leventhal. But there was no one and no matter how often he pulled into an alley or made a sudden U-turn on a busy street, no white van ever braked too hard, no blue sedans with tinted windows turned up twice, no gypsy cab stayed behind him a minute too long. Nor was there any special significance in the choppers that thumped and boomed through the thick brown haze that was building up in the valley. As he made the corner of Victory Boulevard and Beachwood, his cell phone rang. Unknown number. Unknown name.

"Broca."

"*Rick Broca?*" A woman's voice. Familiar.

"Yeah. Who's this?"

197

"*It's Zeffi. You idiot.*"

"Christ, Zeffi. I'm sorry. How are you?"

"*I'm good, Rick. How are you?*"

"Not bad. Any more news about *Cagancho?*"

"*Nothing directly. Rick, the Coast Guard was in here this morning, two of them, a man and a woman. What's a CID unit?*"

"Criminal Investigation Division. What did they want?"

"*They'd already been over to see Enzo Vumbacca. They wanted to know if I knew anything about what happened to the boat. Rick, what happened to Cagancho? They said it had been shot at. Is that true? I thought it was damaged in that storm.*"

"Zeffi, I kept some things from you. I apologize. I ran into a hijack crew, and things got ugly. I was trying to keep it under control. I didn't mean to mislead you. They give you a hard time?"

"*They tried. Is this about the package somebody sent here?*"

Rick pulled into his driveway, shut off the engine.

"The package?"

"*Yes. There's a big brown paper envelope here. It's addressed to you. Rick Broca, care of Key West Marina.*"

"Any return address?"

"*No. It wasn't mailed. It was dropped off here early this morning, by a cab driver, who said somebody in Miami had paid for it to be delivered. He wouldn't say who. He'd been paid five hundred dollars, he said.*"

"Was he Cuban?"

"*Maybe. He was young, a kid really. But he looked Latino.*"

"Did you get the name of the cab company?"

"*Oh . . . no. Pink and lime-green colors. With a flamingo, I think. Or a crane. I'm sorry, I didn't think about it.*"

"Have you opened the package?"

"*No. It's not addressed to me. It feels like paper. And a box of some kind. Do you want me to send it to you?*"

"Was it there when the Coast Guard came?"

"*Yes.*"

"But you didn't tell them about it?"

"*No. I didn't really like them. They were pretty full of themselves, to tell you the truth. They asked to see my visa. Rick, are you in serious trouble?*"

"Yeah. A little."

"*I love it. A little? I think not.*"

"I'll be okay, honey. Really."

"*What about the parcel?*"

"Keep it for me. Someplace safe."

"*How about under my bed?*"

"Is that safe?"

"*It depends on what you're afraid of.*"

"I'd keep it somewhere else."

"*Okay. What about the lockbox at the marina?*"

"Who has access to that?"

"*Just me. Marty's in the Grenadines.*"

"Okay. Put it there."

"*Does this mean you're coming back?*"

"Yes. I don't know how soon."

"*Did you open my present?*"

"Oh, damn. Yes, yes, I did. I have it on."

"*Did it fit?*"

"Yes. Perfectly."

*"And you like it?"*

"Yes, I like it very much. It must have cost you—"

*"It didn't cost me anything. It's been in the family for years. Do you know why they call it a puzzle ring?"*

"No."

*"The story goes that Arab men would give them to their wives as wedding rings. If she took it off, the four inter-locking rings would separate and she wouldn't be able to put them back together. It was supposed to keep her faithful. So you have to be faithful to me."*

"You mean no one knows how to put them back together?"

*"I do. If I see you again, I'll show you how."*

"You will, Zeffi. And please be careful."

*"I'll be here, Rick. You take care too. Please?"*

"I will. I'll see you very soon."

*"Good. Bye, Rick. Love you."*

"Bye, Zeffi. Love."

Love? Bye, Zeffi . . . I love you? What the hell was he saying? Did he love her? He didn't think so. Most of his relations with women were more of a negoti-ation than a friendship. Love had never come into it. Rick had been cured of love a long time ago, by a young woman whose long courageous dying had burned its terrible way through both of them. And just now he had said it without thinking, something he'd never done before. There was something hap-pening here. What it was wasn't exactly clear.

*At least to him.*

He thought about the puzzle ring, and the pack-age, and that word, and about Charles Green and

Zeffi Calderas as he went through the bungalow, with his Colt in his hand, went through it top to bottom, even looking in the dim, dank coal pit that passed for a wine cellar. Nothing. No sign that anyone had been inside the place.

The dead-walrus smell was gone from the refrigerator when he popped it open and got himself a Beck's. Then he opened the old Venetian blinds in the living room to let some sunlight in, checked the tree-lined street for anything unusual and saw nothing out of place. If people were on him, they were good. It had not been his experience that the typical FBI watcher was skilled enough to fool a good cop, but the Cubans were an unknown quantity. He figured, if they were this close, they wouldn't wait around thinking about what they were going to do. They'd have done it already. He went into his bedroom, put his briefcase on the bed, took out the enlarged photo of the Navy vessel, draped his suit jacket over the back of his chair, sat down, and popped the lid on his laptop computer.

He was going to go on Talia's impression that the location of the beach in Green's photo was somewhere in Hawaii, which meant that this ship probably belonged to the U.S. Navy. They probably had a Web site linked to the Department of Defense. He logged on and typed in the DOD address, hit the link, and got a full-color Web page showing ships of the U.S. Navy against a background of the old man-of-war, the USS *Constitution*. Down the page, there was a link to SHIPS that took him to www.nvr.navy,

a Web site called The Naval Vessel Registry. A
search grid ran under the banner that said SEARCH
BY HULL CLASSIFICATION NUMBER. There were several
classifications, from Carrier through Surface Combat, Minesweeper, and Amphibious, under letters
such as CV, CVN, and CVA to CG and FFG, with
hundreds of variations under each class. He found a
grid with a very long list of specific hull numbers,
starting with 146 and running all the way down
to 997.

He found 727 about halfway down this list,
clicked on it. There it was. The ship in the background of Green's photo. The USS *De Haven*, a
destroyer. The notation was brief. The destroyer was
no longer in service, and had been sold to the South
Korean navy in December of 1973. It took Rick
another hour of searching, but he finally established
that the USS *De Haven* was a Sumner-class destroyer
commissioned during the last years of World War II,
and that she had formed part of a Carrier Battle
Group operating on Yankee Station, Gulf of Tonkin,
Republic of Vietnam, from the ninth of March to the
eighth of November in 1973. The lead vessel around
which this battle group was organized was CVA 43.
Even Rick knew this famous ship, the battle-scarred
carrier named the USS *Coral Sea*.

Okay. This fit his take on Green. In his mid-fifties,
Green would have been a young man in 1973. Based
on what Rick had seen of his flying skills, and his
fighting skills, he could easily have been a Navy flier
on Yankee Station in 1973. But even this didn't help

much. The U.S. Navy Web page didn't allow searches based on a general description of what the guy might have looked like thirty years after his service. Better to stay with the USS *De Haven*, and see where it took him. It took him, after another hour, a severe migraine, a backache, and a number of unwilling detours into porn sites that seemed to pop up on the screen like cold sores anytime you typed in a proper noun, finally and quite late in the afternoon, around to the last days of the USS *De Haven* in 1973.

According to a Web page devoted to Vietnam-era naval records, the USS *De Haven*, 727, had been detached from service with the USS *Coral Sea* on Yankee Station in mid-October and ordered to steam back stateside to a naval yard in San Diego, to be stripped of everything secret and prepared for sale to the South Korean navy. Her last official port of call before she reached San Diego in December had been a two-day stopover in Hawaii.

Hawaii. Thank you, Talia.

A two-day stopover. But the reports did not say where, or when exactly. Sometime between October 15th and her arrival in San Diego in December. Nor did it say that this had been the *De Haven's only* visit to Hawaii. Still, if he could narrow down the time frame, if he could date the picture within forty-eight hours, and if he could find out where in Hawaii the picture had been taken, then *maybe* he could locate the actual beach.

If he could do that, perhaps he could put a name on those two girls. He figured his chances of success were a hundred to one, but every search started out that way.

Besides, he had nothing else to go on.

The Navy maintained several facilities in Hawaii. Rick found an atlas, got a pretty good map of Hawaii, and marked the various naval locations. Back into the Web again, where he found a travel page offering hundreds of digital photographs of famous tourism sites in Hawaii, including Pearl Harbor. He sifted through these for thirty minutes before he found one picture that stopped him cold. Low palms. A distant jetty full of cranes and loading gear. Several low gray naval cruisers in the foreground. And a line of craggy cliffs and jagged hills in the distant background, dominated by a pyramid-shaped mountain. He compared the image with the photo of Green's girls—if they *were* his girls. Allowing for the years that had passed, it was the same place.

Kaneohe Naval Air Station, on the north coast of Oahu.

Rick thought about it for a few minutes, and then looked up a number in Washington, D.C., checked the time. It was 4:15 in Los Angeles. It would be 7:15 in D.C. He decided to take a chance on using his cell phone and dialed the number, 202-433-3224.

*"Operational Archives. How may I direct your call?"*

A woman's voice, young.

"Do you have anyone in your records section?"

*"Yes. But it closes in a few minutes."*

"This is important. A police matter."

*"Fine. I'll connect you. One moment."*

A wait. In silence. No taped musical interlude. Then another woman's voice, harried, impatient.

*"Records."*

"This is Detective Rick Broca, with the LAPD."

*"The police? Do you want our shore patrol? CID?"*

"No, actually, miss—"

*"Lieutenant Rickman, detective."*

"I'm sorry. Lieutenant Rickman, I'm trying to establish the date a particular U.S. Navy vessel made a stopover at one of your naval bases in Hawaii."

*"Really. Why?"*

"I have a photo of two missing girls. One of your ships is in the background. I've worked out the name of this ship, and the approximate time it visited this port. If I can pin it down exactly, maybe we can find out what happened to them."

A prolonged pause, then she answered.

*"Of course. I've got a database right in front of me. Do you have the hull numbers?"*

"Yes. It's seven two seven."

*"Okay . . . let's see . . . that's the USS De Haven, sir. She went out of service a long time ago. Back in nineteen seventy-three."*

"Yes. She stopped in Kaneohe Naval Air Station sometime between October and December of that year. Can you find out when?"

*"Maybe. It's a long time ago. And it may not have been an operational call, which means it might not have been logged. Sometimes they put in for shore leave or to transfer personnel. How does this connect with your missing girls?"*

"It's part of the picture. Can you do it?"

"I'll try . . ."

Rick listened to the sound of her shallow breathing, and the click of a keyboard. In the background, he heard a man's voice, young, impatient, and then her voice, possibly with a hand over the mouthpiece, saying, *"Hold on, Colin. It's a cop from Los Angeles."* Then she came back on the line.

*"No, I'm sorry. There's nothing in her log that tells me when she was in Kaneohe. She left Yankee Station in mid-October and reached the decommissioning yards in San Diego on November seventh, nineteen seventy-three, and was sold to South Korea in early January of seventy-four."*

Damn.

"Well, thanks for trying, Lieutenant. Maybe—"

*"Have you tried looking it up in the Shore News Project?"*

"What's the Shore News Project?"

*"It's a digital database that includes archived stories from various base newspapers. Many of the shore newspapers had their copies scanned and digitized by the Naval Historical Society . . . I mean, the Navy provided funds and computers for recognized naval groups who wanted to preserve a record of the daily life of the base. Almost every naval base has a weekly newsletter, or an in-station daily, usually run by the Officers' Wives Club or the base Ops clerk. You know, the homey stuff, intramural baseball scores, dances, who's new, who's retiring, who's been thrown in the brig. You might find a mention of the* De Haven, *when she moored, when she cast off."*

"Would there still be a record of that, after twenty-nine years?"

"*I'll see—wait, Colin, I'll be right there!*"

"I'm sorry if I'm holding you up."

"*This is important. I can search here, see if there was a Shore News publication for Kaneohe Naval Air Station. If there was, and it was scanned, then there'll be a link to it through our Web site.*"

"You have a Web site?"

"*Oh yes. It's navy dot history dot mil slash records.*"

"Will you search it, then? Kaneohe Naval Air Station?"

"*Sure . . . wait a minute . . . this system is slow around this time of day . . . here we go . . . yes.* The Kaneohe Outrigger."

"The Kaneohe Outrigger. And it was scanned into the archive?"

"*Says so here. I hope it goes back that far. Does that help?*"

"Absolutely. Please apologize to the young man for me."

"*He's not a young man. He's my husband. Good luck!*"

Rick went back online and searched the Navy Web page for a publication called *The Kaneohe Outrigger,* found it in less than a minute. It was linked to a Web page run by the United States Marine Corps Pacific Veterans League. Amazingly, original copies of the *Outrigger* had been scanned into the digital archive all the way back to December 7, 1941. The paper was published every Saturday, according to the Contents section. Rick put the cursor on the first Saturday in October, the sixth, and double-clicked.

In a moment, he was looking at the slightly

out-of-focus front page of a typical military base paper, a headline about "TROOPS COMING HOME" describing the slowdown of the Vietnam War, some short columns about Appointments and Transfers affecting base personnel, a few middle pages called Scuttlebutt, which seemed to cover base recreational activities—the Tigers' Little League team had won a semifinal championship against an Air Force team, the bowling league was looking for members, volunteers were needed for the Navy League dinner. He flipped through the pages, looking for a mention of the USS *De Haven*. Nothing in that issue.

He clicked on October 13th. More of the same on the front page—"VIETNAM WAR IN VICTORY PHASE"—and more talk about the Little League finals on page three, and apparently a Mrs. Kinney was having a lawn party for all ranks to raise funds to improve the tennis courts. He opened the week of the 20th, and found a picture of the USS *De Haven* on page four, under the headline:

FAMOUS DESTROYER TO GET NEW LIFE

The picture showed the USS *De Haven* moored at the Kaneohe docks, with all her sailors lined up in Port Arrival formation on the foredeck, saluting the port brass. The article described this as "her first visit to Kaneohe Naval Air Station"—*perfect*—mentioned her pending sale to the South Koreans and the length of her stay. She arrived at Kaneohe Naval

Air Station at sunset on Thursday, October 18th, and was due to weigh anchor for San Diego on Saturday, October 20th.

Rick wrote the dates down, wondering exactly how this was going to help him, and then, to cover the ground, read through the rest of the paper, exited the issue, and clicked on Saturday, October 27th, 1973. The front-page photo stopped him dead.

He was looking at a young Navy flier in his flight suit, standing on the deck of an aircraft carrier with his family. He had his arm around the waist of a very beautiful young woman wearing a sundress in a bold Hawaiian print, long red hair down to her shoulders, a Rita Hayworth smile. In front of them, beaming, holding each other's hands, in matching navy-blue sundresses and tiny white sandals and each clutching a small white leather purse, the two little girls in Charles Green's picture.

Rick studied the man's face, but he already knew the answer. The flier was Charles Green himself, twenty-nine years younger, crew cut, blade-thin, looking strained and weary, all of them looking into the camera in perfect happiness, happy to be together, happy to be standing in the sun on the deck of this wonderful American warship. The caption under the photograph read:

NAVY FAMILY IN HAPPIER TIMES

The story ran underneath the photo.

KANEOHE NAS/NEWS: An investigation into the tragic sinking of a tender carrying several naval families home from an excursion to Sundown Beach on Wednesday evening has concluded that no charges should be laid against the officer commanding the tender or the officer in charge of the minesweeper that collided with the tender. Speaking for the Provost Office, Base Commander Col. John J. Kinney expressed the unanimous opinion of the investigators that the collision and the subsequent sinking of the USS Bowline off the entrance to the harbor was the result of an unexpected fog bank that set in during the evening cruise and a calibration error in the USS Bowline's onboard LORAN receiver. Visibility had been reduced to zero in the minutes before the collision with the USS D'Arcy, and both ships were proceeding at ALL AHEAD SLOW and sounding their horns as required in Ship's Regs. The investigation confirmed that, after the collision, all safety drills were immediately deployed and all of the people on board the Bowline were pulled safely from the water onto the deck of the USS D'Arcy, with the exception of Ruth Kelleher, 24, wife of Lieutenant Charles Kelleher, VF 111 Tactical Wing, USS Coral Sea, and their youngest daughter, Eileen, 2. Both of their bodies were recovered after an extensive search. Lt. Kelleher was serving on board the USS Coral Sea, Yankee Station, at the time of the tragedy and he will be flown in to Pearl Harbor for the funerals later this afternoon. Thankfully, Lt. Kelleher's older daughter, Kathleen, aged three, survived the sinking of the USS Bowline. She was unconscious when pulled from the water but Navy corpsmen were able to revive her and she is now in a coma in a military hospital in Honolulu. Her condition is listed as critical but stable. Sadly, Lt. Kelleher had flown back to the USS Coral Sea a few days previously, after spending some well-deserved R and R with his wife and two daughters here at Kaneohe NAS. Both Mrs. Ruth Kelleher and daughter Eileen will be buried together at Pearl Harbor military cemetery with full naval honors. All base personnel able to be excused from their duties will be provided transport to and from the Pearl Harbor memorial services by MAC/NAS/Pearl Adjutants Office.

Poor Green—no, poor Lieutenant Kelleher. No wonder Green—Kelleher—no wonder Kelleher was carrying that photograph. It was a record of the last time they were all together as a family. As far as Rick could work it out, he must have flown back to the USS *Coral Sea* around the same time that the

USS *De Haven* weighed anchor for San Diego, on Saturday, October 20th, 1973. The accident with the tender happened the next Wednesday evening, which would have been October 24th. Green— *Kelleher,* damn it—it was hard to make the shift. This younger version of the man seemed to belong to another time, an image of someone who had never been a part of that running firefight on the *Cagancho.* But they were the same man. Looking at his young face in the photo, and remembering him as he had last seen him, standing in the shallows off the Key West beach, looking up at Rick, a leathery hard case well past middle age, his face scored and seamed, squinting up into the sunlight, the wry smile and the crisp Navy salute, Rick caught a vision of what it must be like to live that long, and carry such a terrible loss for so many years. Had Green worn a wedding ring? Rick couldn't remember. He didn't think so. But there had been an air of suppressed anger about the man, as well as intense anxiety regarding some element of his wrecked aircraft, or the mission connected to it. But Rick had also sensed something else, perhaps a searing regret, and now he knew why.

He clicked on the next issue, Saturday, November 3rd, 1973, to see if there was a follow-up on the accident, but the screen simply went blank and showed him a notation:

**PAGE CANNOT BE DISPLAYED AT THIS TIME**

Well, it wasn't important. He had what he needed. He hit PRINT and ran off a hard copy of the page, bookmarked the Web site, and logged off AOL. Leaning back into the chair, Rick rubbed his hands across his face. Okay, the man he had pulled off the Cay Sal seabed was really a man named Charles Kelleher. Was he still in the Navy? Rick didn't think so. He could run a personnel search on the Navy's Web site, but he wasn't going to. Were searches like that retrievable? Would Kelleher's name have a trigger attached, like the RTAs that you found on NCIC, hidden links that bounced a signal back to whatever agency had tagged a certain name? It was possible, and the fact that an agency spook like Cam Chennault had come out from the bullpen to short-stop the Seigel case made it damn likely. Thinking about that, he spent a few minutes hunting down and deleting every item in his CACHE register and wiping out all of his HISTORY pages as well. Then he shut it down and rebooted and then used Windows Explorer to confirm the erasures were effective. They were. He was closing the lid on his laptop again and thinking about how he could erase that direct cell phone call to Naval Archives in D.C. when someone knocked heavily on his front door.

# ABAKUA

Picking up the Colt, Rick thumbed the safety off and stepped out into the hallway. He heard movement outside his open kitchen window, someone walking around the side of his house, walking carefully, as if he were trying to do it quietly. Another heavy knock on his front door. At least two men. Cops? Feds? Or somebody else?

Rick went back into the bedroom, quietly opened the bay window, stepped out onto the raised deck of the backyard pool, and dropped to the ground beside the pump house. He heard someone walking up the steps to the back porch, heavy-footed, the old boards creaking under his weight. There was a silence, and then he heard the sound of cracking wood. He could still hear the sound of knocking on his front door. He stepped back around the end of the pool deck and saw a very large black-haired man in faded jeans and a green windbreaker with the words GONZALEZ BROTHERS LAWN CARE stenciled across the back in white letters.

The man was bending over with his back to Rick, a pry bar in his hands, working on the doorframe right next to the dead bolt. Rick came silently over the long grass, his Colt out at his right side—ten feet—five—the man grunted softly as the frame buckled and the door lock gave away. He had his left hand on the screen and the pry bar in his right hand, his foot almost inside the doorway, when Rick pressed the muzzle of his Colt into the back of the man's neck.

"Not a sound," said Rick, close to his ear.

He felt the man's body tensing, his head twisting to the right, and Rick reacted, slamming the barrel of the Colt up hard against his right temple. The man hit the boards hard, a slack deadweight. Rick reached down, clutched a fistful of his long, greasy black hair, lifted the heavy skull. A thick Indian face, darkened by the sun, deeply scarred by smallpox, wheezing through his open mouth. His half-open eyes were like the eyes of a seagull, a pale yellow disk surrounding a tiny black pupil. Blood that smelled strongly of rust and fresh tequila was sheeting down the side of his face and he stank of dried sweat and marijuana. Rick saw something under the blood on the man's left cheek. He used the man's jacket collar to wipe some of the blood away and revealed a scarred patch of skin into which something like red ink had been rubbed. It looked as if the man had done it himself. The shape was strange, resembling a palm tree pierced with a jagged thunderbolt. Maybe a tribal marking?

Rick let the head drop, tugged the man's belt loose and cinched it tight around his elbows, pulling it in tight until he felt the sinews creaking in the man's thick shoulders. Something solid hit the front door, and he heard the lock snapping. Footsteps coming down the front hallway, a man's voice, high, nervous, calling out, *"Ola! Donde esta?"*

Rick stepped into the bathroom, half-closed the door, and watched as a short, thickset dark-skinned male with shoulder-length black hair, wearing a cream-colored suit and dirty white sneakers, light-footed down the back hall, a small stainless-steel semi-auto in his left hand. He stopped, crouched over the man lying in the doorway, went down on one knee. Rick put the Colt up against the side of his head.

"Drop the weapon."

The man hesitated, then tossed the weapon at Rick's feet. Rick kicked it behind him into the bathroom without looking.

"Pick him up."

The man did not react.

*"Señor,* we are only—"

Rick clubbed this one very hard across the back of the head. The man lurched to the left, recovered, and his stony expression did not change much when Rick put the muzzle of the Colt up against the man's forehead, and thumb-cocked the hammer. Looking down at the man over the barrel of his Colt, Rick saw a red scar tattoo gouged into the man's left cheek, a palm tree with a thunderbolt, identical to the one on the first man.

"No talk. Pick him up. Bring him inside."

The man—he looked about forty—sighed, bent

down, caught the man's windbreaker, heaved backward, and managed to drag him inside with a visible effort. Rick, watching the man working as he scooped up the pistol—a SIG-Sauer P-220—judged the big man's weight at two hundred and fifty pounds, all of it muscle and bone. The smaller man gave Rick a puzzled look, patently false, when he stopped in the hall, asked in a mild and unconvincing tone:

*"Dónde?"*—(where you want me to put him?)

His voice was low and flat, a strong Spanish accent, not much of fear in it. Concern. And watchfulness, readiness. He was looking for an opening, however small. Rick kept the Colt on him.

"In the kitchen."

Rick stepped clear and let the guy drag the big man up the hall and onto the kitchen tiles, followed him up. He hesitated, and Rick could see him thinking about a dash for the front door.

"You run, I'll take out your spine."

The man looked at Rick, read him correctly, and sat down on the kitchen floor, his head down, his knees up, his arms resting on his knees, panting slightly from the exertion and from anger. Rick stepped around him, patted his suit-coat pocket over a bulge, put his hand into the pocket, and pulled out a package of plastic cable ties.

"For me? You shouldn't have."

"They are only for the garbage bags, *señor*. We are gardeners."

"Yeah," said Rick, hefting the man's pistol. "I can see."

The man had no ready answer for that, merely shrugged. Rick used two of the cable ties to cord-cuff the man's hands behind his back, kicked him hard onto his left side, and pulled the third one tight around his ankles. He opened his mouth to speak so Rick kicked him in the face, not too hard, but hard enough to make their relationship clearer to the man. Then he trussed the big man up tight, wrists, ankles, knees. Not gently. Rick Broca had always been troubled by a mean streak, and he was very angry. He'd been that way before, and had done things that he deeply regretted; he knew he would have to watch himself. He looked down at the man in the cream suit, dappled with bright-red blood, his white T-shirt stained with it. His small deep-set eyes had grown watery from the pain in his mouth, but he was holding his silence in tight as he glared up at Rick with a killing look, almost feral. Rick smiled down at him, checked the other man. Still unconscious. Maybe.

Rick opened one of the kitchen drawers, took out a small butane lighter, knelt down beside the big man, flicked the lighter on, and held the flame under the man's hand. The man neither groaned nor twitched. He put the lighter away and turned to look at the man in the cream suit, who was staring at him with a slightly altered expression that was harder to read than his war face. Rick went through the unconscious man's pockets, extracting a battered black-leather wallet, a small snakeskin bag with something inside it, and a thin filleting knife about six inches long. The other man watched him with a tight angry expression on his face as Rick dumped the contents of the skin bag into his palm. Some kind of yellow dust that smelled of corn, a few multicolored beads. He poured this back into the snakeskin bag, and opened the wallet.

A Visa credit card issued by Banco Unido del Belize, a color Xerox copy of a Costa Rican driver's license in the name of *Geronimo Suerta,* with a picture that Rick recognized, but it was not the face of this big man on his kitchen floor. Very similar, a relative or blood connection, but not the same man. Yet he knew the face very well. It was a picture of the man whose mutilated body he had pulled out of the water off the Cay Sal Bank, the man with the silver medal engraved to Geronimo. So his full name was Geronimo Suerta. As he studied the shot, he felt the big man begin to stir.

He stepped away and watched as the man opened his pale yellow eyes, blinked, groaned, and then tried to move. When he realized he was bound, he began to struggle, making a harsh mewling sound like an injured cat, straining at the bonds until blood ran from his wrists. The other man spoke gently to him in a low carrying tone.

"*Carlito—Carlito—Tranquilo, ambia. Tranquilo*—sir, his bonds are cutting him. He does not know what—he cannot speak. He is dumb. *Carlito, monina, tranquilo!*"

The big man stopped struggling, twisted his neck to look up at Rick. His eyes widened for a moment, and then he put his head down, his face to the side. Rick didn't buy this for a minute, but he said nothing. He crossed over to the man in the cream suit, searched his pockets, and found two maroon passports issued by Belize, one with a picture that matched the man's face over the name *Narcisse Suerta*, the other passport, issued in the name of *Carlito Vargas*, as well as two thousand dollars in stained and rumpled U.S. bills, a second magazine for the SIG-Sauer, loaded with 9mm rounds, a hypodermic needle, a set of car keys, and a small glass vial filled with an amber liquid. He set all this down on to the counter, and walked away toward the front door, which was wide open, the door lock jimmied, the wood frame split and broken. He walked out onto the stone veranda and looked up and down Beachwood Drive.

Three kids were skateboarding along the far end of the block, and the guy across the street—a lawyer, Rick knew him slightly—was painting his garage door scarlet red. There was a big green van parked by the curb in front of Rick's house, with GONZALEZ BROTHERS LAWN CARE painted on the side.

Rick went down the drive and checked the van. It was full of rakes, lawn food, fertilizers, topsoil. There was a big John Deere riding mower at the back of the van, rusted, ancient, next to a large gas can. A brand-new bright-green wheelbarrow with a brown tarp folded up inside it, still in its plastic wrapper. Rick closed the back doors, looked around the block again. No one had noticed a damn thing. Two men had broken into his house in broad daylight on a busy residential street, and no one had paid any attention at all. He sighed, checked the street again for any sign of surveillance, saw nothing, and went back inside. He could hear the smaller man's voice, low and harsh, talking fast to the other man as he came back down the hall, and the other man's reply, one word, "*Sí.*"

They were both quite still as Rick went past them into his bedroom, picked the silver medallion out of his kit bag, and came back into the kitchen. He pulled out a chair, sat down, looked at the two men, raised his hands.

"Okay. You in the vanilla wrapper. I'm listening."

Suerta took a breath, and dug himself deeper into his silence as Rick watched him, thinking, *So this is the Indian who forced a father to cut off his own kid's hand.* Ottavio. Ottavio Colon. Green—Kelleher—had told him the kid was only eight years old, a fisherman's son.

"Okay. You sure? Nothing to contribute?"

Silence, and the murderous glare. Rick looked over at the big man, got up, picked up the stainless-steel SIG-Sauer, bent over and grabbed him by the web belt that was holding his elbows pinned over the middle of his back, picked him up bodily like a very large and deeply ugly suitcase. When Rick headed for the basement stairs, Suerta found his voice.

"Where are you taking him?"

Rick stopped, still holding the man off the ground. The man was making a high, faint spidery noise as his shoulders threatened to separate from their sockets. Rick, trying hard to pretend the man weighed next to nothing, stared at Suerta, shrugged his shoulders.

"You said he was dumb. Couldn't speak."

"*Sí—es verdad*. It's the truth."

"So he's no use to us, is he? I'll be right back."

Suerta watched as Rick dragged the big man down the basement stairs and disappeared. There was a moment's silence, and then two muffled shots, a pause, and a third. They sounded like someone slamming a door, and then Suerta heard Rick's footsteps on the staircase again. Rick reappeared in the doorway, holding the SIG-Sauer in his left hand, a piece of cloth in his right, dabbing at several small spots of something bright red that had been scattered across his clean white dress shirt.

"Look at that," he said, stripping the shirt off. "That'll never come out. I'll have to soak it in cold water."

He dropped the shirt in the sink, turned on the tap, and stood there watching the water bubble up around his shirt. He spoke without looking at Narcisse Suerta, feeling the man's eyes on him.

"I know what you're thinking, Narcisse. You're thinking I didn't shoot him. That I'm trying to soften you up. Like this is something in a movie and you're the clever guy who has it all figured out. Maybe you are. Then again, maybe I'm the kind of guy who really hates it when people with guns and needles and ugly little fish-gutting knives break into his home. It could be I want to spend the rest of the afternoon making you wish you had stayed in Belize."

He turned the tap off, stirred the shirt with a large wooden spoon, then dried his hands on a tea towel and walked over to Suerta, let the necklace dangle through his fingers. Narcisse Suerta's face lost some color and his eyes widened slightly.

"What's *La Regla de Ocha*?" asked Rick.

"Where did you get that?"

"I'll ask you one more time. What is La Regla de Ocha? The Rule of Eight. What does it mean?"

"I don't know."

"What does that tattoo mean?"

"It is nothing. A game only."

"Your friend has one too."

"Yes. Okay. It is like a club we have."

"The Rule of Eight?"

"I do not know the rule of . . . what you speak of means nothing to me."

"Man, your lying skills need some work. How about this?"

He took the color copy of the driver's license with Geronimo Suerta's picture off the kitchen table, held it up in front of Narcisse Suerta's face.

"Last Friday night, I pulled what was left of this guy out of the water near the Florida Keys. I stuffed his body into a couple of garbage bags and put him in the fish locker on a boat called *Cagancho*. *Cagancho* was a bullfighter, a gypsy bullfighter. Hemingway didn't really like him, but my boss didn't know that.

Later, some people who remind me of you and the late Mister Vargas did their very best to blow my boat out of the water. Now the boat, and my boss, and one of his employees, and a cat named Cisco, well it seems they're all in Havana, and more people like you are probably doing really mean things to them. So I'm not in a very good mood, Narcisse, I'm as cranky as I can be, and it would relieve me greatly if I could take this feeling out on you. You follow?"

Narcisse took the opportunity to shout out for Carlito.

*"Ola! Carlito! Que bola? Carlito!"*

In the following heavy silence, Rick shook his head.

"Carlito can't hear you, Narcisse. I want to know where Mister Green is. Charles Green. He's my friend, you see? So where is he?"

*"No lo conosco. Soy—"*

Rick reached out with his left hand and caught Suerta by the hair, took the small butane lighter out of his pocket with his right hand, flicked it on and moved it very close to Narcisse Suerta's left eye. He could see the tiny curved reflection of the flame flickering deep in the man's dark brown pupil. The man's breathing became shallow and rapid. Many people can resist pain. It passes. Blindness is forever. Rick smelled spiced beef and refried beans on his breath. *Damn,* he thought. *These guys had come straight from lunch.*

It seemed a bit cold-assed, have yourself a nice plate of *chorizos* and beans, a cold beer, and then go off and kidnap some total stranger. Rick decided he really didn't like Narcisse Suerta very much. He moved the lighter in closer. The man's upper eyelashes began to curl in the heat. This got immediate results.

"He is in Miami."

"Where?"

"I don't know. We are looking for him."

"Who's *we?*"

"My . . . people."

"La Regla de Ocha?"

"No. It is like my family."

"Why do you want Green?"

"He killed my cousin."

"Your cousin who?"

"My cousin Geronimo. Jerome."

"Geronimo Suerta?"

"Yes. My cousin."

"The man you gave this necklace to?"

"Yes. He was our *babalao.*"

"What's a *babalao?*"

"A man of much importance in La Regla de Ocha."

"What's the Rule of Eight?"

"It's a . . . we call it a *cabildo.* Like a club."

"A club?"

"Yes. It is a club."

"Charles Green didn't kill your cousin."

"They found his body on your boat. Perhaps you killed him."

"Maybelline killed your cousin, Narcisse."

Suerta blinked, tried to pull back from the flame.

"Maybelline?"

"Yes. Why not take it up with her?"

"Where does she live?"

"In the Florida Keys. I can take you to her, if you want."

Suerta's face was running wet.

"Yes," he said, his voice a whisper. "You take me there."

"It's my heart's desire. Now tell me where in Miami I can find Charles Green. *Señor Verde. A dónde?*"

"I do not know, señor. We are looking too, but we have not found him either. He is in Miami, we think. The flame. Please."

He was telling the truth. Rick could see it.

"Who were the men in the boat?"

"The boat?"

Rick moved the flame again, and Suerta writhed under Rick's grip, straining away from the flame. Rick repeated the question. Suerta's thick neck was rigid, a fat artery in it visibly pulsing. He swallowed twice, his eye on the tiny yellow flame in front of him.

"They are *nanigos,* the men who belong to our cabildo."

"You have a damn big pack of *nanigos* there, Narcisse. A very damn big cabildo. Why did they try to kill me?"

"They did not want to kill you. They wanted to take you."

"Why?"

"To find out."

"Find out what?"

"About the plane."

"What was on the plane?"

"Papers. Important papers."

"Important to whom?"

"To . . . our cabildo."

Now he was lying again. His confidence level was rising. He had half convinced himself that Rick wasn't really going to blind him with the lighter. Rick wasn't so sure.

"Why did you come here?"

"To . . . talk to you. About Señor Verde."

"You were here to take me to someone."

"No, no, we were not."

"The hypodermic. The glass bottle. The new wheelbarrow in the truck, and the tarp. Where were you supposed to take me?"

Narcisse Suerta only shook his head. Rick knew that he was going to have to convince the man that he was serious. So he did.

# SANTERIA

The green van with GONZALEZ BROTHERS LAWN CARE
painted on it sat idling gently inside a circle of bright
yellow light shining down on it from one of the lamp-
posts. Its radio was on, playing a mariachi tune very
loud. The lot was almost empty; most of the people
who had come to the beach and the park had packed
up their kids and gone home after sunset. Now the
lot was deserted and the other three vehicles in the
area looked as if they'd been there since the end of
the last good war. Rick had checked them out anyway.
One was a battered Fiat, a recent wreck, apparently
abandoned here, and the other two were cheap American sedans coated with a greasy residue that stank of
jet fuel. All three had been there a while. A rising
thunder rolled over the grassy dunes behind him, and
then he felt the shock wave hit him as another jetliner
out of LAX boomed its way westward into the night
sky. Rick had timed them. One aircraft every four
minutes. He'd been waiting here for an hour and a
half. That was almost twenty-two planes ago.

Far out on the horizon line, a thin blade of bright orange light marked the end of this lovely late-September evening in Southern California. A hot wind was blowing in off the sea, bringing the scent of kelp and a spray of fine sand off the long, narrow beach. He was sitting in the darkness beyond the parking-lot lights, on a low sandy rise covered with sea grass and windblown garbage from the flats behind him. The grass smelled like kerosene. In the distance at his back, the terminals and hangars of LAX glowed like a city in flames. In front of him, beyond the lights of the parking lot, the Pacific Ocean rolled and boomed out in the blood-warm dark.

Rick was trying to concentrate on the problem in front of him and not the images in his head. What he had done to Narcisse Suerta had stayed with him. Given the right circumstances, brutality opened up underneath him like a seismic fault in his character. Someone who knew him fairly well a long time ago had sat on the edge of a hotel room bed in Saratoga and expressed her strong feeling that Rick had two very different aspects to his nature and that he spent most of his life's energy keeping the hidden one from showing. She had been nude at the time, which had distracted Rick from her basic message, but still he felt there was some validity to this, and he might have had a life-changing insight that evening so long ago if he could only have found it in himself to give a damn. He saw the lights of a car as it turned onto Vista del

Mar and rolled south along the strip that ran along the western end of LAX between the dunes and the beach.

Rick settled into the ground, pulled out the Colt, and waited. The car slowed at the gates, and then turned into the lot, its engine burbling, a low and growling sound, cam-heavy and syncopated. A Corvette, a 1963 split-window coupe, gleaming silver blue. It pulled into a space about fifty feet from the green van. The driver flicked his lights off, and then on again. Twice. Rick knew there'd be no response from the van. Both of the men inside it were dealing with more fundamental issues. He was already moving quietly along the crest of the hill, trying to stay under the glow from LAX.

The mariachi music carried across the lot. Rick, running, heard the Corvette's engine revving up. He was too late. The guy was leaving. But it did not pull away. The Corvette was still sitting there, the engine rumbling, and Rick was less than fifteen feet behind the passenger-side door, moving lightly across the sandy pavement, coming in at an angle, closing fast. He could see the plate number, a California vanity plate, SPLIT-2ND.

He was ten feet away from the passenger side when the driver's door opened, and Cameron Chennault got out, a pistol in his hand. He took a brace on the roof of the car, centered his weapon on Rick's chest. Rick came to a skidding halt, aimed the Colt at Chennault's upper body. They were fifteen feet apart, with the Corvette in between them,

Chennault's lower body sheltered by the car. On the other hand, the only thing that would stop one of Rick's .45 caliber rounds was the engine block, and Chennault wasn't anywhere near it. Rick, however, was wide open. But Chennault did not fire. There was a period of intense silence, while the wind rustled in the sea grass and they listened to the heavy surf booming and crashing.

"Rick Broca," said Chennault, finally. "Always a pleasure."

"Put the pistol down."

"Let's set that aside for the moment. Who's in the van?"

"Narcisse Suerta and his muscle."

"Who's Narcisse Suerta?"

"I was going to ask you that."

"Why me?"

"Suerta was supposed to bag me at my house and bring me here. I offered him a second option. We waited for a couple of hours, and then you arrive. This strikes me as significant."

"Did this man tell you who he was meeting here?"

"Yeah. He said he was meeting you."

This was less than accurate. Suerta had not known exactly who he was meeting here. He had only been told to take Rick here, and wait. But Chennault might not know that. Chennault shook his head.

"I doubt it."

"I don't."

"Yes, you do. You have to. It's not possible.

Whoever he was, he didn't know me. I'm not the man he was waiting for."

"Yeah? Who was he waiting for?"

"A man named Manuel Gonzalez. Rick, let's put the guns away and talk."

"I want to know what's really going on."

"So do I. So do we all."

"Then you put your piece away."

"You first, Rick. I know I'm a gentleman."

Rick considered the man for a moment and then slipped the Colt into his belt. Chennault pushed himself off the roof of the car and threw his pistol inside it. He nodded toward the green van.

"They still alive?"

"Yeah. Mostly. They caught me in a bad mood."

"Can we go talk to them?"

"How about first you explain how you got here?"

"Two men carrying Belize passports got onto a United Airlines seven twenty-seven in Miami early this morning, flew nonstop to LAX. Eventually one of our slightly less moronic airport watchers got word to me here. One of the men, a Narcisse Suerta, had been flagged by our people as a "known associate" of a Cuban-American citizen living in Los Angeles. Manuel Gonzalez. Gonzalez says he runs a chain of maintenance companies, including Gonzalez Brothers Lawn Care, but his real thing is the Cuban exile movement in Miami. Narcisse Suerta works both sides of the Florida Straits. He's a Cuban citizen, lives in Havana, but he has links with the exiles all over south Florida. And yet somehow he manages to get out of Cuba whenever he likes. This is not usually a very easy thing to do. So he's of interest to us."

"What? Like he's wanted? On a list?"

"No. Not wanted. Of interest. We'd rather know where he is and what he's doing. It's what we do."

"Who's 'we'?"

"Us. The government. The good guys."

"The man I found in the water at Cay Sal, Geronimo? He's Narcisse Suerta's cousin."

"Brother, as it happens. We ran the name Geronimo against a list of Cuban exiles active in Miami and he was the only one who fit. The Suertas are both Miskito Indians, from Belize. Cousins and brothers are the same thing in their tribe."

"Why is a Miskito Indian from Belize working for the Cuban exile movement?"

"As far as we can tell, because they'll do anything they're asked to do, and since they believe in *Santeria*, they can be controlled."

"Santeria?"

"All these guys are in the same *abakua*, a secret society. They're *nanigos*, members of the same *cabildo*, or cabal. Santeria is also called La Regla de Ocha. The Rule of Eight. It's like a voodoo thing, came out of West Africa, eventually spread to some of these Miskitos who work for the Cubans. On the surface, it's Catholic, saints' names, the Virgin, even Christ, but underneath that, it's something else. Sacrifices, curses, gris-gris, all that 'walk on gilded splinters' stuff. It's all over Havana. Everybody's into it. This is way too complicated to get into here, Rick."

"That still doesn't explain how you found this place."

Chennault pointed to one of the lamp standards surrounding the parking lot. Rick looked in that direction, saw a small black shape at the top of one of the poles near the far corner of the lot.

"You think, after September eleventh, they're going to let people park under a flight path for passenger jets using LAX without putting in some surveillance? We had Gonzalez and Suerta in the alert system, and the Port Authority cops at LAX saw a Gonzalez truck idling here for almost two hours. They were going to send a cruiser around. I came instead."

Rick nodded. It might even be true.

"So why didn't anybody show up? If they were supposed to meet somebody here? Nobody came but you."

"How'd you get the information out of Narcisse Suerta?"

"Charm. I have oodles of it. Everybody says so."

"If you used force, my bet is he gave you enough information to make you stop, but he left out the *tell*."

"The tell?"

"Yeah. If you're supposed to meet a source, and if the source is compromised, there'll be some signal that either is there, or isn't there. Maybe he was supposed to make a call, or do something with the truck that you didn't do. It's called tradecraft. Covert ops. Now can we talk to your pals?"

All of this could be true. Or Chennault could be a very gifted liar and had come up with a plausible explanation for his arrival during the few seconds he and Rick had been staring at each other down the barrels of their pieces. Rick decided to buy it for now.

"Yeah. Let's."

Chennault bent down and retrieved his pistol, turned off the Corvette, and they both walked over to the van. Rick opened the back doors and flicked on the interior light. Carlito Vargas was lying on the floor of the truck, and Narcisse Suerta was lashed to a strut with his hands behind him. Both men were gagged with duct tape. When the doors opened, Carlito Vargas started to fight the cord-cuffs again, cursing into his gag as he did so, in a muffled Indian or Spanish slang, but Narcisse Suerta only glared at Rick in the dim yellow light, his black eyes bitter cold. Chennault looked at him for a moment, then turned to Rick.

"What happened to his face?"

"He was trying to light a cigarette. Things got out of hand."

"It looks like somebody set his nose on fire and put out the flames with a hammer."

Chennault stepped up into the truck and squatted down beside Carlito Vargas, took out a small Streamlight and shined it down on Vargas's face, let out a slow breath.

"Maybe I should call in the troops. The big guy here looks severely concussed. His pupils are all wrong. And this one's nose looks like a roasted potato. Anybody ever tell you that you have some anger-management issues? Both these guys are going to need medical attention. Soon."

"Your call. Do what you want. I say, fuck them."

Rick went around to the front of the van, picked up his steel briefcase, his laptop computer, and his yellow squall jacket. He had changed into jeans and a white T and a pair of white running shoes. Chennault took a cell phone out of his pocket and tossed Rick a set of car keys. Rick caught them and looked down.

"What's this?"

"Take the coupe. I don't want you involved here."

"Take it where?"

Chennault looked at him, shook his head sadly, and spoke again very slowly, the way you'd talk to a nervous horse.

"Miami, Rick. You're going to Miami, aren't you? That's where the Cuban exiles live. You want to help Jake Seigel and Cory Bryant, start there."

"What am I? Recruited?"

"We figure you're probably one of the good guys. We're hoping you'll help us out more or less on a volunteer basis."

"Who's 'we'?"

"My guys. At State."

"You mean the CIA?"

"Those cub scouts? Tell them to go blow up a car and they burn their lips on the exhaust pipe. I mean my own people."

"What about Dunford Buell? He hates my guts."

"Dunford has some management issues that are making him a tad cranky. You're not seeing his good side. Not that he has one."

"What management issues?"

"He's losing people."

"Losing people?"

"He runs the Cuba desk at the Defense Intelligence Agency. His mandate is to acquire midlevel economic intelligence about Cuba. How our sanctions are working. The effect of those sanctions on the Cuban economy. The idea behind our sanctions is to put economic pressure on the Cuban government, to make problems for them. But they have to be . . . calibrated . . . so we don't have pictures of Cuban children starving in ditches and the UN blaming the Great Satan for all of it."

"Like Iraq?"

"Exactly. Like Iraq. There was a big piece in all the city papers last week. Callista Fry, the UN Human Rights commissioner, is trying to get the Europeans and the UN to pressure America to lift the embargo on Cuba."

"I read about it. She sounds like a complete dork. Castro's the problem with Cuba, not us."

"Right. But she's a high-profile dork and we don't need the crap right now. Keeping Cuba boxed up is part of a larger plan and that's the way it's going to stay."

"A larger plan?"

"Yeah. We need Cuba locked down because Castro

is a dangerous kleptomaniacal creep and he already runs almost all the drug and money-laundering operations in Central America. If he isn't locked down—if he gets free access to global money markets and global travel—then he can get a lot more irritating than he is now. He could turn into another Hussein, this time only ninety miles offshore. He tried it before, with Russia. As long as he's alive, we need to contain Cuba. So Dunford gets status and funding based on the quality of his analysis of the Cuban monetary system. Some of his information comes from changes in international banking rules since the September war began. Some of it comes from sympathetic sources inside Cuba, or from the exile community in Miami."

"Le Tourneau said something about hiring civilians from the exile community. Is that the problem? How many did he hire?"

"No more than five, so far. But no matter who's doing the hiring, every candidate is fully vetted by the CIA and the FBI. They go deep into the prospect's background, all the way to his place of birth. Every document is verified, every source double-checked. Especially important when you're recruiting from a highly politicized population. But you do need that access, and you're only going to get it by using people *in* the community. Buell was only allowed to choose people with a proven record of resistance in the exile underground, people whose sincere opposition to Castro was undeniable, a matter of record. Dissidents, people who had lost family and friends to Castro's secret police. Ex-prisoners, refugees. Anyway, the quality of Buell's information has been deteriorating for years, long before any of these new civilians got involved. You know Buell's boss used to be Elliott Lazarus."

"Lazarus is the new deputy secretary of state."

"Yep. And his last job was running the DIA. Dunford has ambitions."

"Dunford Buell is no Elliott Lazarus."

"No. But he is one heck of a Dunford Buell. He wants to get into the game, sit at the big table. Anybody who gets in the way pisses him off. You stirred things up in a region where he was already having operational difficulties. He sees you as a career impediment. If you ask me, his biggest career impediment is his taste in suits. Man dresses like the mayor of Munchkin City. I mean, plaid? Really."

Chennault shook his head sadly as if in rueful contemplation.

"But he's letting you bring me into this thing?"

Chennault brought his head up, his face hard.

"Buell doesn't *let* me do anything. I run my own shop."

"Really? Why bring me in?"

"You wore a Zegna suit to the FBI meeting this morning. A man with that kind of style is a man I can work with."

"I'm serious. Why?"

"So was I."

Rick had to laugh at that. But Chennault was

right. People discount fashion. If you can't dress yourself, you can't think.

"My dad," said Rick, "used to say that just because we were at war with the commies didn't mean you could get away with vulgar plaids. The seventies nearly killed him."

Chennault grinned. "It's a slippery slope. Next thing we're all dressing like Canadians and there goes Western civilization. Your dad sounds like a smart man. Anyway, about this particular cluster-fuck, you're already in it. The Cubans will come for you wherever you are. I take you off the big board, I lose a chance to see who shows up to kill you. Even if you die, as long as I see who nails you, I still win."

"Charming."

"Ugly game, Rick. Nothing personal."

"Do I get the decoder ring and the X-ray glasses?"

"Get your ass safely to Miami, I'll throw in a free trench coat."

"I can fly to Miami."

"No you can't, my friend. Trust me on that. You're a very big name with the Cubans. Everybody wants your body. You'd never get out of the Miami terminal. Do you have any cash?"

"Yeah. Narcisse there had two grand in his coat."

"Then leave. Don't use your Amex card. Pay cash all the way. And don't try to go home. We'll clean things up there. When you get to Miami, call Diane Le Tourneau's office back here."

"Why am I going to Miami when these guys are linked to a local mutt? Why don't we go find this Manuel Gonzalez guy right here in L.A. and put his dick in a bench vice?"

"I know you meant that metaphorically, right?"

"Why don't we?"

"Because, Rick, we don't have any probable cause. You remember the Constitution, don't you? Long document, on parchment, covered with this spidery sort of handwriting?"

"I'm not a cop anymore. I don't need probable cause."

"True. You don't. You do need to find a good Jungian therapist. I think your inner child has joined the Hitler Youth. Manuel Gonzalez is my end of the python. Your end is in Miami. You go yank on it, and I'll do my bit here. Okay?"

"You care to fill me in on what the hell is going on?"

"If I knew, I'd tell you. Your contact with that Cuban boat is where it all started, unless there's something you haven't told us. Whoever scooped Jake Seigel was expecting you instead. Now they're coping with the political fallout by pretending that Seigel's a spy. What doesn't make sense is the size of their reaction. Normally, the Cubans make loud noises but don't really try to fuck with the United States. We're not the nice guys we were before September eleventh. But this time they seem to mean it. Which means something is at stake, something big enough to justify the risk. In the meantime, we're hearing that the exile community in Miami is all stirred up, but nobody knows precisely why. Yet."

"What's your endgame in all of this?"

"Mine? As in, what does the U.S. government hope to get out of this thing? First thing, we want to get our citizens out of Cuba without kick-starting another Cold War. Much as I personally miss it. This thing with the terrorist cells is way too complicated. I liked it better when we had one big fat target right there in Moscow. We know for a fact that Castro's got a biological weapons research facility in the basement of the Farmacia Internationale del Cubanos in Vedado—not to mention a lot of other weapons research facilities we'd love to bomb the shit out of in and around Havana. Finally, we want to keep Callista Fry and Kofi Annan and the God-damned European Union the hell out of our backyard, so basically that's our game."

"Where do I fit in?"

"No idea. I'd say there's something you know that you don't know you know. Whatever it is, you're more use to me on the outside than in some federal protection compound. You go out there, raise a little hell—for which you seem to have a real gift—and I sit here in the rear with the gear waiting to see what deeply hideous and stomach-turning thing happens to you, at which point I chopper in, scrape up the mess and accept the thanks of a grateful nation. How's that?"

"So I'm bait?"

"Absolutely. Now split. Vanish. Take the car and go."

"What happens to these two?"

Chennault was dialing his phone. He put it to his ear, glanced at the two men in the truck.

"These guys? They just defected."

# MOBILE

Rick had the coupe wound out to ninety-five miles an hour and was running eastbound under a starless sky through the marshy flatlands outside of Mobile when his cell phone rang, startling him out of a slight case of yellow-line fever.

"Broca."

*"Rick, this is Cameron Chennault. We have a problem."*

"Well, that's a shock. What's the problem?"

*"Somebody tagged the cleaners—"*

"The cleaners?"

*"That's what we call the team we use to clean up an incident site. Get rid of the bodies, clean up the blood, take people into custody. Transfer prisoners. Our version of the U.S. marshals witness security thing. When you left, I handed Suerta and Vargas over to the cleaners. Both of them were in bad shape, especially Vargas. I wanted them healthy enough to talk, so I waited it out for twenty-four hours on a suicide watch. Last night around eleven, we called the duty desk at the medical unit, found out they were both in reasonable con-*

dition. I sent three of our cleaners over to transport them to our main facility in Santa Monica. Randy Powell, Trish Conroy and Beau Dietrich. They made the pickup and promptly dropped off the monitor screens. LAPD found the transport van in a culvert off the Santa Monica Freeway about an hour ago. Totally burned. Powell, Conroy and Dietrich in the ditch fifty yards away. Gagged. Hands cuffed behind their backs, banged around but still alive. No sign of Suerta or Vargas, but lots of their blood on the ground at the back of the van."

"Their blood?"

"We're typing it. Takes time."

"No bodies?"

"No bodies."

"Did they get descriptions of the people who nailed the van?"

"Yeah. Indian types, dressed as highway workers. They're looking at faces now."

"Perfect. Lovely. So they're either dead or they're not. That's a big help. What now?"

"I'm giving you a chance to call this off, go home and have children. Buy a barbecue and join the Shriners."

"You have a major hole in your boat, Cam."

"We know we're compromised. We know we've got a rat somewhere inside. We're looking. In the meantime, I figured you needed a heads up. You want to pass? Come back to L.A? This thing is getting snaky. We can't protect you."

"No. I don't."

"Okay. Where are you now?"

Some instinct made Rick hesitate.

"Just outside Saint Louis. Eastbound."

"Okay. Call us at the FBI office in Miami as soon as you get in. In the meantime, watch your back."

"I will," he said.

Golden, he thought, accelerating into the rising light. Fucking golden. He hadn't seen a state trooper since the Mississippi border. The hot night air was as thick as bunker oil and he could smell the salty tang of the gulf a few miles to the south. Mobile city was a distant glow on the eastern horizon. He had the radio tuned to a Mobile station when the hourly news came on. A newsman with a strong Southern drawl was talking about a breaking news story out of Washington, D.C. The Cuban government had announced the arrest and detention of an American citizen.

The man, Jake Seigel, a senior executive with Paradigm Pictures in Los Angeles, and another American named Cory Bryant had been found inside Cuba's territorial waters without proper documentation, and both men were being held by Cuban authorities in Havana. Charges of murder and hijacking were pending. Elliott Lazarus, Assistant Secretary of the U.S. State Department, had refused to comment on the matter, but CNN news in Atlanta had reached a Paradigm Pictures spokesman named Vincent Dyle. Rick heard Vin Dyle's voice in a taped interview with one of the CNN reporters. Dyle was clearly working from a prepared statement, and the CNN anchor was trying to get him to stop doing that. Rick wished him luck.

"Mister Dyle, can you tell us why Mister Seigel was inside Cuba's territorial waters without proper papers?"

"As I've said, at this point in time, we have no information about that, but we're certain that the situation will soon be resolved. The matter is in the hands of the State Department and we don't want to interfere with their negotiations in the—"

"So there are negotiations going on?"

"I'm not aware that there are negotiations going on. I assume that our representatives at State are dealing with their counterparts in the Cuban government. I did not—"

"Has State told you that they're talking to the Cubans?"

"That . . . I mean, one assumes that—"

"So State hasn't been in touch with you yet?"

"Yes, of course—but as to the issues, I can only restate our position that this matter is being handled by State and the FBI, and that they have asked us not to talk about the case in order that—"

"What about these murder charges? Reports from Cuba say there was a dead body on board the boat. A Cuban citizen. Do you have any information on that?"

"I'm not prepared to comment at this time."

"So you have information that you don't want to release yet?"

"No, I don't. I'm trying to say that whatever the situation, it would serve no purpose to speculate in the media and might have the inadvertent consequence of prolonging Mister Seigel's detention."

"Can you tell us anything about Cory Bryant?"

"No, I can't. I don't know the man at all. I'm presuming he was a friend of Mister Seigel. And that's all I can tell you."

The tape stopped at that point. Rick listened to the

newsman telling Rick what Rick had just heard all over again, but it looked as if that was all the information they had. Rick shut the radio off and saw that his hand was shaking slightly. He needed something to eat. He'd covered two thousand miles of ridgeback mountain and desert valleys that shimmered in the blistering heat in twenty-eight hours of nonstop driving, running mainly on McSwill burgers and bitter black coffee, and his insides were beginning to take it personally. He hammered through downtown Mobile as the city was just waking up, crossed two suspension bridges over the mud-brown Chickasaw and Mobile rivers with a flaming orange sunrise showing through the spars and towers of the USS *Alabama*, and pulled over an hour later at a Denny's in some place called Spanish Fort.

It took him a couple of minutes to loosen up enough to get out of the car. He'd been living inside the constant growling rumble of the big 327 for so long that when he finally unwound himself out of the car, the sudden silence made his ears ring. He rubbed two days of black stubble on his cheek, tucked the Colt into his belt, and slipped on the yellow squall jacket to cover it.

Every table was packed with silent truckers or yammering tourists so he sat down at the long counter lined with barstools and ordered a Grand Slam with a large glass of orange juice from a young Mexican waiter who looked the way Rick felt. There was a television on behind the counter, tuned to CNN, the sound off. Halfway through his massive

plate of lemon-yellow eggs and foam-rubber flap-
jacks he looked up to see a woman's face on the
screen, and a blue screen tag under her drawn face
that read Madelaine Bryant—"mother of Cuban
Hostage." He caught the counterman's attention,
asked him to turn the sound up. The woman was
speaking into the camera, obviously being inter-
viewed on a satellite uplink. She was in her mid-
forties, pretty but shopworn, with anxious brown
eyes and lines around her mouth, thick black hair
graying at the temples. It was easy to see where
Cory Bryant got his looks. Her accent was upstate
New York. She was speaking slowly, with a bitter
undertone.

*"No, they're not doing anything at all to help. I've
called several times but they're not returning my calls."*

The camera cut to one of the early-morning news-
readers, a good-looking brunette with large eyes that
looked slightly crossed.

*"Officials at Paradigm say they have no record of any
contractual relationship with your son, Mrs. Bryant. They're
saying he had no connection of any kind with the company,
and that it's possible you're only trying to establish one as
the basis for a lawsuit. Can you tell us why they would be
saying that?"*

In split screen, the woman's face hardened up.

*"I have no idea. Cory told me he was working directly
for Mister Seigel. They were in Hawaii last week, in Maui.
Cory said they were working on a script. I don't know why
they're saying what they're saying. But it's not true."*

*"We've received information that your son had a record,*

Mrs. Bryant. For drug possession. Can you comment on that?"

"No. I mean, yes, Cory got into some trouble last year, but he had himself turned around. He was so excited about this job. He called me last week, from Hawaii, and told me all about it."

"Is it possible that he wasn't telling you the truth?"

"No. It isn't."

"Well, we've called the hotel in Maui that you say your son was staying in, and they have no record of his visit there. The hotel officials say Mister Seigel keeps a suite there, and that he was alone. There are no records of a phone call from the hotel to your number."

This seemed to come as a shock to Madelaine Bryant. Rick watched her face as she took this in, and saw the sudden doubt that showed in her eyes. He got a poignant glimpse of a mother who was used to being lied to by her son. She stumbled for an answer.

"I . . . I don't know why they'd say that."

"Has your son ever been arrested for soliciting?"

"Soliciting?"

"Offering his sexual services for sale. Our sources report that your son had once been charged with that offense, Mrs. Bryant. Can you comment on that?"

Man, thought Rick. This was deeply vicious. Madelaine Bryant seemed stunned by the accusation. Whoever was sinking the blade here, and it was probably Sheila Leventhal, they didn't care much about the collateral damage to Jake Seigel's reputation. And if the Cuban cops got the idea that

Cory Bryant was a gay hooker they'd go out of their way to make his life a complete misery. Even by Vin Dyle's reptilian standards this was truly ugly. He could feel the people around him watching the screen. A trucker in a Freightways cap sitting next to him was grinning into his coffee. Cory's mother was getting no sympathy from this crowd.

The woman finally managed an answer.

*"It's simply not true. Who's telling you this?"*

*"Do you think your son's background had anything to do with Mister Seigel's arrest by the Cubans?"*

*"I . . . I think this interview is over."*

The counterman looked at Rick, lifted his shoulders in a Latin inquiry. Rick nodded, said thanks, and the boy turned the sound down again. The trucker sitting next to him turned a broad red face in his direction.

"You know the woman?"

"No," said Rick. "But I work in L.A."

"Well," said the trucker, in a low whisky drawl, "they're all fruits and nuts out there. And what isn't is—"

"A man could take that the wrong way, sir."

"Oh hell, son. I didn't mean you."

Rick stood up, flipped a ten-dollar bill on the counter.

"You have a nice day, sir."

Out in the parking lot the sun was clear of the horizon line and the heat of the day was building fast, a steaming delta heat; the air was full of the scent of diesel smoke and rotting fruit. The skin of the blue Corvette was already too hot to touch. He climbed inside, started it up, and turned the air-conditioning on to high. It was hard to say which had made him sicker, the lemon-yellow eggs or the way CNN had torn that poor woman apart. He hit the pedal and left the parking lot in a cloud of blue smoke. He was doing a hundred miles an hour three minutes later. He ruffled around in his wallet for the card Jack Cole had given him, pulled out his cell phone, dialed Cole's home number in Los Angeles. It rang five times and then the call was switched over to his voice mail.

"Jack, this is Rick Broca. You're going to want to save this message. I said I'd call you if I had anything useful. When I got back to my house after that meeting with Sheila, two mutts pretending to be gardeners tried to kidnap me. It didn't work and I took them into custody. They were Cubans. Narcisse Suerta and Carlito Vargas."

Rick spelled both names slowly and gave Cole a short physical description of both men.

"I think Suerta and Vargas may be from someplace like Belize, but now they're working out of Cuba. They move around the planet pretty good. I handed them over to Cameron Chennault, the guy from State. Get this. I just got a call from him an hour ago; he tells me some bad guys stopped one of his prisoner transports last night and now Suerta and Vargas are gone. He says maybe they're dead or maybe they're missing. There was blood at the scene, he says. Maybe it's even true. Either way, this situation is out of control, so if you want to make some moves with Wackenhut, get Jake and Cory the hell out of Cuba anyway you can, now's the time. Don't use any of your usual finks. Run this real close in, only people you know personally. Both Suerta and Vargas were connected to a Manuel Gonzalez in L.A. This Gonzalez runs a landscaping company called Gonzalez Brothers Lawn Care. I'm on my way back to Miami to follow up a lead. Since you're the only guy at Paradigm who gives a shit about Jake and I can't trust the feds, I'm handing this to you, and I expect you to do something about it because inside that nifty bespoke suit I think there's a real cop. Okay. One last thing, and hear me on this . . . I watched CNN sandbag Cory Bryant's mother. You know damn well what the Cubans think of gay hookers. You know what their jails are like. You jerk Vin Dyle's leash, call off the pack, or I go to CNN and tell them what I heard in Sheila Leventhal's office. You have any questions, you know my cell number. Have a nice day."

He put the phone down, picked up speed again. He felt a bit better. That call wasn't going to do anything to help Cory Bryant get out of Cuba, but it did help Rick keep the Grand Slam where it was.

# ZEFFI

Rick crossed the Cow Key causeway, made the curve around the shore onto Roosevelt Boulevard and realized that last Friday night at almost the same time he'd been watching Maybelline cruising in the shallows of the Double Shot Keys with that white squall building up south of Cuba. Only seven days ago. In the west he could see the low roofs and painted shacks of the old town, studded here and there with hotel towers, everything drowsing in the early-evening sea breeze, half-asleep under a pale purple sky streaked with pink-and-silver clouds. Big band music was coming across the water from a white Sea Ray moored in the government slip. Zeffi Calderas wasn't in the Key West Marina office when Rick pulled up at the parking lot outside Garrison Bight. Marty Benson was. He was in the back office, a lanky blond kid in his late teens, tanned almost black, wearing faded fatigue pants, shoeless and shirtless. He was roasting a spliff the size of the *Hindenburg*, eyes half-closed, adrift in the middle of a cloud of pale blue smoke, listening to the chatter on the marine radio. When Rick came into the room Marty looked up, processed his arrival as likely not hallucinatory, and pushed the chair upright.

"Whoa, dude . . . I thought you were in Los Angeles."

Rick was looking at the office door. It had been kicked off its hinges, and was propped up in a corner with two of its panels splintered and cracked. And there was a large damp stain in the middle of the room. The realization hit him low in the belly.

"Where's Zeffi?"

"She's . . . like, it's the machine, man. The machine took her. The Matrix. They swallowed her up, man."

Rick moved in closer very quickly.

"Wake up, Marty. Where's Zeffi?"

Marty blinked at him a couple of times through the smoke. His pale blue eyes were red-rimmed and he smelled like a heap of smoldering compost. Marty's main job here at the marina was to monitor the radio for distress calls. God help the desperate boater who needed any assistance from Marty Benson. The fact that he'd shown up at all was, by Key West standards, a tribute to his work ethic.

"She's in the cop shop. Somebody tried to do her, man."

"What the hell are you talking about?"

"Just three hours ago. She was in the office here.

Two guys. I was supposed to take her shift, but I caught a—"

"Two guys what?"

"Two guys, man. I don't know the story. But she was here."

"Which cop shop?"

"Which cop shop?"

"Highway patrol or the locals?"

"Locals. I think. No. The ones at the Salt Ponds."

Rick was halfway out the door and then he stopped.

"Marty, do you have a key to the lockbox?"

Marty pulled at a string cord around his neck, a large brass key hanging from it.

"Totally."

"There's a package for me in the lockbox."

"Dude, I'm not sure . . ." was as far as Marty cared to take it after seeing the expression on Rick's face. He bent down behind the desk, fumbled with something out of Rick's line of sight. His voice came from under the counter.

"What is it?"

"It's a brown paper package addressed to me. A big one."

The sound of paper rustling, Marty's rapid breathing. He popped up with a big flat package in his hands, a brown envelope, wrinkled and stained, put it on the desk.

"This it?"

Rick picked it up. The handwriting was rough and the letters were scored deeply into the paper.

*Rick Broca*
*Key West Marina*

No return address. No stamps. It felt bulky, filled with papers or documents of some kind, and a flat square shape, hard-edged.

"Thanks," said Rick.

"That's cool," said Marty, but Rick was already gone.

The Florida Highway Patrol building was a flat limestone bunker on the airport strip next to Key West International, on the southern shore of the island. Rick reached it in ten minutes, rolled around the big Martello tower on Feraldo, and parked the Corvette in the lot marked VISITORS.

The cop on the duty desk looked up when Rick pushed in through the bullet-proof glass doors, a thick-necked young white kid with a shaved head and a biker's goatee, an amiable mook by Rick's standards—they'd gone out for marlin a couple of times, along with some harness bulls from Miami-Dade—but a tad dim.

"Hey, Rick—how they—?"

"Hey, Bunny. Where's Zeffi?"

"She's in the LT's office with . . . I thought you were back in Los Angeles. Man, I'm hearing your name everywhere. What the fuck's going down, man?"

"Can I fill you in after? I have to see Zeffi."

"Don't know if you can. Wait here, I'll buzz the LT."

Rick paced the visitors' area and watched through the glass walls as Bunny ambled down to the rear of the empty squad room and tapped on a door paneled in frosted glass. After a wait, it opened, and Bunny spoke to the large black man in the rumpled linen suit. The man looked at Rick, said something Rick could not hear, and went back into the room. Bunny lumbered back to the counter—speed wasn't a concept that had taken very deep roots in the Conch Republic psyche—and pressed a buzzer. The glass door slid open and Rick came through into the squad room.

"The LT says wait a minute. You want a coffee?"

"Yeah, Bunny. That'd be great."

Bunny drifted off to the coffee room and began to fumble with the cups and cans inside it. Rick stared at the frosted glass door of the LT's office and tried to control his breathing. Bunny came back, gave him a sympathetic look and a cup of some acrid brown liquid that looked like an oil spill and tasted like burnt toast. Rick was halfway through it when the LT's door opened, and the large black man in the wrinkled suit stepped out of the office, closed the glass door, and waved at him. Rick came across the floor, aware that the man's look was the same look all cops had, detached, wary, willing to dislike you at the first opportunity and arrest you at the second.

Up close, Rick saw the man's age, his hair salted with gray, his skin creased and scored. It seemed to Rick that he had a general air of incipient ruin, and, looking at his sad eyes, maybe a good and private reason for a serious drinking problem, which would explain his obscure posting way down here in the Amnesia Archipelago.

"You Rick Broca?" said the LT.

"Yes." It was a strain for him to leave off the 'sir.'

"I'm Sinclair D'Antony. I'm the CO here. I got a Miss Zeffi Calderas in here, says she really wants to speak to you."

"What happened, Officer D'Antony?"

"First of all, I got a couple of questions."

"Sure. Anything."

"You know of any reason why someone would target this lady? Because this thing didn't look random."

"What happened?"

"Sixteen hundred hours, today. She was working in the office over at Garrison Bight. Two guys come in, Hispanics, early twenties, well-dressed, clean-cut. Hawaiian shirts, Dockers. Spoke perfect English. They walk right into the office and the first guy closes the door behind him and locks it, while the second guy goes right at her."

Rick waited for it. He figured if it had been bad, she'd be at the Trumbo Point hospital and not here in the LT's office.

"She sees this going down, figures it's a robbery, and heads straight for the inside office, locks the connecting door, hits the burglar alarm trigger by the radio desk. Siren goes off. First man kicks the door open and comes straight through."

"What happened?"

"Miss Calderas got a hold of the fire extinguisher and sprayed him right in the face. While he's hacking and coughing and wiping the foam out of his eyes, she steps in and hammers him with it. He goes down. Second man hears the commotion, runs in—sees the situation, takes Miss Calderas out with a backhand, scoops up his pal and drags him out to a big old yellow Galaxy convertible with white leather interior, and they scamper. Fifteen minutes later—fifteen minutes—and finally one of the dockyard grifters stumbles over to see why the alarm is ringing. He finds her out cold on the floor in a pool of foam from the fire extinguisher. Don't worry. She's okay, she's okay. Got some bruising. They checked her out at Trumbo but she wouldn't stay."

"Why didn't your guys answer the alarm?"

"This is Key West, not Palm Beach. It wasn't connected to the station. It was a private alarm company, and the only operator on duty there was across the street at the long bar in the La Concha Hotel with his head jammed inside a bucket of sangria. We're lucky somebody got a description of the car."

"Plates?"

"Didn't have any, according to the witnesses. We never found the car either. Gone up the line, maybe run to earth in Big Pine Key or Marathon. We're running a search. So far, zip. My point is, this was planned, it was directed at her, not the office, she was the target, and I'm wondering why. I ran her, she's a French citizen, born in Morocco, here on a graduate student visa, working under the table like everybody else in the Conch Republic, she's clean, no drugs, no vice record, everybody likes her. So why her?"

"I have no idea. I'd like to see her."

"In a minute. Wednesday afternoon, I had a couple of CID guys from the Coast Guard in here asking me all about you. Wouldn't say why. I told 'em what I knew, which is dick. Ex-copper, quit under a cloud, working in L.A. Nothing known against you. After they bail, I ran you on NCIC and got the whole sheet. No, you don't have to say anything. I saw some of that on TV when it happened and I figured at the time you two was the only real cops on the scene. Anyway, I also pulled this item off the Net, says you were commended by the Royal Navy for a rescue operation last Friday, that big storm."

"And your question?"

"I like this girl in here. She's got nerve and style. The only uncertain thing in her life is standing right in front of me, Mister Broca. You ever hear a song, goes 'there's something happening here, what it is ain't exactly clear'? That's my question."

"Officer D'Antony—"

"Lieutenant."

"Lieutenant D'Antony, can I ask you to call somebody?"

"Sure. Who?"

"The FBI field office in Los Angeles. The number is three one oh four seven seven six five six five. Ask for Agent Diane Le Tourneau. She's the Agent in Charge."

The LT's face had been going through a couple of shifts while he listened to Rick, and it finished with an aggrieved resignation.

"And when I get her?"

"Tell her what went on here, and listen to what she has to say."

"Fine. You wait here."

"Can I go in and see Zeffi?"

"Yeah," he said, not happily. "Go ahead."

D'Antony headed off toward a computer console, and Rick went through the door. Zeffi Calderas was sitting behind the LT's desk, wearing the same pale green sundress she'd been wearing when he'd kissed her good-bye seven days ago, leaning back in the chair, her head tilted up, holding what looked like an ice pack over her nose. She didn't move, and spoke through the pack when she heard someone come in the door. She sounded like someone with a severe head cold.

"Hab you called Rig Broga yed?"

"Zeffi, it's me."

She jumped at the sound of his voice, sat upright, and Rick saw the damage that had been done to her, both eyes surrounded by a greenish black bruise, and the bridge of her nose bloodied, her right cheek marked with a livid red gash. Zeffi stared at him for a second.

"Oh shid," she said, tearing up. "Wonderful."

Rick came around the desk, put out a hand, touched her cheek gently. "I'm sorry, Zeffi. I really am. Why didn't you call my cell?"

Zeffi took his hand, held it. Rick saw bloodstains

under her nails, and more red marks over her knuckles.

"They wouldn't led me. How did you get here? I thought you were in Los Angeles."

"I drove back."

"Drove? Why?"

"That's complicated. How do you feel?"

She smiled, winced, dropped his hand, leaned back again and put the ice pack on the bridge of her nose.

"Oh, super peachy. I guess I look terrible."

Rick told her she looked fine, and she snorted, which apparently hurt her to do.

"They have mirrors here. I know how to work them. I look like a raccoon. Did they catch those two, those *sal cochons,* fucking *merdes.*"

"Not yet."

She looked at him, then at the door, and then back to him.

"Did you get the package?"

"It's in the car."

"Look, Rick, I think that's what they wanted. I didn't tell Lieutenant D'Antony, but the one who kicked the door in, what he said was 'Give me the package'—he had no Spanish accent, but I knew it was about you."

"They might have killed you."

"They were going to do that anyway. When we lived in Agadir, people came to rob my father's shop once, and I remember the look on their faces, that killing look. They had that same look."

"Two guys, right? Did they have tattoos on their cheeks? Like a palm tree with a red thunderbolt through it."

"No. They looked like normal Latino kids from Miami. They looked like college kids."

"Not older? One big and one smaller, but thick in the body. Long black hair? Indian looking?"

"No. They were just—"

At that point, the LT came back into the office, holding the handset of a cordless phone.

"She wasn't in Los Angeles. They transferred the call to the FBI office in North Miami. She wants to talk to you."

Rick took the handset.

"Agent Le Tourneau? You're in Miami?"

*"We flew in this morning. One big happy family. This afternoon during a meeting, Dunford actually pulled an old quarter-pounder out of his coat pocket and ate it right in front of us. It was like watching a toad eat a June bug. Other than that, and dealing with the nest of vipers you stirred up in Cuba, I'm having a jolly time. Such fun. Simply Super. And how are you doing?"*

Apparently Le Tourneau did sarcasm really well.

"Me? I'm peachy too. Fucking peachy. Is Chennault with you?"

*"You could say that."*

"Is he listening?"

*"I couldn't agree more."*

"You know about Narcisse Suerta and Carlito Vargas? Chennault filled you in?"

*"We got the general idea."*

"Well, tell him I'm here in Key West and two Latino-looking college kids just assaulted a friend of mine during an attempted robbery. They were looking for something that belonged to me. I find this coincidence intriguing. Do you find this coincidence intriguing?"

"Utterly. You're quite sure?"

"I am."

"And what was it they were looking for?"

"Mail. Zeffi was going to forward any mail that came in after I left. These kids seemed to know all about that. I'd love to know how."

There was a short silence during which Rick could hear muted talk in the background and the soft cadence of Le Tourneau's breathing, a sound like surf breaking softly on a sandy beach.

"I'll take this up with him."

"Please do. Give him a kiss from me."

"God, there's an image."

"You wanted to talk to me?"

"Yes. I spoke to Lieutenant D'Antony. I told him you were advising us on the Jake Seigel thing, and that we'd keep him informed about the progress of the investigation. I don't think he believed me."

"Golly," said Rick. "Why not?"

"Where are you going?"

"To Miami."

"Are you going to take the Moroccan girl? How is she?"

"She's banged up. And as soon as we get out of the station, I'm going to put her on a jet back to France. Anything more on Jake?"

*"Oh yes. It'll be on the news tonight."*

"What's happening?"

*"Taking the hardest line we've ever seen. The Cubans are charging them both with espionage and murder. They're being arraigned tomorrow morning in Havana. It's death if they're convicted. No trial date yet. We have no idea why they're so determined about this. They're taking a hell of a chance."*

"What's Cam Chennault doing about it?"

*"State has demanded the immediate release of our citizens. We've given the Cuban government forty-eight hours to comply."*

"And if they don't?"

*"Before September eleventh we'd send in the fleet and secretly offer the Cubans a back-channel deal where we lift some of our sanctions after they let our people go. Now that Callista Fry at the UN Human Rights commission is stirring up the Europeans about how our embargo is starving the Cuban people, the president is in no mood to let a cranio-rectal inversion like Fidel Castro—or a hapless nimrod like Kofi Annan—screw around with American lives. He'll do whatever it takes. You follow me here?"*

Rick followed.

# JULY 13, 1994

Zeffi Calderas turned out to have a major malfunction in her obedience module. There was no way in unholy hell, she explained, in a fine, clear, and charmingly French-accented voice that carried wonderfully well inside the huge echoing passenger terminal at Key West International, that Rick was putting her on a jet to anywhere, let alone Paris, and if he pushed it any harder, she was going to tell the airport security that he was a wife beater—*look at my face*—and have him arrested and thrown in jail. And castrated.

Rick tried without success to persuade her that most law enforcement agencies in America were usually rather reluctant to castrate men on the simple say-so of very attractive but arguably highly unstable French tourists from Agadir, but this had zero effect other than to elicit the possibly irrelevant observation that it had been her experience that most American men arrived on the planet already partially precastrated by their mommies and that the rest of the job was usually completed by their wives and daughters.

Rick spent the next few minutes trying to sort that observation out, by which time Zeffi was back in the car park and climbing in behind the wheel of the Corvette. She held her hand out for the keys and after fighting the strong temptation to leave her there and take a jet to Paris himself, he handed them over.

The atmosphere inside the coupe was difficult for quite a few miles. They didn't talk much until they reached South Beach an hour and a half later, although Zeffi did let him light one of her Turkish cigarettes for her a mile outside Matecumbe Key. One hour later, they were fighting the traffic on Collins, trying to reach the National Hotel.

The National turned out to be an eleven-story, pale pink hotel right on the Atlantic Ocean deep in the heart of the Art Deco stretch of South Beach. At eleven o'clock on a Friday night, the bars and cafés that lined the streets were packed with blade-thin Latino punks in pastel Guayabera shirts and wrinkled linen pants, suburban white kids from the inland towns trying to look dangerous, red-eyed college students hammered on draft beer and hashish, shark-eyed gang-bangers in baggy jeans and dreadlocks, muscle-bound street cops in tailor-made blues, jingling as they walked, junk bond hustlers, dentists on the run from their wives, credit pimps, ecstasy dealers . . . the whole crowded and glittering strip lit up like a neon canyon made of polished steel and blue fire by the glow from the hotels' marquees. There was a brightly colored mass of young people gathered around a huge soundstage set up down on the beach; the deep, thudding bass beat coming from the band a thousand yards away was strong enough to feel like soft repeated blows to the midsection.

It took Rick and Zeffi over an hour to move six blocks, with the spotlit façade of the National visible all the way down Collins Avenue, and all the way down the avenue Rick's nerves were wire tight and humming with tension. They were wide open, right out in the front line, as exposed as you could get in a position almost impossible to defend. And they were attracting a hell of a lot of attention. At least, Zeffi was. The split-window coupe with the pretty redheaded girl with the sunglasses in the driver's seat was getting a series of high-pitched compliments from leathery Cuban boys in pastel shirts and way too much gold. Rick had the windows rolled up, but the bass beat was making it hard to think, and Rick needed to think. Zeffi's mood had improved a great deal, however, an unavoidable side effect of being worshipped by total strangers marinating in their own testosterone.

"I guess I don't look as bad as I thought."

"I told you that already."

"You have to say that. The way I look is all your fault. Where are we staying, anyway?"

Rick nodded toward the National Hotel, only a few hundred feet down on their left.

"There. The National."

"Looks expensive."

"It is."

"Why there?"

"Last Monday when I was taking a cab from LAX to my place in Burbank, I was trying to call Jake Seigel's cell phone. Whoever had the phone picked up my number on Call Display and tried to get my home address out of the accounts office. ATT security called me at home. The person who made that call did it from the National Hotel."

"Then he must have known that the number would be traced."

"He had to know it."

"Isn't it risky to show up there? That might have been the whole reason for the call in the first place. To draw you here."

"That's fine with me. The whole idea is to stand out. We don't have time to stumble around Miami hoping to get lucky. We need to bring them to us."

"Who is 'them'? I mean, who are 'them'? No, who are 'they'? Oh hell, Rick—who are we trying to catch?"

"My best guess? People working for the Cuban government."

"Spies, you mean?"

"I guess so. Yes. Spies. And I'm also looking for a man."

"Best of luck. I haven't met a good one yet."

"I told you. The man I'm looking for, Charles

Kelleher. I think he's in Miami. He may be taken by the Cubans, or he may be dead. If I can connect with some of the people who took Jake Seigel, maybe I can find out where this man is, and who's holding him."

"What'll we do if they show up at the hotel?"

"Zeffi. Try to remember that 'we' aren't going to do anything. You're on a jet back to Paris in the morning. Go see your mother."

"I don't like my mother all that much."

"Right now, neither do I."

"Seriously, Rick. What will we do?"

"You can hit them with a fire extinguisher."

"Amusing. Very amusing. Can I ask you a question?"

"If it's 'Do you still think I'm adorable,' I wouldn't advise it."

"Rick? Why are you even *in* this mess? I mean, the Cubans have your boss, and you feel responsible. You want to do something about it, but you don't trust your own government enough to tell them about the man you're looking for, this Kelleher guy. Why, I don't know, but there it is. So you have to do it alone, or anyway, with me. And that means that you and I are checking into a hotel tonight where one of these bad people may be working, and then we're going to wait for them to do something rash, and we're going to take one of them prisoner, or follow him back to his hideout, or do something else clever and cunning that could easily turn out to be fatal. And when we do this thing, it may—okay, it *will*—help you get your boss out of Cuba. Am I getting it right so far?"

"So what's your question?"

"I don't get it. Why don't you tell the government people about—what's his name again?"

"Kelleher. Charles Kelleher."

"Why don't you tell them about Charles Kelleher and walk away from this whole thing? You're a bystander now."

It was a good question, and he owed her an answer. They managed to cover another half-block before Rick answered.

"He saved my life—"

"After you saved his. So you're even."

"And he asked me not to give him up. I think he had a good reason for asking me. He's in some kind of jam, I think, between the Cubans and the American government, and I don't know what it is. If I can find him, I can ask him, and I have to find him myself, without anybody on my case, because the feds or the CIA are going to have their own views about what to do with him, and I won't be able to control the outcome. That's as clear as I can make it."

"You think you owe him all that?"

"Yes. Yes, I do."

"But why? You don't even know the man?"

"No, I don't. When you side with a man, you stay with him."

"Oh please. That sounds like a line from a movie."

"It is. It's from *The Wild Bunch*. William Holden said it."

"And you're taking your ethics from the movies?"

"Damn straight, Zeffi. I'm shallow and unstable and I take my ethics from classic westerns. Now you see why you *have* to bail out."

Zeffi was quiet for a while. They reached the entrance to the National Hotel and pulled up under the portico. A young Hispanic male in a pink Polo shirt and tan slacks opened the passenger door and welcomed them to the hotel. Zeffi gave him a bright smile and told him the luggage was in the trunk. While he was getting it out, she looked at Rick again, reached out and touched his cheek.

"I think you're a lunatic. But I think I might be in love with you and I'm staying around until I figure out whether I am or not."

"You're *not* in this, Zeffi. You're gone in the morning."

"Like hell. I'm the one in the raccoon mask, not you. Anyway, I'm not going, and that's it. There are things I can do. That's flat."

Rick had nothing to say to that. Lately, anyone who'd been stupid enough to hang around him had ended up neck-deep in bitter consequences. Just ask Jake Seigel and Cory Bryant.

No. Zeffi Calderas was on the next stagecoach out of Dodge City, and the sooner he could manage it the better. However, this was not the time or the place to make that point. Zeffi took his silence as a temporary truce, and maybe she was right.

While Rick was making a mental note of the exact mileage on the odometer—62,286.9 miles—she tossed the keys to the valet parking attendant—who was already looking at the Corvette with naked lust—and they walked inside.

The huge lobby of the hotel was designed to re-create the wartime 1940s, with a high vaulted ceiling, a broad marble floor, and heavy brocaded furniture backed by massive gilded mirrors. Big band music was playing on the sound system, something smooth and jazzy by Harry James. Rick felt severely underdressed. A double-breasted pin-stripe with padded shoulders, maybe. And a snap-brim fedora.

The bellman delivered their luggage, Rick's steel briefcase, his laptop computer and the small leather case that Zeffi had insisted in retrieving from her apartment, to the front desk, accepted a fifty-dollar tip from Rick with a broad grin, and disappeared.

Rick put his American Express card down on the countertop and asked the luminous young black woman behind the counter for two double rooms on the ocean side. Zeffi, who had kept her sunglasses on all the way from Key West, leaned across him and offered a conspiratorial smile to the woman behind the counter.

"One will be fine, miss."

"Zeffi, I don't want you in—"

"He's sweet, isn't he?" she said to the woman, who hesitated, looked at Rick. He shrugged and nodded. She gave them a suite on the eleventh floor—all that was available, she explained—and wished them a happy stay. Zeffi took Rick's arm as they crossed the crowded lobby to the elevators. Rick wasn't pleased.

"I didn't want you to be in the same room."

"You want me to sleep in a separate room? How safe is that?"

There was no point in arguing with her—his record in that area was unimpressive—so he didn't. The suite itself was huge, decorated in the same 1940s style as the lobby, with a large living area that opened onto a broad terrace overlooking the Atlantic.

Zeffi walked out onto it and took a deep breath. A yellow moon like a thin curved blade was gliding through veils of high cloud over a limitless stretch of deep blue ocean. Far out on the horizon a cruise ship steamed south, a coronet of tiny lights floating in a dark blue eternity. Below them, on the beachside palisade, a crowd of people was swaying to the bass beat of a reggae band set up beside a long, narrow swimming pool. From eleven stories up, the pool was a slender band of scintillating blue light. The wind off the sea was blood-warm and smelled of salt and seaweed, and where the waves crested on the shoreline, green dots of phosphorescent algae glimmered in the snow-white foam. Zeffi stood there for a while, taking it in, and then turned as she heard the sound of paper ripping.

Rick was sitting in one of the low yellow leather chairs with the brown paper package on the coffee table in front of him, the contents spilled across the blond wood. She came over the soft white carpet and looked down at the table.

"Oh my," she said. "That's a pile of money."

It was. At least fifty thousand dollars in U.S. bills, fives, tens, and twenties. Payment for the *Cagancho?* There was a small black plastic case buried in the pile of bills. Rick pulled the tab, and slid the contents out onto the table, a plastic sheet, and a note. The sheet was covered with black markings. Rick held it up to the light.

[illegible machine-printed bar code pattern covering upper portion of page]

Zeffi was looking at them over his shoulder.

"What in the name of heaven is that stuff?"

"Beats me. It looks like bar codes of some kind, I guess."

"The way it's laid out, the patterns? It has to mean something. What's the note say?"

Rick picked it up, read it, handed it to her.

*Rick, If you get this packet, take the money and do what you can. Things are going on that I don't really understand yet.*

*There are good people involved and*
*only you to help them*
*if anything happens to me.*
*Thanks for everything. Charlie*
*PS—give my regards to Cisco and Maybelline*

"God, I never thought of that," said Zeffi. "Where's Cisco?"

"Cisco? By now, he's probably running a cat house in Havana."

"Who's Maybelline?" asked Zeffi.

"You know her. The tiger shark they were always talking about at Garrison Bight. I think she's the one who got Geronimo Suerta. 'Charlie' is Kelleher's first name. He called himself Charles Green."

"The man you're looking for?"

"Yes."

"A cover name? Why? Who was he working for?"

"That's my whole problem. I don't know."

"Why so much money?"

"He promised to pay for the damage to the *Cagancho.*"

"It didn't cost that much to fix the boat, did it?"

"No. It's way too much money. I have no idea why he sent it."

"These people he wants you to help. Does it have something to do with those sheets?"

"Really? You think so? You're not just a pretty face, are you?"

"Rick, my little friend, there's nothing that makes a man less attractive than adolescent sarcasm. Work it out by yourself, then."

Zeffi stalked over to her purse, extracted one of her sulphurous Sobranie cigarettes, lit it with a short sharp angry gesture, and went off for a wander around the suite, while Rick settled back into the lounge chair, studied the papers, decided that he owed her an apology.

"Zeffi, I'm sorry. I think you're right. This is some kind of script. Look, can you bring me my laptop?"

Zeffi gave him a hard look, and then left the room. While Zeffi was getting him the laptop, Rick set the dead bolt on the main door, then went to the double doors that led out to the balcony, locked them as well, and pulled the white gauze curtains closed. He took one of the dining room chairs and stood on it to reach the smoke detector, popped it off the clip, and checked it for a mike or a pinhole camera. He did the same with every picture. Nothing. Then he crossed to the television set, turned it on to CNN, set the volume up to medium, took his yellow jacket off, pulled the Colt out of his belt, and set it down on top of the coffee table. Zeffi came back with his computer, stopped dead, and pointed to the weapon.

"Is that loaded?"

"If it's not loaded, it's a paperweight."

"Then where's mine?" asked Zeffi.

"Yours? *Yours?* Are you totally nuts?"

Zeffi's face registered some alterations that a

bright guy would have picked up on, the way a bright guy would notice a storm coming in before it damn near sank his boat. In matters of the human heart—particularly the female human heart—Rick was not a bright guy. He lost precious seconds simply staring at her. This did not help.

"If you have a weapon, Rick, I get one too. It's only fair."

"Zeffi, for God's sake. You ever *use* one?"

That was it for Zeffi, whose voice became deceptively soft.

"You really are the complete silly piglet, aren't you? For heaven's sake, Rick, my father was in the Foreign Legion. I spent two years in the Army reserves myself when we lived in Switzerland. We had training every weekend. Everybody there knows how to use weapons. And then we moved to Morocco, you *naïf*. That's in North Africa, in case you didn't know, where every second cab driver belongs to one terrorist organization or another. Everyone in my family carried a handgun and we all knew how to use them. And try to remember that Agadir is a real grown-up city, not some pokey little tourist trap like Key West."

"You were in the Swiss Army? Why didn't you tell me?"

"You never asked. You were too busy trying to get my bra off."

"What's a nafe?"

"A *naïf*. A bumpkin. A boob. Somebody like you."

"Most American women don't like guns."

"Most American women are anorexic snot noses who couldn't fight their way out of a cloud of cigarette smoke. If you don't believe me, try smoking around one of them. And don't you dare compare me to any of those rat-faced little *putains* this country tries to pass off as real women, prattling on about their *vaginas*. *The Vagina Monologues*, God help us. What crashing bores they all are. So, if you have a spare pistol, Mister Broca, you hand it over."

Rick gave it some thought, looking at the line of her mouth and the fierce expression on her face. Zeffi Calderas. The Moroccan pocket rocket. He could see why Sinclair D'Antony had liked her.

"Okay. In my briefcase, there's a pistol in the side pocket. Be careful, Zeffi. It's loaded too."

"If it isn't, it's a paperweight."

"And while you're in there, will you call the concierge and ask him if they have a scanner of any kind?"

"A scanner? Like a radio frequency scanner?"

"No. I meant a digital flatbed scanner. For computers. The best one they have. If they have to send somebody out to buy one at an all-night electronics store, tell them to go ahead, but make it fast. I want to scan this sheet into the laptop."

Zeffi gave him another hard look, softened a bit more, went off into the bedroom. Through the closed balcony doors, Rick could hear the muffled beat of the reggae band, and the sound of people talking. It rose up through the warm evening air, oddly comforting. At least somebody somewhere

was having a good time. He got up, went to the
minibar, and poured two shots of scotch into a pair
of heavy crystal glasses, dropped in some cubes,
took a sip of his, feeling the weight of the crystal. He
recalled holding a glass of scotch in his hand around
the same time last week, getting ready to throw it at
Charles Green's head. Zeffi came back into the
room, barefoot, wearing a white cotton bathrobe,
carrying Narcisse Suerta's SIG-Sauer.

"They'll have one here in two minutes. Did you
want to order up something to eat? They have an
incredible room service menu."

"Zeffi, as long as we're here, we cannot order up
anything on room service. We can eat in the dining
rooms or go out to a restaurant. But no room service food, none at all. Not ever. And if you order up
drinks, wine, pop, whatever, it has to be a sealed
bottle. Never drink anything that comes already
opened. And never let the room service guy pour
your drinks for you. You follow?"

"I follow. Is that for me?"

Rick handed her the glass, watched her as she
sipped at it, considering her shining red hair as it
spread around her shoulders and the butternut
sheen of her tanned cheek. She had put some sort of
makeup on over her bruises, and had found a small
white bandage to cover the gash in her cheek. For
some reason, the bandage, even the bruises, made
her look sexy as hell. She smelled of sandalwood, a
scent that had always reminded him of church. His
altar boy years were a long way back, but never as

far as they were at this moment. Zeffi was perfectly aware of the effect she was having on him. Rick had no intention of letting things get out of control. She was leaving in the morning, one way or another, and he didn't want anything more to regret than he already had. The door chimed softly. Rick walked to the hall, checked the small television monitor by the door, then opened the door. One of the bellmen, older, with a seamed face and small black eyes like pebbles, was standing there holding a scanner.

"Señor Broca?"

"Yes."

"This is for you, sir. With the compliments."

Rick took the scanner, gave the man a twenty. It was a good tip, and it should have made the man happier than it apparently did. He gave Rick a slightly insulting salute, and walked away down the hall toward the elevators. Rick watched him go and made it a point to remember the man's name tag: HONORIO.

He set the scanner up, connected it to the laptop, and booted it up. It took a while to cycle through start-up programs, and while it was working, he watched Zeffi moving soundlessly around the suite, barefoot. He thought she moved very well. It was a pleasure to watch her cross the floor, and the way her hair moved as she bent over to study a water-color painting of a seashell, the way the light rippled across the strands, reminded him of the ocean around twilight. He wished she would stop doing that. It was irritating as hell.

The machine pinged twice, and Rick turned on the scanner input program. It took five minutes to get all three sheets scanned into the computer, during which time he managed not to think of Zeffi for at least thirty or forty seconds. When they were fully processed, he brought the page that looked like a series of bar codes up in an imaging program and clicked on Optical Character Recognition.

The OCR program worked away for about a minute, and then indicated FAILURE TO RECOGNIZE.

"Okay," he said. "Let's see what happens if we zoom."

Rick highlighted the first section of the image:

Then he clicked on MAXIMUM ZOOM, and got . . . something.

Zeffi had walked over to watch, leaned down to look at the screen. Given the effect of the half-open robe, she might as well have been radioactive. Rick could almost hear her body humming with electricity. A basic design problem with American-style cowboy jeans was becoming more evident by the second.

"Can you make it any bigger?" asked Zeffi.

"Can I *what*?"

Zeffi gave him a big-eyed look of puzzled innocence.

"The image. On your screen. Can you enlarge it some more?"

"No . . . at least, not with this program."

"What about a word processing program?"

"A scanned image is simply a picture. It's not read the same way as data that you type in. It sees the whole page as a picture."

"Did you try Optical Character Recognition?"

"Yes. Couldn't read it."

"Is this a Mac or an IBM model?"

"It's a Dell. It runs Windows 2000."

"Really, Rick. You should have a Mac or an Apple."

"I don't like computers that are cuter than I am."

"This thing looks like a slab of granite."

"Yes. That's the idea. It's a manly computer. It doesn't have fruit all over it and it doesn't come in stupid bubble-gum colors."

"See if your manly computer will recognize all type fonts."

"How?"

Zeffi inhaled her Sobranie, then blew smoke all over him.

"Honestly, Rick, how the hell do you manage to pee all by yourself without having to change your shoes afterwards? Go back to your fax conversion program and see if there's an option for that."

He tried it her way, then read the result with a pang of regret: **Save as Word Document?**

This got a triumphant whoop out of Zeffi, who made it worse by belting him between the shoulder blades hard enough to rock him in the chair. Rick managed to squelch an outright yelp.

"Hah! Rick, I *told* you. Put the whole file into your word processing program. Go on, see what happens."

Since he had no better ideas, Rick hit SAVE AS and entered the page into his word program as a text file. It looked exactly the same as before, but when he put the cursor into the body of the image, his taskbar showed him:

**Posse 8**

Damn it! He highlighted the first section again, went to FORMAT, and clicked on FONT. The box indicated a font called MAXIMUS in size 8. He changed the type size to 48, and got this:

# "VENCEREMOS" TUGBOAT MASSACRE "VENCEREMOS" TUGBOAT MASSACRE

Zeffi thumped his shoulder again, and laughed.

"It *is* text. It says 'Venceremos.' Even you ought to be able to read that. Switch it to another font."

"Which one?"

"Any one, you idiot. Go on!"

Rick highlighted the entire text page, went to
FORMAT, and clicked on TIMES NEW ROMAN, and type
size 12. In a second, they were looking at a document in English:

### "Venceremos" Tugboat Massacre
### "Venceremos" Tugboat Massacre

July 13, 1994, at approximately 3:00 A.M.,
72 Cuban nationals composed mainly of women
and children who were attempting to leave the
island for the United States put out to sea from
the port of Havana in an old tugboat named
"Venceremos." The boat used for the escape
belonged to the Maritime Services Enterprise of the
Ministry of Transportation. According to eyewit-
nesses who survived the disaster, no sooner had the
tug "Venceremos" set off from the Cuban port than
two boats from the same state enterprise began pursuing it. About 45 minutes into the trip, when the
tug was seven miles away from the Cuban coast—
in a place known as "La Poceta"—two other boats
belonging to said enterprise appeared, equipped
with tanks and water hoses, and proceeded to attack
the old tug. "Polargo 2," one of the boats belonging
to the Cuban state enterprise, blocked the old tug
"Venceremos" in the front, while the other,
"Polargo 5," attacked from behind, splitting the
stern. The two other government boats positioned
themselves on either side and sprayed everyone on
deck with pressurized water, using their hoses. The

pleas of the women and children on the deck of the tug "Venceremos" did nothing to stop the attack. The boat sank, with a toll of 41 dead.

## Which events occurred seven miles off the Cuban coast on July 13, 1994

The persons who died that morning are: Leonardo Notario Góngora, Marta Cabrillo Vega, Caridad Leyva Cabrillo, Yausel Eugenio Pérez Cabrillo, Mayulis Méndez Cabrillo, Yaltamira García, Joselito García, Odalys Muñoz García, Pilar Almanza Romero, Yaser Perodín Almanza, Manuel Sánchez Callol, Juliana Enriquez Carrasana, Helen Martínez Enríquez, Reynaldo Marrero, Joel García Suárez, Juan Mario Gutiérrez García, Ernesto Alfonso Joureiro, Amado Gonzáles Raices, Lázaro Borges Priel, Liset Alvarez Guerra, Yisel Borges Alvarez, Guillermo Cruz Martínez, Fidelio Ramel Prieto-Hernández, Yaltamira Anaya Carrasco, José Carlos Nicole Anaya, María Carrasco Anaya, Julia Caridad Ruiz Blanco, Angel René Abreu Ruiz, Jorge Arquímides Lebrijio Flores, Eduardo Suárez Esquivel, Elicer Suárez Plascencia, Raoul Felipe Goyri, Susalis Goyri, Omar Rodríguez Suárez, Miralis Fernández Rodríguez, Cindy Rodríguez Fernández, José Gregorio Balmaceda Castillo, Rigoberto Feut Gonzáles, Midalis Sanabria Cabrera, and two other victims who could not be identified.

They read it in complete silence, and in a mood of increasing sadness. When they had both finished it, Zeffi sat down on the arm of the chair beside him, put her hand on his shoulder.

"My God. How terrible. Do you think it's true?"

"I think so, Zeffi. I vaguely remember reading about it."

"I think I did too," said Zeffi. "But it's different when you hear it like this. How could they do such a thing? To children, to helpless women and children? How could they be so fucking cold?"

"The world is packed with people like that."

"But it's so savage, Rick. And people go to Cuba on vacation. I went to Havana when I was in my junior year at the Sorbonne."

"Cuba's a hellhole and anybody who spends his vacation money there is helping to keep it that way."

"I do think the Cuban people are . . . content. You can see it."

"You know this? You know they're all content?"

"Sure. I mean, I asked them. I'm not stupid, Rick."

"Well, that's it then, isn't it? You asked them. End of story."

"Don't be such a sarcastic shit, Rick."

"Then don't be a mindless shill for a pack of totalitarian thugs."

Rick watched her face as she took the blow, her green eyes darkening, the line of her mouth changing, and he felt deeply ashamed. After a long and increasingly uncomfortable silence Rick put his hand out, touched hers gently.

"That was way out of line, Zeffi. I'm sorry. I really am."

Her mouth had hardened into an angry line, and her eyes were moist. The bruising around her cheekbone reddened as he watched. She took her hand out from under his, disengaging.

"Hey, I'm a mindless shill."

"No, you're not. I lashed out. I didn't think."

"Yes. You did. You can be a puzzle, Rick. You're a nice guy, you have a sense of humor, but if somebody crosses you, the switch gets thrown and you come at them with everything you've got. Why?"

Rick was silent for almost a minute. Zeffi waited him out.

"I don't have an excuse. I have a mean streak. I get pushed, or rattled, I push back way too hard. That's why I keep losing people."

"You don't lose them, Rick. You put them on planes and walk away. You're a strong man, I know that, and I admire you for it. But in certain ways you're very easy on yourself. Somebody disagrees, you slip the leash and let your red dog run. You say whatever you want to say and you call it honesty. I got backhanded across the face a few hours ago trying to keep this package safe for you, and I'm here in this room with you, trying hard to help, even though I don't really understand why you're so determined to find Kelleher alone and I think you're mad to try, but what the hell. So I'm a good friend and we've been lovers and I'm on your side and I've proven it several times over, but it was quite okay with you to call me a mindless shill. That's not mean, it's stupid-mean."

"You're right. It's stupid-mean. And it won't happen again."

"It had better not, Rick. I love you, but I won't take it from you. It has to stop now, for you as much as for me. So . . . let's drop it. No, I mean it. Just drop it."

Rick watched her struggling to make peace with him and felt a flood of shame as well as a rush of affection. She didn't go for the throat, didn't say the one brutal thing that had enough truth in it that it can never be unsaid and can never be forgotten. Not even when she had every right to say it; mercy and self-restraint and courage were very rare qualities in the world. This woman had them all.

"I'm really sorry, Zeffi. Believe me. I feel like pond scum."

She softened, smiled at him, and ran her hand through his hair.

"Yes. But you're really superior pond scum. So let's drop this. Why did Kelleher send us this? And why in code? Why not just say so in a note? Too easy. Not spy-crafty enough? There's got to be more to it than that. Whoever you're up against sent two men to steal it from the marina this evening. Do you have any idea what it means?"

"No idea. No idea at all."

"So now what?"

"Now? What's the best way of finding out why these people want this package?"

"We find some of them and ask them?"

"Got it in one."

"And how do we do that?"

"We're already doing it. We're doing it at this moment. That's why we're in this hotel in the first place, remember?"

Zeffi's face changed as she considered the implications again.

"Wonderful. We're trailing a wing, is that it? This is the best plan you could think of?"

"I'm open to suggestions."

"Don't tempt me."

# CHARM

THE NATIONAL HOTEL
1677 COLLINS AVENUE
MIAMI, FLORIDA
8:00 A.M. EDT, SATURDAY, SEPTEMBER 24

Rick spent the entire night sitting at the dining room table with his Colt at his elbow, listening to South Beach brag about itself at the top of its lungs. Around four in the morning the din of car horns and crowds bellowing at each other over the thumping bass beating from passing cars settled down to a muted murmur and Rick could even hear the sound of the ocean rolling in, the hissing curl of surf unfolding along the beaches. The light in the windows changed from deep purple to a pale pink shot through with streaks of gold. And still no one came. No fire alarm rang, the trick he had been expecting. No knock at the door. No voices in the hall. Nothing. It made no sense. They knew he was here. They had to. He had a suspicion that the bellhop, Honorio, would have made sure of that. But the night passed and they did not come.

Around seven, he put on a fresh pot of coffee and

walked into the bedroom to wake Zeffi. The rising sun was filling the room with a delicate pink light. She was lying on her back, her flame-red hair fanned out across the pillow, her lips slightly open. The bruises on her face had softened but they were still visible, and he looked at her for a while with an uneasy, even a guilty heart. After a while she woke up and smiled and reached out for him.

The split-window coupe was waiting for them under the hotel portico, its engine idling and rumbling, a smiling attendant standing beside it with the keys in his hand. The wind off the sea had changed since last night; it was cooler, and the sky was streaked with high cirrus clouds. Out on the street the traffic was light. Rick checked the whole block and saw nothing that looked like a tail. He tipped the kid with the keys, opened the passenger door for Zeffi, and got in behind the wheel. The mileage indicator read 62,301.5 miles. When they had checked in last night, the mileage was 62,286.9.

"Zeffi, please get out of the car," he said, in as calm a voice as he could manage. She stared at him over her sunglasses.

"What?"

"Just get out of the car, honey? Walk away from it. Please."

Zeffi slid out and stepped away from the coupe. Rick shut the engine down, got out as well, carrying his steel briefcase, his laptop, and his keys. He walked over to the valet parking desk. The young Hispanic kid watched him come over, his bright smile fading. His name tag read LUIZ.

"Luiz, has anyone driven this car last night?"

The kid looked surprised by the question.

"Only to the parking garage, Mister Broca."

"You sure? Nobody took it for a joyride?"

The kid looked shocked, then angry.

"Sir, we would be fired. At once. And we are all very well-paid. And bonded. I can assure you, sir, that no one would do that."

"How far is the garage?"

"Just around the corner, sir. At the side of the hotel."

"Show me."

"Sir?"

"Show me the garage. Take me there."

"But . . . of course, sir."

Rick stepped away from the desk and waited while the kid spoke to the other attendant. Zeffi called his name, and Rick walked over to her, handed her the briefcase and the laptop.

"Honey, go back inside the hotel, go to one of the dining rooms, anywhere there are lots of people. Don't go back to the room. Keep this stuff right beside you. Do you have the SIG with you?"

"Yes. Of course I do."

"Okay. Don't let anybody start up a conversation. Have some breakfast. Stay in the public areas. And don't go out on the street. If anybody crowds you, tries to force you to go with them, fight them, scream, create a scene. Shoot them if you have to. Got that?"

"How could I not? What's the matter with the car?"

"Somebody put fifteen miles on it last night. The parking garage is only around the block."

Zeffi listened, paling slightly, kissed him on the cheek, and then walked back into the hotel. The kid was waiting for him by the car. Rick nodded and they went down the drive and out onto the street, the kid leading, Rick a few paces back, watching the street carefully. They reached the end of the block and turned right, down a small side-street lane. At the bottom of the lane, there was a gated entrance ramp. The kid pressed a key pad and the slotted steel gate rose up. There was a booth inside the entrance, with a guard inside. He stepped out as they came in the entrance, a short, muscular black male in jeans and a tight black T-shirt.

"Luiz," he said. *"Que tal?"*

"Henri, this gentleman is staying at the hotel—" Rick cut in.

"Henri, my name is Rick Broca. I'm in room eleven nineteen. Can you tell me how long you've been here?"

"How long?"

"When did your shift start?"

"At six this morning, sir. Can I ask what the problem is?"

"I'm staying at the hotel. I had a car parked here last night. A silver-blue Corvette. Can you tell me if it was moved at all?"

"Moved, sir?"

"Yes. Did anyone take the car out of the garage last night?"

Henri's face altered, became guarded and closed.

"What kind of car was it again, Mister Broca?"

"A silver-blue 1963 Corvette. A split-window coupe."

"And you put it in valet parking last night?"

"Yes. Around midnight."

"Sir, nobody who works for this hotel would have driven your car at all. People think the car jockeys always do that if the car is a fine one, but that does not happen at this hotel. We would be fired immediately if anyone touched your car at all. No one would do it. It was there when I came in and it was there when Luiz came to get it a few minutes ago. Isn't that right, Luiz?"

"Yes, sir. That's—"

Rick stayed focused on Henri.

"And you came on at six this morning?"

"Yes, but the night man . . . he would not move it either."

"Who is the night man?"

"I'm not sure I can . . ."

Rick turned to Luiz.

"Thanks, Luiz. I'll take it from here."

"Sir, do you want me to call the manager? I can—"

"No thanks. Henri can handle it from here."

Luiz looked troubled, but he left. Henri's face was set and hard-looking, clearly angry.

"Sir, with respect. Nobody has touched your car."

"Who was the night man?"

"He was . . . his name is Carlos."

"Do you know him?"

"Know him?"

"How long has he worked here?"

"I don't know. Six months . . . maybe more."

"What's his last name?"

"Anaya. Carlos Anaya. But he's . . ."

"How many people work here on the night shift?"

"Three, until maybe one o'clock. Then only one man."

"And that man was Carlos Anaya?"

"Yes. But he's a very trusted person. His own father has worked for the hotel ever since it opened."

"As what?"

"He's the senior bellman, sir."

"What's his name?

"Honorio. Honorio Anaya."

"Are there security cameras down here?"

"Yes, there are."

"Then let's look at the video."

Henri's face changed from anger to something different.

"I . . . sir, we had a . . . the system went down last night. It is being fixed. Men are working on it."

"So there was no security camera working last night?"

"No, sir. It was . . . May I ask . . . are you a police-man?"

"Not exactly. Where does Carlos Anaya live?"

"I'm not allowed to release the addresses of our employees. I think maybe we need to see the manager. And if you are not exactly a policeman, what are you?"

"I work for the United States government."

"You have identification?"

"You have a green card?"

"I . . . I have applied, sir. It takes . . ."

"Where are you from?"

"From Matanzas, sir."

"That's in Cuba, isn't it?"

"Yes. But I have a visa."

"A temporary visa?"

"Yes . . . but you have no right . . ."

His voice trailed off and he shaded into a definite green. Rick felt like a rat for running this number on the guy, but then maybe he deserved it. Rick moved in closer.

"Where does Carlos Anaya live?"

"He lives . . . in Little Haiti."

"Where in Little Haiti?"

"On Northeast seventy-ninth, where the causeway runs under Highway ninety-five. Twenty-three-seventeen."

"How far is that from here?"

"I don't know . . . maybe seven miles, no more."

Enough for a round trip of fifteen miles.

"Fine. Thank you. I need you to do something for me."

"Yes, sir. Whatever I can."

"I need you to call the American Automobile club and tell them I need a tow truck."

"There is something wrong with your car?"

"No. I don't want to drive it anymore. And, Henri, one more thing. I'm not after you. I don't care if you're illegal. But my people are going to go see Carlos Anaya. If we find out that anybody from this hotel, anybody at all, made a call to him while we were on our way up to Little Haiti, then the United States government is going to go through the staff here like a fire through tall grass. Do you follow me?"

Henri looked completely lost.

"Yes, sir," he said, in an unsteady voice.

When the AAA truck arrived a few minutes later, Rick was waiting under the hotel's awning beside the Corvette. The driver was a middle-aged blond woman with bad skin, a mullet haircut, and the face of a turkey vulture with a secret sorrow. The name NADINE was stenciled onto her uniform shirt. She smelled of gasoline and roses and stale cigar smoke.

"You called for a tow, sir?"

"Yes. Can I see some ID?"

Nadine handed him a laminated AAA card with her photo on it.

"Can you wait here?"

"You want me to hook up the Vette while I wait?"

"No. Just give me a minute."

Rick went back into the hotel lobby. He could see Zeffi sitting at the long bar in the dining room, in a shaft of morning sunlight, sipping at a tall drink of something orange. She didn't look up. Rick opened the yellow pages, looked up the local number for triple A and dialed it. He asked the operator who answered if they had an employee named Nadine

Shoemaker. They did. He asked for a description of her, and it matched. He asked if Nadine Shoemaker was the driver who had answered a call for a pickup at the National Hotel on Collins Avenue. Yes, she was. Nadine was sitting in the cab of her tow truck smoking a cigarillo when Rick came back outside.

"I check out okay, sir?"

"Yes, you did. I'm sorry, but this is a very valuable car. I need it towed to a place where I can go over it top to bottom."

Nadine's small black eyes widened slightly.

"You think it's got a bomb or something?"

"No, nothing like that. I want to check it out."

"We got a shop over on Dade. Got all the tools and a hoist."

"A triple-A shop?"

"Yeah. Franchise. Will that do?"

"I give you the keys, will you see nobody gets near it?"

"You're gonna have to pay rent for the bay. But I can do that."

Rick handed her three hundred dollars in cash.

"Will that cover it?"

"Mister, for three hundred dollars cash, I'll sit with her myself."

"Seriously?"

"Never more."

"Okay. You only. Nobody else gets near it. What's the address?"

Nadine handed him a business card.

"We're right under the Julia Tuttle Causeway,

where it hits one ninety-five. How long will you be?"

Rick was watching a cab cruise by down on the street, lime-green and shell-pink, with a flamingo painted on the side. He remembered Zeffi's description of the cab that had delivered Green's package to the Key West Marina last Monday evening: KEY LARGO CABS.

"Mister?"

"Sorry. It's nine o'clock. I'll be there by two. How's that?"

"Works for me."

Rick left her working on the hook-up while Luiz and a couple of bellhops watched her with worried expressions. He found Zeffi at the hotel bar, a tequila sunrise in front of her, reading a copy of *The Miami Herald*. She showed him the front page.

Above the fold, under the headline "AMERICANS TO FACE MURDER TRIAL," was a color photo of Jake Seigel and Cory Bryant. They were seated at a table and flanked by three Cuban police officers in olive-green uniforms. Jake Seigel looked thinner and more tired than Rick had ever seen, but his expression was angry, defiant, and even dangerous. Cory Bryant's face was bruised and battered, and he seemed sick with fear. Looking at it, Rick felt his chest tighten up. The Cubans were showing every sign of going ahead with the trial.

HAVANA, SEPTEMBER 28: Cuban authorities in Havana have issued a statement that U.S.

citizens Jake Seigel, the CEO of Paradigm Pictures, and Cory Bryant, of Los Angeles, will be put on public trial for the murder of a Cuban citizen. The body of Jerome Suerta was found on Mister Seigel's boat during what the Cubans describe as a security check in Cuban territorial water last week. According to Cuban police officials, the body was hidden in a fish locker and showed signs of mutilation. American government officials have strongly criticized the actions of the Cuban police but have not been able to obtain the release of the two U.S. citizens. Elliott Lazarus, Assistant Secretary of the U.S. State Department, described the Cuban position as "intractable." The deadline expires at eight A.M. Monday, September 30th, but Lazarus would not speculate on what actions the United States would take once the deadline had been passed.

Zeffi watched Rick's face as he read the story.

"This sounds very bad, Rick. What will they do?"

"I don't know, Zeffi. My guess is they want something and they think that putting Jake Seigel on trial will get it for them."

"But you know they're innocent. You pulled that body out of the water yourself. The man was killed by a shark. You can prove it."

"They don't care about the proof, Zeffi. They

already know how Suerta died. What I don't get is why they're so ready to risk a confrontation with the U.S. Bush won't hesitate to go in."

"And if he does, what will happen then?"

"We'll be at war with Cuba."

"Then whatever the Cubans want, you better find it first."

LITTLE HAITI, NORTH MIAMI
11:00 A.M. EDT, SATURDAY, SEPTEMBER 28

Little Haiti was two hundred square blocks of run-down breeze-block bungalows, spray-painted wood-frame shacks, *groceterias,* bodegas, and empty ruined factories that ran from 41st to 83rd Streets in a bombed-out area of north central Miami that ran between Interstate 95 and Biscayne Boulevard. Driving into it in their Crown Victoria, Rick was reminded of Harlem or parts of the South Bronx, except the buildings weren't as well-built and the streets were wider. As they rolled north along Biscayne, scattered crowds of hard-eyed black teens in baggy hip-hop clothing stopped talking and watched them as they passed by. The air smelled of fried food and spice and burning garbage, and the tinny sounds of Caribbean music came through the open doorways of single-story bars made of corrugated tin and scrap lumber. The heat was building fast, and the air was filled with a yellow haze. They had the windows rolled up and the doors locked, and Zeffi was glad the windows of the navy-blue Crown Victoria were tinted almost black.

The car looked official, which was the whole idea, as far as Rick was concerned. That was why she had hunted the model down at several different car rental companies, finally locating one at a dealership a few blocks from the hotel. She'd rented it using her own credit card while Rick had stayed well back from the scene, keeping a careful watch for anyone who looked vaguely like a watcher.

The lack of apparent surveillance troubled him. They were, in Zeffi's phrase, trailing a wing. So why no takers? Not enough people? It was obvious that Narcisse Suerta and Carlito Vargas weren't working alone. They'd had some serious professional help in that hit-and-switch in Santa Monica. Some real cold-assed help. So where the hell were they?

Twenty-three seventeen Northeast 79th Street was a three-story breeze-block apartment building that had once been painted a bright blue. The paint had peeled off in random sections, exposing the concrete, giving the place a mottled, diseased look. A hard, flat light lay on the street side of the building, and some of the upper windows had been covered in aluminum foil. A crowd of skinny black kids were skateboarding along the sidewalk in front of a flight of wooden stairs that ran up to a narrow entrance. They stopped and stared in stony silence as Rick parked the car in front of the building. They had dressed to look federal, Rick in a new off-the-rack navy-blue suit, a white shirt and tie, and Zeffi in black jeans, boots, a tight black T-shirt, with one of Rick's blue dress shirts over that to cover the SIG-Sauer in her belt. She watched as Rick checked his Colt, and did the same with her SIG, handling the piece with an easy familiarity.

"Now what?" she asked, looking at Rick, her eyes hidden behind her sunglasses, her mouth set and hard-looking. Rick reached into the backseat and picked up a small brass cylinder wrapped in dirty rags, along with the two Motorola handheld radios he had bought at Radio Shack.

"We both get out. You stay here, keep the car at your back. You look like La Migre, so I don't think anybody will bother you. If they do, bark them back and call me on the radio. I'm going in."

Zeffi nodded, said nothing, and they got out of the car. Rick threw the keys to Zeffi, walked through the crowd of kids, who made a path for him in complete silence, and went up the stairs to the entrance hall. It was like stepping into a rabbit hole, and it took him a moment to adjust to the darkness inside the narrow wooden hallway, and a moment longer to get used to the stink of fresh urine and stale cooking that choked the squalid entryway. Ten feet down the narrow hall, a flight of wooden stairs ascended into a hazy amber dimness. He could hear music playing from somewhere above, and the sound of a television set. There was a battered tin mailbox nailed to the boards inside the door, with five slots, only two of which, A 1 and A 5, had name tags, *Colibra* and *Guiventa*.

There was no tag for *Anaya*. It had been his experience that it was easier to chase a guy down the stairs than up them, so he climbed all the way up to A 5 at the very top, found the nameplate that read *Guiventa*, and knocked on the battered wooden door. Inside the flat, a radio that had been playing stopped suddenly, and then a slurred male voice called out.

"*Quien está?*"

"*Por favor. Yo quiero Carlos Anaya. Es aquí?*"

"*No le conozco. Salga!*"

"*Abra la puerta, cabrone!*"

"Who the fuck are you? Go away."

Rick delivered a short hard punch to the door-frame, getting a cloud of dust for his troubles.

"*Ola, hijo de la puta, Carlos Anaya, a dónde?*"

"*Cuarto Quatro, cingada!*"

Apartment Four. Rick grinned to himself, tipped his nonexistent hat. That old Broca charm, it never failed him. He went down a flight, and walked softly along the creaking tiled floor toward a door coated in spray-painted graffiti at the end of the hall. He could hear the sound of a television, a loud Spanish commentator shouting something that to Rick sounded like sports coverage. He stopped outside the door, took his old New York State police badge and hung it around his neck on the silver chain, tugged out his Colt, picked out a spot about two inches to the left of the rusted doorknob, and kicked it very hard. The door slammed wide open, banged off the wall, and Rick caught it with his shoulder as he bulled through into the front room with his Colt out.

In the cluttered, dimly lit living area he saw a thickset olive-skinned man clad only in baggy boxer shorts jump up out of a sunken couch set in front of a brand-new flat-screen Sony television, his eyes huge, a large blue-steel semi-auto in his hand. He shouted something at Rick, saw the badge on the neck chain, lifted the pistol, hesitating, but by then Rick was around the couch and on him before he could decide what to do with it, taking him down with a forearm blow to the side of the man's neck. He hit the floor, bounced twice, and then Rick pressed the muzzle of his Colt into the man's temple.

"Police, asshole."

The man locked up tight, while Rick gave the place a quick look over his right shoulder. There was a grungy-looking bathroom off the living room, door wide open, and a section of the back wall that had been turned into a galley kitchen. The couch was covered in stained yellow sheets and reeked of marijuana. Other than this guy squirming under the muzzle of his Colt, the tiny apartment was empty.

Rick gave the guy a quick frisk, tossed the man's pistol across the room, dropped a knee hard into the man's belly and shoved the Colt into his right cheek.

"Are you Carlos Anaya?"

"*Hombre, que—*"

"Ingles! In English."

"Yes, yes, I am Carlos Anaya."

"I'm not very happy with you, Carlos."

"*Por que?* Why? I did nothing . . ."

"What did you do to my car?"

"Your car?"

"Last night you took my Corvette out of the parking garage at the National Hotel and drove it up here. Then you took it back. What did you do to it?"

"I never took your car."

"I just came from a garage, Carlos. Put my car up on a hoist, took out the seats, went all over the chassis. Guess what I found."

Anaya shook his head, said nothing. Rick pulled the small brass cylinder out of his pocket, held the nozzle under Anaya's nose. Anaya's eyes widened and he tried to push himself away from it.

"*Señor* . . . don't . . ."

"This was inside the driver's side air vent. It had a radio trigger attached. What happens when I trip the lever, Carlos?"

Anaya shook his head from side to side, and Rick realized the man was holding his breath.

"Sir, I did nothing—"

Rick cocked the Colt's hammer back, and the man closed his mouth tight, and his eyes. Under his knee, Rick felt the man's muscles quivering.

"I don't have much time to fuck around, my friend."

The man spoke with his eyes closed, his voice shaking.

"You are a police officer. You can't do this!"

"These are ugly times, Carlos. What did you do?"

"I . . . I did nothing."

Rick laid the muzzle up beside the man's left ear and pulled the trigger. The round hit the flat-screen Sony, which imploded in a shattering cascade of glass, the sound of the gun a massive blast in the tiny room. The muzzle flare seared the man's temple. A thin trickle of bright red blood started to run out of his ear. Rick heard his two-way radio beeping. He picked it off his belt, keyed the talk button.

"Yes?"

*"Rick, are you okay?"*

"I'm fine. What's going on in the street?"

*"Everybody cleared out when they heard the shot. Somebody will call the police, won't they?"*

"Not around here. Wait there."

He keyed the set off, and looked down at Carlos Anaya.

"Can you hear me?"

"I . . . yes. I can hear you."

"Who are you working for?"

"We . . . took it for a drive. For fun. I swear."

Rick moved the Colt across the man's face and laid the muzzle up against the man's right ear. Anaya struggled under Rick's grip, tried to pull his head away, but Rick pulled him in tighter.

"Understand me, Carlos. Either you tell me what I want to know, or I blow your other ear off, and then I start in on the really important bits. One more time. Who are you working for?"

"I . . . no one. Only the hotel."

In the distance, they both heard the sound of sirens. Anaya began to struggle, so Rick pressed the muzzle in tight, and set his finger around the trigger.

"Who are you working for?"

"No one . . . *señor*, please."

This kid was more afraid of talking than he was of the Colt. Rick sighed, picked the cylinder up, and held the nozzle under the man's nose. Anaya jerked backward, lips tight, holding his breath. Rick tripped the lever of the tank, spraying the liquid right into Anaya's face. Anaya fought the spray, turned bright scarlet, and then paled to lime green. His eyes rolled upward, and he collapsed onto the dirty tiles. Rick waited for the mist to dissipate, bent down, checked Anaya's breathing. An uneven rattle, but strong. The guy was out cold. Rick's radio beeped, Zeffi's voice controlled but urgent.

*"Rick, the police are coming. I can hear them."*

"Get in the car and get out of the area. Go no farther than two miles, or you'll be outside the range of the radios. I'll call you."

*"But, Rick . . ."*

"Go now!"

She clicked off the air. Rick went to the window, and watched as the dark blue sedan powered away down 79th Street. He stepped over to a telephone on the floor beside the couch, lifted it up, popped the housing, and placed a small FM transceiver inside the phone. He snapped the housing back on, set the phone down, checked Anaya one more time—still out cold—and then left the flat. He took the stairs down to the main floor, pushed past several people clustering in the hallway, and jogged out the back door.

There was a junk-filled alleyway that ran the length of the block. Rick listened to the sirens, gaug-

ing the direction, slipped his badge back under his
T-shirt, put the Colt in his belt, and jogged east
along the alley. When he reached the next block, he
slowed down to a casual walk. At 78th, he looked
back up the street and saw a Miami-Dade patrol car
pulling up in front of the tenement, and two uniforms climbing out, in no apparent hurry. He walked
away in the opposite direction and had covered
about ten blocks when his cell phone rang, startling
the hell out of him. He looked at the call display: ID
BLOCKED. Who the hell . . . ?

"Hello?"

"Rick, it's Cam. How are you? How's Zeffi Calderas?"

"Where are you?"

"We're at the FBI office on Northwest Second. You
never called in. We show you checked into the National
Hotel down in South Beach around midnight. Since then,
nada. Everybody here is wondering what the hell you're
doing."

"I talked to Le Tourneau yesterday."

"That was yesterday. This is now. A bulletin, in case you
missed it? We're going to war with Cuba next week. We're
naming the war after you, since you're the one who started it.
The Rick Broca War. You better come in. Both of you."

"Why the hell would we do that? You and your
guys couldn't hold Suerta and Vargas for twenty-
four hours. You think I'm going to trust you with
Zeffi and me?"

"What are you going to do?"

"When I do it, you'll know."

"How's my Corvette?"

"It's in a triple-A shop under the Julia Tuttle overpass."

*"I don't like the sound of that."*

"Somebody at the National Hotel took it for a ride last night. I took it apart, found a pressurized canister in the air vent, rigged to a radio receiver. Send the signal, it discharges into the driver's face."

*"What was in it?"*

"It smelled like Haldane. We used it in the ESU for nonlethal take-downs in a close-quarter situation. Barricaded EDPs, that kind of thing. It's an aerosol. You spray it on any exposed skin. Takes effect immediately. Depending on the dose, you're out for maybe a half hour, wake up with a killer hangover. Now and then it kills you."

*"How'd you find out?"*

"It had fifteen miles on it that I never put there."

*"Sharp. Very sharp. And the car's still okay?"*

"It better be. I paid a triple-A employee named Nadine Shoemaker three hundred bucks to babysit it. Their garage is on Dade, near the freeway. Tell her I called you."

*"Who took the car? Somebody on the staff?"*

"I wasn't able to find out. You might want to take that hotel apart and get Immigration to check out the staff."

*"We'll send some people there. Where are you?"*

"Never mind. What's happening with Jake Seigel?"

*"He's hurting. Our guy from the Swedish Consulate went in to see him last night. Apparently he picked a fight with one of the guards—cleaned his clock pretty good—so*

*three more guards beat the living crap out of him. You never told me Seigel was such a tough guy."*

"He was snake-mean enough to survive twenty-five years in Hollywood. What about Cory Bryant?"

*"Last news we had, he was in one of their isolation cells. I don't know what they're doing to him, but it's probably nasty. I still think you should come in."*

"No. I have something to do."

*"Anything to do with Charles Kelleher?"*

Rick tried not to react to that, and failed miserably.

*"You called Naval Archives last Tuesday, asking for information on a destroyer called the USS* De Haven. *The LT gave you a link to archived base newspapers. You found something called* The Kaneohe Outrigger. *We picked up on that and ran with it."*

"I don't know what the hell you're saying."

*"October twenty-seven, nineteen seventy-three. 'Navy Family in Happier Times. Naval ace Charles Kelleher loses his wife Ruth and his two-year-old daughter Eileen when the USS* Bowline *sinks in Kaneohe Bay. Three-year-old Kathleen survives but she's in a coma. Funerals at Pearl Harbor.' You're a lousy liar, Rick."*

His cell phone. He'd used his cell phone to call Lieutenant Rickman at Operational Archives in D.C. They'd pulled all his calls.

"I saw it. It meant nothing to me."

*"Then why'd you stop searching at that point? You logged off right after you found it. We traced it through your AOL account. There are no secrets anymore."*

Damn. They were all over him.

"Rick, I told you this in Los Angeles. We turned you loose to see what you would dig up. What's Kelleher got to do with this Cuba thing?"

"I don't know yet. Who the hell is he? Did you run the name?"

"We did. He rang very big bells over at the Pentagon. Up until a few weeks ago, Charles Kelleher was one of the Navy's black ops people, flew all sorts of Intel missions in Central America, Southeast Asia, flew logistics support for the Marine Corps strikes against Iraqi weapons sites all last winter. He was one of their top spook pilots. Then he takes a leave of absence and flat-out disappears. They figured he was off somewhere in Montana. But he isn't, is he?"

"When did he take this leave of absence?"

"Two months ago. Enough talk. Cell phones are worse than bullhorns. You stay where you are. We're sending a car for you.

"Not a chance."

"Buell says you come in or else, and Le Tourneau agrees. You're showing on the grid as somewhere around Little Haiti. That's real close. We can be there in ten minutes."

The cell phone again. They sent out a LOCATE signal every fifteen seconds, looking for the nearest cell to link up with. If the feds had the cell phone's unique radio signature, they could trace it to within a few blocks. Did they have the rental contact on the Crown Victoria as well? He'd have to take the chance. He tried to sound defeated, which was fairly easy to do, since he felt that way already.

"Okay, Chennault. I'll come in. I'm at the corner

of Seventy-eighth Street and ... north Miami. I'll
wait here."

*"Do that. And keep your phone on."*

Chennault broke the connection. Rick stared at
the cell phone in his hand, thinking that the world
was changing faster than he could handle. He
looked across the street and saw the sign for *Farmacia*. He crossed 78th, keeping an eye out for patrol
cars, went into the cool shop—said *buenas tardes,
señora* to the desiccated gnome with the flat black
eyes who was knitting a sweater behind a sheet of
thick bulletproof acrylic—and bought a large brown
envelope. Out on the street, he slipped his cell
phone into it, and then walked east along 77th.
Halfway down the block, he saw a cab coming—
pink-and-green colors—it was a Key Largo cab. Rick
flagged him down, leaned in the driver's window—a
young Latino kid who looked fourteen—the same
guy who had brought Green's package to Zeffi?
Unlikely.

"I have a package I need delivered."

"Are you coming?"

"No."

"Then you have to pay in advance."

Rick gave the boy five twenties. The kid's eyes
widened as he took the brown envelope, and when
he felt the weight inside he gave Rick a hard look
full of suspicion.

"What is it, mister?"

"It's a cell phone. Open it and check if you want.
It belongs to my buddy, and I want you to drive it up

to him. Don't turn it off. If it rings, ignore it, okay. But it has to go there immediately."

The boy slipped the phone out, studied it for a moment, and then put it back into the bag, looking more relaxed.

"Okay. Where do I take it?"

"Las Olas and Sunrise. The Galleria. The security guard there will know what to do with it. But make him sign for it."

"That's in Fort Lauderdale."

"That's why I gave you a hundred dollars."

"I need two hundred. I have to come back empty."

Man. The kid's a bandit.

"Okay, two hundred. But you have to get it there fast."

Rick delivered another five twenties into the kid's grimy paw, accepted a hastily scrawled receipt in return, and got a flash of uneven but very white teeth. He stepped back as the kid powered the old Checker cab down 77th, trailing a cloud of blue smoke. Then he pulled out the two-way radio and keyed the call button.

"*Rick?*"

"Where are you?"

"*I'm . . . at the corner of Biscayne and Northeast 73rd.*"

"Is anybody on you?"

"*No . . . I don't think so. No.*"

"Okay. Stay there. I'm coming."

Seven minutes later, Rick spotted the blue sedan parked in a McDonald's lot across Biscayne Boulevard, engine idling, the windows up. He crossed the street with the light, moving slowly. Zeffi put the car into gear and met him at the exit ramp. Rick got in the passenger side and Zeffi pulled out into the traffic.

"Are you okay?" she asked, her voice reasonably calm.

"I'm fine, Zeffi."

"Did you get the . . . the thingy . . . put in?"

"The thingy?"

"You know what I mean."

"Yes, I did. Go north a couple of blocks, then pull over and park somewhere. We have to stay within range of . . . the thingy."

"Did you hurt him badly?"

"It's safe to say I had his undivided attention."

"Did he tell you anything?"

"I didn't expect him to. I only wanted to scare him."

"Did it work?"

"We'll see . . . okay, stop here."

Zeffi pulled out of the traffic and backed into a parking spot next to a large fruit market at the corner of Northeast 77th. She put the car in park and leaned back with a sigh, laughed softly.

"Your methods are . . . extreme, Rick."

"So I've been told."

"What now?"

"Now, we turn on the receiver and see what happens."

"Won't the cops be looking for this car?"

"I doubt it. My bet is Carlos will get rid of them

as soon as he can. He's not in the kind of business where the cops can help him."

"But other people saw us too. What will they say?"

"They'll say nothing. Most of them are illegals and where they come from, Haiti, Trinidad, Jamaica, Cuba, the police are not the good guys; besides, we looked like federal cops."

"You're sure of this?"

"Hell no. But if we keep moving, we can stay ahead of them."

Zeffi gave him a look but said nothing. Rick set the receiver down on the console between them and adjusted the squelch until the hissing noise abated. Zeffi offered him one of her black-and-gold Sobranies. He had been trying to quit smoking for almost a year. He stared at the slender black cigarette for a moment, then put it in his mouth. Zeffi lit it up for him, then lit hers. Rick inhaled the smoke deeply and expelled it in a harsh cough, his balance reeling.

"Man, what's in this? Freon?"

"No, simply actual real tobacco. Not that dried-out chemical mash you Americans smoke. It's Turkish, I think."

"How long have you been smoking these things?"

"Since I was sixteen."

"Sixteen? You must have lungs of steel."

"My grandmother smoked until she was ninety-four."

"What made her stop at ninety-four?"

"She couldn't reach the matches."

"Why?"

"They were down at the bottom of her coffin."

"I see. What other vices do you have?"

"Opinion varies. I have fourteen in my personal collection."

"So many vices. How do you find the time?"

"I multitask."

"Good for you. By the way, your bruises are almost gone."

"I put makeup on them."

"What kind of makeup?"

"Plaster of Paris. So don't make me laugh. My face will crack off and we'll frighten the children."

"We don't have any children."

Zeffi went all wistful then, and Rick braced himself.

"Children," she said, in a deceptively small voice. "I really love children. Do you love children? I'm serious, Rick."

"Hard to say, honey. So much depends on how they're cooked."

Zeffi sent him a scathing look and he smiled sweetly at her. Then they heard the syncopated thrumming of a heavy chopper—low and close and moving fast. Rick leaned forward and looked upward as a navy-blue Jet Ranger with FBI markings hammered through the hazy yellow air five hundred feet off the deck.

"What is it?"

"The FBI, honey. Looking for me."

"I thought you were on their side?"

"I am. I simply don't want to go home just at this moment."

"Where are they going?"

"Fort Lauderdale. To catch a cab."

He filled her in on the call from Cameron Chennault, and what the State Department had found out about Kelleher's background as a "black operations" pilot for the U.S. Navy, ending with the cell phone trace, and the pink-and-green cab.

"That reminds me, Zeffi. Do you remember telling me about the guy who delivered Green's package?"

"Yes, the young boy in the cab."

"Did it have a flamingo on the side?"

"Yes, I think so."

"I think it may have been Key Largo Cabs."

"I didn't get the name . . . do we go look for the driver?"

"Depends on what we can get out of Carlos Anaya."

Rick was studying Zeffi's face in the slanting light of the early afternoon. Her skin had a soft golden sheen, and her hair was shining.

"Are you really as calm as you look?"

She smiled then, and shook her head.

"God, no. Are you?"

"Hah, I say! Hah!"

"What are you doing?"

"I'm laughing in the face of danger. Want me to do it again?"

"Please don't. How is this all going to end, Rick?"

"I have no idea. I wish I did."

"When it does end, will we still be together?"

"Till death do us part, kid."

"Considering our situation, you might want to rephrase that."

The FM receiver emitted a series of pops and clicks, and then a string of irregular electronic tones, a number being dialed out. Rick watched the LED screen on the control panel: 3 0 5 3 6 1 2 9 7 3.

"Is that the number he's dialing?" asked Zeffi.

"Yes. Let's see if we can get the audio."

They listened to the dial tone, and then the intermittent sound of the connection ringing through. On the seventh, the call was answered, a male voice with a Cuban-Spanish accent, and furious.

*"You are not supposed to call here."*

They heard Carlos Anaya's voice, on the thin edge of panic.

*"Perdoneme. Mi oido. Pienso que soy sordo. Los polis estaban aqui. El me tiro!"*

*"Nada mas! Hang up. Someone will come to you."*

The line went dead. They heard the carrier signal from Anaya's phone running for a few seconds more and then it too clicked off.

"He sounded very frightened, Rick. What did you do to him?"

"I did what was necessary, honey. Wait here. I have to find a pay phone. Lock the door."

Half a block down Biscayne, he found a beaten-up but still-working pay phone on the bullet-pocked wall outside a steel-shuttered lounge called L'Estrella and dialed a Key West number.

*"Highway Patrol."*

"May I speak with Lieutenant D'Antony?"

*"Rick, that you?"*

"Bunny?"

*"Hey, dude, we had some DIA spook named Dunford Buell calling for info on you a few minutes ago. He sounded pissed."*

"Bunny, I need a huge favor. You have to keep it to yourself."

*"Rick, I don't know. You still on the side of the angels?"*

"I am, Bunny. I promise you."

*"Okay, buddy. What do you need?"*

"I need an ANI-ALI check on a number. I need it fast."

*"I'll try . . . what's the number?"*

"Three oh five. Three six one, two niner seven three."

*"Okay . . . wait a minute, I got to boot her up . . . Okay . . . What was the number again?"*

Rick repeated it and waited while Bunny punched the information into his computer. He heard Bunny's shallow breathing over the line and the rattle of his keyboard. A Miami-Dade patrol car cruised by, the black female trooper in the shotgun seat giving him a wary appraisal. He tried to look like a lost tourist and they moved on.

*"Okay . . . here it is. Two sixteen Coral Key Drive. In Key Biscayne. A private residence. Belongs to some corporation. CIMEX Corporation, in Switzerland. There's a notation for the Miami cops in case of a security problem, an address in Geneva. You want both of these?"*

"Yes. Give me both."

"Okay. You got two sixteen Coral Key Drive in Key Biscayne, and the corporate address in Geneva is two thirty-one A Handel . . . strass? Strasse? Handelstrasse—fucking square-head names. I thought they spoke Swiss in Switzerland. Two thirty-one A Handelstrasse SA Geneva Switzerland, then the letters A, Z, W ten. No idea what the fuck that means."

Rick wrote both addresses down on a notepad.

"Okay. Key Biscayne. Thanks, Bunny."

*"You got to keep this to yourself. I told this Buell guy I had no idea where you were. He finds out I lied, he'll gaff, gut, and fry me."*

"I know that, Bunny. Thanks."

Zeffi had pulled out of the parking space and was rolling slowly north on Biscayne Boulevard. Rick caught the door as she slowed and hopped in and Zeffi accelerated into the heavy traffic.

"Take the Dixie Highway. We're going to Key Biscayne."

"What will we do when we get there?"

"Something tactically brilliant. You'll be amazed."

"I will? That's wonderful. I'm so happy."

"Knew you would be."

"So . . . something dazzling?"

"Yep."

"Like what, specifically?"

"I haven't got a clue."

"I didn't think so."

# THE GREEN TURTLE

KEY BISCAYNE, SOUTH MIAMI
4:30 P.M. EDT, SATURDAY, SEPTEMBER 28

They paid the one-dollar toll to a bulky and sullen white security guard wearing the bug-eyed alien sunglasses that all the bulky and sullen white guys seemed to favor these days, and crossed over the two miles of the Rickenbacker Causeway with the long white-sand stretch of Hobie Beach on their right. Out on the curve of the bay, dozens of windsurfers were flitting over ugly-looking saw-toothed rollers under a strong southwesterly gale that had come up out of the Gulf Stream. The weather was changing rapidly, dropping ten degrees in a half hour, and the water was the color of a three-day bruise under a lowering gray sky heavy with the threat of rain. When Zeffi rolled her window down, the scent of rotting kelp and salt air spilled into the car. Up ahead, the long flat key curved far out into the Atlantic Ocean in a southerly crescent several miles long, a rich green island covered in pine and oaks, ringed by a pale line of pink-sand beach. The trees that covered the entire island were tossing and roiling under the seawind, their leaves flashing silver and green, and hundreds of seabirds wheeled and called, skimming above the wave tips. The whole seacoast was full of violent motion, from surf to sand to sky and the force of the south wind was rising every minute.

"Big storm coming, I think," said Rick, as they cleared the causeway and turned left onto Crandon Boulevard, the main line that ran down the spine of Key Biscayne all the way to Cape Florida.

"Do we know where Coral Key Drive is?"

They were traveling southeast down a wide four-lane road almost completely lined with swaying pines, palm trees that bent before the wind, thick hedges of mandevilla, jasmine, and cedar and behind them, block after block of gated estates, huge homes set far back from the road, only partially visible as patches of pink stucco or white marble over the tops of brick walls or wrought-iron fences.

Key Biscayne was a fortress-island inhabited by some of the wealthiest people in the Western world. There were a few hotels on the key and a couple of restaurants, but visitors were not at all cherished by the residents. If they could, they'd close the causeway every night at sundown, and then mine the bay. The island reminded Rick of parts of the Hamptons on Long Island, the same immense estates, the same expanses of money-green lawns that rose up toward Spanish villas, stone manor houses, or white marble temples, and the same long, curving cobblestone driveways filled with Rolls-Royces, Jaguars, BMWs, Mercedes Benzes . . . it struck him that the poor in

America were poor in a thousand different ways but the very rich were all very rich in precisely the same way.

Zeffi repeated her question.

"Rick? Hello? Do we know where Coral Key is?"

"Sorry, kid. My mind was wandering. Crandon is the main line. The rest of the streets are turnoffs along this main road. All of the big estates are strung out along the shoreline. We'll find it."

And they did, about two miles down the line, 216 Coral Key Drive, a narrow wooded lane on their left, on the Atlantic side of Key Biscayne. The lane was marked by a tiny street sign half hidden by a hedge of bougainvillea fifty feet high, draped around a bony framework of steel fencing. Zeffi slowed down and began to pull to the side of the road.

"No, honey, they'll have cameras. After Anaya's call, they'll be looking for surveillance. Go down a ways. I'll walk back."

"And do what?"

"Relax. I'm going to look the place over."

"Okay . . . but take the radio."

She found a turnout next to a power transformer fifty yards down Crandon. She parked the car. Rick gave her a quick kiss on the cheek, got out, and closed the door softly. The wind was so strong that the upper branches of the trees were swaying wildly. The sky was low and charcoal-black, yet shot through with a flickering green light. Rick jogged back up the road, his clothes whipping in the wind, and reached the entrance to the lane.

At the far end of the short palm-lined street, a wrought-iron gate stood across the driveway between two carved marble pillars about twenty feet high. Beyond the fence, a well-tended lawn rolled upward to a large Greek Revival manor, made of what looked to be shell-pink stone, about a hundred yards away from the road. Parked under the portico but still visible from the street was a shiny yellow Galaxy 500 XL convertible and in the rapidly fading light he could make out a couple of men walking through a leafy bower of Spanish oaks to the east of the main house. There was a light on inside the broad stone portico and other lights could be seen in the tall narrow windows along the front of the building.

Rick looked carefully around the main gate and found what he expected to find, tiny security cameras in several positions around the main drive, one of them that seemed to be aimed right at him. But there was no gatehouse, no obvious guards patrolling the grounds. Whatever connection Vargas had to this business, he was keeping a low profile— low for Key Biscayne, at any rate. Rick memorized the basic layout of the main approaches and went back to the car to find Zeffi with her SIG-Sauer on her lap, her face pale.

"You okay?"

"I'm fine, Zeffi . . . we gotta move."

They found a small restaurant about a half-mile along on the main strip, a wood-frame beachside bungalow called the Green Turtle. Zeffi parked the

Crown Victoria in the gravel lot as the sky split open with a huge bolt of lightning, a brutal crack of thunder, and then a torrent of warm rain began to sheet down through the dense forest of elms above them, hissing in the churning leaves and pattering off the shingles of the building. They came inside dripping wet and took a private booth at the back, away from the crowded main room. Zeffi ordered crab cakes and a bottle of white wine for them both. Rick watched her sip at the frosted glass, his mind turning over the possibilities. Since there weren't many, this didn't take long.

Zeffi seemed to read his mind. She put the wineglass down, reached out and put her hand on his. Her skin was cool and smooth, and he thought how good it was to be alive and how much he'd like it to stay that way for both of them.

"That place looked pretty hard to deal with," she said, in a soft voice, barely above a whisper.

"Yeah. Very. I was hoping for something slightly easier."

"Do you know anything about this corporation. The CIMEX Corporation?"

"Never heard of it, but that's where Anaya called, so that's where we have to go."

"It's a Swiss corporation?"

"That's what Bunny said. Based in Geneva."

"Geneva," said Zeffi, with a kind of genteel snort. "My father calls Geneva *'la ville des voleurs,'* the city of thieves."

"I'd like to CIMEX on NCIC or NADDIS."

"What the hell are they?"

"NCIC is the National Crime Information Computer. NADDIS stands for Narcotics and Drug Distribution Information System. A DEA mainframe. They have the best information on foreign corporations in the world, because of all the money laundering. If CIMEX is based in Geneva, they'd have a complete file on them."

"So you're just going to drop by the Drug Enforcement headquarters and ask to use their database? Look, Rick, you need to think this through. The FBI has a chopper out looking for you. This is getting out of hand and there's no shame in calling for help. You've done everything you could do."

"Not yet. Soon, maybe. But not yet."

"You really think that Kelleher's in that house?"

"That's my instinct, yes. I can't see them holding him in some wood-frame rat box in the middle of Little Haiti. If I were going to take a man apart, I'd want to do it where the screaming wouldn't wake the neighbors."

"You think they're torturing him?"

"I don't know. It's possible. Everything that's happened to us tells me that the Cubans still don't have what they want, which, I think, is the exact location of the wrecked floatplane. If they had it, they wouldn't have been bothering with us. They'd be out there, with a salvage barge, bringing it back up. So, if they have Kelleher and they don't have the location yet, you can believe they'll be doing whatever it takes to get the information out of him."

Zeffi filled his glass again, and then hers, shaking her head.

"I don't agree. I don't think you can assume that the people holding Kelleher are working with the Cuban government."

"Okay, why not?"

"Kelleher told you he was going back to Cuba, right?"

"Yes."

"He said if he went back, nobody would bother you. But ever since he disappeared, I'd say you've been bothered quite a bit. So maybe he never made it back to Cuba. Maybe the people who have him are working for the exile underground here in Florida. They hate Castro. If Kelleher had information that would hurt Castro, they could just as likely be the ones working him over, couldn't they?"

He worked that through, staring at the candle-light flickering in the wine. A gust of wind rattled the window beside him, spidery branches raking the glass. Distant thunder shook the roof.

"You're right. At the least, they'd want to know what Kelleher was doing working with the Cubans. If they knew he was flying for them, they'd want to know where the aircraft went down, and what was on it. And he'd be doing his best not to tell them. And the fact that he's gone missing would explain why the Cuban government is so pissed off with America. They're afraid he's gone back over."

"That big white boat that tried to board you near the Dog Rocks? How did they know where you were?"

"I broadcast my location over the marine radio, remember? You heard it yourself. I put it out there for the British coast guard, and for anyone else who was listening."

"Were they Cubans, or exiles?"

"Cubans. Castro's people have already filed a grievance with the UN over the sinking. The boat was theirs. They said so."

"And everyone on board that boat died?"

"I don't know for sure. The Cubans said there were no survivors, but they could have been lying to keep us off-balance."

"So they know where you were, but they may not even know that Kelleher survived the crash."

"I can't say. They could have radioed back to Cuba while they were chasing us. Kelleher was right out there on the stern. If they recognized him, they might have contacted Havana before we sank them. There's no way of knowing."

"Is it possible that the exiles also heard that broadcast?"

"If someone in the exile community heard a conversation like that, they'd talk about it back in port. The word would get around."

"Either way, both the exiles and the Cubans could have a general idea where the thing went down. So they don't really need Kelleher to tell them, do they?"

"A general idea of the location is next to useless. You could run a grid search of the entire area for a year and still miss the wreck. The only way to locate it fast—and it has to be fast—is to have the precise longs and lats. If they want that, they need Kelleher."

"Why are they chasing us around, if they already have him?"

That stopped him for a time. Rick listened to the rain drumming on the leaded-glass windows beside him. Slick palms lashed the glass, shredding in the wind. He put a hand on the wall beside him and felt the deep rumbling vibration. This was more than a wild gale. It was beginning to feel like a major tropical storm.

"Rick, about the wreck, even if Kelleher has told them where it is, I don't think they've even tried to get it yet."

"Why not?"

"Well, how's the weather been? Until today?"

"The weather? Beautiful. Perfect, for days."

"Exactly. Which means no clouds. No cover. Until this storm."

Rick sat back and stared at her.

"Zeffi, that's brilliant. Some of the satellite coverage is infrared, and infrared can penetrate cloud cover, but with a big weather system screwing up the entire basin, they'd at least have a shot."

"That newspaper story said the U.S. Navy has cruisers all over the Straits of Florida. If the Cubans haven't released Jake and Cory by noon tomorrow, there might be a naval blockade of Cuba. Would they still risk a salvage ship out there?"

"The U.S. Navy is going to be busy with Cuban gunboats. They're not going after a U.S.-flagged ship. If they're U.S. citizens, they might be able to talk their way through the Coast Guard or—"

The entire dining room flared up with a blinding white light so intense that everyone in the room seemed frozen in the flash of a strobe—a half-second later, a peal of thunder rocked the entire building so hard that the plates bounced and silverware rattled in the trays. Out in the main room, in the stunned silence, a child began to whine. Then the room lights dimmed—recovered—and flicked off, plunging the entire place into darkness. Emergency lights blinked on over the exit doors, spilling a pale red light across the restaurant, and the headwaiter came bustling out of the kitchen, waving a flashlight.

"Please, everyone. Relax. The power should be back on in a moment. It probably tripped the breaker. It comes back . . ."

As he was speaking, the room lights flared up, died, and then came on again at full brightness. The whiny child switched over to a howl, quickly achieved a grating middle C, and launched himself into a migraine-inducing aria over which the head-waiter had to shout to be heard.

"See, everyone. This happens all the time. Especially at this time of year. So enjoy your meals, please, everyone relax. Everything is fine."

The low murmur of talk rose up again around the room and some thoughtful diner within reach of him must have clubbed the kid with a wine bottle because the earsplitting wail cut off before his crescendo could actually crack their teeth. After a while, when their ears stopped ringing, Zeffi looked up and smiled at Rick.

"Quite a storm. Do you think it will go on for a while?"

"They usually do. This is the hurricane season."

"And you still insist on trying to get inside that house?"

"Yes . . . okay. What's on your mind?"

"I'm going to regret this. While you were out of the car, checking on the gates? Remember where I parked?"

"Yes . . . beside a utility station. A transformer."

It took Rick a couple of seconds to put it together.

"A long shot, Zeffi. A very long shot."

"This, from you?"

# THE CORAL KEY

216 CORAL KEY DRIVE, KEY BISCAYNE
10:00 P.M. EDT, SATURDAY, SEPTEMBER 28

By ten o'clock that evening, the rain sheeting sideways across the road was strong enough to sting and
the wind in the wildly swaying trees had accelerated
to a shrieking howl. The lightning had intensified as
well, jagged bolts of snaky blue fire snapping and
crackling through the shredded clouds racing overhead, or arcing down into the trees behind them
with a sizzling hiss, ending in a huge thumping con-
cussion, the shuddering booming roll of deep thunder following almost immediately. At times, the
lightning was so frequent it seemed to turn the tur-
bulent night into flaring electric-blue day.

All the streetlights along Crandon were reduced to
wavering yellow haloes surrounded by an aura of glowing mist and flying spray. A few isolated cars crept
along the road, their windshield wipers ticking rapidly,
the occupants appearing as dim shapes inside the windows streaming with rain, the cars pushing slowly
through hubcap-deep pools of muddy brown water.
From their position inside a small turnout in a grove of

stunted palmettos, Rick and Zeffi could make out the
entrance to Coral Key Lane. Through gaps in the thick
hedge of bougainvillea they could see a few flickering
amber lights shining in the main house.

Rick had changed into a black T-shirt and jeans,
but the only waterproof coat he had was his yellow
squall jacket, which was far too colorful for a covert
approach. He reached for the door handle. Zeffi
caught his hand, held him there.

"I still want to go with you."

"And if we both get caught? Who calls in the
cavalry?"

"I can help."

"You are helping. One hour. If you don't hear
from me on the radio, don't try to raise me. And if
you get an incoming call signal, don't answer it. Do
not. Respond *only* after you hear *my* voice on the
radio. And the main thing . . . I'm giving you a call
sign. Your call sign is Yankee. What's your call
sign?"

"Yankee. My call sign is Yankee."

"Yankee. Remember it. If I call you Zeffi, if I call
you anything else at all—*anything*—then you don't
say a single word, understand? Put the radio down
and gun this car the hell out of the whole area as fast
as you can. Don't think about it. Just do it right that
second. Run down anyone in your way, don't stop
for anything. Don't use the cell either. Go straight to
the Green Turtle and call Diane Le Tourneau at the
FBI. The number's three zero five, four seven seven,
six five six five. Write it down."

While she was writing the number down, the implication of his warnings began to clarify.

"Rick . . . no one could make you do that. No one."

"I don't think so either," he said, with more certainty in his voice than in his heart. "But it had to be said."

Zeffi looked shaken, but when she spoke her voice was reasonably steady, if a bit weak.

"Ask for Diane Le Tourneau. Tell her everything. Get them down here fast. You've got the paper from Kelleher, the tugboat sinking. Give it all to them, tell them everything you know. Including the floatplane, where it went down, everything we know about Kelleher's flight. All of it. Hold nothing back. That's vital, Zeffi. You're a foreign national. These days that's going to make the feds very nervous. There's a guy named Dunford Buell from the Defense Intelligence Agency—"

"The man who gave you a hard time in L.A.?"

"Yes . . . he doesn't like the idea that you're a Moroccan national. I told Chennault I put you on a passenger jet to Paris, but that won't hold up very long."

This did not please Zeffi. She paled to white, straightened her back and gave him a look hot enough to scorch paint off a wall.

"What? I'm from Morocco, so I'm a terrorist?"

Rick tried to placate her, which was risky. And pointless.

"No, not that. But if you have to call them in,

watch out for Buell. Like I said, cooperate in every way. Completely. You follow?"

Zeffi was silent, but she nodded once, her face set. She was angry and perhaps that was the way to leave it. She might need it later.

"Okay. You have the SIG. Use it if you have to. Don't even think about it. Just do it. Two rounds. Center of the—"

"Visible mass. I know how to shoot."

"Okay . . . what time is it?"

"It's . . . quarter past ten."

Rick looked at his own watch.

"Fine. Remember, Zeffi. One hour. Eleven-fifteen."

Although there was nothing left to say, Rick didn't move. Finally, Zeffi leaned over and kissed him. It was a very fine kiss, thought Rick. He tried to say something comforting, but she shook her head, her eyes shining. Another crack of lightning lit up the interior of the car and he saw her then as if in a photograph, caught in that white flickering moment, already a memory. She kissed him on the cheek and smiled at him, gave him a gentle push.

"No last words, Rick. Too cinematic. Just come back."

"I will," he said. He picked up the tire iron beside him and slipped out into the rain. Zeffi watched him running up the road toward the hydro station as long as she could, then a swaying veil of rain closed over him, turning him into a dark shifting blur. Then there was only the flying leaves and the driving rain and the sound of her own shallow, uneven breathing.

# *LA GAVIOTA*

10:17 P.M. EDT, SATURDAY, SEPTEMBER 28

In less than a minute, Rick reached the squat blue-metal container with the decal of FLORIDA POWER on the side. Kneeling beside it, he looked back down Crandon and then north. No cars, no walkers, nothing moving. The wind was gusting harder than ever and the rain cut into his cheek as he turned back to the doors. They were plate steel, fastened with a heavy padlock. Rick set himself, slid the tire iron between the padlock and the ringbolt, jerked it upward. It gave, but not much. He reset the bar, steadied his grip, blinking away the rain, and heaved upward on the lock with all his strength—pulling—harder—the metal groaned—heaved again—and then the ringbolt snapped off and he was sprawling backward onto the road.

He threw the tire iron into the brush and put the Maglite on the interior. A flat control panel filled with dials. The interior of the box was very warm; it seemed to vibrate with an invisible force. Rick could feel the static electricity in the container crawling over his shoulders and arms like tiny blue spiders. Dealing with a hydro transformer had been part of his ESU training, but the model they had worked with was part of a Con Ed system. This one looked completely alien. And his position here was very dangerous.

He had leather boots on, he was outside in a violent thunderstorm, he was soaking wet, and he was playing with an electric transformer. If his luck ran out, all they'd find were his boots, still smoldering. His calculation—his hope—was that all the estates along this section of Crandon were served by separate transformers. There was no way the owners wanted a parade of grubby serfs from Florida Power wandering over their raw silk Astrakhans looking for a meter. This transformer did have a meter in the panel, which was a hopeful sign. He searched for the big main breaker, finally found it low down on the right-hand side of the transformer housing. Gripping it, he braced himself and waited. The heat from the box was burning his forearm and the smell of ozone was making him dizzy.

He waited, hunched over in the cutting rain and the wind, for three full minutes by the watch on his left wrist. Then a sizzling bolt of blinding light crackled through the streaming clouds right above him and he jerked the breaker down hard. It shifted in its rocker with a solid metallic snap. He looked over his shoulder.

The lights at 216 Coral Key were out. Rick counted three, while the thunderclap pealed and rolled all around him, and then he pushed it back up—he could see the houselights come back on, shining through the flying mists—held it in the ON position for another thirty seconds. Oddly, he found himself counting them off in cadence, a rhythm he'd learned at the Police Academy years ago—walk the *line* and cut no *slack*, just *hook* 'em and *book* 'em, and don't look *back*—when he reached thirty, he snapped the breaker down again, slammed the doors shut, set the latch, raced for the fence, boots splashing through the flooding waters as warm as soup—and plunged into the wiry boughs of the bougainvillea.

The jungle scent was as sickeningly sweet as a funeral wreath—the tangled branches pulled at his clothes—he clawed his way up and up using the heavier boughs—and then he found the steel bars deep inside the hedge—pulled himself up hard and broke through the top of the fence fifty feet in the air—got a glimpse of the darkened house as a brooding mass of stone that was immediately illuminated by a stunning flash of sheet lightning as bright as daylight—it flicked off, leaving the image of the mansion burning in his retinas—he cleared the top and plunged back down into the hedge—half falling, the branches tearing at his face—he felt a sharp pain across his right cheek—still sliding, twisting—and hit the sodden turf flat on his back with a dull thudding smack that punched the breath right out of him.

Struggling for air, he lay on his back for a moment, staring up into the rain that was pouring down on him out of the black sky like a cascade of pepper shot. He rolled to his feet, fumbled for the

Colt at his belt—it was gone—and then another flash of lightning lit up the lawn and he saw it lying in the flattened grass a few feet away.

He scooped it on the run and made a flat-out dash for the side of the big house a hundred yards away over the sloping lawn, his boots sliding and slipping in the mud, his breath rasping in his throat, the shock of each footfall jarring his spine—halfway over the lawn and he threw himself to the ground as a white fork of lightning snaked across the sky and the grounds lit up again—then he was up and running with the thunder booming and rolling.

He reached the house and flattened up against the cold stone at the southern wall. His chest was heaving, his heart slamming around inside a cage of ribs like a crazy red bird, the Colt heavy in his right hand. He looked at his watch: twenty-five minutes after ten.

Fifty minutes before Zeffi called in the FBI.

He breathed in as slowly and as deeply as he could, trying to lessen the flood of adrenaline pouring into his bloodstream, gathered himself and slid along the side of the house toward the main door.

Locked—the door as solid as plate steel. He moved north along the façade and reached one of the tall gallery windows. The interior of the house was dark, impenetrable, but when the lightning came again, he got a flashbulb impression of a broad expanse of polished hardwood floor, a few pieces of furniture, a large white fireplace. The glass itself had a thin ribbon of silver all around the edge, part of the

alarm system. Even with the power off, it would signal the police as soon as he broke the window. He
had forty-five minutes left.

How long before the cops answered the alarm?
In this storm, they'd have more important things
to do. Turning his head away, he tapped the butt of
the Colt against the glass, testing the thickness,
then cracked the lower pane. He brushed away the
shards, pressed on the slider, and the pane pivoted
back on a hinge.

*Way too easy.*

He climbed through it, dropping into a crouch on
the floor, expecting a trap of some kind. But nothing
happened.

Silence; no lights anywhere. He crossed the hardwood and went out into the main hallway. In the
flickering light that came through a fan-shaped window set high over the double doors, he saw a wide
staircase spiraling up to a long upper landing that
faded into blackness and underneath the staircase a
narrow gallery hall leading out into what looked like
a formal dining room. Beyond that, a huge window
wall that seemed to stretch right across the entire
ocean side of the house. He could see nothing
beyond the glass, but the storm pressed up against
the house, rain snaking down the windows.

He went down the gallery, listening to his heartbeat pounding in his chest. The hallway ended in a
broad landing that opened up into a high-ceilinged
open space that stretched the entire width of the
house, at one end a glass-and-steel dining room

table that looked to be forty feet long, in the middle of the room an arrangement of brass and leather chairs and sofas and at the far end another fireplace, this one surrounded by slate rock. In front of the fireplace, sitting on a rumpled sheet of dirty white cloth, a wooden chair.

Rick walked across the room and looked at it. Heavy and crudely constructed out of rough planks, with thick nylon restraints on the arms and more down at the legs, all of them marked with black stains. The crumpled sheet underneath it had blood spattered all over it. Rick had a brief and terrible image: an incoming blow, a man's head jerking sideways, scarlet blood flying from his open mouth.

He bent down to touch the stains. Some dried and crusted, some still damp. And the marks of several boots, also slightly damp and something gritty under his fingers. Sand. Beach sand. He got down on his knees, felt around the sheet. A trail of sandy boot prints led out across the polished hardwood toward the back of the house. Another crack of lightning beyond the window wall threw the entire space into bright silhouette and lit up the stormy shoreline a hundred feet down a slope of grass. Then the light was gone and he was blinking away the afterimages still burning in his vision. The lightning had illuminated something on the glass table; he walked over and saw a scatter of documents and paper. He picked up what looked in the flickering half-glow to be a U.S. passport. He opened it up and saw the name: Charles Green.

He slipped it into his pocket as he reached the long glass wall, opened a French door, moving as quietly as he could across a broad patio of gray slate that was sizzling with hard rain, the drops smacking in and flaring back up as if he were walking across a frying pan full of popping grease.

On the far side of the slate patio the lawn dropped away to a sandy shoreline; in the middle of the shoreline, a stone jetty reached out into the ocean. Huge rollers, visible only by the curling white water at their peaks, were smashing into the jetty, breaking over it with a pounding impact that shook the ground under him.

He moved out of the shelter of the house and into the full force of the storm, the wind driving in sideways, flat and straight off the water, whipping the seas into froth and the heavy rollers running before it, low black clouds rushing south along the shoreline.

In the lee of the jetty, held in tight by the spring lines, he could make out a long, sleek wooden cruiser—sixty feet at least. Her running lights were on and a blurry yellow glow came from a chain of portholes along her lapstrake keel. She was heaving and rolling wildly as the current churned around her, grinding her bumpers on the side of the dock and then lurching away as another breaker struck her on the bows. On the long, narrow foredeck there was a large bulky shape tightly wrapped in canvas, strapped down to cleats in the decking. And she was getting ready to cast off. Through the wind and the spattering rain he could hear the heavy rumbling of her engines.

He came silently down the slope and in the intermittent flashes of lightning he could make out the vague shapes of men—three of them—hunched over on the dockside next to the boat, huddled around a long irregular shape in front of them, apparently trying to lift it into the boat. The shape looked vaguely human.

Moving fast, Rick reached the shore, stepped up onto the stone surface, and ran out along it, as quietly as he could, trusting in the storm to cover him. As he neared the stern, he saw an American flag whipping and lashing on a brass pole, a name painted in gold on her hardwood stern; *La Gaviota*—the seagull.

He was twenty feet away from the cluster of dark shapes when one of the men straightened, turned, saw him coming. Rick broke into a hard run, heard a muffled shout, saw the man reach into his jacket—raise a weapon—Rick, still running, fired at him, the Colt jumping in his hand, the muzzle flare lighting up the figure—the man jerked to the right and went tumbling into the water—the other two men were up and moving toward him—he saw the muzzles of their pistols light up with blue fire and then he was struck—hard—a blunt deadening impact, low on his left side—he staggered to the right—still firing—the Colt kicking—another blue flare and another round lanced across the sloping muscle of his left shoulder—he felt no pain, only the heat of the round—he was six feet away from the men and one of them was down, his hands to his face.

Rick heard a high-pitched squeal and fired again into the crouching shape in front of him. The slide popped, and he felt the dry click of his trigger—the Colt was empty.

Rick hit the man at a full run; they fell back on to the stones together, the man twisting violently as they fell, so that when they hit, he landed hard right on top of Rick—Rick's head hit the stone deck and bounced, stunning him, his vision blurring. He shook it off, shoved at the body lying on top of him—it was solid and heavy but suddenly limp.

Rick rolled the man off him and struggled to a knee, his breathing short and sharp, with a thin blue wire of pain arcing through his rib cage. He reached down, got a handful of clothing on the man's chest, lifted him up, and saw in a crack of lightning a black staring face with wide eyes and red blood in his open mouth, a small hole below his chin where Rick's round had punched through.

There was an exit wound at the back of his neck, wide and ragged, and Rick could feel the sharp edges of shattered bone sticking out of a soft mass of muscle and flesh. The man was dead.

He managed to get to his feet, holding his left side, where a cold numbness was spreading outward from the wound. Blood as warm as coffee was running through his pressing fingers.

He limped back along the jetty to the wounded man, found him lying on his back, body writhing, his hands to his face. Under the rain, his hands were streaming with blood pulsing out from between his fingers. The man was making a sound, almost inaudible, as thin and as high as a gull's cry.

Rick bent down and pulled the man's fingers away from his face. A young Latino male, clean-shaven, dressed in a polo and tan Dockers. In the dim light from the boat's cabin Rick could see that the boy had taken a glancing round off the right cheekbone that had then driven itself down the bone and exploded out the side of the boy's mouth. The entire right side of his face was laid open to the ear, showing the red line of wet molars and the pink joint of his jawbone. His eyes were open and he was staring up at Rick, still making that horrible whimpering sound, his face contorted, his lips shut tight, his whole body twisting and bucking under Rick's hand.

He tugged the boy's belt loose, flipped him on his side, jerked the belt tight around his elbows, pinning him. Then he rolled him onto his back again, peeled off his own bloody black T-shirt, ripped it into several strips, bound them tightly over the boy's ruined face. He knelt down beside him and spoke into the boy's ear, trying to make himself heard over the storm.

"Don't move or I'll come back and kill you."

Rick managed to get to his feet again, reeled, his head full of helium and his vision clouding briefly. He reached into his back pocket and pulled out a spare magazine for the Colt, punched it home, racked the slide, and walked over to the boarding ramp.

He was right. The object that the three young men had been trying to lift was a man, wrapped in a red woolen blanket. Rick knelt beside the figure and pulled the blanket down. He looked at the face for a time before he could be sure who he was, then he laid his left hand on the man's chest. The heartbeat was rapid but steady. The man must have felt the hand on him, because he heaved upward weakly and cried out.

Rick put his lips close to the man's ear and spoke gently.

"Charlie, it's Rick. Rick Broca."

Kelleher managed to open his eyes. They were slits in a purple mass of bruised and swollen tissue, but he could still see.

"Rick?"

"I'm here, Charlie. I'm here."

Kelleher's lips moved again, but the words were torn away by the gale. Rick pulled the blanket away and looked at the man's naked body, his throat tightening. Then he pulled the blanket up again. Kelleher's breathing was short and shallow, his bruised throat working as he tried to swallow some rain.

Rick tried to get his voice under control.

"How many men were there, Charlie?"

Kelleher blinked rapidly, his raw lips thinning, pain in his face. When he finally spoke, his voice was weak and rasping, but steady.

"Six. I think . . . I never knew. They had me blind-folded. I counted the voices but there were two who never spoke."

"You're sure, Charlie?"

"Five, six. I never knew."

"Two are dead. One man is still alive."

"Gonzalez . . . is Rubio Gonzalez alive?"

"One of them is. His face is a wreck. But he'll live."

"Good . . . good . . . keep him real close. We have to go, Rick."

Rick bent down and put his arms under Kelleher's body, lifted him—ignoring the grinding pain in his rib cage—and carried him up the heaving boarding ladder and into the main cabin, set him down on a long couch, peeled the blanket off his battered body, threw the sodden blanket into a corner, stumbled over the moving deck, found a stateroom in the aft section, and stripped the bedclothes off it, pale pink cotton sheets and a soft rose duvet. He brought them back into the living room and laid them carefully over Kelleher.

His eyes opened and his breathing changed again.

"We have to take the boat . . . Rick . . . they're coming back . . ."

Rick looked at his watch. It was three minutes after eleven.

He reached into his pocket and found the radio. He was thumbing the mike button when he felt the cold wet muzzle of a gun pressed up against his left temple. When the hammer cocked back, Rick could feel every metallic click in his temple bone.

"Do not move, Mister Broca."

At the edge of his vision he saw Kelleher's white face staring up at the man beside Rick, the man with his weapon up against Rick's head; in Kelleher's shattered face he saw raw fear and ruin.

"Give me the radio," said a voice, a thick Spanish accent.

Rick handed it across with as little motion as possible. The movies were full of situations like this. Usually the guy with the gun up against his head pulls some lightning fast kung fu move and in the next scene he's standing on the bad guy's chest with the bad guy's gun in his hand and he's saying something clever and dangerous in a low drawl. In real life, what usually happens is the guy with the gun feels it as soon as you tense up and he splatters your favorite memories all over the wall on the far side of what's left of your skull.

"Kneel," said the voice beside him.

Rick went down on one knee and the man stepped back away. Rick looked up and saw the sharp-planed mahogany face of Narcisse Suerta. Looming beside him, holding on to the cabin doorway with a machete in his hand and looking at Rick with a face devoid of any human emotion and the strange pale yellow eyes of a seagull, was Carlito Vargas. Suerta handed the radio to Rick, aimed his heavy gray pistol at Kelleher's face.

"You call the girl. You play a trick with this, I'll kill him and then I'll give you to Carlito. He was in Bahía Honda for many years and has had many boys like you to play with. I have promised him this."

"There is no girl."

"There is Zeffi Calderas, the Moroccan. She's out there in a blue car. I have already sent a boy for her."

"No."

Suerta shrugged, moved the pistol and shot Kelleher in the right leg, in the thick meat and muscle of his upper thigh, the crack of the pistol deafening in the cabin.

Kelleher screamed and twisted, and a thick jet of bright blue-red blood shot out from the wound. Kelleher grabbed a sheet and pressed it into the wound but blood bubbled up all around the cloth. Suerta looked down at the wound and then back at Rick.

"If you call her, I will let you stop the bleeding."

"Fuck you," said Kelleher.

"Fuck me? No, Mister Green. When you're dead I will let Carlito fuck *you*, and I will take pictures and take them to Havana, Mister Green. She will see it all. And then I will give her to Carlito. Or use her myself. You tell Mister Broca to make the call now."

# YANKEE

When the walkie-talkie crackled into life the sound, breaking through the immense pressurized silence that she was wrapped in, sent a galvanic jolt through her entire body. She lunged at the little radio, knocked it onto the floor of the car, snatched it back up. She almost keyed the TALK button and then, remembering Rick's warning, she waited, staring at the little machine as if it were a tarantula sitting in her palm. Then she heard Rick's voice.

"Zeffi, it's Rick. Are you there?"

She caught herself a second before she pressed the mike, her throat tightening, the words pressing against her lips.

"Zeffi, come in. It's Rick."

It was Rick's voice but not his voice. There was a flatness to it, a lack of emotion. She knew then that they had taken him.

She dropped the mike onto the car seat, threw the car in gear, and accelerated into the driving black rain, her tires hissing on the pavement and the engine roaring.

She flashed past the entrance to 216 Coral Key

with her eyes straight ahead, locked on the black tunnel of highway rushing toward her inside the twin cones of her headlights, racing away into the slick black valley of windblown palms and the lashing rain, the windshield wipers flashing like strobes, the engine winding out, a cold slab of granite pressing down on her heart.

A mile down the highway she looked in her rearview mirror and saw a pair of headlights closing up fast. As the car racing up behind her passed through the cone-shaped downlight of a streetlamp she saw a flash of yellow paint and bright chrome. It was the yellow Galaxy that had been parked in the driveway of the Vargas estate. Now it was coming up behind her. Coming up fast, the road ahead of her twisting and turning in the glow of her headlights like a huge black cable. A sign flickered green in the driving sideways rain up ahead. The Green Turtle was six miles away. She looked in her rearview again. The yellow Galaxy was less than a hundred yards back.

As she watched the yellow car flying through the sheeting rain, the night flickered into full blue-tinted day, the palms turned into vivid sunlit green, the bougainvillea beside the road shimmering in blues and reds, and the air hummed with electric fire.

Then total darkness again, the rolling thunder inside it—her retinas pulsing purple with the after-image of the lightning bolt—the immense thunderclap slamming on the roof of her car—the streetlights flickering, flaring bright again—too bright—

then dying out like blown candles as the power cut off, throwing the east coast of Florida into a blackout that stretched from Key Biscayne all the way to Fort Lauderdale. From the weather satellite fifty miles overhead, it looked as if the swirling lightning-filled disk of this tropical storm had just erased Florida's southern coastline.

# CEREMONY

MOTOR CRUISER *LA GAVIOTA*
11:45 P.M. EDT, SATURDAY, SEPTEMBER 28

The lights on the boat had flickered and died some time ago, how long Rick could not tell. Carlito had set candles all around the wounded boy on the rosewood table. In the motion of the boat and the wind that roared and whistled outside the cabin the candle flames flickered and danced, sending lunatic black shadows dancing around the walls.

The young man Rick had shot in the face was lying naked and bloody on the rosewood table, his chest heaving with the effort of breathing, his face wrapped in a blood-soaked bandage, his hands pressing down on the bandage. He was making a high, thin sound that came through the bloody bandages, muffled but maddening, a grating whine.

Outside the walls of the ship's cabin the storm was fully upon them and the entire boat was rocking and heaving. The wind note was rising and falling crazily, racing through levels of deep bass and vibrating baritone to intermittent violent gusts that shrieked and howled at the upper edge of hearing.

Suerta and Vargas were standing on either side of the boy, braced against the pitching and rolling of the boat, looking down at him, their faces thrown into black shadows and planes of brown skin, their eyes hidden in the blackness and then coming back into full candlelight again as the ship heeled at her mooring.

Rick looked over at Kelleher, lying on the floor a few feet away. He was still breathing, a shallow unsteady rasping noise that rattled in his throat. Maybe he was unconscious. The tourniquet on his upper thigh would have to be slacked off in just a few minutes or he'd lose the leg. But he was still alive.

Rick moved in the chair, testing the cord cuffs. They sliced deeper into his wrists and ankles when he did this, and the pain it created seemed to blend with the bullet wound in his right side, so that when he closed his eyes he saw an interior landscape of pain that wavered and floated in his semiconscious mind like colors, bright blue and deep scarlet shot through with lancing violet and sheets of green fire. He felt the room turning and opened his eyes, struggling against unconsciousness.

The last time he'd passed out, Carlito Vargas had brought him back by sticking his index finger deep into Rick's belly wound and jerking it sideways. Rick did not want to pass out again. Suerta turned when he heard Rick's sharp intake of breath and opened his lips, showing his uneven yellow teeth in a thin smile.

"You shot this boy here? And the other two boys? Manolo and Rafael?"

Rick nodded once, his head pounding. He blinked, trying to bring Suerta into focus.

"Yes. I did."

"Too bad. This boy's face is gone."

"Yes."

"He is Manuel Gonzalez's son. Rubio. He has just joined our abakua, our own cabildo. He is only twenty-one years old. I have known his father ever since we were in Angola together. This will be very hard on him. He will be very angry with you, Mister Broca."

"So take him to the hospital."

"You know we can't do that. There is the storm, and all the power is out."

"Where is Zeffi?"

Suerta shrugged.

"She is sitting in your navy-blue rented Crown Victoria wondering what to do. I have sent Romeo to get her. Romeo is the boy she hit on the face with her fire extinguisher. She made a fool of him in front of Manolo, so he will spend some time with her. When he is through and she is here, we will begin."

The boy on the table—Rubio—heaved upward, his ribs and belly muscles flexed, his chest distended. Suerta put a rough brown long-fingered hand on the boy's chest, feeling the heart underneath. He looked over his shoulder at Rick.

"He is in much pain."

"There must be some morphine on board. For Christ's sake, give him a surette."

"Do not blaspheme, Mister Broca. I am this boy's *babalao*. His teacher and protector. Now look at him. You have shot him in the face. He is scarred and maimed. His jaw hangs loose like a broken limb. His teeth are all broken. He is no longer beautiful. Or even useful. You have done a great deal of damage in the last few days. My cousin Honorio's boy, Carlos, his ear is dead because you put a pistol up to his head and fired it. Why are you in this thing, Mister Broca? This had nothing to do with you. You have killed some of our people on the boat. And now you do this? You pulled Mister Green from the water. You know where the plane went down. Tell us where it is."

"I never found the plane. Green was in the water."

"Geronimo was in the water too. You defiled his body and put him in a fish locker. Where is the plane?"

"I don't know."

"Carlito, you are ready?"

Carlito said nothing; his flat pockmarked face shadowed in the weaving light looked like a carved mask of an African demon. Suerta stepped around to the head of the table, took the boy's hands in his own, pulling them out and away. From under the working bandage Rick heard a strangled sound as the boy tried to speak. Suerta pulled the boy's arms straight and set himself against the table.

"This child is useless. His life will be a burden to him and to his family. We will give him to Chango Roja. Chango Roja will make him whole and give him a new life."

Carlito leaned over the boy's chest. He spoke a few words in a language that Rick could not understand and held his palm out. Rick saw that it was full of a fine red powder. Carlito sprinkled this red powder over the boy's chest and belly. It drifted down inside the dancing yellow light, turning, floating, a glittering red and gold mist that drifted down.

A guttural droning noise came from Carlito's throat and his huge chest seemed to vibrate with the sound, a deep bass note that rose and fell rhythmically. He leaned in very close to the boy's face and spoke softly to him through the blood-soaked cloth. The boy inhaled once or twice, and then stopped struggling. A quietness settled over him; he became quite still, his chest rising and falling slowly, even peacefully.

Carlito straightened, looked at Suerta. Suerta nodded. Carlito drew a long slender fillet knife from his belt and gently slipped the glittering blade into the depression below the boy's breastbone at an angle leading upward into the cardiac area. Then he jerked the blade right and left firmly and withdrew it. The boy's chest convulsed once, then it seemed to freeze in the midst of that convulsion, arched and straining. And then it changed and softened and went quite limp, boneless, as if something invisible but tangible had left the body and was floating in the candlelit glow just above the body.

Carlito lifted the wet blade into the glow of the candles, turning it so that the blood on the blade glimmered in the light as if it were red fire. Suerta took up one of the candles, moved the flame slowly along the blade. Rick could see the blood bubbling and searing. A thick burned coppery reek filled the cabin and a slender ribbon of blue smoke rose up from the blade, coiling in the candlelight. Carlito, his part complete, stepped backward out of the light, still chanting, his deep voice appearing to come out of the darkness itself. Rick felt the skin on the back of his neck tighten. It was as if something had come, as if there was now a presence in the air.

Suerta watched transfixed as Carlito's singing rose in pitch. Perhaps it was the motion of the ship and the wind that beat against the cabin walls as he sang, but the thin snake of smoke seemed to move, seemed to pulse in time with Carlito's chant; there was a kind of life in it, a ghostly snake made out of the smoke and the flame and the blood.

Suerta turned to look at Rick, his expression solemn, grave, the face of a priest in the living presence of his god.

"Chango Roja is with us. He will know if you lie. If you do not tell me where the plane is, we will give your Zeffi to Chango Roja too. Where is the plane?"

Rick saw a motion to his left and heard a step. Suerta turned to the open cabin door with a scowl on his face—getting ready to reprimand Romeo for being so long—as Zeffi stepped into the cabin with the SIG-Sauer in her cupped hands, her face white and wet.

Suerta lifted his gun and Zeffi fired at him. He fell backward away from the circle of light, tumbling into darkness. Zeffi fired three more times into the pool of shadow where he had disappeared—the blue fire of the muzzle lighting the interior like a flash going off, the crack of the weapon slamming off the walls, and then Carlito Vargas came out of the dark on her left side, the bloody fillet knife in his right hand—Rick shouted a warning—she turned and fired at him from point-blank range, the round punching into his left cheek.

He reeled and went down hard, shaking the boards as he hit. Zeffi stepped over his writhing body with the SIG held out stiffly in front of her, still covering the complete blackness where Suerta had vanished, picked up the fillet knife and sliced Rick's plastic cuffs. His hands freed, he took the knife from her and cut away his ankle cuffs as Zeffi stood over him, moving the SIG to cover Vargas on the ground.

Rick got to his feet, sick, shaking, unsteady. He moved to the side table, picked up his Colt, looked at Zeffi and then down at Vargas, and she nodded once. Then he went to look for Narcisse Suerta. He came back ten minutes later to find Zeffi sitting beside Charles Kelleher. They had bound Vargas with a ripped-up sheet, and Zeffi was wiping the blood off Kelleher's leg wound. Zeffi looked up as Rick came back into the light.

"Did you find him?"

"No," said Rick. "He's gone. Not on the boat and not in the house. Nowhere. Vanished. Did you call Le Tourneau?"

"No. I was being chased. There was a flash of

lightning, the power went off all over the island. I shut off the car lights and pulled into a lane. The guy went past me and then he came back to look into the car. Only I wasn't in it."

Kelleher was staring at her, the surprise evident even through his four-day beard and his bruised and battered face. He said nothing. Rick, who had never seen this side of her himself but who had been beginning to suspect its existence, asked her what she had done when the man came back to the car.

"I shot him. What else could I do?"

"Jesus," said Kelleher.

Zeffi looked at him, not kindly, and then back to Rick.

"Now what do we do?"

Rick looked around the cabin, at the butchery on the dining room table, at Carlito Vargas lying moaning on the floorboards.

"We get the hell out to sea."

12:35 A.M. EDT, SUNDAY, SEPTEMBER 29

While Zeffi did what she could to clean up the main cabin and Kelleher secured Vargas to a stanchion in the aft cabin, it took all of Rick's strength to drag the body of Rubio Gonzalez out onto the fantail and wrap it tightly into a tarpaulin. He spent another ten minutes dragging their luggage out of the Crown Victoria—Zeffi had apparently driven it right through the gates and all the way down to the beach, where he found it axle-deep in the sand— and getting rid of the other two bodies, one a boneless bloodied shape rolling in the stones at the leeward side of the dock, the other a pile of sodden clothes streaming blood down the side of the jetty, as the driving rain swept the beach and the storm howled beyond the breakwater. By the time he had weighted them down with stones and dragged them into the surging waves, bright red blood was pouring out of his belly wound and the pain inside him felt like a rat was chewing its way out of his stomach.

Back inside the cabin, he found Zeffi wrapping Kelleher's torso with a section of ripped sheet.

When she saw Rick's pale sweating face in the cabin lights she got up to help him, but he shook his head.

"Zeffi, take the con. I'm going to cast her off."

She stopped, shook her head, her face closed.

"No. Enough," she said, meaning the storm, their wounds, the lunatic impossibility of their entire situation.

"We have to. We can't stay here—Suerta may be alive. If he is, he's out there somewhere and he'll already have called in for help—and we can't go back to Miami. The boat's the only way to get Kelleher out. This is a big cruiser. I think she can ride out the storm. Now go."

She hesitated and then headed up the stairs to the pilot's station. Down on the dock, Rick struggled with the spring lines and the wire-tight mains, working with bloody fingers at the soaking wet knots, finally freeing the boat, which immediately pitched sideways away from the dock. Rick made the leap and tumbled through the open gate. Sprawling on the deck, he felt the deep bass vibration shuddering through the hull as the two gas turbines underneath the cowlings spooled up. Then there was a solid jolt that shook the boat as Zeffi engaged the props. The big wooden cruiser dug in by the stern, a spray of white water roared up from her fantail.

He stood up, caught a handrail as she took an incoming roller head-on; the entire pitching deck rose up sickeningly. Then her narrow bow sliced down into the trough and the engines ramped up to full power. The boat rocked from port to starboard, yawed wildly and came up out of the white water again as Zeffi fought the controls. Rick stumbled back into the main cabin, slammed the doors shut. The sound of the wind lessened to a muffled howl as the cruiser gathered speed. Through the rear windows he saw the dock slipping away into the night. The house lit up blue-white in a flash of sheet lightning, then disappeared in the darkness again as they cleared the breakwater, and in another second the squall closed in around them and the shoreline blurred into a featureless wall of driving rain and surging rollers streaked with yellow foam.

Kelleher, leaning on the rosewood table, was looking at Rick's ribs, at the blood sheeting down his belly.

"Rick. Sit down. Now."

Rick twisted to look at his left side. There was a black hole in his belly where Carlito Vargas had shoved his index finger into the entry wound, a thin stream of blood pulsing out of it. He put his hand on his lower back and felt a large ragged exit wound, pulpy and wet with blood. Across the heavy muscle of his left shoulder there was a broad bloody trench about eight inches long, also running with blood. He straightened up, opened his mouth to say something clever yet brave, and everything faded to a lovely pale rose. The cabin floor tilted wildly under his feet. He swayed as Kelleher came for him. The deck rose up at him. He hit it hard.

# CIMEX

MOTOR CRUISER *LA GAVIOTA*
TEN MILES EAST OF CAPE FLORIDA
6:15 A.M. EDT, SUNDAY, SEPTEMBER 29

He was lying on his back in perfect comfort at the bottom of a pool filled with clear warm water, staring up toward the surface ten feet above him. Beyond the surface of the water he could see a full moon gliding through a black velvet sky, a pale blue-white disk, the moonlight shining down through the water in a wavering beam that flickered across his face. Somewhere close by there was music and under the music he could hear a low, steady bass note, so deep he could feel the sound in his chest, a muted rumbling murmur like voices in another room. Under his back, he could sense a rhythmic rising and falling motion. He felt that he should try to reach the surface of the pool, but was unwilling to make the effort. Part of his mind was fully aware that he was lying on a bunk in one of the staterooms on *La Gaviota*, but there was no urgency in that awareness. The illusion of lying in deep water, weightless, warm, free of pain, was too sweet to give up. The moonlight played over his face again, and he closed his eyes, trying to shut it out. He felt a soft tentative touch on his right shoulder, the music swelled and ebbed, quite pleasing to hear; then he felt a gentle pressure, more insistent.

"Rick, please wake up."

So the music was Zeffi's voice. Interesting. Zeffi Calderas. He knew her well. From Morocco. Wonderful girl, Zeffi. Short-tempered, perhaps, unpredictable, even volatile. But all in all, a great broad.

"Rick, you have to wake up."

Pushy, though. A tad pushy.

Rick felt himself being rocked less gently and the warm water around him began to alter, to lighten, changing into a luminous mist, the colors becoming richer and clearer, the pale blue disk of the moon brightening into a warm yellow light. He blinked a couple of times, and the moon changed into a halogen lamp set into the teak-paneled ceiling of a ship's cabin and he was back in the world.

And he was not happy about it.

"Damn . . . Zeffi . . . okay, I'm awake."

"Rick . . . please. Try to sit up."

He turned his head, looked up at Zeffi. Her hair was wild and damp and droplets of water were running down her cheeks. She was pale and tired and she looked worried.

"Hey, babe . . . what's happening?"

"We're in the eye. You need to get up."

"In the eye? Eye of what?"

Zeffi shook her head, set her lips.

"Don't try to sit up. Roll to your right."

Rick nodded, started to move to the right—an electric jolt of blue light flowered in his vision—resolved itself into a volcanic eruption of searing pain that locked him in place with his breath held, his skin running icy cold and beaded with sweat. He looked down at his belly and saw a tight band of cotton strips wrapped around his midsection, traces of cherry-red blood on his skin.

Zeffi put a hand on his shoulder, steadying him.

"You were shot, Rick. It went right through. Charlie doesn't think it hit anything vital on the way. The wound in your shoulder was a graze. Try not to pass out again . . . Rick . . . please?"

Rick closed his eyes, got himself under control, began to breathe again as the waves of pain rippling through his body diminished slightly. He opened his eyes again, offered Zeffi an unconvincing smile.

"Didn't hit anything 'vital'? Everything in here is vital, if you ask me. I'm very attached to all of it. Even the ugly bits."

"We cleaned everything up as well as we could."

"With what? A blowtorch?"

"Charlie poured scotch all over them. Then we opened your side up. Just a tad."

"Great. Now she's Nurse Betty. Opened it with what?"

"There were steak knives in the galley. Charlie said we had to find any bullet fragments, get them out or you'd go septic."

"Who held me down?"

"Nobody. You were out. You've been out for hours."

"What about Charlie's leg?"

"It looked worse than it was. It missed his femoral. Tore up part of his thigh muscle. He opened the wound up while I cleaned it. Then we stitched it. The muscle took most of the force. We found some painkillers in the cabinet and he took a bunch. He'll limp but he'll live."

"You stitched it?"

"There was a medical kit in the galley. He told me how to do it. Now get up. Please."

"What time is—"

The whole cabin lurched to the left, then yawed and rolled as the cruiser worked her way up a roller, her engines laboring, the vibration hammering through her hull, shaking the deck under his bed. Rick looked at the porthole, saw a wall of swirling purple cloud streaked with amber and dark green above a troubled sea whipped by a gusting cross-wind. Zeffi's hands were on him, pulling him up.

"It's a couple of minutes after six. Please try to get up."

It took him two full minutes, but with Zeffi's help he managed to climb into a pair of jeans and slip on a thick white cotton sweater. Zeffi helped him out of the cabin and down the companionway. As they passed the second door in the narrow hall, Rick glanced in and saw Carlito Vargas, heavily strapped into his cot, his ankles and wrists bound with strips of towel, a thick white bandage over his eyes, his face pale and running with sweat.

"How's he?" he asked, nodding at Vargas.

"He'll live. The shit."

Her voice was low and tight, packed with an intensity of dislike that bordered on loathing. Rick looked at her as they went through the living room, Zeffi steadying him as the deck pitched and rolled.

"You all right, honey?"

Zeffi shook her head, her lips set.

"Charlie told me about the chair."

There wasn't much to say to that. Zeffi came up behind him as he climbed the stairway up to the control deck. Kelleher was at the wheel, barefoot, in somebody else's charcoal-gray suit-pants and a heavy black turtleneck sweater. He turned and smiled at Rick, his battered face nearly unrecognizable, his grin deformed by a badly split upper lip. When he spoke, his words were slurred and lisping, his voice cracked and raw, but his tone, though weary, was cheerful.

"Rick, you gotta see this."

He turned back to the windscreen, waved his left hand, taking in the seas all around them, the clouds above. Rick came to the panel, looked out over the long narrow bow. Beyond the bow rail a wild dark-green sea filled with whitecapped rollers stretched away through a strange glowing half-light toward a wall—an abrupt and solid wall—of pale purple cloud that rose straight up into the sky. The wall of cloud was nearly circular and ran all the way around their horizon line, a full 360 degrees of towering cloud thousands of feet high. When Rick realized what he was looking at, his chest tightened and his heart began to pound.

They were in the perfect stillness at the dead center of the tropical storm. It was beautiful and chilling and exhilarating, a phenomenon few people have ever seen from this angle, and it pierced him through the heart. It was like standing in the nave at Saint Patrick's or looking up at the cliff walls of the Grand Canyon from a raft on the Colorado. Rick checked port and starboard and then walked out onto the side deck, got a grip on the taffrail, looked up into the sky. Ten thousand feet above his head, a circle of pink-and-blue sky wheeled in the center of an immense well of swirling cloud with bands of color like the rings of Saturn running through it, streaks of pale green, seams of deep charcoal-black, vivid coral ribbons stretching out and curling inside the main shaft, a multihued band of colors spinning around a shaft of bright cloudless air that must have been at least five miles in diameter.

As he watched, a jetliner flew across that disk of pale blue sky far above him, the light from an unseen rising sun glinting off the fuselage, the sound of its jets lost in the rushing wind and the bubbling chuckle of green water running along the wooden hull below the railing. It occurred to him that a passenger in that distant jet could be looking down at the hole in the sky and seeing a flat circle of green water at the bottom of the storm's eye, with a tiny sliver of white alone on the surface. He leaned over and looked down at the water, saw a school of barracuda lancing through shreds of grass-green seaweed that coiled in the heaving current and ribbons of white foam drawn out on the broad glassy rollers. Wind-ripped fragments of sea foam flew off the wave crests, blown into the sky like confetti.

The working of the ship came through the railing under his hands, the vibrato of her engines, the groan and creak of her wooden hull as she lifted and settled again under the groundswell, the slap and gurgle of the waves as they ran along her waterline, the hissing white fan flying off her cutwater, the spattering dance of warm spray hitting her portholes, sending diamonds of beaded water across her decks.

The air was warm and dense and carried the moldy reek of deep ocean water that had been churned up by the currents and driven to the surface. He looked toward the stern and saw, less than a mile behind them, the trailing rim of the storm, a hard cruel line of solid cloud that rolled over the waves and swallowed them up as if the end of the world were closing in on their tiny circle of blue light and green water. Zeffi was beside him, looking out at the following cloud.

"It's beautiful, isn't it?" she said, after a moment. "And terrible. Have you ever been in something like this? Is this the eye?"

"It looks like one, but if this had been a real hurricane, we'd have never survived it. Never. Hell of a sight, whatever it is."

"Yes, it is. We broke out about a half hour ago. I

don't know how we came through it at all. But you're right. Charlie said it never reached hurricane force and the main body of the storm passed by up to the northeast, or we'd have never made it. The swells . . . you'd get to a crest and you could see nothing but more waves—huge rollers like green glass mountains with white water running down their sides—and the storm everywhere you could see . . . the wind, Rick. The sound it made? It wasn't high, you know, like a shriek? It was a low moaning in the walls and in the hull. You could feel the mad power in it. It was terrible. Simply terrible."

"You did very well, Zeffi. You and Charlie. I couldn't have done it any better. Let's go in. I'll spell Charlie at the wheel."

Kelleher had the boat on autopilot and was down in the galley banging pots and pans. The rich sharp scent of black coffee rose up through the gangway, blending with the smell of chicken soup. Rick sat down behind the wheel, tried to get comfortable and failed, looked at the instrument panel, a complicated array of radar, depth-sounders, GPS data screens, much of it even better gear than Jake had on *Cagancho,* state-of-the-art electronics, digital sonar arrays, Doppler radar, three-dimensional imaging. *La Gaviota* may have looked like a rich man's toy from the outside, but on the control deck she was every inch a working cruiser loaded with serious intentions.

The barometer showed a depressingly low number, but the wind speed indicator registered a reasonable fifteen miles an hour out of the southwest.

They were on a compass bearing of one six five and the rate-of-knots was hovering around twenty. Both engines looked good in the readouts, not running too hot, oil pressure normal and the rpms steady at 3,800. The starboard tank was full but the port tank was half-empty. Zeffi watched him as he flipped the switch to transfer some of the gas to the port tank and trim the ship. The boat felt solid and steady and was running well. The water-level indicator for the bilge was reading at eighteen inches, which meant she was taking in some seawater but nothing the bilge pumps couldn't handle.

Considering what she had been through, *La Gaviota* was in pretty good condition. So far. When the lull passed over and they hit the storm again— even in its reduced fury—they'd be taking brutal crosswinds and the seas could easily run to twenty feet at the crests. If they made it through, it would take everything this boat had to give.

"She's in good shape, Zeffi. Very fine craft. Any idea who she belongs to?"

"She has papers in the navigation desk that say she belongs to the same outfit as the house on Key Biscayne."

"CIMEX Corporation? Doing real well, aren't they? How far out are we?"

"Charlie thinks we're somewhere off the Riding Rocks on the Bahama Bank," said Zeffi, taking a seat in the navigator's chair. Rick nodded, checking the GPS indicator against the chart.

"Okay. Tropical storms run clockwise north of the

equator; we're going southeast down the channel. We've got the Bahamas on our port side about twenty-five miles and the Keys on our starboard by about the same distance. When we hit that wall again, we're going to be taking very strong winds out of the east, right on our port side. If we keep this heading, that puts the Keys in our lee. Lots of shoals and reefs, with the wind pushing us right onto them. Even if we have twenty-five miles, our leeway in a bad wind could eat that up in no time. The reefs would chew us up like a bone. When we're back in the storm we're going to have to turn to port and head straight into the wind, hope we can stay more or less in the same spot, in the center of the channel, try to ride the squalls out until the trailing edge clears. How does she handle?"

"She pitches and yaws a bit because she's narrow, but she's low and heavy so she takes the winds well. Whenever the incoming seas buried her bow, she always came right up again. She dumps water fast all the way along her deck, and the hatches are locked up tight."

"What make is she?"

Zeffi tapped the brass plate on the wooden bulkhead.

"She's a Chris-Craft—built in nineteen forty-one. Sixty feet long. Twin gas turbines. Complete rebuild two years ago, according to her papers. Vargas bought a great deal of new gear—totally updated all the electronics. Something else. See that cargo on the foredeck?"

The cargo on the foredeck was hard to miss, since it took up most of the bow, a low mound under a tightly lashed green tarpaulin.

"I see it. What is it?"

"One of the cables came loose during the night. When I was lashing it back down I—"

"You went forward in the middle of this kind of storm?"

Zeffi shrugged it off.

"Charlie was driving and you were having yourself a nap. I wore a harness and made sure I was tethered. Anyway, it's a minisub and a winch. They have the boat rigged for salvage."

"Zeffi, never go forward in something like this, okay?"

Zeffi gave him a weary look, folded her arms.

"Sure. No problem. I'll stick to being attacked by criminals and hunted by the federal government. That'll be so much safer."

"Does the load affect the way she rises?"

Zeffi considered it for a moment, then shook her head.

"Not really. Maybe she rolls more, but in a way the weight helps, as long as it doesn't shift. Which is why—"

"I got it. Sorry. I know you had to do it. It's very risky."

"Yeah. It is. So's having loose cargo sliding around on the bow and maybe smashing through the forward hatches."

There was a clattering bang as Kelleher dropped

something in the galley. Zeffi stood up to go help him. Rick stopped her.

"How is he?"

Zeffi's smile faltered and came back.

"On the surface, he seems okay. He's taken a terrible beating. They had him for three days, Rick. He won't say exactly what happened. You can see it on his body. He's pretty tough for his age, but he's been through hell. So how is he? He's brittle, Rick. And he's worried sick about something. He won't tell me what."

Rick nodded, let her go down the stairs. He watched the wall of spinning cloud move rapidly north and adjusted the wheel to follow it for a while. The front wasn't moving very quickly and the wind speed was holding at five miles an hour, barely a zephyr. They had time for some food, but not much.

He heard Zeffi and Kelleher coming up the stairs, somehow balancing a tray of heavy mugs filled with coffee and some bowls steaming with soup. Rick watched Kelleher cross the deck. He walked like a man filled with broken glass and when he reached the settee behind the navigator's chair, he settled into it with a grimace, pain flickering over his puffy face. He looked up and saw Rick considering his battered face, tried for a grin, and winced.

"Hey, you should see this from my side. Anyway, you don't look so good either, Rick. How's the belly?"

"It hurts. I hear you poked around inside."

"You've got a pretty good band of real thick muscle there. The round ripped that up pretty good and carved a trough through some gristle, but it didn't get into the peritoneum. You're a lucky man. I can't do anything about internal bleeding, so please don't start."

"What about you?"

Kelleher ran a tentative hand across his jaw and touched his left eye, feeling the damage.

"I can see out of both eyes, which is a big improvement over yesterday. There's something moving around in my rib cage, and I feel like I spent the last week in the spin cycle with a pile of bricks, but basically I'm okay. The leg hurts like hell, but I've got a fistful of Percodans so I don't really care. I guess my looks are shot?"

"Not really. I think they even fixed that problem with your nose."

"I didn't know I had a problem with my nose, but thanks."

"You're welcome . . . what do you want to do about Vargas?"

Kelleher's smile flicked off.

"What I *want* to do is strap him down and skin him with a filleting knife. I have some questions for him, but that can wait for a bit. Zeffi did what she could for his eye—rinsed it out with saltwater and put a clean compress on it. The round blew out his eye but skirted around the brow bone. He has a head made out of solid rock. He'll live, at any rate."

"Has anyone called yet?"

"Not for us, but channel sixteen sounds like an

episode of *Cops*. This storm caught a tournament of
sportfishers out of Matecumbe Key and they're scattered all over the straits squealing for their mommies. We're all lucky this one faded when it did. But
the Cubans, no. Nothing out of Miami for us. It wor-
ries me."

The bow rose as a rogue swell lifted her and a
spray of white water broke across the windshield,
breaking the silence. Rick brought the boat around
into the wind a couple of points and looked at the
edge of the storm, less than a mile away. They'd be
into it again in thirty minutes, at the most, and they
might never see the other side. It was a good time
to ask Kelleher some questions. Maybe the only
time.

"Charlie . . ."

Kelleher raised a hand, stopped him.

"Answers, Rick. You want some."

"We already know a fair amount," said Zeffi.
"Rick, why don't you tell Charlie what we know and
he can fill in the rest?"

Rick gave the distant storm front a swift assess-
ment, turned back to Kelleher, laid out the short version of the whole package from the moment he realized that Jake Seigel had been taken by the Cubans.
Kelleher's reactions were hard to read, other than
when Rick admitted to leaving Geronimo Suerta's
half-eaten body in the fish locker—that got a wide
grin from Kelleher and a wry shrug from Rick—and
he listened to the entire narrative without moving at
all, as if in that stillness there was some kind of pro-

tection. Zeffi, watching him listen, felt that Kelleher was bracing for some bad news, that Rick was about to tell him something that he had been dreading to hear ever since Rick had started talking. When Rick finished, Kelleher sighed and looked up at Rick with a troubled expression.

"So this Chennault guy managed to lose Suerta and Vargas?"

"That's the story. He told me they were dead."

"Confirmed it?"

"He hedged a bit."

"Which was bullshit, obviously. He let them go, way I see it."

"If he did, he had a way of tracking them. Which means he has a pretty good idea where we are."

Rick shook his head.

"Maybe not. Nobody is tracking anything in this storm. If he was on us—"

"Suerta was waiting for you," said Kelleher. "He as much as said so. Which means somebody was feeding him information. He knew what kind of car you were using. He knew that it was you who sand-bagged Carlos Anaya and bugged his phone. You said you wondered why there was no street surveillance. It wasn't necessary. Somebody very professional had a whole team on you from the time you left L.A. You said you got a call from somebody at the National Hotel in South Beach as soon as you got back to L.A. That was a classic setup, a way to lure you back to Miami, where they had a better chance of taking you alive. I think Suerta was waiting for you to show up at Key Biscayne. I was the bait."

"The only person who could do all that would be Cameron Chennault."

"Or someone inside the DIA," said Kelleher.

"Or the FBI," said Zeffi.

"Well," said Rick, "that narrows it down, doesn't it? Do you think Chennault turned Suerta? Played him back at his own people."

Kelleher laughed outright, a bitter bark.

"Hah. They're going to turn Narcisse Suerta? The guy's a Miskito assassin. The God-damn Spaniards couldn't turn the Miskitos into polite little Christians and they had the best torturers in the trade. I think Chennault staged that escape, but I don't think Suerta knows it. And I don't think he has any idea who's feeding him his information. Which means he does think he has a reliable source inside the U.S. government, but he's not sure exactly who it is. Who is this Chennault guy with, anyway?"

"Hard to tell, Charlie. He says he's not with the CIA, but he walks and talks like a spook. He knew nothing about you—or claimed not to—until I triggered the interest by looking you up in the naval archives. I suppose we can be sure he's not Office of Naval Intelligence since you've never heard of him."

"No. I haven't. But you say Dunford Buell was there?"

"Yeah. You know the man?"

"Cuba Desk. I met him in D.C. once, back in ninety-seven. I was giving a briefing on map-of-the-earth reconnaissance flights to some interagency committee. He didn't say much but I got the impression he had some kind of mojo going on at the White House. I know he's tight with Elliott Lazarus and Lazarus was the head of the Cuba Desk before they made him the deputy secretary of state. What did you think of him?"

"A hundred-percent body fat and he smells like a gym sock, but he's damn sharp. He didn't believe a single word I was saying and I'm a very gifted liar, especially when I'm scared shitless. When they ran the satellite feed, Buell noticed that I was returning fire at the same time that I was pulling some wild evasive maneuvers. Called me on it. Said I was 'fucking nimble.' Le Tourneau, the FBI amazon, she kind of liked me and Chennault wanted to turn me loose just so he could track me. But Dunford Buell wanted me buck naked and strapped to a stainless-steel gurney inside a soundproof room. He still does."

"They actually saw us on the satellite film?"

"Living color, Charlie. Amazing."

"I knew the systems were good. I had no idea how good. If I had I wouldn't have been running a flight under the Gitmo Shuttle. I still can't believe you took Suerta down. Zeffi, no offense, but you were lucky with him. I've seen him at work and he's very quick."

"The fifty thousand dollars? Where did that come from?"

"I have a ranch in Denver. I mortgaged it."

"And sent the money to me? Why?"

"The mortgage loan was life-insured. I had a feeling I wasn't going to make it out of Cuba alive. I owed you my life. And I figured if you had the money . . . I hoped . . . that you'd follow up. There are . . . people . . . involved. They need some help. That's why I sent you those coded sheets. And you did. Thing was, moving around Miami, picking up the money to send you, that was how Suerta tracked me down."

"Why me?"

"You weren't connected in any way. I watched you all that night. You have spine. I felt you were the only person I could trust."

"How'd they get you?"

Kelleher made a wry face, shook his head.

"In a cab, believe it or not. Oldest stunt in the game and I walked right into it. Sat in the back, driver turns around and sprays me in the face with some kind of gas. I come around, I'm naked in that God-damned chair. Not a good memory, so let's not get into it."

"Haldane, you think?" asked Rick. Kelleher considered it.

"Smelled like it and it burned on contact. Why?"

Rick told him about the Corvette and the small brass canister hidden inside the vent.

"Fits the pattern, then," he said, when Rick had finished.

"What kind of cab was it?" asked Zeffi.

"The cab I got tagged in? Pink and green, I think. With a flamingo . . . Key Largo Cabs, maybe."

"Where did that coded sheet come from?" asked Rick.

Kelleher hesitated, struggling with some conflict. Rick figured it was a holdover from his spook training. Zeffi had a very different view, but she said nothing about it at the time.

"We—the Navy—we run a couple of sources in Havana. The ONI used to have a cold box—"

"What's a cold box?" asked Zeffi.

"Like a drop box, only it may not get checked by a controller for weeks at a time. A drop is a place where you and your source exchange intelligence material without actually meeting face-to-face. You're running a pickup operation, usually your inside guy is responsible for letting you know if there's a tail. He'll carry a paper in one arm instead of the other, hat or no hat, flowerpots in the window—remember Deep Throat? That's called a tell. If you get the right tell, you know the drop was successful and it's safe to go collect the material. Most drop-box meets, they happen so often that sooner or later you're going to get the attention of the other guys. They put a really comprehensive tail on you and force you to change your routes, your tactics. In order to provide a source with a place to drop material that he doesn't want to hold but that may not be too urgent, we set up locations where that kind of material can be dropped whenever the source feels like it. We check them every now and then, but not on a regular basis. The CIA calls it running a 'trapline.' You look at the cold boxes occasionally to see if anything has turned up. When I got to Miami, that sheet was inside the cold box."

"And you have no idea who put it there?"

Kelleher's discomfort increased.

"I know of only two sources who used that particular cold box, Rick. So it was one or the other."

"Where's the cold box?" asked Zeffi.

"Okay . . . I can't get into locations. Sorry. In Miami, Zeffi."

"Are these two sources reliable?"

"One was usually reliable. The second was what we call a clipper. Clippers take random bits of mid-grade intelligence and shop it around. Sometimes they get something useful."

"So the sheet could have come from either guy?"

"More likely one than the other."

"And you believe the information is important?"

"I do. I just can't figure out why. The tugboat document is extracted from a public transcription of a victim interview conducted by the Inter-American Commission on Human Rights a few months after the incident. We all knew about that when it happened. I mean the ONI. According to our informants in Havana, Hector Preig—the head of the DGI—gave them permission to sink the boat, but we could never figure out why they didn't send in a gunboat and take the thing under tow. There was no reason to sink it that way, and when it happened it brought a lot of international heat down on Castro. He should have been pissed off with Preig, but he wasn't. In fact, he rewarded him. Preig got cut in on more of Castro's financial games the next year. Anyway, it all added up to zip and they eventually folded the file."

"Chilly fuck, this Preig guy, is he?"

"Hector Preig is the head of the DGI," said Kelleher. "He's not going to be a 'group hugs' kind of guy. That was why I tried to get back to Cuba. If I can figure out who was running me, Suerta or Preig, then maybe I can figure out their whole game. I need to know who they are, and I need to get to them fast."

Rick was silent for a time; his expression as he looked at Kelleher had altered slightly. It was wary, tight, and closed.

"So how many missions did you fly for the Cubans?"

"Two. I crashed on the second run."

"What was your stateside destination?"

"I didn't fly into the mainland. They set out a radio beacon and I landed on the water outside the twelve-mile limit. They had a big white cruiser eighty-five me there, they off-load the cargo, kiss me off. I went back to Punta Guarico and waited for the next mission. In a way, it was like working for the Navy. They never told me what I was doing either, or why I was doing it. Just fly the op, get back to your base alive and then shut the fuck up."

"Did you ever see this boat before? *La Gaviota?*"

"No. They had a big Hatteras there. I think it was the same one you and I had the go-round with last week. *La Luna Negra.*"

"And you never had any clear idea what you were flying out?"

"No. Like I said, it was sealed and shrink-wrapped when it arrived, and they loaded it themselves."

"Always the same aircraft?"

"There were two. Identical. Kodiak Twin Turbos. Great machines. I loved them."

"Zeffi and I couldn't figure out if the guys we were up against were working for Cuba or for the exiles. What's your call?"

"I'd say neither. They may be flying Hector Preig's flag, but I think they may be freelancers working some game strictly for themselves. They've got muscle in Havana, but I doubt if Castro has any idea what they're up to."

"Castro's making a real stand over Jake and Cory, isn't he? Would he be doing that if he wasn't working an angle for himself?"

"What else is he going to do? The Cubans seize a boat inside their own territorial waters—at least that's what they're saying—there's a dead Cuban national on board—so they're going to have a public trial—like any other sovereign country—and here comes the evil United States saying no fucking way, give us our people back or else. Castro has to be seen as a tough guy or his own people will eat him alive. He may be the head piranha, but he's still swimming with piranhas."

"Have any theories on what you were carrying?"

"Yes. A couple. It wasn't drugs, because Castro runs the drug trade through Central America. It wasn't guns, because the packages looked wrong. Too squared-off. My best guess was either cash or nego-tiable instruments. Or papers. Documents. Maybe computer files, disks. I figured it was all banking stuff. But that's only a guess."

"Okay. Something you need to think about here. If the cargo was fifteen shrink-wrapped bales of doc-uments on a pallet, there's no reason to believe the cargo sank at all. If it was made of bales containing paper, even at eighty pounds per, it wouldn't sink at all. It would float. And if it floated, the Gulf Stream would have taken it all the way out into the Atlantic, unless some fishing boat picked it up. That cargo could be halfway to Africa, or already in the hold of somebody's salvage boat."

That stopped Kelleher for a moment.

"You're right. Christ. I never thought of that."

"So now what?"

Kelleher turned the question over for a time.

"Well, I'm going to have to assume it sank. It was on a thick steel pallet and I was definitely over-loaded. So maybe the pallet took it down. If the load held together."

"You better hope so. What's your plan if we find this payload?"

Kelleher's hesitation here was almost but not quite invisible.

"My hope? Open it up, see if it tells me who was running me. Go after them directly. Why do *you* want it?"

Rick considered Kelleher's question for a

moment, struggling with the plausibility of his own answer.

"I hope this doesn't sound stupid, Charlie, but I'd like to use it to ransom Jake Seigel and Cory Bryant. If we can pull it off the bottom, I'd like to use Vargas down there to try to negotiate a trade with whoever's behind the Seigel detention, get my people the hell out of Cuba. That's my mission in all of this. Jake Seigel safe at home and Cory Bryant back in his mother's arms."

Kelleher nodded but looked doubtful.

"That's a plan, but remember that Castro's taken a public stand. Whoever was behind the original kidnap may not have the influence to get Seigel and Bryant out even if he wanted to. The situation's changing every hour."

"That's true, Charlie, and it brings me to my most basic question. The thing that kicked off this whole rat-fuck. What the hell kind of bonehead delusion made you ditch the Navy and go fly missions for Cuba? At first I thought you were running a covert operation and didn't want to tell me. Now I know you weren't. So what *was* your major malfunction?"

Kelleher took the question straight and did not miss the dangerous undertone in Rick's voice.

"In the first place, I didn't 'ditch' the Navy. I asked for—and got—a leave of absence. They had no problem with that at all."

"I guess not, since you didn't mention that you were taking a leave of absence so you could go free-lance for the fucking Cubans. Chennault told me you were a black ops pilot, which means you've been in the middle of all sorts of covert operations around the world. How long have you been working that trade?"

Kelleher hesitated, then said, "I got into it while I was on Yankee Station in the Gulf of Tonkin. I was flying cover missions off carriers, some of them into Laos, Cambodia. When the war ended, I stayed on. I've worked missions in El Salvador, Colombia, the Middle East. Insertions. Putting in teams. I flew the first stick of Special Air Service Brits into Afghanistan about a week after September eleventh. I also do extractions. Sometime I cover assassinations. I have no apologies for any of this. I serve my country."

"When you dropped out of sight, what did you think your bosses were going to do? You must have known they'd go bat shit as soon as you dropped off the screen. They'd figure you'd defected. It would shake up every black op in play all over the world. You must have been nuts to even try this. Why did you do it?"

"The Cubans had me in a vice. I had no choice. None at all."

"Give him a break, Rick. I know why he did it."

"Yeah?" said Kelleher, an edge in his voice. "Why?"

"You went because of your daughter."

# STANFORD

Not a question, but a simple statement of fact; it obviously rocked him deeply. He stared at her for a long moment, and when he finally spoke his voice was flat and thickened by suspicious hostility.

"How the hell do you know about Katie?"

Zeffi held his look and returned one of genuine sympathy.

"I don't, Charlie. But Rick showed me that newspaper article about your family, about the sinking of that naval ship in Hawaii. She was the only member of your family to survive and you've never mentioned her name. Not once. It seemed strange to me, since she's all the family you have left. Rick says you were a war hero, yet here you are working for the Cubans. It seemed so unlikely that I thought perhaps you were being forced into it. Threatened. But threats wouldn't work on you. They would have to be aimed at someone you cared about. In your note you said something about 'people involved' that only Rick could help if anything happened to you.

And you mortgaged your house to get enough money that he could do whatever was necessary. Most people would only do that for family. Kathleen was your only family. So, to put it simply, I guessed."

Rick considered her in frank astonishment but kept his mouth shut. Kelleher gave her a hard look, then gradually softened.

"A good guess. A hell of a good guess. If we ever get through this alive, you've got a job with Navy Intelligence anytime you want it. Rick, when you were talking to Chennault and Buell, did the name Kathleen Kelleher ever come up?"

"Not a thing. Is she married? Maybe another name?"

"She never married. It's still Kelleher. So no reference in any document? Nothing from the FBI? She's still a U.S. citizen."

Rick had gotten past the shock. Now he was angry.

"So the Cubans are threatening to harm her to force you to fly covert ops for them? Christ. You idiot. Why in holy hell didn't you tell me all this right from the get-go? It would have made all the difference. I would have done anything to help you. Anything."

Kelleher looked haggard and old; his voice, already cracked and raw, dropped to a toneless whisper.

"I don't know. I guess I thought I could handle it myself. And at the beginning, I was afraid you'd take it straight to the Navy and then I'd never have a chance of keeping her alive."

"Even after this? Man. Zeffi had to pry this out of you."

Kelleher shook his head slowly, said nothing. Zeffi did.

"Rick, try to understand," she said. "Saying her name out loud would be the hardest thing in the world for him to do. Even to us. It's about controlling a terrible fear, isn't it, Charlie? A fear you've had to live with for months. In your life, trusting anyone else is always dangerous. After long enough, it would become nearly impossible."

Kelleher was quite still for a time, and then he nodded.

"Yeah. I guess that's it. I say her name, it's out of my hands then. I have to depend on other people. Other people fuck up. I don't."

"You need to get out of covert ops, my friend," said Rick. "You're freezing solid. That's why I left the state troopers."

"Charlie, how are they using Kathleen against you?" Zeffi said softly. Kelleher looked at her, his face deeply lined, his pain clearly not confined to his bruises and his injuries.

"It's a long damn story."

"So start early. Tell us."

Kelleher drank some soup, stared hard at Zeffi's black Sobranie cigarettes. Zeffi took the hint and they waited while Kelleher lit one up and pulled in a lungful.

"Christ," he said, coughing. "What's in these?"

"Freon," said Zeffi. "Now talk."

"The short version? Or the long one?"

"How about the true one?"

"Okay, Zeffi, it's your dime . . . she was three when the USS *Bowline* sank in Kaneohe Bay in seventy-three. I took care of her after that, at least I did what I could. I was still on active duty and even though the war was over, my decision to stay in didn't sit well with Ruth's parents. They didn't approve of the war in the first place, and when Ruth and Eileen died in a Navy accident they blamed me. That included all of us. The entire service. In the end I had to fight them for custody of Katie. It took four years but I finally won. In four years I'd only been able to see her three times and then only with a court order. When I came to get her . . . well, she didn't want to go. They'd done a number on her, I guess—told her I was a bad man, that her mother was dead because of me. What the hell, she was only seven. What could she do? Maybe I should have quit the service then."

"Why didn't you?" asked Rick. Kelleher lifted his hands, let them drop again, looked up at Rick.

"I was good at it. And I cared about it. Got caught up in the Cold War, I guess. Covert ops. It was what I did; it was important work. It had to be done. Good men are doing it. I still believe that."

"Most of America thinks so too," said Rick.

"But Kathleen didn't?" asked Zeffi.

"She never knew what I was actually doing. I told her I was flying transport and doing training missions. She had no idea I was in covert ops. I got assigned to Quantico and we lived on base until she was thirteen. I never remarried . . . partly because Ruth was . . . I loved her very much . . . and partly because I didn't want to upset Katie. She grew up so fast . . . nothing like Ruth . . . Ruth was like you, Zeffi, a redhead, very alive . . . Katie's slender, dark, intense, smart, but she takes life very seriously. I was away on missions—sometimes for weeks—but the base was filled with Navy families and we had good friends in Virginia and up in D.C.—still, other wives raised her. When I was home I thought we were as close as most teenagers get with their fathers. Then she went away to college. Stanford. Dean's list—whatever that was—graduate studies at the LSE and then in Paris . . ."

"Not the Sorbonne?" put in Zeffi.

"Yes. You know it?"

"I graduated from the Sorbonne four years ago."

The wind was rising and they had to strain to hear him. Rick pulled the bow out of the wind slightly to lessen the angle and the wind's high note dropped off a couple of tones but white water began to splash over the port rails. Kelleher paused, seemed to gather himself to deal with a painful memory, then went on in a soft voice.

"Then it was the United Nations. She decided that the Third World needed lawyers with a grip on international law to help them with the International Monetary Fund and the World Bank. She worked at the United Nations HQ in New York for a while and then went to South Africa as an advisor to the secretariat for developing nations. She specializes in litigation involving reparation payments, human rights abuses. She was at that conference on racism in Durban in 2001. The weekend before they hit New York and the Pentagon. She was one of the only United Nations people with the moxie to tell the Islamic fundamentalists to shove their positions on Israel. Callista Fry, the Human Rights chief at the UN, she tried to have her fired."

"The same woman who's trying to pressure the U.S. to lift the sanctions on Cuba? That would take some nerve. You must be proud of her," said Rick.

"I am. I wish she knew how proud I am. But she doesn't."

"Why?"

"We had a terrible fight around Christmas last year; after that she never returned a call. Never came home for holidays ever again, and in the end she wouldn't even see me if I turned up on campus. A couple of letters, a birthday card last July. Other than that, silence."

"Why would she do that?"

Kelleher shrugged, raised his hands.

"As far as I can tell, it started with the law school at Stanford. The culture of the place. The friends she made there, the professors. They had a strong influence on her. Frankly, I have no clear idea, since I wasn't included in the debate. All I know is by the time she was finished with her last year at Stanford we were on pretty shaky ground. But the final blowup came when she finally figured out I wasn't really running training missions, that I was in covert ops."

"How the hell did she do that?" asked Rick.

"They gave me a mission. When they hit the *Cole*, we had Elint—electronic intelligence—a data stream pulled out of the air by the guys at the National Security Commission at Fort Meade—gave us a precise location for six of the Al Qaeda people who had helped organize it. They were holed up in a village south of Cairo, and the Egyptians wouldn't help us at the time because they were afraid of their own Muslim radicals. So I inserted a team out of Quantico—a HALO drop—High Altitude Low Opening—and flew cover while the team went in and cancelled them. We took a few hits during the extraction. The Egyptians raised it at the UN. Katie got wind of it. The time line was narrow—a matter of days—she realized I was gone during that time line and back with a wound right after it. She's a bright kid. I think she worked it out for herself."

"Did Katie ever explain her hostility? Her reasoning?"

"Reasoning? Reasoning wasn't in it. There was some strangled reference to 'postcolonial theory.' I heard all about it on our last Christmas Eve together. America's support for vicious right-wing dictators and corrupt Saudi princes, my personal and everlasting guilt for helping them do it for so many years. She seemed especially hurt by the fact that I'd lied to her all along, about what I was really doing. She was hurt, disillusioned, angry. Of course, being a God-damn idiot, I lost my own temper then. We said some very hard things to each other and followed it with a long and miserable silence that lasted all night. Christmas morning, she was gone before first light. Left a note, said she was sorry and that she loved me and she always would, but maybe we should give each other some breathing room for a while. That was the last time we spoke. She did write me a couple of letters. I think we were close to patching something together. Then I got pulled into this thing and it was impossible to reach her at all."

"Why? What happened?"

Kelleher looked at her for a time, then across the room at Rick, considering what to tell them while bracing himself on the handrail as the deck began to pitch under him. Rick's cup slid off the counter and he caught it in midair, immediately regretting the twist he put into his torso. The wind was rising and the light fading fast as the clouds moved in.

Rick tended to the wheel, bracing for the incoming squall, and said nothing. Why was no contact possible? He knew the answer to that as well as she did, but he let Zeffi carry this thing. Kelleher's response was spoken in a tone so low Rick could hardly hear it.

"What do you think happened, Zeffi?"

She looked at him sadly for a time.

"She's in Cuba, of course. She'd have to be in Cuba. If she were anywhere else in the world, you could have protected her."

"That's right. I knew the United Nations had

transferred her to Havana. You can't be in Navy
Intelligence without expecting the service to keep a
file on your family. They flagged her on her first trip
in. The brass recommended that I not have any contact with her while she was in Cuba. They were
afraid the Cubans would try to work the connection
in some ugly way."

"But the Cubans found out anyway?"

"Oh yeah. The first guy who contacted me was
Narcisse Suerta. By e-mail, yet. He gave me enough
information on my own unit to let me know he was
serious people, then he sent me these grainy snapshots of her working at the UN office in the Ministry
building in Vedado, or shopping along the Malecon.
I think the pictures were taken by a surveillance
camera—poor light, low-quality shots, but they
made his point clear. They were watching her, they
could pick her up anytime. I was to call a number in
Miami; when I did they laid it out. Fly out some
critical cargo for them, maximum six flights, and
they'd let her leave Cuba. Refuse and they plant
some secret documents on her, rat her out to the
DGI; off she goes to the military prison at Bahía
Honda on espionage charges. It would take a full-
scale military operation to extract her and she'd be
dead when they did. Suerta would take care of it
personally. I believed him."

Rick shook his head at that.

"Why not simply ask the United Nations to recall
her? Make up some excuse to get her out of the
country?"

"The Cuban secret police have her passport. She couldn't leave if she wanted to. And the UN leaks like a cheap diaper. Suerta would hear about it."

"Why pick on you?" asked Zeffi. "Surely the Cubans could find some mercenary pilot to fly this stuff out?"

"Mercenaries are a flaky crowd in general. They knew I was a black-operations professional. And blood ties are stronger than cash. Anyway, the best way to reach Katie was from inside Cuba. I figured, pretend to do what they asked and stay ready for an opening. Get into Havana, get her out somehow, then take one of the cargo planes from Punta Guarico and we're back in the Keys in an hour. But first I had to be in Cuba. So I said yes."

"How did these Cubans find out who you were?" Kelleher looked across at Rick.

"How did they know I was in covert ops? How'd they know so much about my own unit at Quantico? How'd they know that the Kathleen Kelleher who worked for the United Nations was related to me? These are good questions. Very damn-good questions. There's only one logical answer. Somebody in my own outfit ratted me out."

"Any idea who it was?"

"If you walk the data backward, you get someone in the ONI—somebody with high-level access to Naval Intelligence records. I've spent a lot of time thinking about it; I have a short list of about a hundred people. Maybe there's something in the cargo that will help me figure out exactly who it is."

"Why didn't you tell your CO about Suerta's contact? The Navy had already warned you that something like this could happen."

"Same reason, Rick. The mole. I couldn't depend on anyone inside. If a snitch got word to Suerta that I was reporting the contact, there'd be no help for Katie. No way to extract her before the mole tipped the Cubans and they put her out of reach. Like I said, getting her out of Bahía Honda isn't a Special Forces operation. It would take an air mobile operation with serious muscle, and a mole highly placed enough to know all about my covert unit at Quantico would sure as hell get wind of a major military assault on a Cuban prison."

Zeffi shook her head.

"The U.S. is acting pretty forcefully over the Jake Seigel kidnapping. Why wouldn't they act for your daughter? She's an American citizen too."

Kelleher made a sound that started out as a short, sharp laugh but ended up as a low growl.

"Not going to happen. The U.S. isn't going to try to rescue an irritating left-wing nut-bar who's in Cuba of her own free will. I had to do it alone."

"You did have another obligation," said Rick, his tone flat and accusing. "You knew about a mole in the ONI and yet you took a leave of absence to go off and save your daughter without warning your department."

Kelleher's face hardened and a muscle jumped in his left cheek.

"The day my daughter clears Cuban airspace, I

deal with that son of a bitch. But blood's blood. And don't you prod me about my duty, Rick. I was fighting our wars when you were still trying to figure out what your thumbs were for. And if you're such a stars-and-bars patriot, why the hell were you down here in the Keys with the rest of the bums and slackers?"

Rick decided to let that go. For now. Just let it go. Or maybe not.

Zeffi, sensing his rapidly reddening mood, broke in fast.

"Did Kathleen know that she was being used against you?"

Kelleher kept a wary eye on Rick for a moment longer.

"No, Zeffi. Not that girl. It wouldn't fit in with her politics. She thinks Cuba is a paradise and the United Nations is the last best hope of the planet. She despises the covert world. She'd never do it."

Rick looked away from Kelleher and saw the black wall of the storm front racing across a hundred yards of pale-green roiling seas. A gust of cold wet wind slammed into *La Gaviota*'s portside and she heeled sharply to starboard. Another wave crashed over her bow and poured across the decking. Visibility dropped to a few feet.

"Enough talk," said Rick. "Let's button up. Here it comes."

# CHANGO ROJA

MOTOR CRUISER *LA GAVIOTA*
LATITUDE 24 DEGREES 16 SECONDS NORTH
LONGITUDE 79 DEGREES 54 SECONDS WEST
NORTHEASTERN TIP OF THE CAY SAL BANK
8:30 P.M. EDT, SUNDAY, SEPTEMBER 29

Cruising a few hundred yards off the Dog Rocks, on a bruised and sluggish sea under a lowering sky as greasy-gray as a highway underpass, all her pennants gone, her flagstaff broken halfway up and the shredded remnants of the Stars and Stripes snapping on a frayed line, *La Gaviota* looked like a drifting wreck. Her upper decks were coated with slick salt spray; stringy ropes of windblown seaweed drooped across her superstructure and fouled her rails; all along her waterline her once-gleaming mahogany hull was stained with oily green sludge. A thin silvery ribbon of gasoline mixed with engine oil came from the bilge pump outlet at the stern and floated away on the swells in her wake, coiling strands of slimy green and vivid purple that snaked out in *La Gaviota*'s churning wake and lost itself in the spindrift and yellow foam that covered the rolling seas around them. A hundred yards in front of her, the low shoals of the Dog Rocks were visible only as a darker blur against the heavy cloud cover that stretched right across the sky from east to west.

The trailing edge of the storm had passed over around four in the afternoon, moving up the Florida Straits like a spinning top. In the distant west a sliver of the setting sun sliced through a narrow break in the cloud cover. The blood-red beams shone weakly through the dirty portside glass and filled the control deck with a lurid red glow.

Zeffi was down in the cabin with Carlito Vargas, silently—resentfully—spoon-feeding him some beef stew. Kelleher was standing beside Rick, one hand resting on the bulkhead by the instrument panel, both men concentrating on the sonar screen in front of them. In the bright color monitor, the seabed looked like a dense shimmering network of vivid green lines etched on a black velvet background, the lines slowly twisting and reforming in three dimensions as the sonar signal swept across the ocean floor.

They were running along the edge of the drop-off on the eastern edge of the Cay Sal Bank. In the screen, the demarcation point was an abrupt cascade of dense green lines that spilled over into an immense valleylike trough that marked the beginning of the Santaren Channel. On the ledge the seabed was less than two hundred feet down. A few hundred feet to the east and it suddenly dropped away to a depth of nearly thirteen hundred feet. They were closing in on the shelf at the southern edge of the Dog Rocks, following the same debris trail that Rick had followed the week before. It was all there: a broken wheel, a torn-up section of the starboard float, a strut, most of it half buried in shifting sand as the Gulf Stream poured across the shallows. Kelleher was at Rick's side, watching the debris field passing under their keel, his pale battered face tinted green by the glow of the monitor, his expression set and hard.

The crest of coral that formed the Dog Rocks was beginning to appear on the screen, a tightening helix of green lines that flexed and reformed as the boat slid forward through the low swells. Rick looked up and adjusted the course to take them around the shoals to the northern edge. Neither man spoke; both of them were concentrating on the sonar display with a grim intensity. The grid shifted, the green lines snaking and coiling up tighter as the sonar played over the rocky seabed. More traces of the wreck appeared. A few more yards.

And there it was. The wrecked cabin, still canted over on the starboard side, etched in narrow green bars. Kelleher switched on the underwater camera and the floodlights. In the television monitor, they could see the cabin section, half buried in drifting sand, nearly invisible in the murky half-light at fifty feet down.

"Christ," said Kelleher. "That gives me the chills."

Rick nodded, said nothing. It was a night neither man cared to discuss. There wasn't anything you could say that would change the memory, so what was the point? There was turbulence around the shoals and waves were breaking over the sharp coral outcrop that showed above the waterline. Rick put the wheel to starboard and they skimmed slowly past the shoals. In the sonar display, Kelleher watched the cabin section recede as they left the Dog Rocks. The seafloor was dropping away faster, as they cruised northward, looking for more signs of the wreck. They'd talked over their tactics in that deafening stillness that had filled the ocean after they broke out of the southern wing of the storm.

Kelleher's course that Friday night had been, roughly, west-northwest, compass bearing three-one-five, running close behind the C-130. They both agreed that he must have hit the water a few hundred feet off the Dog Rocks, caught a float on a wave tip and tumbled badly as the machine broke up.

Since the debris trail had led Rick to the cabin section, they figured the fuselage had scattered itself in a track from southeast to northwest in the area to the immediate northeast of the Dog Rocks.

If the cargo section was still intact, if it sank instead of floating away on the Gulf Stream—a very big if—it should be located somewhere on the seafloor past these shoals. Using the GPS indicator, they were planning a grid search through the entire debris path, but they all knew they didn't have much time.

On Saturday morning, Elliott Lazarus, speaking for the State Department, had given the Cubans forty-eight hours to release Jake Seigel and Cory Bryant or face an unspecified response. It was around 8:30 on Sunday night. The deadline was 8:00 A.M. Monday morning, less than twelve hours away. If they were still poking around in the Cay Sal Bank scanning for the cargo section by Monday afternoon, there was an excellent chance they'd be up to their gunwales in naval patrols and trying very hard to explain their reasons for being inside a potential war zone. To add to the thrills, the iron-bound north coast of Cuba was only seventy-four nautical miles to the south of their position and the Cuban navy would be aggressively protecting its coastal waters. And there could be Cuban MiGs in the air as well.

So the search here had acquired a degree of urgency that had translated itself into a grim and fixed silence on the faces of the two men watching the sonar display and a deepening enmity between Zeffi Calderas and the shirtless, unshaven and foul-smelling Cuban trussed up on the stateroom bunk down in Cabin 3.

Zeffi spooned another ladle of lukewarm stew into the man's puffy face and watched him work it down, with a bitter expression on her face. She had changed his bandages and swabbed at the livid bullet graze that scored his cheekbone like a furrow in sandy ground; she had done what she could or the ugly crater where his right eye should have been. Bound hand and foot, Vargas had borne the procedure well but had spent a lot of the time describing in vivid colloquial detail precisely what he would do to Zeffi as soon as he got loose.

Since he did this in a kind of Miskito-Cuban patois that had only a passing relation to formal Spanish, Zeffi understood few of the details, but the general message was unmistakable and she was giving serious consideration to poking his other eye out with the soup spoon in her left hand when she heard steps coming down the gangway, and then Kelleher popped into the cabin.

"You okay here?" he asked.

"I'm fine. How is it going up there?"

"Rick's got it under control. I thought I'd look in, see how you were. He'll give me a shout if anything develops. Our man giving you a hard time?" he said, without a smile.

Zeffi got up with the bowl in her hand and stood beside Kelleher, looking down at Carlito Vargas, who was staring up at Charles Kelleher with a rapidly thickening malice, his single eye wide and red-rimmed.

"If I caught his meaning correctly, I think he wants to fuck me in the ass and then feed me to his dogs, but I may have gotten that wrong. He may want to fuck his dogs in the ass and then take me out to dinner.

Kelleher gave her a twisted grin and sat down on the edge of the bed, reached out and tugged the covering off the socket—Vargas grunted something in Cuban-Spanish, which Kelleher ignored.

He studied the damage.

"No infection. Looks okay. He'll live."

"Too bad," said Zeffi. "You want me to leave?"

"Suit yourself. You hearing me, Carlito?"

Vargas made no response but his terrible wound brightened with blood. Kelleher pressed the bandage back in place, smoothed the tapes that held it in place, not gently, speaking in a soft voice.

"Then I have a question for you. You will answer it for me. You will answer it truthfully. Do you understand that?"

No response, other than a twist of his heavy lips and a grunt.

"Do you know where Kathleen Kelleher is?"

Vargas shrugged, exhaled, his breath sour and rank. Kelleher considered the man for a while. Vargas showed no kind of unease, seemed almost content to settle into a morose silence. A beating wasn't going to crack him open.

"Do you know how Geronimo died?"

Kelleher was watching Vargas's single yellow eye. Something deep inside it flickered, the black pupil narrowing.

"I saw his body. You gave him to a shark."

Kelleher nodded.

"I did. I can call this shark."

The yellow eye again, the pupil contracting.

"No one can call a shark."

Kelleher, deciding, looked at Vargas for a time. There was a fear there, buried, controlled, but a fear, nevertheless. Kelleher stood up and pulled Vargas to his feet.

"Come. We'll call her together."

A minute later, Kelleher had Vargas out on the fantail and strapped into one of the fighting chairs bolted to the decking. The ship was cruising slowly over a rolling sea, the gas turbines rumbling under the deck, the props churning at the stern board. All around them the shreds of the tropical storm were drifting against a steel-gray sky shot through with purple, a bruised and damaged sky above a turbid and restless sea.

The waves were short, sharp and choppy, stirred by a crosswind that brought in the scent of kelp and dead fish. Vargas was looking at the long tarpaulin-wrapped bundle on the floor of the stern deck, his face a rock wall, but his one yellow eye very wide and his barrel of a chest rising and falling in short rasping breaths. It came to Zeffi, watching the two of them, that Vargas was afraid of Kelleher, afraid of what he was going to do next.

Kelleher checked the handcuffs and the ropes that bound Vargas into the fighting chair, sent Zeffi a warning glance—*either say nothing or leave*—and then he stepped to the taffrail and looked out over the heaving ocean. The surface was clouded and opaque, with streamers of greasy foam floating in the hollows and troughs. The bloated bodies of bonita and snapper killed in the storm bobbed in the wake of the boat. The sea smelled of rot and death, as it always does after a storm.

Kelleher leaned out over the railing and saw what he had expected to see: a brown stain running down the scuppers where the blood of Rubio Gonzalez had drained out of his body and dispersed into the following sea. He looked closely at the surface and saw a deep strong ripple, wide and fast, running counter to the wake. Something huge was down there, waiting, drawn by the blood. He turned and looked at Vargas, who was staring at him with a terrible understanding.

Kelleher bent down and tugged at the fold of the tarpaulin, jerking it upward. Gonzalez's body flopped over the deck, dead skin pale blue with a face as gray as ash. Zeffi stepped back into the cabin behind her and stood in the doorway, trying to control her expression.

Kelleher picked up Gonzalez's limp body in his arms, carried it to the railing and hurled it into their streaming wake. It hit the surface heavily, rolling in the current, settled onto its back, Rubio's face ghastly, staring open-eyed up at them from the water, his slack mouth gaping. A heartbeat, then an explosion of broken water as Rubio's body leapt skyward in a convulsive jerk, lashed brutally from side to side, and then was dragged beneath the surface.

Kelleher and Vargas saw the flash of steel-gray skin, a rounded muscular flank, a gray-white belly and a coal-black eye as dead as Rubio's. The big mako arched and drove the body down with brutal power, leaving the surface roiling with eddies and whirlpools that slowly settled and flattened out. The ocean closed over it, the wake fanned out and away, the engines rumbled in the deep. A silence, with the wind tugging at the guy wires and ruffling Carlito

Vargas's cotton shirt, stirring his long, greasy black hair.

"Where does Katie Kelleher work, Carlito?"

A hesitation, then an answer.

"At the Ministry of External Relations."

"In Havana. Off Calzada. The Vedado district?"

"Yes."

"Is my daughter still alive?"

"I . . . she is. Yes she is."

"You know this?"

"Narcisse said she is alive."

"Is she well?"

"Well?"

"Is she unharmed? Is she in a prison?"

"No. She works in the ministry all day and goes home to her house at night."

"Where is her house?"

"In Havana Vieja, on El Callejon del Chorro, near the Cathedral of San Cristobal. Top floor."

Kelleher changed direction abruptly here.

"Do you know of a man named Jake Seigel?"

"He is the American film producer."

"Do you know where he is?"

"He is with the authorities. In Havana."

"My friend Mister Broca tells me that someone from the National Hotel in Miami called the company that gives him cell-phone service. This man wanted to know Mister Broca's address in Los Angeles. Do you know who that was?"

"It was Honorio Anaya."

"How did he get Mister Broca's cell-phone number?"

"It was on the phone."

"Which phone?"

"Mister Jake Seigel's phone. His cell phone. In the list of 'missed calls.'"

"And how did Honorio Anaya come to have Mister Jake Seigel's cell phone?"

"It was on his boat."

"The *Cagancho*?"

"Yes. The *Cagancho*. It was on the table."

"Honorio Anaya was on *Cagancho*?"

"Yes. When they took him."

"When they took Mister Jake Seigel?"

"Yes. And Mister Cory Bryant. When they took them."

"Who took Mister Jake Seigel and Mister Cory Bryant?"

"The men in the other boat."

"Which boat was that?"

Vargas swallowed once, staring at the racing water beyond the railing, straining at the plastic cuffs by which he was held.

Then he answered.

"It was this boat."

"How did you get near the *Cagancho*?"

"We pretended to be in trouble. On the sea, when you are in trouble, people usually try to help you."

"Why did you want to get close to *Cagancho*?"

"It was concerning the sinking of our boat. *La Luna Negra*. On the Cay Sal Bank. Many men of our *cabildo* died. We were angry."

"Did you take Jake Seigel to the Cubans in Havana?"

"No. We only towed the boat into the waters."

"The waters of Cuba?"

"Yes."

"To hand Seigel over to the Cubans?"

"No. To hand him over to our own people."

Kelleher considered that surprising answer for a time.

"Yet he is in the custody of the Cuban government. Castro is putting them on trial. If you didn't hand Seigel over to the authorities, how did they get him?"

"When we got to the rendezvous, a gunboat was waiting for us. They towed the boat into Marina Hemingway."

"So the gunboat was a surprise to you?"

"Yes."

"Were you in radio contact with the boat that was supposed to meet you?"

"Yes."

"What was your password?"

"It was . . . *avispa*. Wasp."

Kelleher recognized the oblique reference to a highly secret Cuban counterespionage unit called Avispa Roja, the Red Wasp. In early 1995, the analysts at ONI had identified Avispa Roja as a special operations unit working directly for Fidel Castro, a unit deliberately isolated from the rest of the Cuban spy networks, including the DGI.

"Are you a member of Avispa Roja?"

"No. We use the name to . . . *como se dice? Por mofarse el commandante.*"

"You used it to ridicule? To make fun of Castro?"

"*Sí* . . . yes."

"So you work to free Cuba?"

"Yes. My cabildo does."

"And you do this by kidnapping people and by threatening to rape and then kill their daughters? You help Cuba in this way?"

"There is a struggle. It is like a war."

"If it is a war, you have very good relations with the enemy in Havana. How is it that you are working with the exiles and yet you can come and go in Cuba whenever you want?"

"There is an understanding. Even in a war sometimes you have to deal with the enemy."

"Is Manuel Gonzalez in Los Angeles in this war?"

"He also works to free Cuba."

"With whom does he work to free Cuba?"

"I do not know everyone in our cabildo."

"Tell me the names you know."

"I know only a few. There is a member named Onassis Goyri, who is the Cuban representative with the United Nations and a very great friend. There are others. We are not allowed to know them all."

"Do you know who owns this boat?"

This brought Vargas to a stand; he looked away, trying to find an answer that would keep him out of the water and yet give nothing away. Kelleher stepped in and Vargas spoke quickly.

"It is owned by a company, not a man. The CIMEX Corporation."

"And who owns the CIMEX Corporation?"

"I . . . do not know."

Kelleher stepped around behind Vargas and began to loosen the ropes that held him to the chair. Vargas lurched backward, twisting his head around, his eye wild.

"No, *señor*—wait . . . it is owned by Onassis Goyri and Hector Preig."

"Preig? The head of the Cuban secret police?"

"*Sí*, Hector Preig."

"Only those two? Remember, you will be with us to the end of this. We will find out everything. I am with the U.S. government and we can easily find out who owns this company. If you lie, you go into the water just like Rubio."

Vargas was breathing heavily. Zeffi thought he was trying to find the courage to go into the water instead of telling Kelleher what he wanted to know. In the end, he chose to stay alive and it seemed to break him.

"My father also owns this corporation."

"Who is your father?"

A long, defeated silence, ending in a kind of stoical despair. The tension seemed to flow out of him and he slumped in his bonds.

"His name is Roymundo Vargas. He lives in Geneva. He runs the business."

"Are all these men members of La Regla de Ocha?"

Vargas went on, in a flat lifeless tone, as if he were beyond saving.

"We are all in Santeria. But we are men of differ-

ent *orishas*—different gods. Our *orisha*—the god of
our cabildo, the cabildo of the Vargas family is
Chango Roja, who is the husband of Ochun. Jerome
Suerta was also of Chango Roja. His death made
many of our people very angry. They feel you killed
him. Or Mister Broca killed him. We were to bring
you to Cuba so you could answer for his death."

"A shark killed him. You saw it yourself."

"We think you put him to the sharks."

"Why would we do that?"

"To . . . find out about your daughter. To force
him to talk. As you are doing to me."

Kelleher reached into the pocket of his jeans and
drew out a silver necklace that Zeffi recognized as
the necklace that Rick had taken from Geronimo
Suerta's mangled corpse many days ago. Kelleher
held it up in front of Carlito's face, dangling it over
the racing water.

"Do you know what this is?"

"It is the medal of Saint Christopher. For traveling
safely with the protection of God."

Kelleher turned it so that Vargas could read the
inscription.

> *Por Geronimo*
> *Y la regla de ocha*
> *—Narcisse—*

"*Sí*—yes. That is the medal of Geronimo. He was
our *babalao*. Now Narcisse is our new babalao."

"What is the secret name of this god?"

"The secret name?"

"He is an *orisha*, Saint Christopher. What is his true name?"

"It is . . . *Aggayu Sola*."

"What is your current password?"

"It is *Por Yemaya*."

"How many different cabildos are in your network?"

"There are four."

"The Gonzalez family is of Ochun. Who else is of Chango Roja?"

"Mister Goyri and his people."

"Onassis Goyri?"

"Yes. He is of Chango Red."

"Is your father in your cabildo?"

"Yes. Mister Goyri is one of Chango Roja's people too."

Kelleher had heard of Chango Roja. He was a snake god who was supposed to live in the tops of royal palms and send thunder and lightning down on his enemies. He was the god of punishment and betrayal and commanded the birds and the reptiles and the insects.

"What was in the packages I was flying out of Cuba?"

Vargas, who had been slumping into his chair, suddenly straightened and stared out to sea in the direction of the Dog Rocks. He held the look for a while and seemed to be listening. He drew in a deep rasping breath, let it out slowly. Then he looked at Kelleher, sadness and a kind of strange exhilaration in his face.

"I will say no more. It is coming for me."

"What is coming?"

"The punishment is coming. From Chango Roja."

Vargas closed his single yellow eye.

"Do you want to leave, Zeffi?"

"I don't know," she said. "Do I?"

"I think so."

# THE EDGE

Rick was at the wheel, his face tinted a ghostly green in the glow from the sonar display. Beyond the windscreen the night had come down and a few stars pierced the thick mist that lay on the seas around them. *La Gaviota* was cruising without any running lights showing. The cloud cover was breaking up. This was worrying Rick since it exposed them to the surveillance satellites. He turned and watched Zeffi as she came up onto the control deck.

"Hey, kid. . . . How's Vargas?"

"Charlie is asking him some questions. I decided to be somewhere else while he did it."

Rick glanced at her face and said nothing.

"How's it going here?" she asked.

Rick tapped the screen, drew his finger along their route.

"Lots of debris down here. I'm running along the edge of the banks. You can see the drop-off. Most of the stuff I'm seeing is the general clutter you find anywhere in a sportfishing zone, but some of it is fresh and looks like pieces of Charlie's aircraft. So far, no cargo pallet. If it went over that ledge, it dropped into a valley more than a thousand feet deep and we may never find it. How you doing?"

Zeffi was rubbing the faded bruise on her cheekbone, her eyes a luminous bright green, her red hair weirdly violet in the strange light.

"I'm very tired, Rick. How does your side feel?"

"Sore. Damn sore. I find if I don't breathe, it doesn't hurt as much. But then I faint more than I'd like."

Zeffi stared down at the screen, apparently watching the sonar image unfold as they worked their way up the eastern edge of the shoal, but Rick knew her mind was out on the fantail with Vargas and Kelleher. Finally, she spoke.

"Carlito Vargas took Jake, Rick. And Cory Bryant. The Gonzalez family helped. They used this boat to catch him."

"How did they do that? This boat could never overtake the *Cagancho,* and Jake was always on the watch for a hijack. That's what the Remington was for. They'd never have gotten close."

Zeffi told him what she'd heard, ending with the reference to Chango Red and the *nanigos* of Santeria. Rick thought about it for a while and came around to the same question that had been bothering them all along.

"These people say they're with the exiles, but they have a hell of a lot of contact with the Cuban government, don't they?"

"Are they spies, Rick? Double agents, isn't that the word?"

"Spies? I don't know. They're working for someone in Cuba with a lot of power. Not necessarily Castro. But somebody in the government. No one else could move in and out of Cuba like that."

"You say they're not working *for* Castro. He's a dictator. If you're not working for him, you're against him. Wouldn't Castro know about it if anyone inside Cuba was . . . freelancing?"

"Maybe. Maybe not. Castro's been sick lately. Even made the news. He fainted during a speech. The trouble with strongmen is they only hold power as long as they're strong. Show any weakness and the knives come out. There's no way of knowing who these people are really working for. But I have a gut feeling it's not Castro."

"But Castro is the one who's refusing to release Jake Seigel and Cory Bryant. If he's not the man behind all this, why is he helping them at all?"

"My guess is he's operating on what he's being told by people he trusts. I don't think he knows the real game at all."

"You mean they're using Castro . . . how?"

"As muscle. They've told him we killed a Cuban citizen. They've got the body and they've got real Americans to blame. Castro would go for that in a heartbeat. Now that he's drawn the line, made it a matter of national pride, he couldn't back down and keep himself in power. He's being used, but he doesn't know it."

"Rick, back there, Vargas used the word *avispa* as a password. They were contacting a Cuban gunboat, the one that towed *Cagancho* into Marina Hemingway. Kelleher asked him if he was a member of something called Avispa Roja. What's that?"

"Hang on . . . I can show you."

Rick checked the time, reached for the ship-to-shore and switched the radio to the shortwave frequency. He hit the SCAN button and they both listened in silence as the radio flickered through a series of shortwave radio broadcasts. Rick stopped it when it reached 30.3221.

"Listen to this."

He adjusted the gain and turned up the volume. It was a woman's voice, speaking in Spanish.

*"Atención. Atención. Cuatro seis siete ocho uno. Cuatro seis siete ocho uno. Atención. Tres cinco nueve seis seis ocho. Tres cinco nueve seis seis ocho. Atención. Trescientos cuatro ciento triente. Trescientos cuatro ciento triente . . ."*

"They're numbers," said Zeffi. "She's reading off a list of numbers. She repeats each set twice, says 'attention,' and then reads off another list of numbers. What is it?"

"It's on every night around this time. The broadcast comes from Havana. Shortwave. Same thing every night. Numbers and numbers, always in the same format. Goes on for thirty minutes and repeats."

"It sounds like some sort of code."

"It is. It's directed to Cuban agents working in the United States. You remember Brothers to the

Rescue? Those exile flights out of Miami that used to do reconnaissance flights in the Florida Straits, looking for Cubans trying to escape on rafts, drop leaflets, that sort of thing?"

"Yes. Two of their flights were shot down by Cuban fighters a couple of years ago. Four people died."

"That's right. The routes those rescue planes fly are always a carefully guarded secret. A few days before the planes were attacked, this broadcast contained special instructions to Red Wasp agents in the exile movement. The same guys who told the Cubans what the flight plans were going to be. The number sequence was two one two two two three two four. According to Kelleher, who knew some of the ONI guys on the brief, the numbers were meant to tell them what days they should *not* be on one of those planes. The planes were shot down on November twenty-fourth. That's what the Red Avispa does."

"Who runs the Red Avispa?"

"Who do you think? Fidel Castro."

"Not the DGI?"

"Kelleher thinks Castro separated the Avispa Roja from the other intelligence systems around the time they sank that tugboat. According to the ONI, Castro oversees Avispa Roja himself. They punish his own particular enemies, in and out of Cuba. The DGI is isolated from it, along with the rest of the enforcement wing."

Zeffi's face went through a change; when she spoke her voice was low and her tone uncertain.

"Rick, did you ever do anything to a prisoner? I mean, to get information or something? To save someone innocent?"

"I was never in that position. I wasn't a detective."

"Would you have? Say you had someone you knew had kidnapped a child and if he told you where the child was, you could save her. What would you do?"

"If I was certain he knew?"

"Yes. There was no doubt."

"Then I'd do whatever it took."

"But it's still torture, isn't it?"

"Yes, it is. You do what's needed. Afterward you try to live with it, if you're a good man, and if you're not, you miss it."

"When good men do things like . . . this . . . doesn't it stay with them? It must. How do they live with it?"

Zeffi was talking about Charlie Kelleher, but Rick's mind was back in Albany, standing over Donny Thornborough's coffin. His closed coffin. Seeing through the polished oak to the ruined face beneath the surface. The face Kelleher wore often reminded Rick of an oak plank, but he had no idea what lay underneath it.

"How do they live with it? Sometimes they don't. And maybe that's why we all die eventually. For some of us, it must be a relief."

"Is Charlie a good man, Rick?"

"I'm counting on it."

"Will he still be a good man after this is over?"

"Will any of us?"

Zeffi was looking at the screen again, this time with real attention. The sonar was scanning a section of the seabed thirty-one fathoms down. She tapped the monitor over a vague jumble of what looked like abandoned oxygen tanks nearly buried in the sand.

"What's that?"

Rick looked at it hard, trying to read the image.

"I don't know . . . it's heavily silted. It's been there a long time. It's not the cargo pallet, anyway. Check the charts."

Zeffi stepped over to the navigator's desk and unrolled a series of laminated paper charts, found the one she wanted, held it under the chart light on top of the desk. Rick heard the sharp intake of breath and looked over at her.

Zeffi was tapping a point on the map right at the northern curve of the Cay Sal Bank. The chart showed a circle of dots and beside it a notation in fine print which read:

Unexploded Bombs—Reported 1967.

"Am I reading this right?"

Rick craned to look at the chart, nodded.

"The Navy trains in a big area south of the Dry Tortugas and there are military flights all over the basin. Planes in trouble dump their ordnance. I guess that's what we're looking at down there."

Zeffi didn't find this encouraging.

"Let me understand this. Sometimes my English gets all muddled up. Are you telling me the entire seafloor in the Florida Straits is covered with unexploded bombs?"

"No . . . not at all. Just here and there."

Zeffi's eyes narrowed, and Rick saw that tiny red spark deep in her green eyes. Her fuse was officially lit.

"Just here and there?" she said, in that soft tone Rick had learned to recognize early on. "And you say they're not dangerous?"

"No. Not if you leave them alone."

"And this is where we're poking around looking for this mysterious lost cargo? In an area littered with unexploded bombs?"

"Zeffi . . ."

"Rick, this is *incroyable*. Flat-out lunacy."

"Honey . . ."

"Don't 'honey' me. If you find this cargo pallet, who's going down in the minisub?"

"I am. Or Kelleher—*ow!*"

Zeffi had jabbed him in the left side. In his wound. Rick tried to convince himself it was accidental but couldn't manage it.

"Christ. What the hell did you do that for?" said Rick, outraged, his wound throbbing painfully.

"There's a phrase for you two in my language. You're both *hors de combat*. Neither of you could drive a tricycle down a staircase without a hard shove from your nanny."

"What's a 'whore de goombah'? An Italian hooker?"

"Don't be flippant. This is for real. That leaves me. And I'm supposed to do all this in the middle of a dumping ground for unexploded bombs? Oh, I think not."

"Have you ever driven a minisub?"

"Have you?"

"I asked you first."

"You asked me first? What is this, kindergarten? Why not say 'double-stamp it and touch blue'?"

"Yes," said Rick, too firmly. "I have."

"You drove a minisub? When did you do this? Where did you do this? And Disneyland doesn't count."

"I took an underwater search course when I was with the ESU. I'm fully checked out on minisubs."

"Are you lying to me?"

"Yes, he is," said Kelleher, who had come into the gangway while they were talking and was standing behind them. He led a silent and brooding Vargas down to an aft cabin and lashed him to the steel bed frame. He came back up the stairs and sat down on the navigator's chair, looking dead tired.

"And neither of you are taking the sub down. I am. Unlike Rick, I really am checked out on mini-subs. Including the model on the foredeck. We have one shot at this. I have to do it."

"You're in no shape to—"

"Maybe not. But there it is. I have a question. Does the name Roymundo Vargas or Onassis Goyri mean anything to either of you?"

"Vargas?" said Rick. "Carlito's last name is Vargas."

"And the name Goyri sounds familiar," said Zeffi. "I think there was a Goyri on the list of victims that drowned in the *Venceremos*."

"Roymundo Vargas is Carlito's father. You ever hear of the CIMEX Corporation?"

"CIMEX?" said Zeffi. "They own this boat. The papers are in the navigation desk. CIMEX also owns the house in Key Biscayne."

"They're based in Geneva," said Rick.

"Well, it looks like Carlito's father runs the business with two partners. One is Onassis Goyri. Vargas says he's Cuba's envoy to the United Nations. The other partner is Hector Preig. I'd like to know what kind of business these three guys would have in common."

"They have one thing in common," said Zeffi. "Fidel Castro."

"Castro?" said Rick. "How?"

"She's right, Rick. Preig is the head of Castro's secret police. Onassis Goyri is Cuba's representative at the United Nations. Both of those jobs would have been personal appointments from Castro himself."

"That doesn't mean that Vargas connects to Castro," said Rick.

"I doubt very much that Castro would let either man go into business with someone he didn't approve of. I think we can assume Roymundo Vargas is involved with Castro."

Zeffi was shaking her head.

"It's possible that Castro doesn't know a damn

thing about CIMEX. It's based in Geneva, not Havana, isn't it?"

"We don't know," said Kelleher.

"But we could find out," said Rick.

"How? We can't ask the government."

"Zeffi, does this boat have a weather fax?"

"Yes. It has a satellite uplink too."

"Give me a piece of paper, will you?"

She ruffled through the charts and came up with a section of graph paper. Rick took the sheet and wrote down a quick note:

> URGENT FAX FOR JACK COLE
> JACK . . . CAN YOU RUN A SEARCH
>    OF THESE NAMES ASAP?
> THE CIMEX CORPORATION /
> ROYMUNDO VARGAS / GENEVA
> ONASSIS GOYRI / UNITED NATIONS
> THIS CONNECTS DIRECTLY TO JAKE
> FAX US BACK NO RADIO CALL
>    RICK BROCA

Kelleher and Zeffi read the note over his shoulder, Kelleher shaking his head.

"Who's Jack Cole?"

"He's the head of security at Jake's film company. Ex-LAPD. He's a trained investigator and he gives a damn about Jake Seigel."

Kelleher shrugged.

"Worth a try. If you can get it through. Remember the NSC monitors every radio transmission. What if Chennault picks this up?"

"Fuck Chennault. We keep moving, he'll have to play catch-up anyway. We sit still, he's onto us. It's worth a try. Zeffi, will you fax this out? Here's his private fax number."

She took the sheet, nodded, and went down to the radio room. Kelleher watched her go and turned to say something, but Rick held up a hand. "Okay—hold on. Look at this."

Kelleher stepped up to look at the sonar screen. The dense matrix of green gridlines indicated a squat squared-off shape lying inside a crescent-shaped rubble of coral rocks. Drifting sand had piled up on the side sheltered from the Gulf Stream, but the image was fairly clear: a slab-sided, boxy shape lying at a crazy angle on top of a jagged crest of coral. The sonar indicated a depth of thirty-one fathoms. A fathom is six feet. If that was the cargo pallet, it was 186 feet below *La Gaviota*'s keel.

Rick reversed the drive, and the boat's bow dipped as she came to a hover over the shape. The green lines on the sonar screen were dense and tightly packed around the image. A few yards to the east, they dropped away into a black nothingness.

"It's right on the ledge," said Kelleher.

"Yeah," said Rick. "Does that look like the cargo?"

Kelleher studied the image, shook his head.

"It's square, all right. Can we try the camera?"

Rick flicked on the underwater floods. It was full
dark, with a few stars glittering through the thinning cloud cover. They saw the white glow light up
the water around her bow. Rick adjusted the hull-
mounted video cameras. A joystick mounted on the
dash controlled the camera direction. He watched
the television screen as he moved the cameras. The
water was murky and seemed to be flying past the
camera driven by the force of the Gulf Stream. The
light from the floods moved across the distant
seabed, and then they were looking at a large square
shape lying on pink coral. It was coated with sand,
but in the dim light of the floods they could discern
the lurid pink of shrink-wrapped plastic bundles and
a band of metal strapping.

In the television image, they could see wavering
ribbons of sand being driven over the cargo pallet;
the current was very strong that far down. Whoever
went after the cargo pallet was going to have to fight
a minimum ten-knot current running from southwest to northeast all the way to the bottom. And
when the sub reached the pallet, the operator would
have to maneuver it around the rocky terrain, still
fighting that current, somehow get close enough to
the pallet to attach the cable from the winch on the
foredeck of La Gaviota. Get fouled up with the strapping or make any one of a hundred other tactical
errors, and that pallet could ride down the rocky
slope of the ledge and tumble two thousand feet into
the deep, quite possibly taking the minisub with it.
And all of this would have to be done in the dark

using only the lights on the minisub. The chances of doing it at all ranged from fashionably slim to out-and-out anorexic.

Rick looked at Kelleher with his smile on crooked. "Charlie, let's not fight about this," he said. "You go get it."

# LOUISIANA

As so often happens in the Caribbean after a major storm has lashed its way through the Straits, the heaving seas flattened out into a placid sheet of dark green glass and then a drifting pall of dense fog seemed to rise out of the ocean itself. It cut off the shredding clouds in the night sky and wrapped *La Gaviota* inside a ghostly sphere less than fifty feet wide, the upper half filled with a rich amber glow from the spotlight on the foredeck, the bottom half of the globe filled with black water, rippling witch lights playing across the surface like pale fire, and in the center of this isolated world, the long narrow boat with her engines muttering as Zeffi, weary to the bones, stubbornly fought the insistent north-easterly current of the inexorable Gulf Stream.

In the glow from the forward spotlight, Zeffi could see Rick and Kelleher as they struggled with the electric winch, trying to raise the fourteen-foot-long gray steel minisub off the mountings. They were cruising in two hundred feet of water here so there was no hope of mooring. The only way to stay positioned above the cargo pallet on the seabed was for Zeffi to put the bow into the running current of the Gulf Stream and give *La Gaviota* enough throttle to hold her in place.

She was using the sonar image to keep her station, which called for a fine—and constant—touch with the throttles, but it left Rick and Kelleher with the heavy lifting out on the foredeck. The fact that the sea had flattened out was a blessing, thought Zeffi. There was no way those two cripples could have done the job in a heavy groundswell.

It took them close to a half hour of silent effort, but they finally got the minisub in position, suspended over the black water on the port side by a thick corded-steel cable. The sub looked like a shining slate-gray torpedo with a fighter-jet canopy made of heavyweight Plexiglas covering a narrow pilot's station. Rick held the sub steady while Kelleher climbed slowly into his wet suit and strapped on the emergency air canister. When he was ready he straightened, wincing from the pain in his leg, looked at Rick, his face pale and his bruises vivid in the sulphurous light from the spot lamp.

"Damn," he said. "I'm not looking forward to this."

"It's only at one eighty-six," said Rick, secretly hoping that Kelleher would reject his next proposal. "And your leg is worse than you're letting on. Dick Butkis moves faster than you. I could do that as a scuba dive. Take a weight down along with the winch cable, hook it up, then kick off for the surface."

Kelleher shook his head with a certainty that eased Rick's troubled conscience.

"Can't be done. That's a heliox dive if you have to spend any time at all down there. Dead dark and only you—there's only one system on this boat—and anyway, none of the air supply is heliox. I checked it myself. Out of the question, but thanks for thinking of it. I have to take the minisub."

"I could probably do it," said Rick, understanding completely what Kelleher was going through. The last time he'd gone down in these waters it had almost killed both of them. Kelleher smiled at him.

"No, you can't. If you could, trust me, I'd let you. You're a young guy and nobody'd miss you. I'm adored by all."

"You're adored by you, anyway," said Rick.

Kelleher got a grip on the fold-down ladder on the hull of the sub, set himself, sighed deeply, looked back at Rick.

"Watch the sonar, hah? If you see anything . . . big . . . I'd like a heads up. You follow?"

"Big? You mean Maybelline?"

"She lives in these waters, right?"

"Charlie, you're in a fourteen-foot minisub. What can she do?"

"I don't know. Maybe she'd want to mate. Just keep an eye on the sonar for me, there's a good lad."

"*There's a good lad?* What's this, suddenly you're Irish?"

"I was always Irish. Some days more than others."

"Charlie, what I said a while back? About duty? I was totally full of shit, okay. I hope you know that."

"That you're totally full of shit? I had no idea. I would have guessed maybe three-quarters, max."

"Well, you never know."

"Apparently not. Anything happens to me . . ."

"Nothing will."

"Yeah. But in case, you'll remember Katie, won't you?"

"Count on it. I'll get her out."

"One last thing . . ."

"Don't jinx this, Charlie."

But Kelleher was pulling something out of the collar of his wet suit. He lifted it from around his neck and held it out to Rick. It was Geronimo Suerta's necklace, with the medal of Saint Christopher hanging from the end of the loop. Rick took it from Kelleher, his uncertainty showing in his face.

"I got what I needed out of Vargas with the help of this thing. It carried a lot of power in Santeria. You should wear it."

"Wear it?" said Rick, suppressing a morbid tremor. "Why?"

"It might get you out of trouble."

"How?"

"Just wear it, okay? And remember your promise."

"I will," said Rick, slipping on the silver necklace.

Kelleher gave him the same crisp military salute, began to climb into the minisub. Rick had no idea how he was supposed to engineer Kathleen Kelleher's safe exit from Cuba. But then he had no clear idea how he was supposed to help Jake and Cory either. So far, dumb luck seemed to be working for him. He knew the "dumb" would hold out, but he wasn't sure about the "luck" part.

He didn't say this to Kelleher.

Kelleher climbed up the ladder, stopped at the top, and waved to Zeffi, who was watching them through the windscreen, a worried look on her face. She smiled unconvincingly and waved back. When Kelleher settled into the cockpit a cold electric snake of preflight jitters slithered across his belly.

He was looking at an instrument array that reminded him of the controls of a Harrier jump jet; the matte-black panel filled with backlit gauges in ruby-red depth and sonar indicators, fuel cells, compass and range indicators, battery charge levels, air tank capacity, buoyancy regulators, even the center-mounted joystick and the foot pedals for pitch and yaw. The cockpit smelled of silicone and latex and rubber and engine oil. On the upper left of the panel there was a thumb-switch and a red button marked STARTER. Kelleher nodded to Rick and closed the canopy hood.

It settled over Kelleher with a hiss and an audible click as the seals snapped in place. He heard the rush of air as the cockpit pressurized and felt a slight lurch as Rick began to lower the sub into the water. It settled into the waves until the water was lapping around the canopy bubble; then there was a hydraulic pop as the cable connection bolt snapped open. The sub was free of the cable and floating on the surface. Kelleher hit the STARTER button and the electric motors came on, a muted humming vibration that ran through the hull. He checked the gauges—they all indicated NOMINAL—and shoved the joystick forward. The whine of the engines increased in pitch, and he felt the craft glide forward through the water.

He edged the sub closer to *La Gaviota*'s hull. Rick leaned down over the railing, the winch cable in his left hand. Kelleher pushed the sub in closer and watched as Rick put the winch cable hook into the right manipulator claw in the nose of the minisub. Kelleher closed the claw around the hook and locked it in.

He looked up through the canopy, already misting over, and saw Rick's black shape silhouetted against the floodlight. He picked up the sub's radio and keyed the button.

"Zeffi, you read me?"

"*I do,*" said Zeffi. "*Are you okay?*"

"I am. You can kill the spot."

"*Okay,*" she said; the floodlight snapped off, darkness complete, pressing in on the surface of the canopy. He was alone in a tiny world lit by the ruby-red glow from the instrument panel. A chill rattled through his chest and shoulders and he adjusted the sub's heater, flicked on the dive lamps. Two solid gray cones leaped out from the bow of the sub. One of them played along the wooden hull of *La Gaviota*, the other lanced out into a limitless darkness, a wavering cone of blue-white light filled with drifting motes that somehow made the surrounding darkness more intense. He edged the craft away from the hull. Rick's voice came over the radio.

*"Charlie, you read me?"*

"Five by five. We still in position?"

*"We are. The shelf is right underneath us. One hundred and eighty-six feet. We have a thousand feet of cable on this winch, so you have lots to play with. The current is running northeast at around ten knots. Can you feel it?"*

He could. The sub was already sliding northward along the hull. He corrected her drift with the joystick controls, listening to the tone of the electric engines change as the props feathered.

"I can feel it. It's pretty strong."

*"How you want to do this?"*

"Let the cable drum freewheel. I don't want any tension on the line, or it'll snap the claw off. Just see that the line doesn't run out too easily or I'll get tangled up in the slack."

*"I know. Just like trolling. Only you're the lure."*

"Thanks for the comforting image. Diving."

*"Ten four. We're here, Charlie."*

"Yeah. Just be here when I get back."

Kelleher pushed the joystick forward. He watched as the twin cones of white light swept away from the hull. The sub pitched as he fought the current. He increased the speed and bled the buoyancy tanks. He heard the gurgling rush of bubbles as the tanks emptied and he felt the sub settling into the water. He put her nose down. She slid forward and slipped beneath the waves; the deep breathing silence closed around him.

He spiraled downward in a lazy looping curve, listening to the hydraulics working, the cabin pressure increasing as he went down, his rasping breath unnaturally loud in his ears, aware of his own heartbeat. The depth gauge ticked off the numbers in a slow ruby flicker.

Fifteen feet.

Twenty feet.

Thirty feet.

In the sonar screen the seafloor looked like a slanted rocky hillside, glowing bright red in the display. He turned on the sub's bow camera and studied the image in the tiny television screen. Nothing yet. Just a field of drifting motes and the wash of sickly light that died away ahead of him. Beyond the cones of light there was only the infinite blackness of the deep. He could have been the last man alive, drifting through space in a pod, cut off forever from the world of light and air. These were not helpful thoughts, and with an effort he shut them down. The radio crackled to life.

*"Charlie. Everything okay?"*

"Yeah. Have you got me on sonar?"

Up in the cabin, Zeffi and Rick were staring at their own sonar display. On their screen the minisub was etched in tiny green lines, a tiny cylinder drifting downward through a maze of green wire toward the distant seabed. Rick's voice came back to Kelleher through the minisub speakers as slightly strained and tinny.

*"We have you, Charlie. How's the sub handling?"*

"Solid. Lovely machine. If I live, I'm keeping it. I'm showing a hundred and fifteen feet. Check?"

*"On the needle. Can you see anything yet?"*

Kelleher was concentrating on the sonar screen. The floor was rising up out of the deep. It seemed to be coming up at him in a rush. He slowed the descent and leveled out a couple of degrees.

"No. Just the seabed."

*"We've got you at a hundred and fifty-six feet. You should see the shelf pretty soon."*

Zeffi and Rick watched as the packet of green lines leveled out and slowed as it neared the higher part of the slope. Kelleher's voice came out of the shipboard speaker again. He sounded tense and strained and a billion miles from home.

*"I've got it. Switching to the camera."*

"You're about eighty feet west of the pallet," said Rick. "If you keep running east on that course, you should see it in a minute."

Kelleher adjusted the camera and watched the tiny digital screen set into the panel as the lights swept across the darkness. Something mound-like and gray rose up out of the darkness, spread itself outward beneath him. He looked out through the canopy and saw the seafloor gliding underneath him. It dropped away in a steep pitch, a silted field of jagged coral outcroppings and limestone plateaus, here and there a clear stretch of sandy floor, all of it angled down and away more and more sharply as the sub cruised over the bottom. He pulled the joystick back and cruised over the shelf.

In his sonar screen, Kelleher could see the drop-off into the channel. It was less than a hundred feet ahead of him. Where the hell was the cargo pallet? He felt the sub gaining speed as he closed in on the edge of the shelf. Some trick of the Gulf Stream? He throttled back, but the sub was still picking up speed. The seabed underneath him was slipping by in a rush. His forward-speed indicator was showing twenty knots. The current down here was brutal.

Up ahead the twin spots picked up a squared-off shape, bulky and squat, canted over on one side. The sub rushed at it as Kelleher tried to slow down. He pulled the joystick upward and gained some height, but he could not slow the sub down. He was doing eighteen knots when he flew over the cargo pallet. It slipped by underneath his hull only ten feet below him. The ledge was right in front of him, a yawning black emptiness.

His belly muscles tightened and he felt a sharp stinging pain lance through his ribs. He shot out over the ledge and into the blackness beyond it, caught inside the terrible current that was spilling down the slope and out over the ledge. Fighting it was like standing on the edge of a skyscraper and leaning against the wind that ripped across the roof. The electric motors were howling as he fought the stick and put the sub into a slow curving turn to starboard. He felt an unreasoning fear of that thousand-foot drop under his hull, a fear of tumbling helplessly into the abyss, a fear of what things there may be at the bottom, looking up at him with pale dead eyes. Rick's voice came over the radio, low, steady, calming him.

*"Charlie, take it easy. I think you overshot it."*

"I know. The current is much stronger down here. I think there's some kind of venturi effect along the ledge. It's running at least twenty knots down here."

*"What are you going to do?"*

Out over the deep, the current was much slower. Kelleher had the sub under control and was cruising back toward the shelf.

"I'm going to have to come at it upstream. It's easier to handle the current that way. I'll come in from the east and set the cable with her nose into the current."

*"That's risky, Charlie. If you snag your claw, you could draw the load down the slope after you. You'd be right in its path. With the current pushing it, that load could take you right over the edge."*

"I can't do it backward, Rick. I'm not good enough. I'm out of practice with these damn things."

Rick apparently heard the undertone of fear and anger.

*"Charlie, you want to come up and take a breather?"*

Kelleher looked at the battery gauges.

"No. We'd have to recharge, and that means we couldn't go back down until after sunrise. It's already past four in the morning. The deadline for Cuba is eight o'clock. By dawn, the Navy will be all over us. They're probably already in the area. It has to be done . . ."

*"Okay, Charlie. Standing by."*

"I'm going to set the winch hook and back off. Keep the slack in it. I don't want it lifting off the floor while I'm still downstream."

*"Ten four."*

Rick and Zeffi watched in silence as the tiny green image fought its way eastwards toward the edge of the shelf.

"This isn't going well, is it, Rick?"

Rick looked at her, shook his head. The cargo pallet was lying on its side on the eastern edge of the banks, less than twenty feet from the lip of what amounted to an underwater cliff a thousand feet deep. And the Gulf Stream was washing over that edge at twenty knots. Coming upstream against it would be like swimming up a waterfall. If Kelleher misjudged it, or if he caught the mechanical claw in the strapping, the load might shift. If it broke loose, the current would push it over the edge. The only safe way to approach it was from upstream, reversing the props to keep the sub in position, while he set the cable hook into the strapping. That way, if the load shifted, he could simply release the claw and pull clear as the load slipped away from him down the ledge toward the cliff. But Kelleher was at the controls. Only he could judge the best way to do this.

"He's a pro, Zeffi. He'll be fine."

Zeffi shrugged, looked away from the screen and out across the bow. The fog lay flat and thick on the windscreen, glowing green from the control panel. The engines murmured in the dark. From down in

Cabin 3 they heard Vargas moaning, wrapped inside a drug-induced sleep. Rick looked at Zeffi.

"Want me to take the wheel?"

Zeffi shook her head.

"He's been fed, he's been drained, and he's been sedated. You want to go read him a story, you go ahead. I'll stay here."

"Not really."

"Then fuck him," said Zeffi.

Down in the well of blackness, Kelleher's whole world had come down to those narrow cones of white light that led back to the abrupt limestone cliff that marked the edge of the shelf and the squat bulk of the cargo pallet that lay on the rocky floor twenty feet up that slope. He pushed the joystick forward as the sub moved back into the current. The vibration of the props increased and the dials jumped as the sub nosed into the current head-on.

"Like a salmon spawning," said Kelleher to himself. He fought the bow's tendency to veer to port or starboard and slowly closed in on the cargo pallet. He crossed back over the edge ten feet off the floor. Now the pallet was dead ahead and slightly below the blunt nose of the sub. He dipped the stick and increased the throttle. Although his hull-speed indicator showed twenty knots, he was actually covering the ground at less than two knots.

In the pale light of the forward floods, the seafloor changed from dull gray to a sandy yellow, tinted here and there with pink and black as he got closer to the bottom. Now he was three feet off the shelf and gliding slowly up the slope, the pallet less than fifteen feet away. The current held at a steady twenty knots, although he felt some turbulence near the ground as the Gulf Stream tumbled over the rocks. He closed in on the pallet.

At ten feet the spots picked out the bright pink of the bundles, still strapped securely to the pallet by the metal binders. The load lay on its side, having tumbled as it fell, and the lee side had silted up. But he could clearly see the crossover point where the nylon straps converged on the load. If he could get the winch hook underneath that section, they'd be able to put some tension into the line and slowly right the pallet. He was less than five feet away.

The engine tone changed and the sub picked up speed so fast he had to jump at the throttles and pull them back. He'd moved into the lee of the cargo and its bulk was protecting him from the full force of the current. But the water pouring over the top of the load was still running at twenty knots. And he'd have to move out into that current to set the hook properly.

He looked overhead and saw the cable line bowing in the current, rising up into the darkness. Somewhere up there, 186 feet away, *La Gaviota* was holding her position in the same current. He looked at the bowing cable again.

"Rick."

"*Charlie?*"

"I need you to take the cable up a bit."

"*How much?*"

"I can't say. I can't see the whole length of it. Just run it back until I tell you to stop."

*"Ten four. Hold on."*

Kelleher held his position for thirty seconds, seeing Rick in his mind's eye as he crossed the bow and hit the cable drive.

*"Taking it up, Charlie."*

Kelleher watched the curve of the cable and saw it tighten up as the slack came out of it. The sub began to lift as the cable tension on the mechanical claw increased. Kelleher compensated as the minisub's nose came up.

"Okay! Stop there."

The cable stopped tightening at once. He checked the grip of the claw and edged the joystick to starboard. The wall of pink bundles slid to the left as he neared the edge of the load.

Almost there. Another two feet and he could feel the current tugging at his starboard fin. He increased the push and moved out into the stream. Immediately, the sub began to yaw as the nose caught the current, but he was ready for it. He moved the sub forward along the load, concentrating on the center of the strapping where it crossed over the top of the load. He could see a gap between two of the bundles, an opening of less than six inches.

He extended the mechanical arm, holding the winch hook tight in the claw, working to hold the minisub in position with his left hand while he worked the claw arm with his right hand. A ribbon of silt was flowing across the canopy bubble, slightly obscuring his vision. The gap was close . . . a foot . . . six inches . . . he held the claw steady and touched the joystick gently—very close . . . almost there . . . the broad blade of the red hook dug into the gap and moved forward. He set it in and raised the claw, watching carefully as the red-painted hook engaged the network of nylon webbing. There was a spring-loaded retainer clip on the hook. He eased the throttle forward and put some more pressure on the retainer. There was an audible snap as the clip closed. He had done it. He released the claw and allowed the sub to slip sideways away from the pallet.

It looked solid. Time to set the hook.

"Rick."

*"I'm here."*

"The hook's in. Take it up slow."

*"Okay. She'll swing when she lifts. You better back off."*

"Ten four. Go slow, Rick. If I say stop, stop."

He let the sub slide away from the load about ten feet, keeping an eye on the hook. The long curve of the cable began to tighten again as Rick worked the winch. Up on *La Gaviota* he felt the hull take the weight as the cable began to tighten. Kelleher had estimated the load as twelve hundred pounds on the dock at Punta Guarico, but it would weigh a lot less in the water. Those bundles were shrink-wrapped in heavy pink plastic. Completely airtight. Kelleher could see where the material had been sucked in even tighter as the air trapped inside the bundles had compressed during the tumble into the deep.

Something didn't fit here. The pallet was loaded

with bundles that—inevitably—contained some air. While each bundle may have weighed around eighty pounds on dry land, it was entirely possible that each one of those bundles would have floated if it had been dropped overboard. Archimedes figured that out in the tub. And the buoyancy effect wouldn't be diminished simply because the bundles were down at 186 feet; compressed air was still air and even compressed air was still lighter than water. There were fifteen bundles on that pallet, each one of which was—presumably—buoyant.

So why wasn't the cargo floating?

Considering the problem, he recalled that the takeoff from Punta Guarico had been very difficult. The plane—normally an agile and powerful airframe—had lurched into the air like a Canada goose with a buttful of buckshot. At the time, he'd put it down to Geronimo's massive weight. Now that wasn't so convincing.

There were only two explanations: either the bundles carried something a great deal more dense than documents or paper, or the pallet weighed a lot more than it had to weigh. He tried to remember what the pallet actually looked like when he had seen it on board the plane. It had appeared to be some kind of light metal: aluminum or titanium. That made no sense. Either metal was much too light to hold this load down. So why was it still here?

He finally decided, the hell with it; they'd figure it out when they got it to the surface. The weight would be well within the winch-load rating. But when the cable pulled taut and the pallet righted, they'd have to factor in the sideways drag of a twenty-knot current. And the cable itself, which was run out to over three hundred feet. Three hundred feet of one-inch cable weighed five hundred pounds. The drag factor of the cargo pallet was an unknown, but if the numbers added up wrong, the results would be spectacular.

Kelleher watched as the curve in the cable gradually straightened out. The hook lifted slowly, set in tight, began to take the weight of the cargo load. He heard an ominous creaking as the straps shifted. The pallet groaned, a sound he could hear over the whir of the electric engines and the churning rumble of the props. A puff of silt rose up and flew away in the streaming current as the load shifted on the seafloor. The load began to rise and the pallet shifted again.

There was a gravelly rumble as a small avalanche of pebbles broke loose and tumbled down the slope. He backed away some more as the cable went taut. If it snapped, the backlash could smash the sub. The pallet shifted—then abruptly broke free of the bottom and came swinging massively toward him, a huge pendulum headed directly at the sub's canopy. Kelleher powered to port as the pallet swung heavily past his canopy, missing it by a couple of feet.

Up on the deck Rick saw the cable running forward through the water and he felt the whole ship tilting slightly to port as the winch took the load. The winch groaned, an animal sound, almost alive, the cable thrummed in the pulleys. He had a hand on the RELEASE lever. It wasn't the weight, it was the drag—the force of the twenty-knot current pulling at the load and straining the lift mechanism. If the deck tilted any more, or the cable snapped, they were in trouble.

*"Charlie, what's happening?"*

"It's loose. It's swinging. How is it up there?"

*"We're heeled over badly. But she's holding."*

"Tell Zeffi to take her forward with the current. That should ease the drag somewhat. And keep pulling her up."

Rick signaled to Zeffi, pumping his right hand and pointing to the bow. Zeffi turned the floodlights on and pushed the throttles. *La Gaviota*, still leaning to port, began to move through the water, chasing the cable. Rick watched the angle of the cable as they slipped through the water. It was very much like trying to land a marlin. If the marlin weighed two thousand pounds. The cable angle changed and when it reached nearly perpendicular, he signaled to Zeffi to slow her down. The winch groaned loudly as it took the load again.

A hundred and sixty feet down, Kelleher watched the pallet lifting up, swinging less now that they were out of the strongest part of the current, rising more steadily through the dark water. He was off the shelf and a long way out over the drop, following the movement of the ship overhead as Zeffi headed out into the channel. He could hear the cable creaking and the retaining straps on the pallet were stretched tight. But the load was holding.

"Zeffi."

*"Charlie?"*

"We're running way out into the channel."

*"I know."*

"Try to come around. Slowly, Zeffi. Slowly."

*"Okay."*

Zeffi turned the wheel a few degrees to starboard. The deck tilted crazily. The load was still dragging badly when they turned it back into the full force of the current. It was like trying to drag an umbrella through the water. Rick keyed his handset.

*"Charlie, she can't turn yet. The current is still too strong. The drag will pull us over."*

"We're over the Santaren Channel, Rick. If the cable snaps or the strapping goes, she drops thirteen hundred feet."

Kelleher was cruising a few yards away from the rising load, every nerve humming, willing the cable to hold. Underneath the sub there was nothing but black water.

*"It's no good,"* said Zeffi. *"The whole ship is listing."*

"Okay—put her back into the current," he said. "But try to take her up some more. The shorter the cable the less she'll swing and the stream seems to back off as you get closer to the surface."

Rick watched as the cable steadied and the angle went back to ninety degrees as Zeffi brought the boat around into the northeast, running with the current again. The winch had stopped groaning, and the deck tilt had diminished. Kelleher, hovering near the load, rising with it, began to breathe easier.

"Okay . . . it looks good. Steady as it goes."

The cable was nearly vertical, but as the load ascended, it was rising out of the worst of the current. It looked good. They were—

"*Charlie!*"

Zeffi's voice sounded thin and strained.

"What?"

"*Okay . . . there's something weird in the sonar here.*"

"Where?"

"*I can't tell what it is. Something strange.*"

"What's the bearing?"

Kelleher was staring at his own sonar screen. In the small red display, he saw only the luminous ruby sweep of the needle. There was nothing registering on the minisub's sonar but the stony cliff of the Cay Sal Bank a good five hundred yards to the east of his position. Zeffi's voice came back over the sub's speakers; this time her concern was palpable and growing.

"*The bearing . . . is one five six. Charlie, it's headed right at you. I can't tell what it is. The return is totally clouded.*"

Kelleher checked his screen again and saw nothing at all.

"I'm getting nothing, Zeffi. What is it? What do you see?"

Kelleher was thinking about Maybelline. It wasn't a pleasant thought. He knew he was safe—relatively safe—inside the fiberglass and steel hull, but Maybelline was a very impressive fish and she had a reputation for creative responses to vexing dinner-time questions. He craned his head and stared into the black water to his right, but he saw only a darkness rapidly filling up with an unidentified threat. Rick's voice came over the speaker, controlled but intense.

*"Charlie, whatever it is, it's coming right down the channel. It's moving at about fifteen knots and it's down around two hundred feet. It's six hundred yards out. Can you see anything?"*

Kelleher moved the joystick and put the nose of the sub around to starboard. There was still nothing on his . . . yes, there was something starting to register . . . oh Christ . . .

*"It's closing in fast, Charlie."*

"I've got it," said Kelleher.

He was staring at his sonar screen. The sonar field was rapidly filling up with an image, indistinct and shapeless, but definitely something real and it was moving very fast. Rick's voice came over the radio again, packed with urgent warning.

*"I'm getting an unidentifiable return at one hundred and ninety feet down and five hundred yards out. Closing directly on your position and steady at fifteen knots. You're right in its path, Charlie."*

Kelleher was already taking evasive action. He had pulled the joystick back and accelerated upward, his eye fixed on the red cloud growing larger in his screen, getting closer with every sweep of his sonar. Holding the stick close, his feet on the rudders, his breath coming in short sharp gasps, Kelleher counted off the seconds.

He was climbing at speed and the canopy was creaking with the force of the air expanding inside the sealed cockpit. His eardrums were starting to hurt and he could feel pressure building in his lungs. Exhale, Charlie. Exhale. He pushed the air out of his lungs as hard as he could and the pain inside his chest lessened.

Rising—still rising—

*"Charlie, it's almost on you. Keep climbing!"*

"I am climbing, people. Calm down."

Kelleher kept the sub's nose up, watching the black water rushing past the canopy and chasing his own gray cone of light upward out of the deep. More than a hundred feet above, in the pilot's deck on *La Gaviota*, Rick and Zeffi were standing at the controls and staring at their sonar screen. Kelleher's sub registered as a tiny packet of distinct green lines rising up through the hundred-foot level about fifty yards off their port side. They could even see the smaller sonar image of the cargo pallet itself, a squared-off boxy grid swinging in the current at a hundred and fifty feet down, the thin green return that was the cable running upward from it.

But spreading across the entire screen, less than a hundred yards off and closing in fast, was some sort of foggy green return running—as far as they could determine—generally southeast down the channel at a hundred and fifty feet, its probable course on a line running directly underneath the minisub.

"What is that thing?" asked Zeffi, her eyes locked on the screen, her voice strained and thin. The unknown bogey seemed to pulsate, changing its shape as it moved, swollen and egg-shaped, then drawn out and slender as a barracuda, never taking a recognizable form. Rick, his mind racing with possible interpretations, watched as the return withered into near-transparency and then blossomed like a sudden green lotus right across the upper half of his screen.

Looking at it, Rick felt the first tremor of an atavistic awe rising up, a shivering sensation of unreasoning fear that he recognized at once—although he had never before felt it—as the kind of terror brought by ghosts and monsters: simple superstitious horror.

"I have no idea," he said, fighting the loss of control. "It's not a boat of some kind. There's no engine noise at all. No sound at all, not even whale cry, or the beeping sound porpoises make. Just absolute silence. It could be a thermocline—a barrier line created where two bodies of water with different temperatures collide. It could even be superheated water from a subterranean vent. Christ, Zeffi, I don't know. I can't read it at all. Maybe a big school of fish. Maybe a whale. I have no idea. It's like nothing I've ever seen before."

"If it's a whale, is it hunting Charlie?"

"Could be. It may think he's a dolphin or a tuna. I don't know. I don't even know if it *is* a whale, Zeffi. The return is . . . unreadable."

Kelleher's voice came over the speakers again, calm, controlled, the voice of the airline pilot talking the passengers through unexpected turbulence.

*"Okay, folks . . . let's calm down. I think I see it."*

Rick looked at the screen and saw the two images converging.

*"Whatever it is, it's eighty yards away, Charlie. It's going to pass right underneath you. Can you see what it is?"*

*"I'm trying to get the lights on it. Keep your eye on the ball there, Rick. Have you still got the cargo?"*

"Yes."

*"Make sure you stay with it—damn!"*

The image field bloomed into a bright green flare—they heard a low buzzing hiss that rose in intensity until it shook the speakers and then the two sonar images—the minisub and the green cloud—merged into one return, shapeless and shifting, then Kelleher's radio transmission disappeared into a sustained burst of loud static—they picked out a couple of words—*Rick*—*passing too*—more static and a loud humming sound that burred out from the speakers, underneath that a faint signal—Kelleher's voice—*pressure*—*seven*—*crackle*—*four three*. Rick keyed the handset, speaking slowly, his breathing unsteady, his tone unconvincingly calm.

"Charlie, can you read us?"

A huge burst of static . . . and then silence.

"Charlie, come in?"

"Rick," said Zeffi. "Look at the cargo."

Rick glanced away from the pulsating sonar return where Kelleher's minisub image had merged into the unknown bogey. He saw the thin green line of the cable stretching away down into the deep, but at the end of it there was no solid square shape. Only an indistinct tangle. A few seconds later, a low but extremely powerful wave reached *La Gaviota*'s port side, a surging groundswell that shoved her directly sideways for several yards, the deck lifting underneath them as the boat heeled over sharply.

"What the hell was that?" asked Zeffi.

"It felt like a pressure wave of some sort."

"Pressure from what?"

"Maybe an earthquake. A plate shifting."

Zeffi was staring down at the sonar screen.

"Rick, where's Charlie?"

They both looked for that clear tubular shape outlined in sharp green lines, but it had never emerged from that bizarre cloudy return that was filling up the sonar screen like a living green tide. In a few seconds it had completely obscured the sonar display. All they could see was a field of glowing green light, empty of detail. The speakers were hissing steadily, the pitch almost painful. Rick turned the volume down, gave Zeffi a look. She was shocked but steady. He put a hand on her shoulder, felt her muted tremble.

"Take the wheel," said Rick. "I'm going to run the cable in."

Out on the bow the fog was still lying heavily on the ocean, but the surface was heaving and rough as some kind of powerful wave force moved through the water.

As Rick leaned over the railing and looked down into the water, an explosion of air bubbles erupted through the surface, a huge burst that stretched from the cutwater all the way to the stern, as if the entire boat was adrift in boiling white water.

He felt another, a deeper, chill run along his belly and shoulders and had the fleeting impression that there was some alien unknowable *thing* moving through the deeps right underneath their keel. He had never seen anything like it, and it quite literally chilled him to the spine. He stood by the turning drum and watched as the cable slithered up out of the water, dripping, throwing salty spray as it spooled onto the drum. There seemed to be only slight resistance and hardly any drag at all. Rick's heart grew heavier with every yard that clicked off on the indicator. As he watched the cable spinning onto the drum, he felt the heaving waves subside and the hull steadying.

Whatever was still on the end of this line, there was a lot less than they had started out with. A few seconds later, the end of the cable broke the surface and rose up into the glow of the floodlight. It hung there above the churning water, spinning gently. It was the pallet itself, still intact. But the nylon strappings that had secured the bundles were hanging loosely off the steel frame, snapped and frayed and shredded. One nylon strap was still looped around the cable hook.

But everything else was gone. All fifteen packages had tumbled free of the pallet and were lost in the Gulf Stream. He swung the pallet inboard and lashed it into place beside the winch. Trying to shift it into position by himself he realized it was brutally heavy.

It was twelve inches thick, six feet square, and made of solid metal plates that looked something like titanium.

Very overbuilt for the job. A wooden pallet would have done the job as well and weighed a hell of a lot less. As he knelt by the pallet, a second pressure wave, this one much weaker, rolled underneath the keel and rocked the boat. Then the fog settled back on the deck and the night closed in around him. He got up in the bitter yellow glare of the floodlight and walked back into the pilot's cabin.

Zeffi was sitting at the wheel, her face drawn and weary. The muttering burble of the engines coming up through the wooden hull was the only sound in the room other than the constant hiss of static coming from the bulkhead speaker. As Rick reached her she keyed the handset again and held it close to her lips.

"Charlie, this is Zeffi. Please answer . . ."

The static hiss wavered and flickered slightly. Rick looked at the sonar screen. It was clearing up, the green cloud receding quickly as the distance increased. The unknown return had passed directly below their hull at a depth of a hundred and eighty feet and a speed in excess of twenty knots. It was moving steadily away down the Santaren Channel, visible now that the screen was clearing, but still a maddeningly indistinct shape. As it pulled away down the channel, the hissing gradually subsided. A few minutes passed and the screen was back to normal. The speakers were silent. Aside from this mysterious return, fading to nothing, there were only the cliffs and valleys of the seabed and what looked like a small school of fish far off in the channel. "Charlie, please answer," said Zeffi.

Silence.

The hiss and crackle of random static.

"Charlie . . . please answer . . . Charlie . . . ?"

# DRIFT

For more than five hours Rick searched the rolling sea and scoured the sands far below in a profound and weary silence, his heart a leaden weight and his mind empty of thought, the only sound the dull rumble of the twin diesels as *La Gaviota* worked her slow and ponderous way through the building swells, her narrow bow pushing the seas aside, a constant spray of ghostly white water flying out from her cutwater. As the night died away, around the boat the light had changed slowly. When they began the search for the minisub, there had been only that all-surrounding blackness and the fog itself, glowing in the gray funnel of the spotlight as Rick played it over the surface of the water. Now, as the polished brass chronometer above the pilot's station reached 8:20 in the morning, the fog was thinning out rapidly, had become a thin veil of mist suffused in a pale pink glow as an unseen sun rose above a horizon still only theoretical, like a hooker's promise of a day that might never come.

Rick's head was pounding with fatigue, his eyes burning with the effort of looking. Behind him, on the settee, Zeffi lay wrapped in a blood-stained pink comforter, the same one she had used to cover Kelleher's naked and battered body when they had pulled him off the jetty back at Key Biscayne a thousand years ago. Across from Zeffi's mounded form, shapeless underneath the quilt, Carlito Vargas sat upright in the other couch, cuffed and bound, his head nodding as he dozed, a towel around his shoulders, in torn and bloodied jeans. As he had for the last hour, Rick picked up the radio handset again and keyed the thumb-switch, an action that had become increasingly robotic as hope had died inside him.

"Charlie . . . this is *La Gaviota*. Come in."

And as it had for the last five hours, the radio gave him back only a static-filled hissing silence.

"Charlie, this is *La Gaviota*. Come back?"

Rick was using the citizen's band frequency that connected only with the minisub. Now and then he switched to the main SSB at 2,182 kilohertz, trying to pick up any information about the situation in the larger world outside this floating island lost inside the glowing pink mist all around them. Twenty minutes ago, 0800 hours, the American ultimatum had run out. After that moment, as Elliott Lazarus had asserted, the United States would take "severe but unspecified action" against Cuba in an effort to force the Cuban government to surrender two American citizens, Jake Seigel and Cory Bryant. Whatever the

United States had planned, they were going to do it right here in the Florida Straits.

And as far as he was concerned, Rick was ready to let them do it. Losing Kelleher like this had drained him of resolve, emptied him of the arguably lunatic belief that he could ever have accomplished anything at all. Zeffi Calderas had been right all along; he should have seen that days ago. He might have saved both of them a great deal of pain.

Yes, Charlie Kelleher might have died an ugly death inside that big house on Key Biscayne if he and Zeffi hadn't freed him. But he was dead anyway, wasn't he? They had only prolonged his life by a few hours. Whatever it was that had come down the Santaren Channel—and they still had no idea what that . . . *thing* . . . had been—it had ripped the cargo loose with the force of its passing and very likely sent Kelleher's sub spinning down into the depths of the channel, out of control, breaking up, lost. If that's what happened, then Kelleher's death was probably as terrible as the death he would have met at the hands of Carlito Vargas and his associates back in that big white mansion at 216 Coral Key Drive. Futility was not Rick Broca's best emotion; he did it badly, he was resentful and grudging, resisting it every foot of the way. That was why, a few minutes after the last try, he sighed deeply, rubbed his belly where the bandages around his waist were cutting into his wound and keyed the handset again.

"Charlie, this is *La Gaviota*. Come in."

More hissing crackle . . . a few weak clicks from some distant repeater—more likely from a solar flare—and then that slow reptilian exhalation of empty static that he'd been listening to for the last five hours. Out of habit more than interest, he switched back over to the single sideband channels and immediately cut into this transmission.

"—*ota* repeat La Gaviota *a donde?* La Gaviota, *estamos aquí a dónde—ola, Carlito—estamos aquí. Que bola?*"

At the sound, both Zeffi and Carlito Vargas had jerked upright, Zeffi's hair wild and her face still creased from the quilt, Vargas's one visible eye widening. Zeffi held her hand up to him warningly and jumped off the settee, dragging the quilt along behind her as she crossed to the pilot's chair.

"Are you going to answer, Rick?"

"That's why *he's* still here," said Rick, indicating Vargas.

"You can't let him answer," she said. "It was Charlie he was afraid of. He'll warn them somehow. Have you heard anything?"

Rick shook his head, his face drawn and weary.

"Of Charlie? Nothing," he spoke, in a low whisper. "Honey, we have to respond."

"Then you do it. Not him."

"My Spanish sucks canal water. It has to be Vargas."

"*Ola*—La Gaviota. *Responda por favor. Estoy—*"

"Please, Rick. You have to say . . . what was the word?"

"Now would be a good time to remember it," said Rick, very aware of Vargas across the room, of his bright attention.

Zeffi, sensing this, stepped over to the man and put Rick's battered Colt up against his forehead, pressing the muzzle in tight, jamming his head back against the paneling.

"What's the word?" she hissed at him.

"*Yoruba,*" he managed to say through gritted teeth. Zeffi was hurting him a lot and he wanted very much one day to repay the debt.

Rick thumbed the switch, raised the mike.

Zeffi stopped him.

"No! Not *yoruba*. It was . . . *por yemaya.*"

"Ya-may-yah?"

"Yes. Charlie got it out of him. It was *por yemaya!*"

"Okay—Carlito, a warning here. You speak one word, she'll kill you right there. You follow?"

Vargas, staring into Zeffi's cold green eyes over the blue steel barrel of the Colt, shrugged and leaned backward into the couch.

Rick keyed the transmission.

"*Ola—esto es* La Gaviota. *Por Yemaya.*"

The response was instant.

"*Viva La Señora de Regla! Que bola, bonco?*"

Rick was manipulating the "squelch" button to inject some much-needed static into the irritatingly clear transmission. Where were these guys? Close? He was on single sideband out here. They could be a hundred miles away, or they could be just over the horizon.

"*Sta*—crackle, hiss—*y usted. A*—hiss—*donde ustedes?*"

"*Somos en Habana! A donde Señor Suerta? No esta aquí?*"

"They want to know where Narcisse Suerta is," said Zeffi. The voice went on.

"*La flota Americana nos bloqueara por la mañana. ¿Dondé está el cargo? ¿Usted lo ha encontrado?*"

"The cargo," said Zeffi, in a whisper. "They want to know if you found the cargo. They say the time is running out fast. Something about the American Navy coming at dawn."

"*Todavía no,*" said Rick, grinding the squelch key back and forth, filling the transmission with a random interfering hiss.

"*Buscamos—somos—*" Rick cut the SEND button in midsentence, sat back in the chair, blew out a ragged breath. The receiver crackled right back with an urgent response.

"*Digame—Carlito—a dónde está Señor Suerta—*"

Rick changed the channel back to the minisub's CB frequency and the stream of insistent Spanish cut off abruptly.

"What do you think?" he asked Zeffi.

"I don't know," she said, still pressing the muzzle of the Colt into Carlito's forehead. "They don't seem to know anything about what happened in Key Biscayne. Maybe Suerta really is dead. You tried to warn them, didn't you, Carlito?"

Rick saw her trigger finger whitening as she increased the pressure on the trigger.

"Zeffi, don't."

Her face was set and pale, her fading bruises vivid

as her blood pressure rose. She was going to do it. Even Vargas could see that.

His eye closed and he lowered his head.

"It doesn't matter," he said, with his head still down. "I will die either way. Chango Roja will send the punishment. I have seen this. There is nothing to be done. I am dead."

"Zeffi," Rick began—and again that faint sound came out of the speaker, familiar but meaningless, the same series of barely audible clicks that Rick had been hearing intermittently for the last few hours. It was a solar flare. Or distant lightning. Perhaps a fuse somewhere below getting ready to pop.

Yet . . . was it oddly rhythmic? Repetitive?

Rick grabbed the mike.

"Charlie . . . is that you?"

The speaker filled with a burst of static and settled into a prolonged hissing that wavered and dipped. Rick remembered the squelch controller, adjusted it to normal. The transmission cleared up and resolved itself into another series of clicks, again very faint, but undeniably regular. The pattern seemed to gain conviction with Rick's response and repeated itself quite steadily.

A click followed by a pause and then a click, a pause and another click. Over and over again. After the third repetition Rick recognized the Morse Code signal of a dash and a dot followed by another dash. It was the signal to transmit.

"It's Charlie," said Rick, his heart leaping inside his chest.

"Charlie, my Morse sucks. If you can hear me, click twice."

*Click. Click.*

"Okay. Two for yes, one for no. Are you afloat?"

*Click. Click.*

"Do you know where you are?"

*Click.*

"Are you in deep water?"

*Click. Click.*

"Do any of your instruments work?"

*Click.*

"Are you hurt?"

*Click.*

Rick turned the radar on and set it to a thirty-mile range. He watched the screen as the arm swept across the dim orange field, picking out the shoals of the Dog Rocks far to the southwest of their position. Rick had been searching for the minisub in the northeasterly flow of the Gulf Stream for over five hours—on the assumption that Kelleher was drifting inside it, either on the surface or on the bottom somewhere along that track.

They had cruised a long way in their gloomy, hopeless search and were well out into the Santaren Channel, running northeast a few miles off the edge of the Great Bahama Bank.

Kelleher seemed to be signaling that he was afloat but without instruments, which meant he was likely without much battery power either. So he was basically a big log drifting in the Gulf Stream and that meant he was probably close. The weakness of the CB signal supported that interpretation; they'd have to be within a few miles to pick it up at all.

Zeffi had come to stand beside him, her face bright with renewed hope as he studied the radar sweep, watching for the tiniest blip. If the sub was floating—and Kelleher indicated that it was—very little of it would be above the waterline. Finding it against the litter of tiny rocks and shoals that studded the radar return all along the edge of the Great Bahama archipelago would be like finding a single diamond in a bed of gravel. But he was still alive. So far.

"Charlie, is the sub stable?"

*Click.*

"Is it taking on water?"

*Click. Click.*

Christ . . . he was sinking.

"Do you have flotation gear?"

*Click.*

"Charlie, we're real close. Just hang on. We're coming."

*Click. Click.*

And they had better be damn quick. So where was he?

According to their instruments, the Gulf Stream was running northeast at an average speed of fifteen knots. They had lost contact with the minisub—Rick checked the chronometer—exactly five hours and twenty-six minutes ago at a position about three miles north-northeast of the Dog Rocks.

"Zeffi, see if they have a marine chart for all of this sector. It'll be number one one zero one three."

Zeffi riffled through the rolled-up charts on the navigator's table, found one detailing the entire region from the tip of Florida to the Grand Cayman islands south of Cuba. She spread it out on the table and looked expectantly across at Rick.

"Okay . . . find the Dog Rocks."

"Got them."

"Look for those unexploded bombs."

"Here," she said, laying a pencil point on the tiny dotted circle.

"All right . . ." Rick paused, checking the GPS indicator.

"Okay . . . we've been cruising northeast for five hours and thirteen minutes on compass bearing three one at five knots per hour. But we've been doing that inside the Gulf Stream, which is moving at fifteen nautical miles an hour, which gives us a net forward motion over the ground of twenty nautical miles an hour . . ."

Rick paused again, working it out. He was using dead reckoning—a navigational calculation that combined current, hull speed, and wind drift to arrive at an actual distance over the seafloor—and although it looked simple, there were a lot of variables. In this situation, an error of a few hundred yards would be critical.

"So we've covered . . . what? Over a hundred nautical miles," said Zeffi, working the compass and the dividers. "That puts us two miles off the Riding Rocks at the edge of the banks. The chart says there's a navigation light on the Riding Rocks. Ask Charlie if he can see a light anywhere on the horizon line."

Rick picked up the mike again.

"Charlie, this is Rick. You okay?"

*Click. Click.*

"Can you see a navigation light anywhere on your horizon?"

A pause . . .

*Click.*

"Okay, Charlie. Wait one."

"Look," said Zeffi, "we've been cruising at five knots. Charlie has been drifting without power. So he's only making whatever the current is making, right? He's moving inside the current."

"Yes. Which means he's covered . . . at the most more than seventy-eight nautical miles."

"Less if the sub is dragging."

"Yes, but we don't have to think about the windage. The breeze has been light all morning and that sub is probably low in the water."

"So where is he?" asked Zeffi.

"Start where we lost the sub . . ."

"Here. Just by the unexploded bombs?"

"Northeast of that. Right at the curve of the banks."

"Okay. Got it."

"Find compass bearing three one and draw a line along that bearing for seventy-eight nautical miles. Where are you?"

Zeffi worked with her head down, the navigator's light shining in her hair, her hands moving in the glowing circle on the chart.

"Here we are. On the edge of the banks, a shoal called Munnings Knoll, near Orange Cay."

Rick looked up at the brightening sky. The sun was well up and the last of the pink haze was rapidly burning away.

"So we've overrun him."

"Yes."

Rick keyed the mike.

"Charlie, you there?"

*Click. Click.*

"Is the water under you deep blue?"

*Click. Click.*

"Are the waves long rollers?"

*Click. Click.*

"Are there smaller top waves that seem to be running diagonal to the main waves?"

A pause . . . Rick could see Kelleher in his mind's eye, leaning out to study the surface of the ocean around him.

*Click. Click.*

"Are those surface waves running westerly?"

*Click. Click.*

"Okay . . . those are reflections from the shallows. They're bouncing off the shoals and coming back out to the channel. That means you're close to the banks. Can you see the sun?"

*Click. Click.*

"Okay. Look into the east. Look for a faint green glow far off in the east. In the sky above the horizon line. There might be a bank of clouds above it; the green will be on the underside of the clouds too. Do you see it?"

*Click. Click.*

"Good . . . that's Andros Island. She glows green in the east around this time of the morning. You can see it if there's a mist. Is that green glow due east of you?"

*Click.*

"Is it in the southeast?"

*Click. Click.*

Rick reached for the wheel, cranked it hard to starboard, and gunned the diesels so hard that Zeffi stumbled to keep her balance and Vargas rolled right off the settee, landing on the teak deck with a meaty *thwack,* groaning in complaint. White water blew out around their stern as the bow rose up and the boat shot forward. Rick raised his voice to be heard above the deep roaring of the twin diesels.

"Charlie, you're in deep water a few miles west of Munnings Knoll in the Great Bahama Bank. We're less than fifteen miles away from you. We'll be there in minutes. Can you signal us with anything?"

*Click.*

"Think, Charlie. We need a signal. Do you have an air horn?"

*Click.*

"A cloth? A rag?"

*Click.*

"Zeffi, get the flare box."

Zeffi ran down the companionway, fumbled in the crate by the engine compartment, returned at a run with a box of emergency flares. She set them down in front of Rick.

"Charlie, in about five minutes, Zeffi's going to send up a flare. It will be red. If you see it, click twice. Got it? Five minutes. That cheap Timex of yours still ticking?"

*Click. Click.*

"Five minutes, Charlie. A red flare."

*Click. Click.*

They ran *La Gaviota* at her best speed of thirty knots, faster than she'd been run in years; the boat seemed to love it, the classic Chris-Craft slicing through the rollers with twin bright rainbows of diamonds flying in two clean pure arcs off her lean destroyer bow and the carved narrow keel hissing through the sparkling blue water, the deep vibrato of her engines rising up through the wooden decks and humming in their bones.

Rick leaned over the wheel with his hard club-fighter's face set and his blue eyes narrowed, scanning the distant horizon as they boomed into the southeast toward the edge of the Bahama Bank under a tourmaline sky streaked with opalescent clouds. Zeffi was out on the bow, braced against the taffrail forward of the winch, the stubby flare gun in her left hand, her right hand raised to shade her eyes as she watched the knife-edge demarcation between sea and sky, where whitecaps showed as tiny white ripples against the shimmering deep blue of the ocean. Rick checked the chronometer and looked at the hull speed, reached for the loudspeaker mike.

"Okay, Zeffi. Fire one."

She turned in the wind with her red hair flying and waved to him, took a brace on the bow railing and raised the squat pistol-shaped flare gun into the sky. The gun popped and a brilliant red flare flew straight up into the blue sky, streaking through a flock of gulls and scattering them like scraps of white paper. Rick turned the speaker volume to FULL and listened for a signal from Charlie Kelleher.

Nothing but silence.

He ran off another five nautical miles on the indicator and told Zeffi to fire a second flare. It sizzled skyward two thousand feet and cut a slow ruby arc across the pale blue sky as it fell back into the sea a half-mile away. And the speaker clicked twice. Two hard decisive snaps that rattled the cloth over the speaker above his head.

"Charlie, you saw that?"

*Click, Click.*

If a man could signal jubilation with a dry electric snap, Kelleher had managed it, the two crisp signals coming in a rapid sequence. Rick felt his lungs easing as the fear and the tension drained out of him. He got on the loud-hailer to Zeffi.

"He saw that. Send another."

Zeffi fired the third flare. It snaked into the sky and fell lazily southward, a spark of bright red light twinkling into the churning blue of the rising seas.

*Click click click click.*

"Charlie, don't blow your batteries. Click once if

we're north of you, twice if we're east, three for south, four if we're to the west."

*Click. Click.*

Rick was running southeast. He told Zeffi to hang on and cranked the wheel to port. The hull canted starboard and a huge white wall of churning foam flew out from her bow as she changed course at speed. Running straight again, she was head-on into a running green sea filled with white rollers, and she banged over each of them with a hard smacking explosion of white foam as she cut through.

Zeffi was holding on with two hands and bending at the knees as the hull lifted and slammed down and lifted again. Rick could see the rigid concentration in her body as she watched the incoming sea, looking for a small black shape somewhere in that huge glittering plain of light and color. She turned out of the wind and waved to him, and then pointed out to sea a few degrees off the starboard bow. Rick heard her clear voice floating back to him on the rushing wind, a faint cry like a gull's call. *"There! Rick, there!"*

Rick strained to see what she was seeing, scanning the channel to his right . . . and saw a tiny black dot rise up out of a corrugated plain of churning waves—it disappeared as it sank into a trough and he lost it again. Zeffi was still calling to him in that faint ringing voice, then he saw the black sliver again, a dull streak silhouetted briefly against a rising green wave, a flicker of movement in the center.

*Click click click click click.*

"We see you, Charlie. We see you."

*La Gaviota* boomed over the water, running straight at the tiny black shape. Rick watched it with his heart in his throat, willing it to stay afloat for two more minutes—one more minute—he had the throttles pressed down so hard his knuckles were white and the hull was booming like a bass drum as the boat pounded through the sea, leaving a spreading white arrowhead wake behind her as straight as a thrown lance. Now the black shape was clearer and he could see the smaller black outline of Kelleher's body in the low-lying hull. He slowed the boat to a cruise, afraid that the forward wash of the hull would swamp the fragile hulk of the minisub.

In another minute they had him along the port side—Kelleher's grim face wreathed in a sun-burned grimace showing white teeth and eyes hooded against the hard sun. Zeffi, standing at the portside gangway, threw him a long loop of white line. It landed with a splash in the water beside him, and Kelleher snatched it up, pulled it so tight that it snapped up out of the water and ran in a straight line from his hands to Zeffi's, dripping beads of water. Waves were breaking over the minisub as they pulled him in. It tipped and flooded and Kelleher was in the water as the minisub sank underneath him.

The sub slipped beneath the waves with a ripple and a breathy explosion of trapped air; then he was

alone in the heaving seas and Zeffi was pulling him
into the boarding ladder. She caught him by the
hand, literally jerking him bodily out of the water.
They fell back together on the gently rocking deck
and he was safe on board again.

# ODALYS

It was a straight run of fifty-three nautical miles from Munning's Knoll, where they'd fished Kelleher out of the water, to a little-known supply port on the northwestern tip of Andros Island known as Flat Iron Shoals. Rick had been fretting about their dwindling reserve of diesel fuel ever since they started their search for Kelleher; the Garrison Bight brigade of roustabouts and rumrunners had told him various lurid stories about the semipiratical nature of Flat Iron Shoals—a smugglers hangout, a no-questions-asked semilegal backwater—so he figured the run for fuel was worth the risk of out-harbor gossip reaching back to the mainland. While they were making the run, Kelleher lay back on the settee behind the wheel and laid out the whole story, while he worked his way through a large glass jug filled to the brim with cold sangria.

"It was the *Louisiana*," he said. "I saw the hull

484

numbers. I called them out to you, didn't I? *S S B N* seven four three? Before I rolled and lost her."

"You broke up," said Rick, shaking his head. "All we heard was static. Why couldn't we get a sonar return?"

"She was using her Escape and Evasion systems. The *Louisiana* is a nuclear missile submarine. She's attached to the Sixth Fleet out of Norfolk. I even know her captain, Cyrus Kaltenborn. I flew off the *Kitty Hawk* when he was her XO in the South China Sea. She's packed with . . . well, with the kind of hardware that can cloak her presence under any circumstances. Don't ask me what they are because I don't know. Anyway, her sensors would have picked up the sonar pulse off *La Gaviota* and she'd jam back automatically. If Cy wanted to cloak her completely, she'd register as an indistinct shape—maybe a school of fish, maybe a warm-air anomaly. These nuclear steam turbine subs run totally silent so you'd never hear a whisper. The props are—let's say they're designed to make no noise at all, even at flank speed. They don't cavitate, they don't rumble. Huge props and they turn in total silence. Amazing thing to watch. So, if you kept scanning her, they'd up the evasion systems and jam you out totally. The jamming would flood your screen with unreadable anomalous returns. It's routine procedure."

"I've run near U.S. Navy subs before and never been jammed."

"You heard the radio. The Navy's blockading Cuba. They always jam when they're in a combat deployment. I guess she was simply running down the channel to get into position and we had the bad luck to be in her way. Man, you should have seen her when she came out of the dark. High as an office tower and that big black nose—she's almost six hundred feet long, displaces eighteen thousand tons. It was the bow wave that did me in. Along with the cargo pallet. Shoved me out of the way like I was a cow on a railroad bridge. I spun out and the canopy cracked wide open. Drowned the electrics right there. It was all I could do to blow the lift tanks and hope for the best."

"Couldn't they tell you were there?" asked Zeffi. "I thought these things were bulging with sensors. They ran right over you."

"Under me, actually. It was like riding a rocket. I'm amazed the sub held together as well as it did. By the time the pressure wave coughed me up on the surface I was a mile out in the stream and bailing for my life. Did they pick me up on their screens? I'd say yes. Did they know what I was? Maybe. Did they care? Nope."

"How'd you make that signal?" asked Rick. "The click?"

"The CB radio was in a portable waterproof module. The exterior antenna was gone and the max power was only eight watts. But I turned it up as high as it would go and kept keying the transmit button. I knew you'd be looking for me, and I hoped you'd figure out what the clicking was."

"Why didn't you use Morse?"

Kelleher gave him a look.

"What? Broadcast an SOS or send some other help signal in Morse? That would bring on any boat in the area. I only wanted to hear from you. So I clicked in a pattern I figured you'd recognize as deliberate. And you picked it up."

"Took me long enough."

"Doesn't matter. You found me."

"Yeah . . . and we lost the cargo."

"Maybe," said Zeffi. "It's still out there."

"The bundles?"

"Yes. You said they'd float and perhaps that's what they're doing. They're floating somewhere in the Gulf Stream. We could go look for them."

Rick gave it some thought while Kelleher finished off the sangria. Finally he shook his head.

"We can't, babe. You're talking about a stretch of ocean sixty miles wide and a drift path that is at least a hundred miles long. Do the math. We'd need a fleet to search a grid like that. And in the meantime we'd have the U.S. Navy asking us what the hell we were doing in a blockade zone. Not a chance, Zeffi."

"We found Charlie."

"I clicked," said Kelleher. "The packages don't."

"How long would they last out there anyway?" asked Rick.

"It was heavy-grade shrink-wrap. Salt-resistant. Months, I'd say. Possibly years. Provided they don't snag on something, or get chewed up by some freighter's prop wash."

"Would they stay more or less together?" asked Zeffi.

Kelleher thought about it.

"Define together," said Kelleher. "Chaos theory."

"Chaos theory?"

"Each packet will have surface anomalies that would affect the way it drifted," said Rick. "And there are variations inside the Gulf Stream. Water temperature. Salinity. Groundswells versus crossing waves. Some of the packages would weigh more than others, so they'd float lower in the water, which would affect the way the wind worked on them. Given a long enough time, they'd gradually drift apart. Look out there. Every day—every hour— the sea changes. Never the same twice. As far as we're concerned, those packages are off on an around-the-world cruise. Some of them will make it to shore on the coast of Scotland next spring and some of them may get snagged on a Bimini reef later tonight. Either way, for our purposes, they're gone."

There was a silence while the three of them considered the consequences of that loss. There were no happy interpretations.

"Man," said Rick, finally, "is this project cursed?"

"No," said Kelleher, shaking his head and smiling. "It's business as usual. I've never been on a black op that didn't have at least three screwups bad enough to make your ears bleed. You cope and 'Charlie-Mike' it like a good little spook."

"'Charlie-Mike it,'" said Zeffi. "What's that?"

"Continue the Mission. Charlie. Mike."

Zeffi rolled her eyes at that and said, "Now what?"

"Now?" said Rick, his attention alternating between Kelleher's story, the dwindling supply of fuel in the tanks, as well as the distance between *La Gaviota* and the narrow stretch of palm-lined shore that was barely visible on the horizon line. "Now we find some diesel and the propane tank is empty. We need supplies."

"And soap," said Zeffi, looking at them both in a meaningful way. "And shampoo. And fresh water. Enough to shower in."

Rick had been right to worry, because they reached the Flat Iron Shoals marina on diesel fumes—*La Gaviota* literally ran dry, coughing out as they were coasting through the breakwater a hundred yards from the dock. An onshore breeze and what was left of their forward motion kept them gliding across the placid diamond-clear water of the inner lagoon toward the tiny clapboard village scattered across the limestone plateau; the same steady breeze ruffled the dry leaves of a few stunted palms that marked the line of the white sandy beach.

They touched the end of the dock at noon precisely, the only big boat around other than a battered wooden junk sagging at anchor fifty feet off the dock. The black morning shadows had all crawled under the available cover; the hard white light of midday bled the color out of the town, firing the stony pavement with dry heat.

The windows and doors of the rambling collection of painted shacks were black holes in the bleached white walls. No one was out in the cobbled street, but they could hear tinny music coming from the Black Dog as they tied *La Gaviota* to a sagging piling and set the spring lines to keep her from grinding at the jetty.

Since Zeffi was staying on board to guard Vargas while they hunted down the dockmaster to locate some fuel, Rick left her with his Colt semi-auto. Although they still had Narcisse Suerta's SIG-Sauer, they were out of nine mill rounds, but Kelleher had found a big Smith revolver in one of the staterooms on *La Gaviota*, along with a hundred rounds of .357 Magnum. He took that with him as they went up into the town looking for fuel and supplies.

If there were any to be had.

Looking around at the huts and lean-tos and the rusting fuel pumps on the dock, Rick wondered if there was anyone here at all. The place looked like a ghost town, the kind of dusty outpost village you'd find on the lost coast of Belize or along the barren desert beaches of the southern Baja. No customs officer showed up to take their papers as they stepped out into the sunlight, but a large gimp-legged tabby cat with one yellow eye and a blood-stained coat that looked like a flop-house bath mat limped slowly over to the gangway, yowling at them as Kelleher and Rick came down onto the dock. The stray cat, ignored by both men, took a resentful swipe at Rick's leg as he walked past, getting one claw tangled in Rick's frayed cuff.

Rick reached down, deftly snagged the cat by the

scruff of his neck, hoisted him up to eye level, a nimble move the cat repaid by trying to slice Rick's nose off. He pulled his face back in time to feel the cat's second strike whisper past his eye. The animal twisted in Rick's grip, amazingly strong. Rick held him at arm's length, watching the animal struggle to get his hind claws into any available flesh. His jaws were half-open showing a set of fangs that would have made a vampire sick with envy; he was hissing at them like a boiling rat, his one yellow eye slit almost shut, the other puffy and sealed with dried blood, his tattered ears flat against his delta-shaped skull.

Kelleher, who had walked away toward the bar, looked back.

"Rick, I need a drink. Throw the little freak in the bay."

But Rick continued to hold the cat up, studying him.

"Charlie, guess who this is?"

Kelleher came back and gave the yowling ball of evil intentions a closer look. Comprehension dawned slowly in his drawn unshaven face; he smiled suddenly.

"Is this Cisco?"

"I think it is. I think it is. Damn, Cisco, is that you?"

The cat stopped struggling in Rick's grip, emitted a low yowling growl that rose through the octaves and ended with a steam-whistle shriek that brought Zeffi out onto the portside deck.

"Rick, what are you doing to that cat?"

Rick held him up for Zeffi to see.

"Who is this, babe?"

Zeffi shaded her eyes against the flat white light. "Bring him here."

Rick walked him back to the rail. Zeffi leaned over and inspected him closely, her face breaking into a wide grin.

"I think it's Cisco. What happened to his eye?"

Rick folded the cat under his arm, locking him down while he tried to pry open the cat's left eye, swollen shut under a mound of puffy tissue. He got it partially open. Cisco yowled with pain.

"It's in there. He's been scratched. Finally lost a fight. You really think it's Cisco?"

Zeffi came down the gangway and took the cat out of Rick's hands. The cat immediately closed its one good eye and settled into Zeffi's softest places with what could only be taken as a look of pure self-satisfaction. Zeffi put her face in his fur, breathed him in, something neither man would have done for a case of Cuervo.

Two cases maybe. No. Three.

"I think it is . . . where did you find him?"

"Where do you think? He was waiting by the dock."

"How did he get here?"

Rick was silent for a moment, looking at the cat, who showed every sign of falling happily asleep with his ugly mug buried in Zeffi's left breast—who wouldn't?—and considered the variables.

"Charlie, did you ever ask Vargas what happened to Cisco?"

"Never occurred to me."

"I think Cisco recognized the boat."

*"La Gaviota?"*

"Yeah. It was the boat they used to take down *Cagancho,* wasn't it? Vargas told you that, didn't he?"

Kelleher nodded.

"Which means *La Gaviota* put into this port."

"At least once."

"Which means . . . I don't know what it means."

"Neither do I. Let's go find out."

"You two do that," said Zeffi, more interested in Cisco than in either of them. "I'm going to take him inside. He needs some attention."

"Looks to me like he's getting all the attention he wants," said Kelleher, looking at Cisco's face buried in her breast.

"He's frightened," said Zeffi.

"So am I," said both men, nearly in unison. Zeffi gave them both a warning look and walked back up the gangway, cooing softly in Cisco's ear. Both men watched her go, admiring her geometry.

"When I die . . ." said Kelleher.

"Me too."

The interior of the Black Dog was darker than its name. They stood in the doorway, waiting for their eyes to adjust to the shadowy room. The place smelled of salt spray, spilled tequila, rotting wood. A long rickety bar fronted with corrugated iron and topped with a slab of wood six inches thick ran the length of the rear wall, in front of which an ad hoc collection of stools and chairs were arranged in no particular order. Over the bar a string of Japanese paper lanterns hung crazily askew, swinging softly in the wind off the sea, casting a shifting mix of multi-colored light down on the scarred and battered surface of the bar. A few card tables and some folding chairs had been set up around the room, which was floored with a combination of beach sand and the same kind of rough limestone cobbles that had been used to line the street outside.

In a far corner an antique Wurlitzer playing a forty-five rpm recording of Santo and Johnny doing "Ebb Tide" bubbled away noisily. In one of the sash windows a machine that might at one time have been an air conditioner wheezed at them, sending a withered plume of chilly air dusted with black mold curling into the smoky atmosphere. On a shelf behind the bar an old Motorola marine radio hissed and popped with muted cross talk on channel sixteen. There was no one visible anywhere in the bar, but behind it they could see an open door; beyond that, bleached white in the midday sun, there was a small stand of stunted palms.

An intermittent chuffing sound was coming through the door; as they watched, a spray of sandy soil flew past the doorway. Someone—or something—was out in the back, digging. They rounded the end of the bar, passed through a tiny smoke-blackened kitchen area that would have gagged a Norway rat, stepped out into the limestone hardpan at the rear of the building.

A slender black woman wearing a brightly colored

cotton dress in a wild red-and-green parrot print was on her knees, her back to them, digging furiously in the hard-packed soil, chopping at it with a large rusted meat cleaver, the effort of the work making her breath puff out with each stroke, her sinewy forearm bright with sweat. She must have heard them coming because she spoke over her shoulder without turning, still hacking away at the ground.

"You come too late for that assassin. I will kill him today. He is an evil black-hearted murdering pig. I will boil him alive for it."

Neither Kelleher nor Rick answered her. She stopped digging, turned around to face them, still on her knees, froze in place, her sharp-featured young face turning stony and closed in a second.

"You are not Mister Vargas?" she said, in a thick Bahamian accent.

"No, ma'am," said Kelleher. "We're friends."

"I saw his boat coming in. Where is he?"

"On board. He has been in a very bad accident. We put in to see if you had any medicine or bandages."

She leaned back on her haunches and stared up at them suspiciously. "What kind of bad—"

Then her expression changed abruptly, sunlight burning through a fog; she grinned hugely, pointing at Rick's throat.

"You are of *San Cristobal! Of Aggayu Sola.*"

Rick looked down at Geronimo Suerta's silver necklace.

"Yes. Saint Christopher. And you?"

She pulled out a string of beads and held up a

gold medal hanging on the end, an image of the Blessed Virgin, finely carved.

"I am of *Odudua,* of Our Lady of Mercy. And you?"

She was staring at Kelleher, clearly expectant. Kelleher shook his head sadly.

"With respect, ma'am, I am no one in the rule. Just a friend of Mister Vargas. An employee. A person of no importance."

The woman dismissed Kelleher with a gracious inclination of her head, turned back to Rick and, with the solemn intensity of a priest—admittedly a priest stoned on *ganja*—she intoned the sacred name, her face rapt, her eyes shining; *"Por Yemaya!"*

*"Viva La Señora de Regla,"* he answered, narrowly avoiding an actual genuflection, the altar boy in him still very much alive. Her carved mahogany face reflected a momentary ripple of something very much like adoration; then she frowned again, a beautiful girl's petulant frown.

"Look," she said, indicating something on the ground behind her. "Look what your friend's *tigre malo* did to my poor Ton-Ton."

She shifted to clear their view. A midsized black mongrel with a grizzled muzzle, sharp bony ribs like a beached schooner was stretched out on its side on a pallet of dried palm leaves. A chain of red-and-blue beads was wrapped around its neck. It was motionless, clearly dead. The woman leaned over, raising the dog's limp head to show the terrible gash that had been carved deep into its throat from below its left ear all the way to its shoulder. Dried blood

matted the dog's black fur, a flood of it by the size of
the stain, although she had clearly tried to clean the
animal up before she put him in the ground. Since
Kelleher had already declared himself to be an
employee of no importance, Rick decided he had
better step up to the plate here.

"Ma'am, let me do this for you. The ground is very
hard. No one should bury a beloved friend alone. Let
me say an orison."

She looked up at him with grateful reverence
shining out of her like the candle inside a lantern.

"Babalao," she whispered, as in a prayer. "You are
a priest."

Rick let it pass with more than a ripple of shame;
if it gave her comfort, he would be a babalao. He
knelt down beside her, aware of her scent as he got
close, a heady narcotic mix of lime, spicy perfume
blended with some very powerful ganja. Her deep
brown eyes were moist and filled with loss. She was
very beautiful in the way of some fine-boned
Bahamians, combining the delicacy of porcelain with
the graceful planed features of an Ibo River mask.
She smiled at him and tears came into her eyes, running down her cheeks, leaving two shining tracks of
polished topaz through the dust of her digging. She
sat back, sighing, and watched him with a sweetly
stoned affection as Rick began to pound away at the
yellow dirt, every blow a knife blade in the bandaged
belly wound hidden beneath his white T-shirt.

When she wavered slightly, from fatigue or from
the ganja, Kelleher stepped around him and offered

her a hand up. She put her languid hand in his and let him draw her to her feet. Brushing the dirt off her thin cotton dress, she arched her back to work the stiffness out, the gauzy material defining the nakedness beneath it perfectly, and offered them something to drink from the bar.

"I have cold beer, rich black rum, even some tequila. Sirs?"

Rick looked over his shoulder at Kelleher and said, "I'll be through here in a moment, Charlie. You go ahead."

Kelleher and the young woman walked back into the cool of the bar, leaving Rick to bury the dog. He looked at the animal's wounds—mostly deep tearing gouges delivered to the dog's head and chest area, but the coup de grâce was obvious, a ripping raking gash along the dog's carotid that had torn it wide open. It had been a face-to-face fight, a fair combat, but death would have come in minutes.

Rick made an educated guess concerning the most likely suspect and sighed a weary sigh for all the poor unwitting victims in the world. In a few minutes he had laid the dog gently into a shallow grave and built up a low mound of limestone cobbles to mark the place. He placed a few sheaves of dry palm across the cobbles, made a small cross in the middle of the sheaves with white stones from the woman's sad little garden. Standing up again was a challenge he was almost unable to meet—his belly wound had flared up into a red-hot bar under the bandages and his ribs hurt like hell.

He found Kelleher and the woman sitting together at the long bar, talking softly the way people talk at wakes. He noticed that while Kelleher was working his way slowly through a pitcher of ice water, the woman was on her third bottle of Red Stripe. The beer, combined with the ganja she had been smoking all day long, had made her only very slightly maudlin but it had greatly enhanced her willingness to talk. She held her grief with dignity; they listened in respectful silence while she sketched a brief history of Ton-Ton's uneven life and his role as the official mascot of this *cantina* at Flat Iron Shoals.

"He was why they called this The Black Dog Oasis," she said, raising the glass of Red Stripe to her lips, sipping delicately. "He was here when I came, when they gave me the job of being the bar girl here. I was only fifteen. Ton-Ton became my first friend here. Now he has died. What will I say to Onassis Goyri when he comes? He will say, 'Odalys, you have let a cat kill poor Ton-Ton and I no longer have faith in you,' but it was he and Carlito who brought the cat here. I do not know how I could have stopped that . . ."

Here, her descriptive powers were overwhelmed by her distress; they sat quietly and watched as she dabbed at her eyes with a pressed linen cloth she had drawn from a pocket of the sundress. While she cried Rick and Kelleher composed their faces in sympathetic lines while in each man's mind rang the name *Onassis Goyri*.

After a few moments she had recovered and,

through the liquid glimmer of the tears in her eyes, offered them a bright smile of genuine solicitude.

"But I am being tiresome. You say Carlito has been hurt? I can offer nothing, but one of the men who lives here was a doctor in France and perhaps he can help. But no, he has gone. All gone. Everyone has run away."

"Yes," said Kelleher, "I was wondering about that. Where is everyone? You seem to be alone here."

Odalys shrugged, indicated the bright sparkling plain of the Caribbean through the open doorway.

"They have all gone to Nicolls Town in their boats because of the war. All the fishermen, the smugglers, and their girls. They will not be back until the war is over."

"The war?" said Rick.

She looked at them in blank amazement, waved a delicate pink-palmed hand in the direction of the antique Motorola marine radio on the shelf behind the bar.

"The Americans have gone to war with Cuba. How could you not know this? Listen to the two-way radio over there. It is the news everywhere in the islands. The Cubans have arrested two American movie stars for murder. They have taken Brad Pitt and Robert Redford to a prison where they are abusing them. President Bartlett has declared a big war on them. Soon there will be a big warship here and the Americans will arrest everyone who has been bad in his life. I think they will arrest me too. I asked the men to take me but they said no, since I am

Onassis Goyri's girl I must go with him when he comes."

"When will Mister Goyri come?"

Again, the hopeless shrug, the fatalistic acceptance.

"When he comes . . . I have not seen him since last week."

"How do you reach him? Do you telephone?"

She laughed at that, gave Rick a playful push.

"Telephones? There are no phones. We use the marine radio, sometimes Mister Goyri answers. Sometimes he does not."

Kelleher sent Rick a look that he understood completely. They had to be careful not to signal an unhealthy interest in Mister Goyri. Partly to deflect the course of the conversation, partly out of morbid curiosity, Rick asked her which cat it was that had attacked Ton-Ton. Her face hardened to a brittle ebony mask while her deep brown eyes blazed with sudden outrage.

"Who else? That tiger cat, the big male with the yellow eyes who came on *your* boat a week ago. He was standing on the bow beside Mister Suerta. He jumped off the boat before it touched the land, came right up to my door. In without a bow. Everyone was here having lunch. He jumped up onto the bar and walked along it with his tail up like a mast. Django swiped at it, but the cat clawed him for his impudence. Ton-Ton chased him out the door, not very far. When the boat left the cat stayed. He and Ton-Ton grew to dislike one another. I kept them apart,

of course, but when all the men went away . . . I was
lonely. I drank some of the beer. I woke up this
morning to find Ton-Ton lying in the street. I hunted
for the cat, but he knows how to stay out of reach.
He is an evil thing. When I catch him I will spill his
blood across Ton-Ton's grave and pray to Odudua
to take him into the underworld with her and torment him."

"Do you know the name of the cat?" asked Rick,
unconsciously falling into her slightly Elizabethan
cadences. She shook her head and wrenched the cap
off another bottle of Red Stripe as if she were jerking the head off a cat.

"No—he has no name, or answers to none. I
asked Carlito—the name of the cat, but he said he
did not own the cat. He said that the cat was a
vagabond gypsy cat who roamed all over the
Caribbean and belonged only to himself. It is true
that the cat left Carlito as soon as he arrived here
and would not come back to the boat even when
they called. He has stayed here to be a scourge to us.
I have prayed to Chango Roja to burn him with the
lightning, but he has not answered me yet. You,
sir . . . ," she said, fixing Rick with a ferocious stare,
"you are a babalao. Can you cast this animal out?"

Rick, on shaky ground when it came to the powers of a Santerian priest, simply said, "When we go,
we will take him with us and throw him to the
sharks."

She put a thin dry hand on. Rick felt the heat in
her skin. "You promise me? You will give him to the

sharks? But how will you catch him? Will you magic him?"

"He came to the boat on his own. He's there now."

"With Carlito?"

"Yes."

"Is there a woman?"

"Yes. Why?"

She looked pensive then, oddly wistful. Rick realized that she and Carlito Vargas had been lovers of some kind. Speaking of Vargas had brought them back to the question of his injuries.

"What happened to him?"

"He has lost an eye," said Kelleher. "In an accident."

She did not seem unduly distressed by this. Whatever they had been to each other, he had left no imprint on her soul. This did not surprise either man; anyone crazy enough to get emotionally tangled up with Carlito Vargas would have only one thing in common with him: they'd both be in love with pain.

"There is no doctor here anymore. Do you want me to look at him? I used to help Monsieur Duplessis when he would take the fishhooks out of a man's hand or dress a knife wound."

Time to redirect, thought Rick. He wasn't sure whether or not they should put Carlito Vargas and Odalys into the same room yet.

"Do you have fuel here? We need some diesel for the boat."

"And propane?" said Kelleher. "For the galley stove."

"There is diesel fuel in the tank at the dock. The propane we keep on the old junk boat in the harbor, so it won't blow us all up. We have lots of it. And we have a spring for the water which runs all the way from the interior. The boat comes with fresh supplies, so we have also frozen shrimp and oysters and fruit in season. There is also fish, of course. Snapper and bonita and wahoo, even tuna. It is a pretty good place to live. Really."

Her tone had grown wistful when she spoke of her life here.

"How long have you been here, Odalys?"

She sighed, poured some of the Red Stripe into a fresh glass. She sipped at it and set it down, turning the glass in a circle of wetness on the beaten surface of the bar.

"Very long. Forever. Once I was taken to Bimini and last year they let me go in a fishing boat so I could look at America from the water. But I have no papers. Mister Goyri allows me to stay here."

"Where are you from?" Rick asked softly.

She looked back through the door to the glittering sea beyond it. A trick of the light sent a shaft of reflected sunlight playing across her face, and tiny green lights flickered in her brown eyes.

"I am from Remedios," she said simply, the way an exile would say the name of a homeland forever lost.

"In Cuba?"

"Yes," she said. "In Cuba."

"When did you leave Cuba?"

She glanced at a faded Pemex calendar on the wall.

"What year is this?"

Rick told her. She nodded, her feelings confirmed.

"I came here in nineteen ninety-four. I was fifteen. I have been here ever since."

"Why did you leave Cuba?"

She gave him a sly up-from-under look.

"No one wants to leave Cuba, sir. It is a paradise."

"Yes," he said. "It is. So you were taken away?"

"Yes. We lived in Havana then. My mother and my brother wanted to go to America. So we got on the big ship and we sailed away. Only they chased us. In boats, they chased us."

Rick and Kelleher found that they were not moving or breathing. Both men lifted their glasses and drank in silence while they got their emotions and their voices under better control. Odalys was far away inside a ganja-driven dream of her youth. She had noticed nothing in either man. Her face was a dark pool of unhappy reflection.

"Who chased you?" said Rick, speaking in the softest voice he could find, as if the force of his words could shatter the air between them, as if he was speaking into a gossamer narrative web so delicate that a single breath could destroy it. Beside him Kelleher's profound silent attention was an electric force in the surrounding air.

For a long time, Odalys drifted inside her memories, staring out at the sea but seeing the plunging waves in the moonlight, the twin white wings of foamy water that shot out from under the blunt prow of the boat that chased them through the black water, while the women on the boat cried and the men stared back at the oncoming iron prow with stony lost faces. When she finally answered Rick her voice was weak and tentative but carried an undertone of anger.

"The others chased us. We left Havana in the middle of the night, but they caught us in La Poceta and sprayed us with water until we sank. The women tried to ask them to stop, but they put the hoses on them and drove them off the deck. There was a coast guard gunboat nearby but they did nothing, only watched. I was swept into the sea. There was an empty water bottle in the sea. I held on to it. At first our ship would not sink, but then they drove the big boat onto our boat and crushed it. Then it sank pretty fine. Some of us they pulled from the water, the others they ran down with their boats until there was no one on the surface anymore."

"They pulled you from the water?"

"Yes. The coast guard boat. They say forty-one people drowned. My mother was one of them. I don't know if my brother Joselito lived, but if he had, I think he would have tried to find me. So he is gone too. I was saved by the coast guard men, along with some others. The other people were put on another boat, the men, the old women. I was kept apart."

"Why you?"

She shrugged and lifted her dress up, oddly dispassionate about her own nakedness, let it billow around her and settle again.

"I was fifteen. A pretty girl. They found me convenient."

"And the others?"

"All girls. All of us."

"When did this happen?"

"In the summer. In July of that summer."

"Where did they take you?"

"They put me on the big boat. We sailed north. Out by the shoals at Orange Cay, the big boat met Mister Vargas's boat—*La Gaviota*—far out in the ocean where there was no land to see. Mister Goyri told the men on *La Gaviota* to bring me here. I never saw the others again."

"Who brought you here?"

"Men working for Mister Goyri."

"What was the name of the big boat, Odalys?"

"It was called the *Polargo Five*."

"Was Mister Goyri the captain of that boat?"

"No. But he was the *jefe*, the boss man. He was the one who came downstairs when the sailors had finished with me. He took me to his room. He was very kind to me and treated me as if I was his daughter, except when he lay with me. That is how I came to be here."

"And your mother? What was her name?"

"Her name was Yaltamira."

"And your name?"

She looked at him in confusion."

"My name. I am Odalys."

"I meant your complete name."

A tremor passed over her. Her eyes widened.

"Mister Goyri says I am not to tell anyone my name."

Looking at her face then, Rick felt they had taken this as far as they could; to ask more questions would not only be cruel but unnecessary. They had Kelleher's decoded documents on *La Gaviota,* in the bags that Zeffi had taken from the rented car the night they found Kelleher in Key Biscayne.

He had an idea that her full name would be there, part of that long list of people who had drowned on the *Venceremos* on July 13th, 1994, chased down and deliberately sunk by two Cuban fireboats seven miles off the Cuban coast. In Kelleher's silence Rick sensed the same thought. He put a hand on her arm and held it there.

"You are right, of course. Mister Goyri would not want you to talk about this. But we haven't told you why we're here."

She looked unfocused, confused, caught between the painful remembrance made even more painful by the intensity of the ganja and the responsibility she felt to be the girl in charge of Onassis Goyri's cantina. She gathered herself with a visible effort and pulled her arm away gently, disengaging herself not from Rick but from the effort of recollection, from the images that the act of remembrance had brought to vivid hurtful life again in her mind's eye.

"You are here for fuel and to get some help for Carlito."

"Yes. But we are also here from Mister Goyri himself. He wishes us to take you away before the Navy gunboats get here. He wants you to be in a safe place."

"What safe place?" she asked; Rick saw fear suddenly awake in her soft brown eyes. "What safe place is there?"

"There is America," said Kelleher, speaking for the first time. She looked at him in surprise.

"America? I have no papers for America. They took all of our papers before they let us get on the boat. That is why I cannot ever leave Flat Iron Shoals. Not in my life. Not even to go to Nicolls Town."

"They took your identity papers?"

"Yes," she said, speaking to Kelleher as you would speak to someone who has already identified himself as someone of no importance, a trace of impatience in her voice. "We all had to give our papers to the official at the dock in Marina Hemingway."

"What kind of papers?"

"All of them. Whatever we had. Our birth certificates, our citizenship cards. Those who had driver's licenses had to surrender them. Anything with a picture on it. We were told that the Americans would give us brand-new papers when we got to Florida, that we did not need them anymore. They took my student card, my medical card. Family albums. Pictures from school. My record of inoculations for smallpox and measles. Anyone who had a passport had to give it up. Visa photos. Anything that was official paper. Letters. Cards. They had already taken our rings, our watches, our jewelry—whatever we had in our bags. They took it all. Everything."

"All of you?" asked Rick. "Everyone on the boat?"

There had been seventy-two Cuban nationals on the boat. Forty-one of them had been reported as drowned when the *Venceremos* sank. Nothing in the document that Rick had read said anything about the confiscation of their papers. If what she was saying was accurate—although she was only indifferently educated, she seemed to be an intelligent woman—then thirty-one survivors had gone back to Cuba and into the detention camps reserved for runaways.

But forty-one people had died without their identity papers. Why had their identity papers been taken *before* they got on the *Venceremos*? He glanced at Kelleher and saw the same unspoken question.

"Odalys, you don't need papers to go with us," said Kelleher. "We have the papers ready for you on the—"

The jukebox had burbled into silence a while ago, so the unmistakable sound of the shot that rang out then—a solid muffled crack—made them all jump. Rick was out the door and racing down the path toward the dock before the echo of the shot had rattled around the wooden walls of the town, his feet scuffling on the cobbles, his heart slamming. He was vaguely aware of Kelleher pounding along behind him, falling behind as Rick flew over the shoreline stones and ran up onto the dock. As he reached the sharp wooden bow of *La Gaviota*, Carlito Vargas came stumbling out of the starboard cabin door with Rick's big Colt 45 in his left hand, his blood-stained bandages flying in the sea wind.

His battered face twisted in rage when he saw Rick coming; he fired at him four times, each percussive crack raising dust off the hull of *La Gaviota*. Rick felt one round buzz past his skull like a hummingbird and heard another round smacking into the stony ground at his feet and ricochet into the air with an ugly metallic whine. Vargas steadied himself on the railing, leveled the Colt at Rick's head again, this time taking careful aim. Rick jumped sideways into the shelter of the ship's tumble home, huddling into a ball as another shot slammed into the ground where he had been standing. From somewhere close behind him he heard Kelleher shouting a warning. Three rapid booming cracks split the dense air over his head. He heard Carlito grunt, an explosive huffing sound as if he had been punched very hard in the belly, then his own blue-steel Colt tumbled down the gangway in a clatter. Vargas staggered back and leaned up against the deck rail, his hands crossed over his belly, blood bubbling out between his fingers. He lifted his hands away from his wound, looked at his bloody palms, lifted his hands out to Rick.

"*Nada más,*" he said and turned to his left, facing the dock. He began to walk down the gangway; Rick went to confront him. Vargas stopped at the bottom of the walkway and looked at Rick with a kind of weary reproach.

"Leave him," said Kelleher, close behind Rick. "I'll go look for Zeffi."

Vargas waited for Rick to step out of his path, his

eye fixed on the seaward horizon. He lifted his head and sniffed at the sea air, his blunt battered face tight with pain. He turned at the base of the ramp and walked out along the jetty, Rick following behind him, the Colt in his right hand. Vargas made it to the end of the jetty and stood there, weaving slightly, staring out beyond the breakwater. Rick stopped about ten feet behind him. Vargas turned to look back at him.

"It is coming."

"What is coming?"

"The punishment. I have broken The Rule of Eight. You should not be here. You go back. It is over between you and me. It is decided. You go back to the others."

Vargas turned away then, straightening himself as he looked out to the rippling field of the sea as if preparing for some ceremony. Rick looked beyond his massive shoulder, out to the pure blue ocean beyond the breakwater. There was nothing at all on the flat knife edge of the horizon line. No. There was . . . something. Rick had seen this before, a trick of the light, a sun-gall the sailors called it, a glowing circle of sunlit cloud or haze, hovering on the horizon. They were a kind of mirage, a thing made of floating mist shining with a pale reflected light from the sidelong sun. He stared out at it past Vargas's huge sloping shoulders. The sun-gall had all of Vargas's attention now. He was leaning slightly forward, holding his belly wound with crossed hands, breathing harshly. The sun-gall seemed to float somewhere in the luminous air between the horizon and the breakwater. Rick tried to blink it away but could not.

He heard a rapid *click-click* sound and looked down into the clear water by the end of the dock. Crabs, small pink-and-gray spider crabs, were crawling around on the wet boulders and broken concrete slabs beside the jetty. There seemed to be a lot of them, but no more than you always saw at the tide line or along the shore when the evening sun was coming on. A few dozen, perhaps a hundred. More coming from under the dock. And the white sand seabed showed a black wavering mass that could have been others.

He looked back up at Vargas and saw that he was staring down at the spider crabs with a pale sheen of perspiration on his thick pockmarked face. He looked back at Rick; in his red-rimmed yellow eye there was a kind of animal supplication, a bull-in-the-slaughter-pen look. Vargas blinked once and sighed and then stepped forward and pitched into the deep water beyond the jetty. He sank immediately, limp, turning. The crabs seemed to follow him down. Others appeared from under rocks and sunken logs. With an effort Rick tore his eyes away from the water. He looked out to sea. The sun-gall had faded, now little more than a curved space in the shining air. He walked back toward Zeffi and Kelleher, who were waiting in silence.

"Is he dead?" she said, her face white and strained.

"Yes. He is," said Rick.

"I've never seen anything like that," she said. "The light out on the water? Was it real?"

"I don't know and I don't want to think about it ever again. I know Vargas is dead. Are you okay?"

"I'm sorry," she said, trying to get her breathing under control. "All my fault. I was tending to Cisco. He got loose somehow. Came into the galley with your Colt. I'm okay. Really, I am. The son of a bitch. He took one shot—missed me—I jumped into the bay."

"He missed. God, Zeffi. How did he miss?"

"I distracted him."

"Distracted him with what?"

"I threw the fucking cat at him."

# THE BLACK MARLIN

They pulled what was left of Carlito Vargas's unrecognizable body out of the surf and buried him without ceremony in a shallow rock-lined grave under a
stunted jacaranda at the farthest end of the breakwater, marking his grave with a turtle's bleached-
white skull. When they got back to the town Odalys
was gone. She wasn't in The Black Dog when they
looked for her there, nor did she answer when they
called her name through the streets and alleyways.
Even when Zeffi went alone into the town and called
her, all that came back to her from the empty shacks
and the churning sea of palm trees in the limestone
flats beyond the bay was the distant hissing of the
wind and the rolling boom of ocean surf pounding
against the breakwater. They asked Zeffi to stay with
the boat while Kelleher and Rick walked the perimeter of the village. By two in the afternoon they had
reached the seaward edge of the low forest of stunted
palm groves that ran inland for several miles across

the limestone flats. There was no sign of Odalys anywhere, not even footprints in the sandy earth. They stood there at the edge of the tree line and looked into the sun-dappled clearings and tiger-striped shadows of the palm-tree forest.

"Odalys," Rick called. "Please . . . come out."

Only the dry palms rustling and tossing in the rising wind.

"She's frightened, that's all," said Kelleher.

"She thinks Chango Roja sent the punishment to Vargas. We may never see her again."

"We can't leave her here," Kelleher said, flatly. "If Onassis Goyri comes back, it will be only to kill her. She was supposed to have died on *Venceremos*, but he kept her alive. She's a witness to an incident that links directly to Roymundo Vargas and Hector Preig. Now that we know about her, he'd want her dead. The fact that she's alive and he brought her here means he had something to do with the sinking. He's with the United Nations. A story like that, from the mouth of a victim, would ruin him. Why he let her live I'll never know."

They were a mile from the shore, well beyond the last outpost of the ramshackle town. The wind had risen during the afternoon and the palms were bending and lashing in the gathering force of it, their leaves hissing and rattling. A fine salty sand was on the wind. It stung what skin it could find. Over the sound of the wind and the lashing palms they heard the low moaning sound of the ship's horn.

"That's Zeffi," said Rick. "Let's go."

They turned away from the palm grove, walking back down the slope and through the empty town. Zeffi was standing on the stern of *La Gaviota*, holding Cisco in her arms, waiting for them. When they came out along the jetty, she walked around the port side to meet them, concern in her weary face, a piece of paper fluttering in her hand.

"What is it?" asked Kelleher.

"This fax just came in. It's for you, Rick. From Jack Cole. And there's something on the radar screen. Coming this way."

They went inside and gathered around the radar screen. It was set to maximum range, almost fifty miles. At the farthest edge of the sweep five blips glowed bright red. The bright green arm swept around three times. Each circuit brought the five blips several miles closer. Kelleher went back out onto the bow and looked out over the sea toward the west, with his hands on the bow rail.

The sea smelled of kelp and fish and salt; the wind carried a fine mist that beaded on his skin. Far out over the dazzling field of bright churning light he could make out five black dots low in the sky, in the band of shining haze that separated the ocean from the cloud-streaked sky.

"What are they?" asked Rick, standing behind him.

"Hard to say. Probably Rhinos. Super Hornets. If the *Louisiana* has been deployed against Cuba, you can bet they'll have a carrier group in the Straits as well. Oh yeah. Here they come. Brace yourselves. They're right on the deck, the crazy bastards."

The five black blips resolved themselves into five
sleek fighters coming in at speed off the Santaren
Channel. They were on them in a matter of seconds,
flashing in at less than a hundred feet off the water.
They could see the markings on their fuselages, U.S.
NAVY, and even make out the helmets of the pilots as
the fighters flickered by overhead, banked sharply,
disappearing into the southeast. A half-second later
the sound of their jets tore the air apart and buffeted
them as they stood there, wrapped inside a prolonged
booming roar that drove the breath out of them, leaving them half-stunned and silent.

"Cowboys," said Kelleher, watching the tiny delta
of blips as they winked out of sight in the hazy
southern sky.

"What was that all about?" said Zeffi.

"Showing the flag," said Kelleher. "I guess the
blockade is officially on."

He looked down at the fax sheet still in Rick's
hand.

"What did you get out of Cole?"

Rick handed him the sheet.

RICK BROCA/FAXMAIL/PARADIGM

Rick this is what I got. Keep me informed.
Jack.

EXTRACT—INTERPOL/NADDIS
BANCO FINANCIERO INTERNATIONAL
FOUNDED 1984 IS RUN OUT OF **CIMEX
CORPORATION** WITH BRANCHES IN US

CANADA AND EUROPE. **CIMEX** ADMIN-
ISTERS OPERATIONS OF FUNDS KNOWN
AS COMMANDANTE'S RESERVES, FIDEL
CASTRO'S PRIVATE FUNDS. AFFILIATED
WITH EL BANCO D'INVERSIONES SA
LOCATED IN SOMEILLAN BUILDING IN
HAVANA, PART OF MECHANISM THAT
MAKES LOANS TO CUBAN CIVIL GOV-
ERNMENT AT HIGH INTEREST RATES.
**CIMEX** ACTS AS TRANSFER AGENT FOR
COMMANDANTE'S RESERVE FUNDS,
MOST OF WHICH DERIVE FROM THE
LAUNDERING OF DRUG MONEY AND
ASSORTED CONFISCATORY OPERA-
TIONS CARRIED OUT UNDER THE PER-
SONAL CONTROL OF FIDEL CASTRO.
**CIMEX** AND BANCO FINANCIERO INTER-
NATIONAL HAVE THREE OPERATING
OFFICERS; **HECTOR RODRIGUEZ
PREIG,** DIRECTOR OF OPERATIONS
FOR THE DIRECTION GENERAL
D'INFORMACION—THE CUBAN CIA—
**ROYMUNDO VARGAS,** A CITIZEN OF
SWITZERLAND RESIDENT IN GENEVA
WITH HOLDINGS IN CUBA AND THE
UNITED STATES, AND **ONASSIS GOYRI,**
OSTENSIBLY THE CUBAN ENVOY TO
THE UNITED NATIONS BUT SUSPECTED
OF USING DIPLOMATIC STATUS TO
COURIER LARGE CASH AND CREDIT
TRANSFERS FROM THE COMMAN-

DANTE'S RESERVES TO CASTRO'S PRIVATE BANK ACCOUNTS IN GENEVA.

"Okay," said Kelleher, handing the sheet back to Rick. "Now I'm really confused."

"Come in and eat," said Zeffi. "We have to decide what we're going to do."

She had dinner ready for them, laid out on the big rosewood dining room table in the lounge—scrubbed and bleached six times by Rick himself—everything she could find in the kitchen of the Black Dog; mangoes and oranges and limes, fresh salad and a mound of fresh shrimp on a bed of rock ice, even a frosty silver bucket with a bottle of chilled Soave and several more Red Stripes, half buried in the snowy ice. They sat down around the table and for several minutes ate and drank in a calm soothing silence.

Zeffi had shut off the marine radio—the constant chatter of overexcited sportfishers and trawlers was irritating as hell—heated-up war talk on everybody's mind, all the tiresome birdbrained backchatter from the left-wing dopers and One World numb-nuts out of Key West. She had found some bossa nova CDs and she was playing a Stan Getz number, low, jazzy, with a silky trumpet line.

The sun shone in through the slatted wooden blinds that covered the cabin windows. It lay in glowing bars of amber light across the table. The sea breeze was strong enough to cool them while filling the gently rocking cabin with the scent of lemongrass, eucalyptus, and sea salt. After a while Rick pushed his plate away and leaned back in the deck chair. He looked around the table at Zeffi and Kelleher, at Cisco sitting up in one of the chairs, mildly outraged that he had been offered nothing. As Rick watched, he put a huge paw out, extended his blood-stained needle claws, deftly snagged a big fillet of red snapper right off Rick's plate. Then he bolted away into the galley to enjoy the kill in privacy. When Rick looked back at the others, they were both looking at him. Kelleher sighed, rubbing his face with both hands; he put his head back and closed his eyes.

"Let's review, kids. We can start with Odalys. Have you got the sheet listing the victims of the *Venceremos* sinking?"

Rick got up to find it. While he was gone, Zeffi stood up and looked out the cabin window toward the town. The shadows were growing longer as the day passed. The colors of the painted shacks, the lime greens, the royal blues, the tomato reds that had been bleached out by the midday sun were glowing vividly in the slanting afternoon light. Beyond the town the field of palms was weaving and tossing in the wind; the surf was booming out beyond the breakwater. In the town, nothing moved. They had told her the story of Odalys, and what her story meant; her heart went out to the young woman who was hiding in abject terror somewhere out in the palm groves. Whatever the men decided, Zeffi had no intention of leaving the woman here.

"Neither do we," said Kelleher, reading her thoughts.

Zeffi turned to look at him, saw an old man with a ravaged face, bruised and tired beyond belief.

"You mean Odalys?"

"I do. We have to bring her with us. They'll kill her."

Rick came back into the room with the two documents Kelleher had taken out of Cuba. He spread them out across the table and they leaned forward to read them again. Kelleher pointed to the list of the victims. "Read that," he said. "They're all there."

Rick turned the sheet around and read the last paragraph.

## Which events occurred seven miles off the Cuban coast on July 13, 1994

The persons who died that morning are: Leonardo Notario Góngora, Marta Cabrillo Vega, Caridad Leyva Cabrillo, Yausel Eugenio Pérez Cabrillo, Mayulis Méndez Cabrillo, Yaltamira García, Joselito García, Odalys Muñoz García, Pilar Almanza Romero, Yaser Perodín Almanza, Manuel Sánchez Callol, Juliana Enriquez Carrasana, Helen Martínez Enríquez, Reynaldo Marrero, Joel García Suárez, Juan Mario Gutiérrez García, Ernesto Alfonso Joureiro, Amado Gonzáles Raices, Lázaro Borges Priel, Liset Alvarez Guerra, Yisel Borges Alvarez, Guillermo Cruz Martínez, Fidelio Ramel Prieto-

Hernández, Yaltamira Anaya Carrasco, José Carlos
Nicole Anaya, María Carrasco Anaya, Julia Caridad
Ruiz Blanco, Angel René Abreu Ruiz, Jorge
Arquímides Lebrijio Flores, Eduardo Suárez
Esquivel, Elicer Suárez Plascencia, Raoul Felipe
Goyri, Susalis Goyri, Omar Rodríguez Suárez,
Miralis Fernández Rodríguez, Cindy Rodríguez
Fernández, José Gregorio Balmaceda Castillo,
Rigoberto Feut Gonzáles, Midalis Sanabria Cabrera,
and four other victims who could not be identified.

"There she is," he said, tapping the sheet. "Odalys
Muñoz García. Just after her mother, Yaltamira
García. And Joselito García. All listed as drowned on
the thirteenth of July, nineteen ninety-four. Only
she's not drowned. Odalys is alive and living in Flat
Iron Shoals."

"Any Goyris on the list?" asked Kelleher.

"Yes," said Zeffi, pulling the sheet around so she
could read it. "When I heard the name, I thought I
remembered it. Yes, here they are. There are two of
them. Raoul Felipe Goyri and Susalis Goyri."

Kelleher tapped the sheet.

"So Odalys García connects with Onassis Goyri,
and Onassis Goyri connects to the Manuel Gonzalez
outfit, and the Manuel Gonzalez outfit connects to
Roymundo Vargas."

"Okay," said Rick. "Charlie, why didn't your damned
secret source tell you about this CIMEX thing?"

"Because he didn't know."

"Where does this source work?" asked Zeffi.

Kelleher had to fight his covert instincts for a moment.

"He works inside the Defense Intelligence Agency. Over the past ten years the DIA has experienced a serious degradation of its intelligence capabilities. Agents have disappeared. Intelligence has been inaccurate. Freelancers have stopped talking to them at all. At the ONI, we've been wondering why. So we contacted one of their guys who used to be Navy and asked him to run a kind of watching brief for us. The guy who gave me this works in their Caribbean section. He's an analyst. Just like Buell."

Rick picked up the paper and studied the list of victims again.

"Odalys says they took all their identity papers *before* they got on the boat," said Rick. "Is that normal?"

"I don't think so," said Kelleher. "In this case, it would have made the people damn suspicious. Seventy-two suspicious people can cause a lot of trouble. I'm surprised they took the risk. There had to be a damn good reason for confiscating all their papers like that. I can't think what it is. It makes no sense."

"I have a question," said Zeffi. "What happened to the people who officially survived the sinking? The ones who were taken out of the water by the Cuban coast guard?"

"Castro put them all in the prison at Bahía Honda," said Kelleher. "According to our sources in

Havana, most of them were never heard from again. A few made it back home to their villages, but they never talked about the prison. They were only sent back when they were ruined. Broken. It was a way to make the point. Don't try this ever again. We'll hunt you down and kill you for it."

Zeffi was quiet for a while, looking at the names.

"Okay," she said, finally. "There's another way to look at this. It's not a question of who drowned and who didn't drown. Maybe there had to be bodies found. There had to be deaths, real deaths. And it had to happen inside Cuban waters so there'd be no outside agencies involved in the recovery of the bodies. So there'd be no accurate and independent *count* of the bodies. And why not?"

"Beats me," said Rick. "Why not?"

Kelleher was staring hard at her, listening intently.

"Because the dead bodies wouldn't add up to forty-one. They were all meant to die to cover up something else. I think they were meant to cover up for people who were never on the boat in the first place. Bodies lost at sea. Unrecoverable. Disappeared."

"But what does that get Onassis Goyri?" asked Rick.

"It explains why two of his own family members were no longer around. Susalis and Raoul. They drowned on that boat. At least, that's what Goyri wanted it to look like."

"Explains it to whom?"

"To Fidel Castro," said Kelleher, smiling at Zeffi. "Goyri was getting his family out of Cuba. It's all about the money. And I think the only man in a position to help Vargas and Goyri get their families safely away from Castro is Hector Preig. The question is, What did Preig get in return?"

Zeffi was checking the list of victims.

"So there's no one on this boat connected to Hector Preig?"

"Preig's a total loner, Zeffi. The ONI established that Preig was estranged from his entire family for years. Ever since Castro had General Arnoldo Ochoa executed in eighty-nine, Preig steered well clear of any 'unpatriotic' connections. Especially family. They were rumored to be having some kind of contact with the exile groups. He dropped them all flat. He even went so far as to divorce his wife. We had the whole sheet on him. Dumped his wife, dumped his sisters and even his own son. Since then he's a total hermit, sees no one, had no kind of private life at all. The complete spymaster."

"What was his son's name?" asked Rick.

"His name? Christ, this was years back. It was . . . José . . . Marcel . . . I don't know what it was. How am I supposed to remember his damned name after all this time, Rick? And why?"

"Look, we're all agreed that Onassis Goyri couldn't have done this without help from inside the Cuban intelligence network. What Cuban agency controls the merchant marine?"

"Man . . . I think it was the Maritime Services Enterprise."

"So they'd have been the people in charge of the

fireboats that sank *Venceremos* at La Poceta. Who runs the Maritime Services Enterprise, Charlie?"

"The Ministry of Transportation."

"The Ministry of Transportation. That's a civil authority isn't it, and in Cuba the civil authorities are all supervised by . . . ?"

"The DGI," said Kelleher.

"Right. That means Hector Preig. So what was his son's name? Think."

"I'm trying. It was a long time ago. I wasn't in the analysis section. I'm a pilot for Christ's sake. A grunt."

"You say he divorced his wife in eighty-nine?"

"Yes."

"What was her name?"

"Man . . . I can't . . . was it Mavis? Malice? Alice?"

"How about Mayulis?"

"Yeah. Mayulis. It could have been Mayulis."

"There's a Mayulis right here."

Rick tossed the list over to Kelleher, who scanned the names with a hard searching expression on his dark face.

"Mayulis Méndez Cabrillo. That doesn't mean she's the Mayulis who was married to Hector Preig."

"She's the only Mayulis on the list. It's not a common name in Los Angeles, and it wasn't in New York either. There are four people traveling under the Cabrillo name on this list. Marta Cabrillo Vega, Caridad Leyva Cabrillo, Yausel Eugenio Pérez Cabrillo, Mayulis Méndez Cabrillo. You said earlier that the name of Preig's son might have been something like José or Marcel, right?"

"Yeah. And . . . ?"

"How about Yausel?"

"Yausel? Could have been, Rick. Could have been."

"So what are we looking at, Rick?" asked Zeffi.

"I have a gut feeling that Hector Preig faked the divorce from wife and kid. If I wanted to get my family out of the country without Castro's permission, then I'd need a damn good cover story. I think this is it. I think Goyri and Preig used the sinking to cover up the disappearance of their own families."

Kelleher took that in, then shook his head.

"One problem. Let's say we're right. Let's say this was some kind of double operation that Preig was running. He'd still have to sell Castro on the idea of letting the boat sail and then deliberately drowning everyone on board. Castro's sensitive to public opinion in the world. He has trade sanctions he wants lifted, he has funds around the world that he wants to keep access to. Sinking that boat was an atrocity. When it happened, he was condemned around the world. The only reason it slipped off the front page was Rwanda, the massacres; they happened around the same time and everybody forgot about the *Venceremos*. Otherwise Castro would have had a rough time."

Rick cut in, his tone more urgent.

"But if Preig could sell him on it—how I have no idea yet—then the sinking of a huge tugboat would work beautifully. You'd need all the bodies you could get. Put them on board, take all their papers, then run the boat down seven miles out. Bingo. The wife and kids—who you've already pretended to divorce—are safely out of Castro's reach. He's not even going to look for them. He thinks they're all dead and gone. Neat stunt. Chilly, but neat."

"Why would they want their families out of the country?" asked Zeffi. "They're powerful guys, Goyri and Preig. Why bother?"

Kelleher's expression had altered.

He gave Zeffi a wolfish grin.

"How about because Preig and Goyri are planning to defect and have been for years? It's the only explanation that fits all the facts. Castro's fading fast. But he's still the *commandante*. If I were going to take a powder on Castro, first, I'd take steps to get my loved ones out of the country, and then to keep them safe in exile, I'd want to take everything I could that Castro would want kept secret. Anything I could threaten him with if he came after me."

"And he would," said Rick. "The Cubans have killed several defectors in Miami over the last few years. Castro would come after them both with everything he had if he thought they had been stealing from him. You'd need some serious blackmail to hold him off."

"That's right," said Kelleher, his voice rising. "I'd fly out espionage records, bank records, agent lists, computer files, hard drives, cash, gold—by the way, have you guys cracked that pallet yet? While I was floating around out in the ocean in that damned minisub, it hit me why the cargo didn't float, why that pallet was overbuilt. I'll bet it's stuffed with gold bars or silver ingots."

"No, it's not," said Zeffi. "I looked."

They stopped and stared at her.

"You were out hunting for Odalys. I used a wrench to open up one of the panels. You know what's inside it? Watches, jewelry, wedding rings, diamonds, emeralds, pearls, rubies, coin collections . . . it all looks like it belonged to hundreds of families. Heirlooms, personal effects. Tens of thousands of dollars worth. It's terrible."

"Christ," said Rick, looking at her. "Taken from . . ."

"The disappeared," said Kelleher, simply. "All the disappeared ones. All over Cuba. Year after year after year . . ."

A silence fell around them. It lasted for quite a while. There was nothing to say in the face of the horror of it. After a time, Zeffi spoke again, her voice changed and hushed.

"So Preig and Goyri staged the whole thing to cover the escape of their families because they're both planning to defect. Is that what you two think?"

Kelleher was silent for a while; then he shook his head.

"Remember, I said Preig would have to sell the idea to Castro. Sinking that boat would have to give Castro something that was worth all the bad publicity. The hook. Something that Castro would love, something that would distract him from Preig's real game."

Kelleher broke off here, his face went blank.

"Okay," said Rick. "I'll bite. What is it?"

"I think Preig's irresistible offer to Castro was to make 'legends' for him."

"Legends?"

"Look, if you want to give an agent—a spy—a good cover, you need to start with something—with someone—who was real. Somebody who lived a real life and left a trail of actual documents. You can always alter them, but nothing beats the real thing to start with. If I was going to insert a network of agents into a country, the first thing I'd want is genuine life histories to work with. Real birth certificates. Real baptismal certificates. Graduation diplomas. Driver's licenses. Passports. Smallpox inoculation records. School photos. Everything I could get from all the real people I could find. Of course, the people whose papers I was using would have to go away."

Rick and Zeffi sat motionless in the chairs while the amber bars of dying light crawled across the table and worked their way up Kelleher's body, his face hidden in shadows as the sun settled into the golden haze of the evening. His voice was low, oddly soothing, as he laid it out for them. The wind had died away to a zephyr. The breakers on the jetty were a rhythmic whisper.

"Go away?" said Zeffi. "You mean, drown?"

"Yes. Disappear. Drown. That's why they took everyone's identity papers. Odalys said so. They took everything. Even family snapshots. You'd need all of that to create a 'legend' for whomever you were going to insert."

"But all these 'legends' would be 'legends' for people who were officially dead. How would that help you?"

"Officially dead to whom? The Cubans can doctor anyone's record. There's no way any of us at the ONI were able to verify a single name on the list of the dead on that boat. How could anyone else? And that's not the point. When you have all those original documents, you begin from there. You also have their past lives. Lives that were really lived, lives that left a path, a trail of names and dates and people. Then you change the names, you falsify around the edges, you stay as close as you can to the truth because the truth is always persuasive and far enough from it to avoid being caught. You give this new 'legend' to an agent. Then you try to place that agent in a situation that has access to intelligence. Sometimes you put the agent in for years. You wait until he finds himself in a useful job and then you activate him. A mole. Everyone does this. Hell, we do it."

Rick took this in and asked one final question.

"If you're right, Hector Preig and Onassis Goyri smuggled their families out of Cuba in the summer of nineteen ninety-four. Yet here you are flying their cargo out years later? Why wait so long?"

"Look at Jack Cole's fax, Rick. Castro put CIMEX in charge of Banco Financiero in 1984, right after he executed Ochoa. A lot of money has been made since then, and I'll bet you that not all of it got to Castro. My guess is that Goyri and Vargas have been skimming Castro's funds for years, with Hector Preig's help. Now that Castro's sick, now that it's all starting to fall apart, it's time to get out from under it. My money says Preig's family is in Geneva, close to their money. Vargas's people are already there. Along with Goyri's family."

"It all makes sense," said Rick. "In a totally fucked-in-the-head kind of way. All those people. What chilly fucks these guys are."

"Yeah," said Kelleher. "That's what I've been saying."

"But if it's even halfway true, then we have these sons of bitches right by the sphericals. All we have to do is contact Le Tourneau—tell her what we know—she uses a back channel to let Preig know we're onto his game and if Jake Seigel, Cory Bryant, and Katie Kelleher aren't on the next flight out of Gitmo, we drop a word in *el commandante's* shell-like ear."

"Not that simple," said Kelleher. "We still have to think about the mole. First of all, there's Chennault, who let Suerta escape for reasons I can't figure out. Maybe Chennault *is* the mole. He gives Preig a quick heads up and Preig's people snag Katie off the street. Preig sends a message back to Le Tourneau. Rat me out to Castro and Katie Kelleher dies. Your plan gets Seigel and Bryant out, but Katie Kelleher dies in Bahía Honda prison."

"Charlie's right," said Zeffi. "As long as Katie's

still in Cuba and the mole is still in place, Preig can get to her before we can."

"Then what the hell can we do? Go to Cuba? How? The U.S. Navy is blockading the entire island. We can't get in, and even if we could, what are we going to do? Scoop Katie off the street and smuggle her all the way across Cuba to Guantánamo?"

"That was more or less my plan," said Kelleher.

"Any thoughts on how we beat the blockade?"

"None. Yet. But the night is young."

"Christ," said Rick, his frustration maxing out. "We need to figure out who the mole is before we can do anything else. Maybe he's using one of the legends that Preig made for Castro. We can follow up every name on this list, see if anyone in the DIA connects. We take out the mole, then we move against Preig."

"That's not the kind of background check we can run over a marine radio. We're still going to need help from some outfit in D.C. You still trust Diane Le Tourneau at the FBI?"

"I trust her," said Rick. "I think she's straight."

"Who runs the FBI?" asked Zeffi.

"The Justice Department," said Rick. "Why?"

"Alone?"

"No. It answers to the president. And Congress."

"And what about the DIA? Who runs that?"

"The State Department."

"Can the FBI investigate the DIA without permission?"

"No. They'd have to clear it with the secretary of state."

"Then I'm afraid we still have a problem. Vargas told you there were four cells, four networks, each network was loyal to one of the gods, one of the *orishas* of Santeria. The Gonzalez cell was affiliated with . . . ?"

"Ochun, the wife of Chango Red."

"And Vargas is of Chango Red himself? The thunder god who lives in the royal palms?"

"That's right."

"And Onassis Goyri's cell?"

"Odalys said they were of Odudua," said Rick.

"That's three," said Zeffi. "You said there were four cells."

"Yes. The fourth cell was affiliated with *Babalu Aye*."

"There's a book about Santeria in the library here. It was originally a West African ancestor cult that started in the Yoruba tribe. In order to protect themselves from the Spanish Christians, they used Christian cover names to conceal the true names of their gods. The book lists all the *orishas* and their Christian counterparts. Rick's Saint Christopher medal is connected to Aggayu Sola. Odalys and Goyri have the *orisha* Odudua and her Christian identity is the Virgin Mary. Ochun, the Gonzalez family *orisha*, is also known as Cuba's patron saint, the Virgin de la Caridad del Cobre. Chango Roja, the Vargas *orisha*, has a Christian identity as Santa Barbara. That's three cells. What did Vargas say the *orisha* of the fourth cell was?"

"Babalu Aye."

"Do you know the Christian identity of Babalu Aye?"

"He's the *orisha* of disease."

"Disease? What, like smallpox?"

"No. Leprosy. His Christian identity is Lazarus."

# MIDNIGHT SUN

The delicate purple light of the evening was dying into a deep velvety indigo off in the western sea; a full moon was gliding high above the palm groves beyond the town, casting a pale light down on the palm sheaves, cutting hard white shapes out of the black shadows deep inside the groves. Out on the stone jetty, the lights of *La Gaviota* were amber squares against the black shape of her long hull. The muttering burble of her engines came across the water, dying away inside the soft whispering wind that moved through the leaning palms and stirred the dry grasses that covered the ground inside the forest. Rick was moving carefully through the palm trees with every sense alive to the surrounding night, passing like smoke from moonlight into darkness, then back into the silver moonlight again.

The cool evening air was full of the scent of unseen flowers, the darker musk of rotting palm leaves. Under his feet, the limestone was still giving off the heat of the day, a warmth he could feel through the soft leather of his sandals. He was aware of Kelleher's silent shape slipping soundlessly through the trees a few yards to his left.

It was time—it was past time—to leave Flat Iron Shoals. The fuel tanks were topped up and the propane tank that ran the galley stove had been refilled. They had fresh water and fresh food, and it was time to take Odalys García off the island. If they left her here, Goyri or one of his people would have her killed, just to get rid of her story. Whatever they were going to do about Katie, and they hadn't worked that out yet, they couldn't do it in Flat Iron Shoals. They needed to get safely back to Key West. Rick and Kelleher had been searching for Odalys over an hour; there was no trace of her anywhere.

She was a woman of this town, they knew; in her years on this flat palm-covered island she would have walked over every low rise of stone and swum through every hidden lagoon. They had already searched the town building by building and hut by hut, picking through the threadbare belongings of the fishermen who had run away to Nicolls Town; they had found the tiny cabin where Odalys lived, a corrugated-iron hut roofed in dry palm sheaves, a wooden sleigh bed in the corner covered in white cotton blankets, a few sticks of secondhand furniture, a tiny kitchen with a propane stove, the one-room cabin floored with limestone cobbles, the entire place swept spotless. In one corner they had found her shrine to Odudua, a lump of pink-and-black coral covered in glass beads, a votive candle in the broken bottom half of a red glass jar guttering low, almost gone in a pool of melted paraffin, the burnt scent of it drifting inside the empty cabin. But they had not found Odalys and they were running out of time. If they left her here, sooner or later Goyri or his people would come to kill her. And there was nowhere else on the deserted peninsula where she could be hiding. She had to be in this huge sprawling palm grove somewhere.

Zeffi was at the wheel of *La Gaviota*, waiting for them, listening to the marine radio, watching the radar screen in front of her, looking for any sign of an approaching boat. She had one of their portable two-way radios on the countertop beside her, next to Rick's heavy Colt pistol. Cisco was curled up in the navigator's chair beside her, snoring loudly. Now and then she would walk out to the stern and look inland toward the black mass of the palm-tree forest and worry about Rick and Kelleher and Odalys.

Almost a mile away from her, kneeling down in a clearing, Rick was looking at his watch, lifting it into a shaft of moonlight; it was a quarter past ten. Kelleher, sensing Rick's movement, drifted in so close Rick could smell Zeffi's Turkish cigarettes on his leather jacket and spoke in a soft whisper.

"We can do this without her."

"We can't leave her here. And we need her, don't we?"

"We don't need her at all, since you ask. We have everything we need to finish this thing. We're not trying to prove this in a court of law. We just want to know enough to force Preig to let us get our people out alive. I'm not trying to undermine Castro. I could give a shit about Castro. Or Preig. I want Katie out and you want Jake and Cory out. That's the mission. We just can't stay here. Remember the Indigo satellite. It's right up there and the night is as clear as spring water. Chennault could be looking at images of *La Gaviota* this second. They have to know we took her from Key Biscayne. They could send in a Blackhawk from Trumbo Point. As long as that mole is still in place we can't be taken."

"I know. Please, Charlie. It's her life. Fifteen more minutes."

He saw Kelleher's head move in silent agreement and watched as the man slipped noiselessly away into a pool of blackness beyond the grove, the moonlight pouring down through the palm leaves dappling his back with silvery ovals as he disappeared. Rick sighed and moved forward himself, brushing aside a feathery stand of pampas grass, moving deeper into the palm forest.

In a few minutes he had worked his way through a slow rise and reached a stretch of higher ground where the palms were much older, very much taller, their leathery trunks leaning crazily askew, their spreading tops riding on the sky far above him, the black angular blades of their outspread fronds stark against the moonlit night and the faint dusting of stars beyond. The broad pink river of the Milky Way showed above the treetops. The huge palms began to sway gently in a sudden freshening of the wind off the sea.

He felt a tremor of wind running through the ferns around him when the same sea breeze filtered down through the palms and stirred the grasses in front of him, carrying with it the strong scent of rot and kelp that came from the sea when the tide was pulling back from the shorelines. He breathed it in, held it, stopped moving.

The sea scent was salty and biting, but there was something else in it, a stronger, richer scent. He turned to face the wind and raised his head, feeling the spidery touch of the moonlight as it lay across his face, his body still in deep shadow. He pulled in another breath, taking it deep in his lungs. There was something strange in that wind.

A few feet to his left, a shadow moved through a wall of low ferns and came silently across the clearing to kneel beside him.

"You smell that?" said Kelleher.

"I do," said Rick, his heart oddly heavy in his chest, his throat filling up with the scent, the fresh reek of copper and salt.

"It's close," he said.

"This way," said Rick, checking the wind direction and getting to his feet. He moved away into the wind, gliding softly through the clearing toward a stand of royal palms a few hundred feet to the south. Here the ground continued to slope gradually toward a kind of crest or coppice. At the top of the crest they found a bowl-shaped depression in the limestone, surrounded by a ring of royal palms that rose up a hundred feet, swaying slowly back and forth in the wind, their ancient trunks creaking and groaning in the night.

Here they found Odalys. She was lying on her left side in the middle of this depression, her face turned to the sky but her body huddled and curled inside her flimsy parrot-print dress, as if she had been trying to stay warm as the evening cooled and the winds rose. Her throat had been cut so savagely, so completely, that her head was almost severed from her body, the wound gaping wide under the grinning horror of her face. Her dead eyes caught the moonlight, glittering like black onyx.

The shallow sandy bowl had soaked up most of the blood that was in her, but there was still enough of it in a pool around her body for its scent to drift a long way on the wind. Kelleher knelt beside him; they looked at her for a time in silence.

Then Kelleher touched his shoulder.

"She must have called Goyri. On the radio. We have to go."

"We can't leave her like this."

"Rick, she's still warm."

Rick turned to look at Kelleher, lit up by the moon glow, his eyes two black holes in the hard granite of his face. He picked up the two-way radio, flicked the TALK button.

"Zeffi," he said, in a hoarse whisper. Relief flooded through him as her voice came right back, low and calm.

*"Rick. I was worried. That stupid cat's acting like he's seen a ghost. He's staring at the walls and hissing at nothing.*

*A second ago he ran outside. This silly cat is really freaking me out. Are you—"*

"Zeffi, listen to me. They're here. Cast off and go."

*"Rick, what's the—"*

Rick cut her off.

"Zeffi, listen. They killed Odalys. They're here. *Go.*"

They both heard a feathery rustle to their left. Rick flicked the radio off, rolling away into a pool of black shadow as Kelleher rose to meet a dark shape racing at them from the tree line. They slammed into each other with a huffing breathy impact in the middle of the clearing. Rick saw a silvery flash of steel blurring against the two black shadow figures struggling in the clearing. There was a sudden muscular twist and one of the figures hit the ground hard on his back; the bright steel flashed out in a sideways arc that ended in a violet flaring of liquid droplets and sparkled like tiny rubies in the moonlight. They made a distinct spattering sound as they flew out across the sand. Rick picked up a flat stone and raced toward the kneeling figure, lifting it to strike at the skull. Kelleher stood up in a fluid motion and caught Rick by the forearm, hissing at him.

"Take this. I have the Smith."

Rick looked down at Kelleher's hand. He was holding out a long narrow-bladed knife with two curved guards, the hilt wrapped in strands of soft leather. The blade of the knife was nine inches long and tapered to a needle point. The shining steel was slick with fresh blood. Kelleher flipped the knife into the air, caught it by the blade, held the hilt out to Rick.

Rick took it and felt the fresh blood on it as warm as spilled black coffee. He looked down at the figure sprawled in the sand, at the arc of blood drops that stretched out in a line over the moonlit sand. It was no one he knew, a large well-muscled man with vaguely Indian features, in a black T-shirt and jeans, barefoot. A terrible gaping slash had opened his throat from his breastbone to his left ear and part of his collarbone glinted wetly in the moonlight. When Rick looked up again, Kelleher was gone and he was alone in the whispering glade. He glanced at Odalys, lying in the sand, felt a bitter surge of pity and regret; then he padded off into the forest in a low crouch, moving in the direction of the shoreline and thinking only one clear thought . . . *Take the boat, Zeffi.*

*Take the boat and run.*

Then from somewhere to his right, much deeper in the palm grove, he heard the muffled boom of Kelleher's Smith. He saw the blue flash of the distant muzzle in between the trunks and another rolling boom as the sound of the second shot reached him. Rick slipped into the tiger-striped shadows under the palms, heading for the sound. The sand was cooler here, silky under his feet, and the silence that followed the gunshots pressed in against him.

As he moved through the grove he searched the shadows and pools of light around him, looking for anything man-shaped, the knife in his right hand, tip out, double-edged blade flat. He felt the rising flood of fear coming up his body. The skin across his back tightened. His knee shook slightly. As the adrenaline coursed through his veins, his breathing accelerated and his heart thrummed in his chest. He swallowed and tried to concentrate on the act of walking forward when a great deal of his mind was arguing for headlong flight.

No. Leaving Kelleher alone in this moonlit grove was unthinkable. There was no worth at all in a life made unlivable by a shame you could never redeem. And yet to go forward into this quiet moonlit glade with nothing but a narrow blade . . . Rick found that it was a very hard thing to do.

Still, he went; the silence seemed to grow more profound until his own breathing seemed unnaturally loud and he could feel the blood singing in his ears like the sound of the sea in the turning pink spiral of a conch shell. And then, above that nearly inaudible singing of the blood, he heard something else—a soft rustle of sand—coming from a shadowed area under a stand of ferns a few yards up the trail.

Rick slipped softly into a pool of blackness and waited. The faint whispering sound came closer, and in a moment Rick saw the dappled shape of a man moving down the narrow track toward the clearing that looked out on the sea. As the man moved from light into darkness and back into light, the pale oval of his face became clearer, his eyes dark and the line of his mouth set hard. He did not recognize this man either. The man reached a place near Rick and settled into a crouch, turning on the pads of his feet, breathing deep, his face in the air as if he were trying to catch the scent of a man.

*Do I kill this man?* Rick thought. He had killed before this but not like this . . . this was cold-blooded killing. Intimate. Skin to skin and breath to breath. The man froze in place as if he had sensed Rick's unspoken thought. Rick moved slowly toward the man, who then turned suddenly to look back up the trail he had come down, perhaps to see if he was being tracked. Rick was within two feet of him and yet the man had still not sensed him. The man lifted his face to the moonlight again and ran a hand over his eyes as if he were trying to clear his vision. Rick saw the pistol in the man's hand, a silver glimmer in the light.

The man tensed and began to turn in Rick's direction, the muzzle following the motion, and then he swiveled around on his toes to look behind him, and then Rick was at the man's back, so close he could feel the heat of the man's body and the smell of tequila on his skin. The man began to turn again— *he will kill you and then he will kill Zeffi if you don't move now*—he reached out with his left hand, caught the man by the mouth, covering it, feeling the stubble of his unshaven skin, jerked his head sharply, pulling the man backward onto the tip of the long knife in his right hand, the blade sliding in easily through the muscle underneath the right shoulder blade—a slight grating vibration moved up the shaft of the blade as the edge ground a path over a rib—it all passed in one silent motion—as the man's body tightened to resist and he struggled to open his mouth to call a warning to his friends, the needle-sharp tip of the stiletto reached his heart and stopped it the way you stop a swinging pendulum.

Rick held him in a close embrace, squeezing him into his own body, feeling the heat of his body, the rapid humming vibration of the man's living spirit fluttering madly against Rick's chest.

*Hush . . . hush. . . .*

Rick repeated the words, breathing them into the man's left ear; he held him in this embrace for a timeless interval, measured at first in two separate heartbeats but ending in only one. In another few seconds the man's body changed from a hot breathing thing to a slack deadweight on Rick's thighs. He let go of the man. The corpse slipped noiselessly onto the ground, the breath coming out of its wet open mouth in a prolonged sighing hiss.

Rick stood up, breathing hard, heard the sound of a shot—and another—two clear hard cracks coming from the jetty. He recognized the distinctive muzzle blast of his own Colt 45. Zeffi was shooting at someone. He began to run through the palms with the knife in his hand—the trees flashing by him and the gliding moon flickering through the palm trunks as he ran—then another sound reached him, the sudden growling roar of the twin diesels as *La Gaviota* accelerated away from the dock.

He reached a clearing and stopped, breathing hard. Down in the shallow bay he could see *La Gaviota* running flat-out on a straight course for the breakwater, her lights gleaming, the sleek arrow-shaped hull slicing a lacy white V out of the moonlit water. As he watched, *La Gaviota* reached the break-water and flashed through it into the open sea. He heard a high-pitched howl coming from somewhere out beyond the breakwater, and then two Zodiac boats zipped in toward the speeding cruiser, narrowly missing her as she blew by them. They turned into *La Gaviota*'s wake and chased her, their engines wailing with a high buzzing note like angry wasps.

*La Gaviota* was racing at her best speed, her destroyer bow cutting through the waves, running straight as a lance out into the open sea, two white wings of flying spray arcing out from her cutwater. She was gaining distance while he watched. He heard a series of tinny chattering sounds coming over the water and saw blue flames flashing at the bow of one of the Zodiacs. Bright red sparks glittered and zipped around *La Gaviota*'s stern as the rounds struck home but the ship neither slowed nor wavered in the slightest. It flashed over the rollers like a sea bird and Rick remembered that *La Gaviota* meant seagull. She was well-named. *That's it, Zeffi. Fly. Fly away as fast as you can.*

Far off in the groves behind him a man screamed in agony—a long rising shriek of terrible pain. In a second, Rick was pounding through a tall stand of ferns, the leaves whipping at his chest and the sandy soil slipping under his sandals. When he cleared the ferns something moved in his peripheral vision—he turned as a man came up at him from the ground— his arm extended—Rick saw the shape of a heavy pistol in the man's hand—he charged straight at the muzzle—the man fired—the muzzle flared up bright blue with a red spark in the middle of the flame—Rick felt a round humming past his right ear and then the booming sound of the shot—Rick hit the man at a dead run and the impact carried them both in a tumbling fall down a sandy slope. Rick could smell the man's fishy breath; the salty odor of dried sweat was in his nose as he got a grip on the pistol in the man's hand and wrenched the muzzle skyward—the man fired again with the muzzle an inch from Rick's left ear. The sound of the shot blew Rick's eardrum apart and his left hand went icy cold and numb. They hit the bottom of the slope in a vicious tangle.

Rick felt the man's powerful body flexing as he heaved at Rick—Rick, fighting him down, felt his belly wound split open and a shaft of red fire arced across his chest—the man brought his knee up sharply, catching Rick solidly in the lower ribs—the breath exploded out of him and the light around them seemed to change as he struggled for air—in a dim red rage he struck at the man's body with his right hand—a ripping upward blow with the long, thin knife twisting in his grip—the hilt still slick with blood—he felt the blade punching through muscle and ribs—the man's face was inches from his own when he screamed—a squealing cat's cry of pain and rage—Rick stabbed him again, feeling the thin blade slicing into meat—again—the blow of the blade punching into the man's body so hard Rick could feel the man's belly muscles jumping against his fingers clenched around the bloody hilt—the screaming cut off suddenly and the man went limp under Rick's body.

Rick pushed himself off the man and stood looking down at him. The man was on his back, staring up at the wheeling star-filled sky above him, gasping for air, his eyes wide and blinking rapidly, his mouth working like a gaffed shark in the bottom of a boat. Rick stood there for a timeless period—the fight had lasted less than thirty seconds—until the man stopped breathing; then he turned away and staggered a hundred yards down the slope toward the edge of the palm grove. He could still hear the sound of *La Gaviota*'s engines, much fainter, coming from a great distance away.

He reached the sandy shelf above the town and looked out over the jumble of rooftops toward the open sea. Far out on the shining moonlit horizon he saw a tiny ripple of amber lights flying away into the night and heard the distant muted humming of twin diesels running fast. Zeffi Calderas was still out there, still flying away across the water toward Key West.

He stood swaying in the sea wind while the blood ran down his legs, watching *La Gaviota*'s tiny yellow lights glimmering across the miles of ocean until they seemed to blend into the luminous haze at the farthest reach of the horizon line, finally disappearing into the deeper blue band of haze that shone between the sea and the stars. Four seconds later, a white hot blaze flared up abruptly and spread along the horizon line at the point where *La Gaviota* had disappeared. The fireball expanded and pulsed blue-white and violet—a midnight sun—then shrank again into a churning pyramid of red and yellow flames sharply cut by the black line of the distant horizon.

A few seconds passed, then a deep rolling boom like distant thunder came out of the ocean and rumbled in the air all around him. He watched the fireball shrink even further until it was nothing more than a dim yellow torch burning like a tiny spark far out in the glimmering plain of the Santaren Channel. When it finally wavered and dimmed into nothing he kept on staring at the place where that light had been, although the only sign that it had ever burned at all was in the bright purple after-image still floating on his retinas.

That too slowly faded and he was alone with the booming of the surf on the breakwater, the sighing of the wind in the dry leaves of the palm trees behind him and the relentless, pointless beating of his own heart.

# MOONLIGHT SERENADE

## MIDNIGHT ON FLAT IRON SHOALS, ANDROS ISLAND
### TUESDAY, OCTOBER 1

Kelleher found him sitting in the sand at the edge of the tree line a few minutes later. Rick heard him crossing the sand, but he didn't look away from the sea. Kelleher sat down beside him, breathing hard. He smelled of fresh blood and worse. Kelleher shoved the Smith into his belt and said nothing for a few minutes, while they both looked out at the shimmering moonlit sheen of the Caribbean. The moon had risen in the star-filled sky and was hanging directly above the town. The light from it lay all across the harbor, delicate, silvery, extraordinarily beautiful. Rick looked down at his own hands. The moonlight made them glow like wax candles. His left hand was dripping blood. He leaned over—the effort made him wince—and scooped up a handful of rough sand. He ground it between his hands and then let the clumps fall to the ground between his feet. The bleeding slowed and stopped. Kelleher finally spoke.

"I heard an explosion."

Rick nodded, his throat working hard.

"*La Gaviota.*"

"What happened?"

"They tried to get on the boat. I think she shot one. I heard the Colt. Two Zodiacs. Maybe four men. She led them away. Straight out into the reach, full throttle, rock steady. I could see her running lights. They were firing on her but she never wavered. Straight on into the deeper ocean. She made it a long way, Charlie, all the way to the horizon. Then a light, it flared up. Later the sound came in. Like a tropical storm. Then there was nothing. I think a round hit that propane tank for the galley stove."

Further speech became impossible for Rick, and Kelleher could think of nothing at all to say that would change any of it. But something had to be said. He put a hand on Rick's shoulder.

"She was a serious woman, Rick. A serious woman."

"She was," said Rick in a thick voice. "A serious woman."

Ten minutes passed slowly as they listened to the crashing and booming of the Caribbean rollers on the distant breakwater. Rick sighed and spoke in a hoarse whisper, his voice steadier.

"I killed two men back there. With this."

He lifted the stiletto and turned the blade in the moonlight and then rammed it hilt-deep into the sandy ground at his feet. They fell into a silence again, each man alone with what he had done.

"You could have stayed out of it," said Kelleher,

after a few minutes had passed. "I had the Smith."

"And then what? Go back to L.A.? Live out my little life?"

Kelleher nodded in the moonlight. There was nothing more to be said about it. It has never been true that it's always better to live.

"Hell of a thing, Rick," he said after a while.

"Yes. It is a hell of a thing."

Kelleher blew out a breath and ran his fingers through his tousled hair, raining sand down on his shirt. He looked out across the empty sea under the moon, then back at Rick.

"Well, what do you want to do?"

"Now?" said Rick, sighing and struggling to his feet and looking back at Kelleher. "We get the hell off this island."

"How do we do that? If you're thinking of the propane junk down in the harbor, she's a hulk. The first sea roller will sink her."

"Suerta got here."

Kelleher thought about it and then struggled to his feet.

"It'll be beached somewhere south of here. They would have had to come in over the shoals, so it won't be a big boat."

"I want to be a thousand miles from here when the sun comes up tomorrow. I don't give a damn if it's a basket made of reeds."

# LAZARA

Less than a mile down the windblown shoals they found a dark blue Kodiak seaplane moored in a deserted lagoon, rocking gently in the beach break. They came up on it quietly, but there was no one aboard. Kelleher stepped up onto the float and opened the pilot's door. A last supper of *huevos revueltos* and refried beans that had been eaten by the dead men in the palm grove was still congealing on paper plates scattered around the floor of the passenger cabin, surrounded by a small platoon of empty beer bottles. But the basic plane was still there underneath the grime and the mess. Kelleher saw that her tanks had been topped up recently and her galley locker was full of food. Rick found a battered but serviceable M-16 in a wooden crate at the back of the passenger cabin along with four thirty-round box magazines of 5.56 Military Ball. There were some first-aid supplies under the copilot's chair, and even a spare magazine that fit the SIG-Sauer.

They sat down on the starboard float with their

backs up against the struts and stitched whatever could be stitched, poured hydrogen peroxide on what couldn't, then wrapped the results in clean bandages.

"You know this plane?" asked Rick.

Kelleher nodded.

"It's the second plane. We had two. Identical models."

"How the hell did they get it out of Cuba?"

"My guess is it wasn't in Cuba. It was in the Keys."

"The Vargas connection. Was Suerta a pilot?"

"No. One of the others, I guess. Back there."

Kelleher straightened up and reached for the cabin door.

"Come on, Rick. Let's go."

Rick got to his feet with difficulty, cast off the mooring line, climbed into the copilot's chair and slammed the door. Kelleher did a quick systems check and switched the engine tabs to ON. He cranked the starboard and it snarled into life, followed the port. He feathered the props and the uneven rumble of the engines settled into a smooth throaty growl. He let the aircraft drift around until its nose was pointed out to sea, then he increased the throttle and it began to slide forward toward the shoal water outside the reef. When the plane cleared the reef, Kelleher shifted the pitch and they floated over the water toward Flat Iron Shoals, the prop wash kicking up a thin spray of white water from under their wings, the floats beginning to hiss in the surf as they cut through the swells.

"Where to, sir?" said Kelleher. "Cuba or the Keys?"

Rick shook his head.

"Let's go back to the town first."

"Why?"

Rick shrugged, said nothing, but Kelleher got it.

"Christ . . . you want to go back for Cisco?"

Rick smiled.

"We don't leave our guys on the beach, do we?"

"Rick, those damned Zodiacs will be coming back any minute. Anyway Cisco's not a 'guy.' He's a cat. And a cold-blooded killer."

Rick's smile faded away.

"And what are we, Charlie?"

Kelleher digested the concept in silence. In a short while, they were opening the lagoon at Flat Iron Shoals and the darkened town was gliding into view. Kelleher killed the engines and the floatplane drifted across the inner harbor. They reached the jetty in a silent glide, and Rick went out to warp them along the dock. He tied the plane off on a stanchion, ran a spring to the tail wing mooring hook. Kelleher stepped down onto the float and considered the deserted village. He could see what Rick was thinking. Cisco was a survivor. He'd be around here somewhere. Rick turned to face him directly.

"Charlie, I have a question."

"Sure. Run it by me. I'm a fucking fountain of wisdom."

"Zeffi was right, wasn't she? Elliott Lazarus might be the mole. He fits the profile, anyway. But so does Cameron Chennault, and Dunford Buell. Maybe even Diane Le Tourneau."

"Right as rain. Also fifty other people."

"And what does Hector Preig want?"

"Preig? If we're right about all this, Preig wants out of Cuba."

"And Onassis Goyri?"

"Same thing. Out of Cuba. A happy reunion with his money."

"So let them have it."

"What?"

"We make it possible for both of them to defect."

"How do we do that? It's no good asking for U.S. help. The mole, remember?"

"We don't need the feds. We need our own people."

"Who? The Navy? Forget that. They—"

"Not the Navy, Charlie. We need Hollywood."

"Hollywood. What the hell can Hollywood do?"

"Get on the radio and raise the Marine operator. Ask for a patch-through to an American landline."

"And when I get it, what then?"

Rick poked around in his pocket and extracted his wallet, fished out a business card, flipped it over to Kelleher. Kelleher read it and then looked up at Rick with a wary expression.

"Jack Cole again? What can he do?"

"I told you. He's the head of security for Paradigm Pictures. He's ex-LAPD and the only guy at Paradigm who gives a damn about Jake Seigel. Back in Los Angeles, he proposed a back-channel deal with the Cubans. Give them whatever they want and get Jake back. We know what the men behind this whole thing want. They want to get out of Cuba alive with all their toys intact."

"Getting them all out of Cuba—including Hector Preig and Onassis Goyri—that's going to take the kind of global logistical reach that not even Paradigm Pictures has. You need your own choppers and your own Learjets and you need people experienced in hostage negotiations. Ex-military or ex-FBI. And you'd need enough clout to make the government go along with the extraction after the fact. Who the hell can do all that?"

"Wackenhut. They do it all the time."

"You'd have to tell Jack Cole everything we know. They'd need all of that to force Preig and Goyri to go along with it."

"That's fine with me. We wouldn't have figured out the CIMEX connection without his help anyway."

"It's not fine with me. It's too risky. Preig could take Katie out just for insurance. Personally, no offense, she's all I care about here."

"Yeah. I know. And here's my answer. If we take Katie out of the equation, then there's nothing Preig can do to her. Let Jack Cole worry about the rest of this. He's a pro. He's up to it. Charlie, let's go get Katie. You and me. We do it tonight. We take this plane and go get her. We fly into Havana and pick her up. Then we fly the hell out. We can be in Havana in two hours."

Kelleher studied Rick's face in the moonglow.

"You're serious?"

"I have nothing left to lose. Let's finish this thing tonight."

"It's three hundred and forty nautical miles from Andros to Havana. We'd have to fly this crate at over two hundred and fifty miles an hour less than ten feet off the deck. The whole area around Cuba is blockaded at the twelve-mile limit. Even with the antiradar paint and the stealth color, it's a fifty-to-one shot, at best. Hell, if the Cuban MiGs don't get us, our own guys will probably shoot us down."

"Yeah. You're right. It's totally nuts. So the fuck what?"

Kelleher was silent for a long time. The plane rocked gently on her floats and the lines creaked from the tension. Shell-shaped ripples curled along the sides of the floats. Finally, he grinned at Rick. "This is you all over, hah? Fuck all the rules. Death or glory. It is a good day to die. Am I as crazy as you are?"

"Are you?"

"Yeah. I probably am."

"Good. Great. Call Jack Cole. Call him. Get him on the sideband and lay it all out for him. Leave Katie out of it."

Kelleher nodded, handed Rick the Smith, and climbed back into the plane. Rick could hear him calling the Marine operator as he stumble-walked down the cobbled hill and into the town. His left hand was throbbing and every time he took a step he felt a jab like the point of a knife, which took his mind off the bullet wound in his belly.

"Cisco. Cisco, you mook. Cisco. Come here."

He walked down into the town calling Cisco's

name, his left hand cradled up and his head tilted a degree to the left, as he favored his shattered eardrum. In a few minutes he reached the steps that led up to the Black Dog bar, where he stopped in the rectangle of warm yellow light that was shining out the open door. Zeffi Calderas was sitting on a stool at the long bar, her wet hair wrapped in a damp towel, her knees up and a long yellow-cotton sweater pulled down around them, a huge, round frosted glass of something pale green in her right hand, a black Turkish cigarette smoldering in an ash-tray made of a cylinder head sitting on the bar close to her left hand. Underneath the stool, coiled up in a loopy tangle of damp fur and muscle, was Cisco. Zeffi smiled at him, lifted her glass and said:

"Hello, sailor. Buy a girl a drink?"

"Zeffi . . . for Christ's sake. How the hell . . . ?"

"I set the autopilot. Then we both jumped off, didn't we, Cisco? Cisco was very . . . Rick? Rick, you don't look at all well."

# HAVANA

AIR SPEED 250 MPH
COMPASS BEARING 237
ALTITUDE SEVENTEEN FEET
TWENTY-FIVE MILES OFF THE NORTH
COAST OF CUBA, INBOUND
4:04 A.M. EDT, TUESDAY, OCTOBER 1

They were running in the dark, all their exterior lights out and the cabin dimmed. The flat wall of the ocean was racing by underneath their windscreen, a streaming blurring plain of flickering moonlight, jagged curling whitecaps, long indigo rollers rising up to meet them and dropping away under the wings. On the port side of the plane, just aft the rear stabilizer, a faint milky-pink stain was spreading across the soft blue velvet of the eastern horizon far behind them, a deeper, truer white in the center of the rising light.

Through the windscreen beaded with spray and out beyond the heaving surface of the ocean constantly rushing toward them, there was a faint glow of warm yellow light shining on the underside of a bank of low cloud. Inside the cabin, the air was cold and clear, the interior lit only by the orange-and-red glow of the instrument panel, the muted howling of the engines filling the small space with a sustained humming vibration, steady and strong, a purring bass note that had almost faded out of their awareness. Kelleher's creased and haggard face at the controls was shadowed, his eyes black holes in the weird amber glow of the instrument panel. Zeffi was curled up in the copilot's chair on the starboard side, a blanket over her, snoring softly, Cisco asleep in her lap.

Rick, in a fold-down jump seat behind the pilot's chair, was leaning forward with his arm on the back of Kelleher's chair, staring out at the onrushing waves, his face set and stony-looking.

"Those lights," he said. "Is that Havana?"

"Not yet," said Kelleher, his voice soft, barely audible above the deep vibrato of the engine noise coming through the hull.

"Probably Cárdenas or Matanzas. There's a big naval port at Cárdenas. We're about forty klicks out of Havana. On this bearing, we should pick up her shore lights almost dead ahead in maybe five minutes. I'm going to take her right down on the deck when we cross the twelve-mile limit. Their short-range radar sucks."

"Take her down? We *are* down. We clipped the top off a roller only a mile back. You'll catch a float and we'll skip like a flat stone all the way into Marina Hemingway. You can't go any lower."

"Rick, with respect, is this a fucking boat?"

"No. Not yet, anyway. Go any lower and we'll see.

Where the hell is the blockade fleet? All we've seen since we left Andros are two cruise ships and some sportfishers over the Cay Sal Bank."

"They're blockading at the twelve-mile line. All their attention is inward, toward the Cuban coast. They're keeping the Cubans in. I don't think they're paying much attention to traffic outside that line. Otherwise, we'd never have made it this far. You made a good call."

Rick looked over at Zeffi, watched the rise and fall of her breathing and the way the light lay on her sleeping face.

"I wish she had let us put her ashore at Nicolls Town."

Kelleher made a low noise that might have been a laugh.

"Oh yes, that went really well. Next time you bring it up, do it when I'm in another time zone, okay? I have a weak heart."

Zeffi's response to that suggestion had been . . . forceful. Clear and forceful. Kelleher had begun a mild observation that could have been interpreted as weak support for Rick's position. The brief but feral look he got from Zeffi had him checking his face for burn marks. What was it going to take, she had said, to get them to understand that her life belonged to her and no one else and it was hers to risk as she damned well pleased, and what was it going to take for them to accept the fact that she was as important to the . . . well, mission seemed to be the right word . . . as either of them. This was said without excessive fire, but with a latent indignant ferocity that carried every argument away and made both men ashamed of their condescension. She was sleeping, looking like a young girl, a cat draped across her lap and a blanket around her shoulders, but neither man considered her at all childlike.

Rick was leaning to the right, looking out the starboard cabin window, thinking about Zeffi Calderas and what, if any, future they might have together when a shred of low cloudbank lifted and he saw something out on the ocean: a low island of white lights, visible just at the edge of the horizon line, maybe five miles to the west of their position and a few miles closer to Cuba.

"You see that, Charlie?"

Kelleher looked out to the right, saw the lights, and immediately shoved the stick forward. The plane dipped and the streaming surface of the ocean was only six feet away.

"Christ, Charlie. What the hell?"

"That's a Cuban gunboat."

"How do you know it's Cuban?"

"Because we're still alive. We'd never have gotten within sight of any American ship. One of their Harriers would have lit us up before we got within ten miles."

At that moment a huge black shape slammed through the sky less than a hundred feet overhead; a second later, a shattering roar shook the whole plane. Kelleher pulled up on the stick and the Kodiak swooped up sickeningly as a large wave rose up at them from the churning seas. They clipped the crest with a float as they passed over it, the airframe lurched and recovered; sea spray scattered itself across the windscreen. Then a second black shape boomed by close enough to leave the floatplane weaving in the backwash, followed by a second huge roar of jet engines. Both shapes were streaking away from them, heading right for the gunboat.

"What was that?" asked Zeffi, wide awake and sitting up.

"Harriers," said Kelleher. "Off the *Ticonderoga*. They're going to buzz that Cuban gunboat over there."

All three of them watched as the pair of Harriers hurtled across the deck toward the little island of white lights five miles away. Kelleher reached for the radio controls and hit the SCAN switch. Within seconds they were hearing a laconic American voice talking to the Cuban gunboat.

*"This is Bobcat Niner Four to the Cuban naval vessel. You are in a blockade zone. Repeat, you are in a blockade zone. Come about to bearing one niner zero and return to your base immediately or we will fire on you. Acknowledge."*

An immediate and defiant response came back from the gunboat, a deep voice in heavily accented Spanish.

*"Bobcat Niner Four, you are approaching Cuban airspace. If you do not leave the area at once you will be shot down. Acknowledge."*

They didn't hear what the Harrier pilot of Bobcat Niner Four had to say because in the next second a vivid fiery streak of golden beads erupted from the deck of the gunboat and sprayed wildly across the night sky.

"Christ," said Kelleher, who'd been on the other end of that kind of fire. "Golden BB's . . . antiaircraft fire."

*"Bobcat Niner Four to Base. We are taking hostile fire from the Cuban gunboat. Permission to engage."*

*"Roger, Bobcat Niner Four. Permission granted."*

*"Roger, base. Bobcat Five, let's go."*

*"Roger, Bobcat Leader. In hot with guns."*

The sound of jet engines spooling up came through the windshield, drowning out the sound of the Dakota's turbos; they saw a shape like a black shark briefly silhouetted against the stream of golden fire arcing up from the gunboat. They heard the distant rattle of automatic fire coming from the gunboat.

"They're going to regret that," said Kelleher, his face bright and avid.

Before he had finished speaking, two black shark shapes flashed across the water near the gunboat. Both Harriers erupted in twin streaks of blue-white fire that zeroed in on the gunboat. Seconds later, they heard a long ripping sound like silk being torn apart. The lights of the gunboat flickered, the golden stream of fire ceased; a moment later the entire ship rose up on a white flare of internal explosions, a fierce red blaze shot up for two hundred feet, and then the boat capsized and settled, wallowing in a wash of white foaming water. The assault had taken less than ten seconds.

*"Bobcat Leader to base. Target destroyed."*

*"Bobcat Leader, roger that. Bobcat Leader. You have bogies at your six, repeat three bogies at your six."*

*"Roger, base. Three bogies at my six."*

"Cuban MiGs," said Kelleher, in the stunned silence of the cabin. "Out of Cárdenas, probably."

"Can they take out the Harriers?" asked Rick.

"They won't get the chance."

The gunboat was gone, her place in the ocean marked only by a small flickering ball of yellow flame. They could hear the sound of the Harriers booming across the water, climbing fast.

*"Bobcat Leader, this is Bobcat Five. I have bogies on my tail."*

*"Roger, Bobcat Five. Here comes the cavalry."*

A new voice, also American, younger, equally dry and calm.

*"Bobcat Leader, this is Tango Flight Leader."*

"Who are they?" asked Zeffi. "The Cubans?"

"No. Probably a couple of Rhinos. Watch this."

*"Tango Leader to Tango Four. We have three MiGs approaching at two thousand. Engage."*

*"Roger, Tango Leader."*

*"Tango, this is Bobcat Leader. We're outta here."*

*"Roger that, Bobcat Leader. Mind your skirts, ladies."*

"Are MiGs up to Rhinos?" asked Rick.

"Until a war starts," said Kelleher, his voice tight with frustration. "God, I wish I were up there with them. Super Hornets have twenty-mill cannons, but the killing gets done with Sidewinders. They'll lock on and . . ."

"*Tango Leader, I'm locked. Fox one. Fox two.*"

"He's fired two Sidewinders at the MiGs," said Kelleher.

"*Tango Four. Fox one. Fox two.*"

"His wingman."

Four bright blue streaks arced overhead, ending in one . . . then a second . . . two yellow flowers opening in the dark sky thousands of feet above them. The flowers blossomed and glimmered and winked out. A few red-hot sparks tumbled earthward.

"*Tango Leader to base, the third MiG has done a one-eighty. Permission to pursue.*"

"*Permission granted.*"

"Christ," said Kelleher. "They're going to chase that MiG right into Cuban airspace. There they go."

Far up in the gradually lightening sky they saw a blue-white flare of an afterburner, followed by a second. The air was full of a prolonged roaring thunder as the fighters shot straight into the sky over Cuba. Kelleher looked down at the ocean and saw the lights of Havana stretched out across the coast, a chain of yellow pearls on a low black coast, clouds lying on the dark mass of the Mesa de Mariel behind the city. They were closing in fast, less than two miles out. Kelleher told them to strap in and get ready for anything.

"Damn, it looks like we're going to make it," he said, tightening his strap. "I guess the Cubans are busy with the Rhinos. I can put her down anywhere around here and we can taxi to the dock."

"Won't there be more gunboats?"

"Likely. I see one off to our left but he's steaming out to sea. And there goes another. I guess they're scrambling whatever they've got. We couldn't have asked for a better diversion. Rick, you have the luck of the God-damn Irish. God, look at that. The harbor's jammed with boats. There must be thousands of them all over the bay. All lit up too. What the hell . . . ?"

"What's our plan?" asked Rick.

"Plan?" said Kelleher, laughing. "What plan?"

"I thought you had a plan?" said Rick.

"I thought *you* had a plan. Hey, Zeffi, do *you* have a plan?"

"God," said Zeffi, mainly to herself. "Americans."

Kelleher eased the stick down and set the flaps. Their airspeed dropped and the glimmering surface of the bay, yellow shore lights reflected in the water, came up beneath them. The floats touched, skimmed, Kelleher dropped the airspeed and feathered the props, and then they were down, a broad fan of white water surged ahead of the floats and they felt the forward shift of their own weight.

The Kodiak settled into a slow glide over the water, her props churning like two silver disks and the lights of Marina Hemingway flickering inside the silver disks. Soon they were among a huge fleet of cruisers, sailboats, small craft, fishing boats, hundreds and hundreds of them, all drifting idly through the calm waters of the harbor, each boat carrying as many people as it could hold, boys and girls, whole families. People were out on their decks, all of them staring up at the night sky, mothers with babies in their arms, pointing up at the heavens like a scene from *Close Encounters*.

Kelleher popped his side window and a warm breeze rolled in, carrying the bright clear sound of music playing, the scent of gasoline, garlic, oil slick, raw sewage, burning bread, and under that the sharp tang of pine and eucalyptus and the sweet rot of the tropics.

*"A dónde va, amigo? Tenemos cervezas fria?"* came a hail from a nearby trawler, several thin dark men clustered on the bow, music coming from somewhere in the boat. Zeffi recognized the liquid sensuous piano of Rubén González.

"How's your Spanish, Zeffi?" said Kelleher, in a low voice. "Ask them what's going on."

Zeffi leaned forward and popped the copilot's window. She exchanged a few words with the young men on the fishing boat, ending with a bright laugh and a wave.

She closed the window, still laughing.

"What's so funny?" asked Rick, whose Spanish was only marginally better than his Martian.

"It's a *fiesta*, Rick. The whole town—all of Havana—has turned out to watch the war. All the gunboats have gone to sea and the soldiers are all down in the old town guarding the *playa central*. They say Castro's gone into hiding and even the *douanieros* are drunk."

"It's a party?"

"Looks like it," said Zeffi. "God, I love the Cubans."

Kelleher had the props feathered and the engines throttled back, slowing the plane to a four-knot cruise through the crowded harbor, looking for a place to moor. He saw a blue-and-yellow buoy bobbing in the wake of a big sportfisher a hundred yards off the pier.

"Rick, I'm going to run her into there—the blue-and-yellow buoy. We'll tie her up there and ship the inflatable. One of you is going to have to stay with—"

They all heard the sound of a heavy chopper hammering through the damp seaside air, the syncopated thrumming of the blades and the heavy drone of the turbines. A ripple of alarm went shooting through the people in the boats all around them—Zeffi put her head out the cabin porthole—someone from the marina dock was shouting to the flotilla—and then Zeffi saw a large twin-rotor chopper rise up over the low buildings along the marina shoreline—people in the boats nearby were gunning their engines and pulling up their anchors—Zeffi watched the chopper level out and bank to the right—it was coming out over the harbor—she saw letters painted along the side of the fuselage— GUARDIA CUBA FEDERAL—

"It's a coast guard gunship," said Kelleher, killing the props and turning off the running lights, letting the turboprop glide silently through the water toward the mooring buoy. They were in a crowd of fishing boats, and the smoke from a nearby barbecue had settled down into a low bank riding on top of the water. They drifted through this smoke bank in a sudden and ominous quiet, only the sound of the rotors beating, and watched the big Russian-made chopper lumber slowly out across the bay at a hundred feet off the water.

As it passed over the boats, they pulled away from its path, clearing a lane under the machine as it came, a white spray fanning out from it as the rotor wash hit the surface of the harbor. It reached the middle of the harbor and hovered, turning slowly around a fixed point above the flotilla; a bright blue searchlight mounted on the nose cone flashed on and began to flicker around the boats, a fifty-foot circle as bright as sunlight; a voice came booming out of the bullhorn.

*"Atención! Atención! Todos las barcas a la playa immediamente! Todos las barcas a la playa.* All boats to the dock. Everyone is to leave the harbor. *Atención! Atención—"*

About twenty feet to their left, an old man lurched unsteadily out onto the bow of a large silver trawler, something blunt and tubular in his hand. He raised it up and pointed it in the direction of the chopper—

"Oh God," said Kelleher. "Don't do it."

The man shouted something in Spanish—a garbled incoherent cry of drunken rage—he steadied the flare gun—the chopper pilot must have seen the motion because the searchlight flickered across the forest of spars and radar masts and zeroed in on the shouting man in the bow of the fishing boat. Then they heard a warning from the chopper just as the man fired the flare, the luminous arc racing at the chopper, glowing bright green at the flaming tip like a tiny meteor. Almost at the same moment, a stream of red fire flashed out from the chopper's open bay door and they heard the chatter of a heavy machine gun. The flare smacked into the armored nose of the gun ship and ricocheted—tumbling away—just as a rippling swath of twenty-mill rounds tore a path through a line of boats. Rick got a momentary glimpse of a young woman coming apart in a halo of bright red blood inside the blue-white cone of the searchlight and then the row of fire reached the man in the bow—cut him in two—and kept coming toward them. People in the boats were jumping into the water—Zeffi saw a small boy struggling in the wake of a speedboat that was gunning away toward the breakwater. A moment later he disappeared under the prow of a big trawler and then the chopper was turning—fixed in place and rotating while the gunner in the bay sprayed machine-gun rounds all over the inner harbor—the rounds smacking into the water like a hard rain, punching into the hulls of the wooden boats, slicing through people in the water—women, boys, babies. The gunner was laying down a murderous fire while the chopper floated above them—a scene from hell. Zeffi felt the plane lurch and turned to see Rick stepping out onto the starboard float, something long and black in his left hand—an M-16 rifle.

Rick braced himself on the strut, steadied the rifle, and squeezed off a three-round burst. Three red sparks glanced off the nose and the machine gunfire

stopped abruptly as the gunship pivoted and rose—
Rick slipped as the plane bumped into the mooring
buoy—got his stance again—the chopper was moving
straight toward them and Zeffi could hear Kelleher
shouting something over the thrumming beat of her
rotors—Rick squeezed the trigger again and a stream
of 5.56 rounds raked the pilot's window—Zeffi saw
the window glazing as the rounds punched through—
the chopper soared up, stalled, banked crazily left and
slid sideways toward a houseboat that was powering
out of the way—it grazed the houseboat roof and
smacked into the black water on the far side, rotors
slashing up a fountain of white water—then it settled
and rolled completely upside down, bobbing in
the waves.

In the sudden silence, a figure in olive drab
climbed out of the water and crawled onto the
underbelly, got to his knees—a very young man—
brown-skinned and thin as a rake—he waved an
arm—Rick moved the M-16—put the iron sights
over the man's military shirt—a hundred-yard
shot—squeezed off three rounds—the boy jerked
backward into the water, a cloud of pink foam floated
in the air above the chopper—a gush of escaping
air—and the entire gunship sank below the surface—the waves settled and closed over it. The
sound of ragged cheering and a smattering of
applause came across the water.

"Welcome to Broca's War," said Kelleher, while all
around them the flotilla was breaking up in every
direction, some boats slowing to pick up people

struggling in the water, others running them down without a pause, everyone getting the hell out of the harbor any way they could.

A long, low cigarette boat, matte black with a purple thunderbolt on the hull, rumbled and popped by a few yards to port, three teenaged men in the cockpit, wearing colorful Hawaiian shirts, kahki shorts, tanned, beardless faces shining with sweat, shocked and staring as they went by the plane.

Rick called to them.

"*Ola—aiude me? Quieremos—*"

"*No habla,*" shouted one of the teens. "We don't speak Spanish," the accent unmistakably American.

"You're Americans?" said Rick.

"Yeah," said the blond kid at the wheel. "We came in from Bimini last week. They wouldn't let us leave because of the blockade. You with the American Army, man?"

Rick nodded.

"We're here to extract an American woman. She's in the old town. Can you help us?"

The kids looked at each other blankly, then back at Rick, standing on the float with an M-16 in his hand and at the red-haired woman standing in the open cabin door behind him. The blond kid at the wheel grinned suddenly and lifted a can of Bohemia.

"Hey, dude . . . what do you need?"

# LAS VIEJAS

LA HABANA VIEJA
5:00 A.M. EDT, TUESDAY, OCTOBER 1

After a heated exchange followed by a low and whispered conversation, Rick agreed to stay with the floatplane, Kelleher's argument being that someone who knew the whole story had to be able to get out of Cuba or the entire effort would have been in vain and that an old man traveling with a young woman in the Havana streets would draw less attention than two men, both of whom looked as if they'd just come from a losing war. When they cleared the marina, Zeffi had looked back and seen Rick standing there on the float, staring after her, his face hard and filled with resentment.

During the run it became clear that sporadic fighting had broken out all along the Havana waterfront. As they cruised slowly eastward a few hundred yards off the broad avenue of Malecon they could see tracer rounds streaking into the air from the center of the town. The popcorn sound of small-arms fire drifted out across the water, punctuated with the heavier thump of grenades and the wail of sirens. As they cleared the breakwater by the old town harbor a pair of U.S. Navy F-18s flashed in a few hundred feet off the deck going inland. Seconds later they saw a string of small yellow fireballs spraying upward in a weaving line, Cuban antiaircraft fire from a position somewhere near the national assembly. Far off in the east the sun was rising and it was growing light enough to see smoke rising from several fires scattered around the vicinity of Vedado.

As they watched, three U.S. Navy Tomcats flashed in from the north and disappeared behind some buildings. A few seconds later, they heard a deep rolling boom. The shock wave hit them next, a concussive blow like a solid thump in the chest and belly. A huge plume of black smoke and orange flame rose skyward. Then another *flash-bang* and a second deep booming explosion. Then another. More plumes of black cloud and thunder in the air.

"Guys, are we in a war?" asked one of the American kids, a boy named Brad, a senior from Florida State. The cigarette boat—*Black Angel*—was his father's, borrowed for a two-week getaway. Kelleher looked at the kid's face and considered his answer. The boys seemed happy to help, but if they were caught by the Cuban authorities it was likely they'd all be stood up by a wall and executed right there.

"No," said Kelleher. "Those are Navy Tomcats taking out antiaircraft, I guess. And some buildings too, it looks like. The small-arms fire is probably just fighting between military units. Castro's managed to get most of the guns away from the people. Unarmed civilians don't have much of a chance against an army."

"Then who's doing all the shooting?" said Zeffi.

"Factions inside the military. Or the police. Maybe they think they're fighting an American incursion. Confusion. Panic. Untrained soldiers badly led. Some are drunk. Some are looting, I'll bet. I doubt the civilians are doing anything but hiding out and waiting."

Brad was pointing toward a long, low concrete dock.

"Sir, that big channel there is the entrance to Bahía Habana. They usually have a customs house on the point, right underneath the fort on the far side. They'll stop us if we try to go in there. And we could get trapped. Where do you want us to moor?"

Kelleher was studying the seawall that ran in front of the old town walls. A ripple of surf was curling along the battered stonework. The seawall itself seemed deserted.

"If you can tie her up just west of the mole we can walk into Vedado. Katie's apartment is close to the monument. Less than ten blocks from the sea wall."

"Will she be there?" asked Zeffi.

Kelleher said he hoped so but it sounded like a prayer. Brad brought the cigarette boat in at a dead crawl. Trey, the black kid, stepped off and lashed a coil around the bollard, pulling the bow in.

Dalton, the third kid, a lanky Texan, threw Trey the spring line and snugged the boat along the jetty, where it rocked gently in the swells that curled along the stonework. Trey stepped up to the edge of the dock and gave Kelleher a hand up. He was in rough shape, moving like a cripple. Zeffi looked at him.

"I should do this alone."

"No," said Kelleher. "Not a chance."

The three American kids kept their mouths shut, waiting for the decision. Finally, Zeffi stepped up onto the deck beside Kelleher, opening her mouth to say something pointed, when a burst of small-arms fire opened up from somewhere inside the old town. It was answered by a heavy thumping rattle that ran on and on. Then another massive boom as one of the Intruders took out something big. The three kids looked worried as hell.

"Can I count on you to stay here?"

"Yes," said Brad, after looking at his friends. "We'll be here."

"Count on it," said Trey.

"Good men," said Kelleher, shoving his Smith into his belt and pulling his shirt down over it. "Zeffi. Now's the time."

# OJOS VERDES

APARTMENT SESENTA Y OCHO
VISTA DEL MAR Y SOL
EL CALLEJON DEL CHORRO

Zeffi and Kelleher worked their way through the side streets and deserted *calles* of the old town, keeping away from the main streets. The narrow, cramped blocks of the old town were filled with Spanish-style stone and brick buildings built in the last century, most of them leaning toward one another over the narrow cobblestone streets, lines of washing fluttering in the hot sea wind, filigreed balconies stuffed with clothes or mattresses, but all the windows shuttered and barred and no one in the streets at all and a hot airless silence hanging over it all.

It seemed quiet now, as if the bombing runs had stopped. The silence was palpable, a pressure on the ears, after all the explosions. As they passed by one pink stucco apartment they heard a window sash slam shut and then the sound of an iron bolt being driven home. At the corner of Via Cielito and Cabron they flattened up against a wall as a pickup truck loaded with soldiers raced past the corner, heading for the national assembly. A few seconds later a light Cuban chopper passed overhead, going in the same direction. Fire alarms as well, and sirens now and a pall of gray smoke that hung in the hot wet air, drifting out from the direction of Vedado and Centro Habana to the west of them. The sound of distant gunfire followed, a short sharp exchange, then silence. Silence everywhere and the sound of their own shoes scraping on the bricks. More of this creeping and scuttling advance with Zeffi's nerves twanging like bow strings, and then Kelleher stopped Zeffi with a hand signal at the edge of a tall, narrow brick building.

"That's her apartment," he said in an over-the-shoulder whisper. Zeffi came up behind him and looked over his arm. The apartment building was across the narrow cobbled dead-end lane from something called The Galleria Victor Manuel; it was old, maybe two hundred years, a leaning tower of crumbling French and Spanish stonework, faced with wrought iron and peeling wooden fretwork. In the east they could see the spires of the Cathedral of San Cristobal rising above the buildings at the open end of the street, part of the plaza, empty, a car burning, black smoke rising in a pall, covering the center of San Ignacio street.

"Will you go?" said Kelleher.

"She doesn't know me," said Zeffi, a little surprised.

"I have to watch the street. Hold on."

Kelleher moved a little forward and studied the

long, narrow street. Parked cars, mainly old Fords and Chevies from the fifties, rusted, painted bright primary colors, dashboards crowded with statues of the Virgin or Jesus Christ. Five buildings on the left, across from Katie's apartment, all floors shuttered tight. No open windows. No one in the cars. No shadows on the roofs.

"Clear, as far as I can tell. Do you want the radio?"

"No," she said. "If anything goes wrong, you can use it to warn Rick and the kids."

"All right. If you don't come down with Katie, I'll come in. Zeffi, when I come in, hit the floor. You have the SIG?"

"I do," she said, pulling her T-shirt up. The big stainless-steel pistol looked huge against her tight brown belly.

"Okay then. Go. Be safe."

"I will."

She stepped out into the street, crossed the lane at a slow easy walk, went up the cracked and sagging concrete steps, pushed open the stained-glass door and stepped into the hallway. Faint music—salsa—was coming from an apartment somewhere down the shadowy hall, along with the smell of burnt grease and cigar smoke. A flight of wooden stairs stretched up into darkness. They creaked and groaned and complained under every step, sounding to her like the old women who sat in the shadows under the stalls in the bazaars of Agadir. It occurred to her then that she was homesick.

She reached the third floor, fully aware of the

fatigue that was weighing her down. The door was solid oak, carved into angels by someone prone to vivid nightmares. The knocker was a lion's head. She heard music playing through the door, a tango of some sort.

After the third knock boomed through the wood, she heard latches working and then the door cracked open an inch and a young woman with the greenest eye Zeffi had ever seen examined her over a steel security chain. Air flowed out through the open door, bringing the scent of her perfume and the smell of fresh shampoo. The woman's face was damp, her hair in a towel. She was getting ready for work, Zeffi realized, a young woman whose life was about to change dramatically, blissful and unaware.

"*Buenas días,*" she said. "*Que tal?*"

"Miss Kelleher?"

The eye narrowed, closed, and opened again, a wary light glimmering deep inside the forest green.

"Yes. Who are you?"

"My name is Zeffi Calderas, Miss Kelleher."

"How do you know my name?"

"I'm a friend of your father's."

"Daddy?"

"Yes. May I come in?

The green eye darkened, and Zeffi heard the woman's breathing increase. Down the hallway, someone was fumbling at a lock and a baby's furious complaint rose up from a lower floor.

"How do I know you're from my father. I don't think . . ."

She paused and watched as Zeffi put a hand into her pocket and fumbled for something. She found it and lifted it up so the young woman behind the door could see it clearly. It was Kelleher's faded snapshot of his two little girls, taken on the beach at Kaneohe Naval Air Station. Zeffi sensed the gasp and saw the emotion rising in that strange green eye, surrounded by lashes the color of cedar.

The door closed suddenly, leaving Zeffi standing alone in the hallway, the picture of Kelleher's little girls almost forgotten in her left hand. Then the *click-snap* of the latch, the sound of a dead bolt being drawn, and the door opened wide. A tall young woman was standing in the doorway, wearing a bathrobe, her hair up in a towel. Her expression was grave, wary, closed, but oddly self-contained.

She stepped back from the door and motioned for Zeffi to come inside. Zeffi came in and the woman closed the door softly, but did not close the dead bolt.

The flat was long and narrow, a railway flat, probably a bedroom at the rear, a small kitchen in the middle, this front room overlooking the street, lightly furnished with canvas deck chairs and a low, painted wooden coffee table with a ship's model on top. Through the barred windows there was a narrow view of the plaza, filled with long shadows by the rising sun and the tall bronze pillar of the monument. The place smelled of fried rice and chicken soup. She came into the center of the front room and turned around. Katie Kelleher was still standing in the hallway outside the room. Narcisse Suerta was standing next to her, a pistol in his outstretched hand, the muzzle up against Katie Kelleher's right temple.

"Welcome to Havana, Miz Calderas."

There was a sound from the front hall—a floorboard creaking. Suerta turned to look, and Katie Kelleher dropped to the floor as Charles Kelleher stepped into the hall, his weapon up—firing—he put five rounds into Narcisse Suerta—stitched them down the man's body from the forehead to the throat to the breastbone—the hammer working—the muzzle flaring white and blue—the sound slamming off the wooden walls—the belly—his crotch—Suerta twisting as he fell back into the narrow hall—he hit the floor hard and bounced up and hit it again, splayed out, his pistol still in his hand. Kelleher stepped over the crouching body of the young woman, stood over Narcisse Suerta.

"You okay?" he said to the woman, his voice flat and steady.

"I am," she said, coming to her feet, strangely calm. Unmoved.

"Good," he said, leaning down over Suerta's body. He pressed the muzzle of his Smith hard up against Suerta's forehead and pulled the trigger. The blast lifted Suerta's skull off the floor and drove it back down, flattened out and misshapen, like a dropped melon.

A pool of blood ran out from under it and began to spread across the shining wooden boards.

"That's it," said Kelleher. "Let's go."

# REUNION

At full throttle, the *Black Angel* boomed out like a jet, a spreading white wake cutting twin furrows out of the green chop of the shallows. Brad hit the trim tabs and the boat leveled out onto a plane and picked up speed, reaching forty knots—fifty—the wind tearing at them—the roar of the engines brutally loud, speech impossible. Behind them large parts of Vedado and Centro Habana seemed to be burning. But the gunfire and the bombing runs had stopped. There were no more fighters in the sky. No planes of any kind.

In six minutes they had opened Marina Hemingway and were banking—bouncing across the rollers with everyone braced in their seats or clinging to the rails—and the seaplane was still there at the blue-and-white buoy, surrounded by a small fleet of pleasure boats filled with people. Three small brown boys were sitting astride the port float and one little girl was perched on the starboard wing, preparing to dive. Zeffi saw a long, low boat—forty feet at least—moored behind the floatplane, a thin plume of exhaust rising from her stern. When they reached the plane, Rick Broca was waiting for them, grinning, a new light in his eyes.

He kissed Zeffi as she stepped off the *Black Angel* and shook hands with the woman they had come back with—Kathleen Kelleher. Kathleen shook his hand in a firm, dry grip and stepped into the floatplane, saying nothing, showing no surprise at all, not even breathing hard. She had been like this all the way from her flat in the old town; Kelleher seemed equally odd—distant, reserved. Guarded.

Rick sensed nothing of this, his mind filled with something else entirely. He took Zeffi around to the starboard float and held out his arm, indicating the cruiser moored beside the plane.

A long, low boat, her engines idling steadily, filthy, covered with seagull guano and littered with garbage. Good lines, but . . .

Rick shook his head at her blindness, stepped off the float and onto the stern. He leaned over the taffrail and wiped some spindrift off the sternboard, clearing it of clotted brown slime and harbor scum and revealing the large Roman letters carefully rendered in formal gold leaf seven days ago:

CAGANCHO

Kelleher had come around the port side of the floatplane. Katie was already in the passenger seat of the floatplane, strapped in, not even looking down at them. She puzzled Zeffi. Her reactions were cold, and she hadn't said ten words to Zeffi since they got her out of Havana. Kelleher looked at the *Cagancho* with a set grim expression.

"Rick, you can't take her out of here. The blockade's still on."

Rick shook his head, still grinning.

"I sure as hell can. The Navy owns the sky around here. No gunboats that I can see. There's no way I'm leaving *Cagancho* here."

"Rick, we have to take the float and go. We have to go right now. There's room for you and Zeffi if you want, but we're leaving."

"What about the boys?" said Zeffi.

Kelleher looked over at the *Black Angel*. The three American kids were talking to the Cubans. As they watched, Trey cracked a beer and handed it to the father of the little girl.

Kelleher called out to them.

"Brad. You want to get out of here?"

Brad said something to Trey that they couldn't hear and then called back.

"Is the war still on?"

"No. I think it's over," said Kelleher. "How about it?"

"Yeah, we're gonna go."

Brad patted the *Black Angel*'s hull.

"We'll take this."

"There may still be gunboats," said Zeffi.

"Fuck the gunboats. *Black Angel* can do sixty knots. Nothing can catch her. I'll fly the U.S. flag. If we run into the Navy, they're not gonna hurt us, are they?"

"Not likely," said Kelleher. "You tanked up, then?"

"We are. Cold beer. Righteous weed. Fritos and salsa. The basic food groups."

Kelleher turned and surveyed the harbor. No one in the area looked official. They could still hear distant gunfire coming from the center of Havana, but it was quiet in the harbor. Kelleher looked down at the boys.

"You better go now. If you see a U.S. Navy ship, raise them on sixteen. Tell them who you are. You have passports?"

"Yeah."

"Have them ready. Read the numbers over the radio. And show that flag. If you're going, go now. Don't wait for the Cubans to show up. And when the Navy picks you up, don't have that weed on board."

"Hey, dude . . . don't worry. It won't last that long. *Adiós*, guys. *Viva Cuba Libre!*"

To a round of cheers from the Cuban kids all around. Brad started up the engines, the props churning up the murky harbor water. The sun was well up now and the sea beyond the harbor was shining with golden light. Trey and Dalton strapped themselves in their seats. Brad reached down into the cockpit and pulled out a can of Bohemia beer, lifted it high, pushed the throttles, and the boat powered out to sea, up on plane in seconds, leaving a spreading V of churning white water in her wake, the fading sound of rolling thunder.

Kelleher looked back at Rick.

"You really want to take *Cagancho?*"

"I do," said Rick, sensing a shift in Kelleher's mood, a distance. A stony reserve.

"Okay. Do what Brad's going to do. Fly the Stars and Stripes. Head for the first battle group you can see on the radar and call them on channel sixteen. Don't stop for any Cuban vessel. Katie and I are taking the plane. Look, Rick . . . there's a lot I would like to say. You and Zeffi went through this for me."

"And for Katie," said Zeffi.

The phrase seemed to sting him.

"Yes. And for Katie."

"You have something to say, Charlie," asked Rick. "Something bothering you?"

"Yes. I do. You saved my life, Rick. You too, Zeffi. I want you to know how much that means to me. It's a debt I can never repay."

"We got into this with our eyes open," said Zeffi. "I don't regret it. Do we need to regret it?"

"Sometimes things are not . . . clear. We do what we have to do, and we try to live with the results. You weren't told—I was not honest with you. I think Zeffi knows that. You will too."

"Hey, Charlie," said Rick. "Are we having an Oprah moment?"

"Will you shake my hand?" asked Kelleher.

"I will," said Rick, taking his hand and gripping it tight.

"And you, Zeffi?"

She did and then kissed his cheek.

"Whatever it is, Charlie," she said, "you're forgiven."
Kelleher studied her calm steady face.

"You're a remarkable young woman, Zeffi. I'll always remember you."

"Remember her?" said Rick. "Hell, we'll see you in America."

"What you did here, Rick. It was a fine thing. A very fine thing. You should be proud."

"Hell," said Rick, laughing. "I'll settle for not being indicted. Now go. Give my best to your daughter. We'll see you stateside. And you're buying."

"Yes," said Kelleher, looking down at them from the open cabin door, the rising sun behind him, his face in shadow, the sea wind in his silver hair. "See you stateside."

# BREAKING NEWS

ASSOCIATED PRESS, OCTOBER 4TH: In a surprise conclusion to a dramatic international confrontation, Cuban government officials working with a hostage negotiation team from Wackenhut Security secretly arranged the unconditional release of Hollywood executive Jake Seigel and his associate Cory Bryant. As a result, the U.S. Government lifted the blockade of Cuba immediately and ceased its overflights of Cuban airspace. Mr. Seigel was flown in to Miami airport from Havana by private jet at some time last night, although American officials will not release the exact details of the arrangements. Mr. Seigel appeared to be in excellent health in spite of signs of injury evident during the press conference held in a VIP room at Miami International Airport. When asked about a black eye, Mr. Seigel jokingly replied that "since the Cubans were so crazy about Hemingway, they should have expected an American to know how to punch. Now they do. And, Fidel—give me back my boat or I'll come and get it." This drew a round of applause from the entourage accompanying him, which included Jack Cole, his security chief, and his wife, film executive Sheila Leventhal, who told reporters with a tearful smile "This is the happiest day of my life."

The Cuban official who accompanied Mr. Seigel on his flight out of Cuba, Hector Preig, refused to elaborate on the deal that resulted in the release of the two Americans, saying only "When I was finally made aware of the actual charges I soon became convinced of their complete innocence. I made it a matter of honor to see that justice was done whatever the personal risk to myself."

Mr. Bryant arrived in a separate plane and was taken to a nearby hospital where he is said to be recovering from injuries sustained while in the custody of Cuban police officers. His condition is listed as stable and he is expected to make a full recovery. His mother, Madelaine Bryant, has expressed her thanks to the United Nations for their assistance in negotiating the release of her son. Accompanying Mr. Bryant on his flight out of Havana was Cuba's envoy to the United Nations, Onassis Goyri. Mr. Goyri credited the release of Mr. Bryant to the influence of Kofi Annan, the much esteemed Secretary General of the United Nations. Mr. Goyri said, "Mr. Annan took a personal interest in Mr. Bryant's case" and was "materially instrumental" in obtaining Mr. Bryant's release. It was suggested that

Mr. Annan may have telephoned Castro to plead the boy's case, but this has not been confirmed at press time. Mr. Goyri left the clinic shortly afterward. Sources have told us that he was prebooked on a flight to Geneva "to consult with senior Swiss banking officials on behalf of Mr. Annan's plea for more open banking as part of the global war on international terrorism."

# VERONICA

There was a ninety-foot windjammer sloop in port with a load of party cruisers, which meant the long open bar was duly crowded with half-corked German tourists sunburned into a staggering daze and hammering back tumblers full of the kind of drinks that hangovers are named after. Under a roof of dry palm fronds a Jamaican marimba band was doing something undeniably fatal to a pop song about Key Largo, while in the center of the dance floor a glitter ball sent shards of crazy diamond lights spinning over the dancers and fluttering over the bamboo walls like a flock of Tinker Bells stoned on crack cocaine.

Out on the broad wooden deck that overlooked the shining waters of the Caribbean Sea there was a quiet corner where a group of wicker lawn chairs had been set up around a private piano bar, but no one was at the keys. Rick Broca and Zeffi Calderas were leaning back in their wicker chairs at one of the round tables, a couple of dead champagne bottles floating in a silver vase in front of them. Zeffi looked at her watch for the third time and then around the room.

"They should have been here an hour ago."

Rick, who had the clearest view of the dockside lounge all the way to its entrance, lifted his champagne glass and tilted it toward the door: "Here they come."

Zeffi turned around as Diane Le Tourneau and Cameron Chennault came through the entrance lobby. Le Tourneau spotted them out on the deck and came through the crowd with a broad smile, Cameron Chennault following at a distance, looking a little uneasy but well turned out in a dark blue three-button jacket over a pale blue shirt, open at the collar, that set off his tan and his long blond hair perfectly.

As usual, Le Tourneau was dangerous to look at without sunglasses on, this time manifesting herself in a tight-fitting sheath of jade-green Thai silk. Her blond hair swayed with each step and Rick watched her cross the floor with a look on his face that Cisco would have understood completely. She reached the table and beamed a searchlight smile at them. When they were seated again, with more drinks on the way, Le Tourneau sat back in her chair and pulled an envelope from her gold silk handbag and set it on the table in front of Rick and Zeffi. Rick picked it up, but did not open it immediately.

"The mole?"

Le Tourneau inclined her head and offered a hint of a smile. Chennault said nothing, sitting back in his chair, studying Zeffi from under slightly hooded eyes.

"Buell. Please. Or Chennault here."

She shook her head and silvery highlights rippled in her hair.

"Regrettably, no. It was one of Buell's civilian advisors."

"Which one?"

Chennault put his glass down, leaned forward into the circle of light from the lantern hanging over the table.

"His name was Flores, Rick. Buell had recruited him from the exiles, but it wasn't only his fault. We were to blame as well. The CIA and our people were responsible for vetting all of the DIA's recruits."

"But you missed this one?" said Zeffi, not sweetly.

Chennault nodded without smiling. Le Tourneau looked past Rick at Zeffi, who returned her smile with less warmth than she might have managed if Le Tourneau had arrived looking like an overweight lesbian yak in a seersucker pantsuit, which was what she had been expecting from an FBI agent. Le Tourneau spoke directly to Zeffi.

"The name we knew him by—Alejandro Lebriijio Flores—was a man whose family members are all on the list of the dead from the *Venceremos* sinking. There's a Jorge Flores, and the others are all relatives of his by the name of Suarez."

"What was his real name?" asked Rick. Chennault answered.

"We're working on that. Preliminary readings suggest something Latvian or Russian. Possibly even a Chechyn."

"Will Preig tell you?"

Chennault laughed then, the first break in his reserve.

"When we get to him. You caught us completely flat-footed with your Wackenhut operation. We had intended to scoop Preig when he tried to escape Cuba. You had him flown out by private jet. Now he's out in Los Angeles hiding behind a couple of Paradigm lawyers. He's applied for political asylum. Until that's adjudicated, we can't get near him."

"Los Angeles," said Rick, his head beginning to pound. "What the hell is he doing out in Los Angeles?"

Le Tourneau gave him a sympathetic look.

"You're going to find this hard to believe."

"That was never in doubt. Tell me anyway."

"Jake Seigel hired him."

"*Hired* him? To do what?"

"According to what his lawyers told our people at INS, he's hiring him as a script consultant. Seigel's doing a movie about his 'captivity' in Cuba and Preig's going to be the technical adviser."

This took some time to sink in. Zeffi found her voice first.

"Peachy. What about Cory Bryant? Does he get a role?"

"Apparently not," said Le Tourneau. "Jake Seigel said he was all wrong for the part. But he is paying the kid some sort of settlement. Undisclosed. Turns out the kid had a copy of his contract scanned into his laptop. Vin Dyle rolled over when he heard that."

"So Hector Preig gets away clean with this?" said Zeffi.

"You made the deal, didn't you? Not us," said Chennault.

"What about Onassis Goyri?"

"He's in Geneva somewhere. With Roymundo Vargas."

"Can't you get to them?"

Chennault looked at her, smiled warmly.

"Zeffi, he's a fucking hero. Kofi Annan says so. And Roymundo Vargas is Castro's own banker. We can't touch him."

"What about Buell?" asked Rick. Le Tourneau shook her head.

"As we said, Dunford has chosen a career in the private sector."

They savored that for a while. Zeffi had a question.

"The *orisha* for one of the cells was named Lazarus. Why?"

"We don't know exactly," said Chennault. "But Flores got himself into the DIA while Elliott Lazarus was still the boss, so maybe it was a coded reference to the agency."

"But Elliott Lazarus didn't know?"

"How could he? Flores was Buell's personal pick and we all thought we had done a complete excavation on the guy. We all believed the 'Flores' legend that Preig worked out for him. As Diane says, we wish Dunford every success in the private sector."

"So he's taking the fall?"

"Oh yes," said Chennault. "At least something good came out of this whole project."

"Project?" said Zeffi. "What project?"

Chennault, looking uneasy again, shook his head. "Sorry. I meant this affair."

Rick set his glass down and nodded at Zeffi, who took it as a cue. He reached down under the table and lifted a packet off the floor, set it in front of Le Tourneau and Chennault.

"What's this," she said, raising a single eyebrow.

"Open it."

Le Tourneau gave them both a puzzled—slightly wary—look, and pulled at the seal. She dumped the contents of the envelope on the desk: several computer CDs and a fax sheet. Chennault leaned in close to look at the pile.

"Read the fax first," said Rick. "Out loud."

Chennault unfolded the fax sheet and read it out in a low tone.

Rick . . . I ran the names you sent me and I found the same thing . . . the November 3rd edition of the Kaneohe Outrigger had been deleted from the on-line archives by the system controller. But I was in the USMC myself and I got a buddy to ask around and see if anybody had any of the original copies around. One of our Gunny Sergeants had been in Kaneohe and he

had most of the copies of the Outrigger.
He faxed this to me and I'm sending it on
to you. Hope it's useful.

Jack Cole.

PS: Jake wants his boat back.
Semper Fi.

KANEOHE NAS/NEWS/SATURDAY, NOV. 3,
1973: The body of three-year-old Kathleen
Kelleher will be laid to rest beside her
mother and sister in a full dress ceremony
at Pearl Harbor this Sunday evening. In a
tragic sequel to the accidental drowning of
Lieutenant Kelleher's wife Ruth and their
daughter Eileen last week, Lt. Kelleher's
daughter Kathleen—who had been in a
coma since she had been pulled from the
wreck of the USS Bowline—slipped away
quietly on Friday evening in the ESU ward at
Pearl Harbor Medical Wing. All base personnel able to be excused from their duties will
be provided transport to and from the Pearl
Harbor memorial services by MAC/NAS/
Pearl Adjutants Office.

Chennault finished reading the fax and placed it
on the table in front of her. Then he looked up at
Rick and Zeffi.

"I see," was all he said.

"Do you?" asked Zeffi.

"What is there to say?" put in Le Tourneau.

Rick's attention was now fixed on Cameron Chennault.

"Was Charles Kelleher really Charles Kelleher?"

"Yes," said Chennault.

"And his background? Navy flier. Covert ops."

"All true. In any legend, you stay as close to the truth as you can. That way there is less chance for confusion."

"Who was the woman we risked our lives to get out of Cuba?"

"One of ours. I recruited her myself."

"Why was she there?"

Chennault glanced over at Le Tourneau, who nodded.

"Okay. We had information that indicated a highly placed figure in the Castro regime was trying to arrange his departure. We knew this person had a lot of documents and goods he wanted to take out with him. We didn't know who he was. It was decided that we'd place one of our people in Havana with the legend that she was the estranged daughter of one of our covert pilots. Then we let it be known inside our own intelligence community that this situation had developed and that we were concerned that one of our pilots might be vulnerable to pressure from the Cubans because his daughter was in Havana. The mole—Alejandro Lebriijio Flores—got word to the Cubans. A few weeks later, Narcisse Suerta sent his first e-mail to Charles Kelleher."

"Why did we have to go in and get her?" asked

Zeffi. "If she was a professional? Why not let her get out on her own?"

Le Tourneau answered that.

"Having Charles Kelleher move heaven and earth in an apparent effort to get his daughter out of Havana reinforced Suerta's belief that she was really Katie Kelleher. Besides, it actually was the best way to get our agent out—Suerta had a good idea that you were going to come for her. We all figured he'd be waiting for you at Katie's apartment, that he'd rather have you in Havana than outside his reach. We don't like to leave agents behind. Kelleher knew Suerta would be waiting for you in Katie's flat."

"So he sent Zeffi up to die?"

"No, Rick. He sent Zeffi up to distract Suerta. It had already been arranged that our agent would leave her door unlocked. Kelleher was right behind Zeffi all the way. He would never have let Suerta hurt Zeffi. You have to believe that, Rick. It's the truth."

"Christ," said Zeffi. "The truth! You people are just making up the truth as you go along. How could you let Rick get so far into this thing?" Le Tourneau smiled at her.

"Your Rick, dear, is not very easy to control."

"You turned Suerta loose after I gave him to you. Why?"

"Cam and I disagreed about that, Rick."

Chennault took a sip of his drink, put the glass down.

"I did say you were bait. I wanted Suerta out

there, I wanted the whole thing still in play, all the pieces moving. I gave you a choice when I called you in Mobile. I told you they were—"

"Dead," said Rick, cutting in. "You told me they were dead."

"There's that," said Chennault, a sudden grin flashing out. "Actually, I think I said 'dead or missing,' but let's don't quibble. I'm slime. I freely admit it. I blame my upbringing."

Zeffi sent him a killing look and spoke to Le Tourneau.

"You knew Kelleher was being tortured by Suerta?"

"Hell no, we didn't. We weren't even sure they had him. Kelleher was unwilling to keep in close contact because he was afraid the mole would find out where he was. And then your stunt with the cell phone and the cab—you sent the kid to Fort Lauderdale—very sneaky, Rick—that foxed us totally. We had no idea where you were after that. You were off the chart and then that damned storm hit. We couldn't locate you until one of our Indigo satellites saw *La Gaviota* heading out to sea from Key Biscayne."

"So you weren't feeding Suerta information on our movements?"

"No. But Alejandro Flores was. He knew you were at the National and he was aware of the cell phone trace we were running on you. He was part of the reaction team for the project."

"I thought you couldn't use surveillance satellites in a storm."

"You were given that impression, Rick," said Le Tourneau.

"Yeah, and in our first meeting back in L.A., Chennault here told me that he couldn't get permission to track *Cagancho* by satellite after the first sighting. Is that the 'truth' too?"

"No," said Chennault. "We can always track a target, once we have it fixed. If we get clearance to divert the eye."

"And did you?"

"That's classified. Sorry."

"I was wondering how Suerta's people knew where *Cagancho* was once Jake had taken her out of Key West that morning. Did you tip the Cubans off just so you could manufacture a major incident?"

"Jesus, Rick. You cut me. Flores had access to the satellite data readings as part of the project. We did track *Cagancho* all the way into Key West Marina, that's true. But we couldn't afford to keep watching one boat. We logged the GPS numbers. I guess Flores got them out of the system and fed them to Suerta. If Suerta knew where *Cagancho* was, he could lie outside in the Stream and wait for Jake to take her out. I may be a rat, but I'm not a *sadistic* rat."

"You had no idea? Even afterward, when you pulled me in?"

Chennault shrugged.

"My conscience is clear. We did what was necessary."

"What about tracking *La Gaviota* out of Key

Biscayne? Did you manage to get clearance to do that as well?"

"Rick, when we saw *La Gaviota* heading out to sea from Key Biscayne we sent a team to the Vargas residence. It was clear there'd been a firefight and that you and Miss Calderas and Kelleher had escaped. From that point on the mission was really in your hands."

"The mission," said Rick.

"What *was* the mission?" asked Zeffi.

"We call it a Veronica," said Chennault. "You remember I told you that we knew Castro had a biological-weapons facility in the Farmacia Internacionale del Cubanos in Vedado?"

"Yes. I remember. You said there were others as well, in and around the city."

"Yes. Well, not anymore."

"Not anymore?"

"No. We took them all out. You were there."

"Those Tomcat flights? I thought they were hitting antiaircraft emplacements?"

"No. The Hornets took out the antiaircraft sites so the Tomcats could hit the buildings. They did the heavy work. They hit a total of sixteen locations in Havana. Secondary explosions. Satellite confirms total destruction. One hundred percent successful."

"Are you saying our whole mission was simply to provoke an international incident just to give you an excuse to hit these targets?"

"Not exactly. When Kelleher went down and you got involved, we just sort of let Kelleher freewheel it.

Remember, we were taking heat from Callista Fry and the UN Human Rights commission?"

"So it was all just a distraction," said Zeffi. "A ploy?"

"No," said Le Tourneau. "It was a legitimate, even a vital operation. America is safer now than it was last week. Thanks to you both."

"Jesus," said Zeffi. *"Quelle infame."*

"Not an infamy," said Le Tourneau, gently. "It was necessary."

"Was it?" said Zeffi. "How much of what you've just told us is the truth?" Le Tourneau began to answer but Chennault leaned in.

"Almost all of it, and, Miss Zeffi, I have to say that, in this business, getting that much truth at one sitting is very rare. We're here as a measure of our high regard for what you've done and as an expression of our gratitude. Charles Kelleher is grateful as well—"

"Then where the hell is he?" asked Rick.

"In the hospital, or he'd be here in person. And when I mean 'gratitude,' I mean our sincere and un-ironic gratitude. You're angry for having been . . ."

"Led," said Le Tourneau.

"Yes . . . for having been led. That is, regrettably, the nature of this kind of combat. I wish it were not so. But it is."

In the following silence the sound of the sea came floating on the evening air, the ruffle and boom of surf, the wind in the palms and stirring the bougainvillea and magnolias.

"So the world is a better place, is that it?" said Rick. "Good for us. Except the bad guys still walk. Preig and Roymundo Vargas and Onassis Goyri seem to be out of your reach. Scot-free."

"So far," said Le Tourneau. "The night is young."

"Maybe not," said Rick.

"How would you like to nail them for fraud, for money laundering, for all kinds of breaches of international banking regulations?" said Zeffi.

"We'd adore the opportunity," said Le Tourneau.

"Fine," said Zeffi. "We have proof that Hector Preig, Roymundo Vargas and Onassis Goyri have been skimming Castro's funds for years."

"What kind of proof is it?"

Rick reached out and tapped the small avalanche of computer CDs on the table. Le Tourneau picked one up and turned it in the light. It shimmered and changed color, and the light was reflected in all of their faces as they watched her.

"Where did you get this?"

"You know we dumped Kelleher's payload when the *Louisiana* ran us down in the Santaren Channel?"

"Kelleher told us about that. All the parcels on the pallet were lost, as we understand it?"

"Let's say this material has recently surfaced."

This was quite literally true; he and Zeffi had found two of Goyri's pink plastic parcels grounded on Long Boat Shoal, a few miles south of Bimini. They were betting on more up the Gulf Stream.

"I love it when you're enigmatic, Rick," said Le Tourneau. "Will there be more?"

"Possibly. Zeffi and I are going for a nice long cruise."

"Sounds divine. And how will you beguile the tedious hours?"

"Wander the beaches looking for treasure," said Rick, smiling at her. She understood him completely, gave him one of Salome's best up-from-under looks—she was driving Zeffi totally bats and she was enjoying that very much—finger-tapped one of the disks.

"Rick, even if this is conclusive proof that Goyri and Vargas and Preig stole money from Castro—"

"And it is," said Rick. "It even lists the account numbers."

"Fine. I accept that it's proof they embezzled Castro's funds. We send this to the U.S. Attorneys, or The Hague, it will still take years to make a case. Goyri, Vargas and Preig will fight it with Castro's own money. We'll be pensioners by the time they get into court."

"Then don't send them to the U.S. Attorneys," said Zeffi.

"So who *do* I send them to, sweetie? Kofi Annan?" she asked.

Zeffi showed her a tight and steely smile, leaned into the light.

"Castro, darling. Send them to Castro."

SIMON & SCHUSTER
PROUDLY PRESENTS

# *COBRAVILLE*

## CARSTEN STROUD

NOW AVAILABLE IN HARDCOVER
FROM SIMON & SCHUSTER

TURN THE PAGE FOR A PREVIEW OF
*COBRAVILLE*. . . .

The navy blue envelope lay on the polished oak table in the center of a pool of warm yellow light, the embossed crest of the National Security Agency in its center gleaming like a fifty-dollar gold piece. During his six-year tenure as a senator attached to the Intelligence Oversight Committee, Drew Langan had been handed several navy blue envelopes exactly like this one and he had learned through bitter experience that what was contained inside them was often dangerous to know. Gunther Krugman was sitting on the other side of the low round wooden table, watching Drew through half-closed gray eyes in which a pale light glittered. They were in the Library Bar of the St. Regis Hotel. It was Krugman's usual base of operations; where you looked for him if you needed him, where he waited until you did. The richly detailed wood-paneled room was nearly empty on this rainy Monday evening. It was the last full week of the August Recess and those few government staffers still in town were safely back in Georgetown or Cherrydale or Adams Morgan.

Drew Langan's Secret Service escort was parked at a table a few steps away: Dale Rickett and Orlando Buriss, two sleek young hard-cases with gelled hair wearing Hugo Boss suits and Armani glasses, as alike as a pair of artillery shells. They were both tactically deployed; one man facing the service door behind the long wooden bar, the other watching the entrance to the lobby of the hotel. Black coffee steamed untouched in white porcelain cups on the tabletop between them. He knew very little about them and he intended to keep it that way. Cigar smoke was curling and rising through the yellow haze and Krugman was watching it with an air of Zen-like calm, as if he had a universe of time to burn. Drew sat back in the chair and studied Krugman's blunt irregular face, the skin cracked and seamed, the pale eyes slightly hooded, the jawline clear-cut and lean, his bloodless lips thin and tight, as if their only purpose was to seal his mouth—the result of a lifetime spent keeping other people's secrets.

Krugman returned Drew's look with the unblinking self-possession of a tombstone. An artery pulsed slowly on the left side of his throat where the perfect white linen of his shirt collar cut deep into his leathery hide. His tie was a silken ladder of Egyptian hieroglyphs in bright copper against a deep ochre field. Hieroglyphs, thought Drew, one of the first ciphers. A nice touch. A Django Reinhardt number was floating faintly through the cigar-scented air: Cole Porter's "Night and Day." A distant echoing murmur was coming from the lobby, the milling stamp-and-shuffle of guests, the crystalline ping-ping of the bellman's signal and, whenever someone opened the French doors that led to the street, the hissing rattle of rain drumming on car roofs and pooling in the gutters.

"Who sent this?" asked Drew, feeling that he had lost something by speaking first, the scotch working on him now, a smoky burn in his throat and belly. He was tired and he needed to sleep. He'd felt this way for longer than he could remember. Krugman put the cigar down onto the crystal ashtray in front of him, his long fingers moving precisely. He had no fingertips at all, just ten blunt fleshy conclusions at the ends of his fingers. Krugman had never told him how he lost his fingertips, but then Drew had never asked him directly. Krugman's military service had been as an Intelligence Officer in the Marine Corps during World War Two. He had served in the South Pacific, in the same unit as Drew's father, Henry Langan. Once, a long while back, Drew had asked his father what had happened to Krugman's fingertips. The old man's demeanor—usually quite genial—had immediately altered: he said nothing, and a cold and distant expression hardened his face. Drew never raised the subject again. Krugman's tone was one of polite regret.

"Obviously this is from the National Security Agency. The specific sender wishes to remain anonymous."

"Why? I can figure out who sent it by what's in it."

"You can infer what pleases you."

"So he wants . . . what? Deniability?"

"There is no such thing. And I didn't say it was a 'he' at all."

"Fine. Tell me what you think is the reason for this contact."

Krugman gave the question his glacial consideration.

"Well . . . actually I think it's a warning."

"A warning? A warning to me?"

"Not necessarily to you."

"Then someone connected to me? Someone on the committee?"

"Possibly."

"Do you know this?"

"I suspect it. That's why I agreed to deliver it."

"Why to me? Helen McDowell is the chair. If I have the protocols right, she has to approve every rated release, doesn't she?"

Krugman closed his eyes and inclined his head gravely. Drew took this for agreement and restated the question.

"So why is this coming to me?"

"Let us say that a decision was made to deliver this directly to you. I assume that the same communication will find its way to her desk in a timely way. I infer but cannot define a specific reason."

"You understand that by accepting this document

I may be committing a breach of the Oversight Committee protocols?"

"I take full responsibility for that. You will be indemnified."

"Even from Helen McDowell."

"Particularly from her. She has vulnerabilities."

"McDowell? What sort of vulnerabilities?"

"I'm not at liberty to say. But I assure you they are sufficient to keep her at bay, even in a protocol breach."

"You're a cryptic old bastard, aren't you?"

"I prefer to think of myself as discreet."

Drew picked up the envelope, weighed it in his left hand.

"What's the rating?"

"VRK . . . Umbra," said Krugman. His voice was a breathy whisper in a throat burred by heavy smoking. Drew shook his head and forced a counterfeit smile.

"Spare me, Gunther. Please. Almost everything is Very Restricted Knowledge now. And everything that isn't Gamma or Zarf is Umbra. If it isn't a Goddam press release, they code it VRK. We're not on good terms with the intelligence sectors and you know why. You read the Findings from the Select Committee. Everybody did. It was all about shifting the blame to another agency. Even the nontactical geeks at NIMA and the National Reconnaissance office, for Christ's sake."

"Hindsight is a wonderfully pleasant opiate."

"Hindsight! You could see the threat building. You said so yourself. It was exponential, starting with the embassy bombing in Beirut back in eighty-three. They send in Captain Crunch and he ID's Elias Nimr—and what does the CIA do with that nasty bit of Lebanese crap? They let him walk and fire Keith Hall for treating him badly and a year later the same group—funded by Nimr—kidnaps Bill Buckley, Hall's station chief. They torture him to death and send us the video. And what do we do about *that*? Not a damn thing. Except Clinton issues a directive forbidding the CIA to associate with unsavory sources, which effectively killed any chance they ever had of tracing real terrorists. And all through the nineties the CIA lets the DEA suck up their operational resources so they can be pissed away on The Never-Ending War On Drugs while a bunch of Saudi killers take flying lessons in the heartland. And in the end—after September Eleventh—they all lied like wild dogs, burned their own people, the field people, the operational troops. The analysts blamed the operational people, and the agency brass blamed anybody but the men in their shaving mirrors. They tried to save themselves by torching the only real talent they had in this game. And what happened to the senior officials at the FBI and the CIA, the mutts who let this atrocity happen on their watch? The hapless drones at the top, who should have been frog-marched out of the building by a platoon of security guards?"

"That's a bit harsh, Drew. Some very strong private condemnations have come out of the Executive Branch. Quite a few senior people saw their careers wither in the chill that followed."

"Chill? Hardly that. Most of the people who appeared at our hearings have either been promoted or retired with honors."

"My point exactly. Promoted out of operational areas or retired. That's how it's done. We don't put them up against a wall."

"Maybe we should. And now somebody at the NSA wants to back-channel this thing to me? I've been here before and I always get screwed one way or another. I'm being worked for somebody's endgame and I'm getting tired of it. Tell me why I should care about one more eyes-only packet of disinformation from the NSA."

"You are free to regard this in any way you choose. I have no brief for or against it. In this matter, I am merely the courier. However, in my view, it may have some intriguing implications."

"What exactly is it?"

"It's an intercept from the Kunia listening post in Hawaii. They rated it a CRITIC flash at three-eleven this afternoon."

"What was the originating language?"

"Tagalog. Not a native speaker. A senior Reader translated it."

"They gave it to a senior Reader. Why the urgency?"

Krugman shrugged, reached for his cigar, drew on it. The ring of red fire in the tip glowed and spread up the shaft of the cigar. Krugman's face was briefly obscured by the smoke, then slowly rematerialized through it like a drowned man rising in a lake. He said nothing, merely shrugged his shoulders and smiled. In his heart, Drew wanted Krugman's package to mean nothing. He wanted to go home and crack a bottle of Gamay and let that sanctimonious old gasbag Larry King irritate the hell out of him until he fell asleep on the sofa.

"Look, Gunther, if it's rated CRITIC the President already has it. He gets them within ten minutes. Then they show up on the National Sigint File website. If it's relevant to our brief I'll get it when the security advisor hands it to the oversight committee."

"I think that would be a bold decision. In this case, time is a critical factor. Something in this has implications for someone on your side of the debate."

In Krugman's vocabulary, "bold" meant stupid and risky. And the "debate," as Krugman put it, probably meant the antagonism that had arisen between the Congress and the Executive Branch over what people on Drew's side of the House saw as the deepening worldwide morass that had started out as a War on Terror. Aside from the ongoing complications that had resulted from the destruction of Hussein's regime in Iraq, there were combat troops in Afghanistan and other American military elements engaged in over seventy "advisory missions" all around the world. Even the chronically commitment-phobic UN had managed to get itself buried up to its wheel-wells in a nasty little Peacekeeping mission in the Southern Philippines—for once body bags were coming home in places farther away than Terre Haut and Laramie—and The Hill was trying to get the current Administration to define an endgame, a point where the States could get out of the ugly—and so far worse than thankless—task of saving Western Civilization, without any substantial success. The idea that American soldiers were out in the global swamp trying to reshape a hell-bound world into a Republican pipe dream of good order was a constant goad to him.

"I take it you've read this already."

"I have. I never deliver a packet I haven't read; people who do that kind of thing sometimes end up being blamed for what's inside."

"And . . . ?"

"And this is hardly the place. Drew, as a longtime friend of your family, and for your father's sake at least, who is one of my oldest friends, my earnest and heartfelt recommendation is that you take this envelope with you and read it at home, with your Beringer Gamay. Then do whatever seems required. It may be that nothing is required. It has been my experience that many of life's truly vexatious problems go away of their own accord, without any action ever being taken against them. We can but hope."

A brief revelation of his long white teeth, his canines prominent. He pushed the envelope closer, picked up his antique rosewood cane with the solid gold horse-head, and got to his feet, breathing heavily, favoring his left hip.

"You'll forgive me if I slip away; I'm being stalked by Britney Vogel. *The Post* thinks that I'm vain enough to let myself be profiled in their weekend section. Now, are you in touch with Cole at all?"

Drew suppressed his startled reaction to this unexpected mention of his son Coleman—their relationship, already strained by Cole's mid-term departure from Harvard to enlist in the U.S. Army, and further complicated by his equally sudden resignation from the army after a long combat tour in Iraq, was now almost nonexistent, an estrangement of which Krugman, an old family friend, was perfectly aware. After a prolonged pause during which Krugman regarded him with detached amusement, Drew shrugged.

"Cole and I don't talk. Haven't for over two years. I think he's in Thailand on a walking tour. At least that's what his mother tells me."

"Thailand, is it?" said Krugman, nodding absently as if this confirmed something he already knew. "Well, if you do hear from him, give him my very best, will you?"

Drew said that in the highly unlikely event that

Cole ever called him, he'd convey Krugman's regards, and rose with Krugman, taking the envelope from the tabletop and holding it under the light. It felt solid and heavy—NSA packets were usually lined with inert metals as a security measure—and seemed to contain a plastic disc. Krugman extended his hand and Drew shook it. Krugman's skin was hot and dry, his palm leathery, his grip hard. He held Drew's hand in that tight grip for a moment longer as he leaned forward and slipped a silver cigar tube into the breast pocket of Drew's suit jacket. Krugman then spoke very softly, his breath scented with cigar smoke and scotch, his whisper barely audible.

"Read the report, Drew. Look at the CD. Enjoy the cigar. I think you should have it tonight. I really do. I'll say good night now. And if we don't see each other for a while, I want you to know that I have always been proud to have been be associated with your family. I'll take my leave now and I wish you good luck."

He smiled then, perhaps at Drew's visible surprise at such an intimate expression of friendship from a man so famous for his wintry heart. Krugman offered him a half-ironic faintly Prussian head bob and a smile that seemed strangely off, almost regretful. Then he turned unsteadily and cane-walked away towards the lobby, the slender rosewood shaft flexing under his weight. Drew watched him go—Krugman's ambiguous smile floating in his mind—

and promptly felt the heightened attention of Rickett and Buriss, like heat on the back of his neck. Krugman's last words felt like a farewell to Drew and he wondered if the ancient cold-warrior might be sicker than he let on. Rickett and Buriss were staring at him, taut and at the ready. "Okay," he said, as the men got to their feet. "Take me home."

# Visit
❖ **Pocket Books** ❖
## online at

# www.SimonSays.com

Keep up on the latest new releases from your favorite authors, as well as author appearances, news, chats, special offers and more.

SIMON & SCHUSTER
A VIACOM COMPANY
www.SimonSays.com

Pocket
Books

2381-01